Anonymou

Proceedings. Of the Association of Municipal and Sanitary Engineers and Surveyors

Vol. I

Anonymous

Proceedings. Of the Association of Municipal and Sanitary Engineers and Surveyors

Vol. I

Reprint of the original, first published in 1875.

1st Edition 2024 | ISBN: 978-3-38538-389-0

Verlag (Publisher): Outlook Verlag GmbH, Zeilweg 44, 60439 Frankfurt, Deutschland
Vertretungsberechtigt (Authorized to represent): E. Roepke, Zeilweg 44, 60439 Frankfurt, Deutschland
Druck (Print): Books on Demand GmbH, In de Tarpen 42, 22848 Norderstedt, Deutschland

PROCEEDINGS

OF THE

ASSOCIATION OF MUNICIPAL AND SANITARY ENGINEERS AND SURVEYORS.

VOLUME I.—1873-4.

EDITED BY

LEWIS ANGELL,

M. INST. C.E., F.R.I.B.A.,
HONORARY FELLOW OF KING'S COLLEGE, LONDON,
PRESIDENT OF THE ASSOCIATION.

LONDON:
E. & F. N. SPON, 48, CHARING CROSS.

NEW YORK:
446, BROOME STREET.

1875.

PREFACE.

THE history of the ASSOCIATION OF MUNICIPAL AND SANITARY ENGINEERS AND SURVEYORS is soon told. Engineering knowledge and sanitary science were not among the qualifications expected of the "Town Surveyor" of the last generation. The Public Health Act of 1848 called into existence another class of officers, protected by the General Board of Health, under whose auspices considerable progress was made in the sanitary condition of the country. In 1858, the Public Health Act was "amended," the General Board of Health suppressed, and the "Local Surveyor" handed over to the tender mercies of the omnipotent ratepayer. The consequence was that, with the exception of a few of the larger towns, the office was degraded and, for the most part, avoided by those whose professional knowledge and character would have been of service to the country. In 1869, it occurred to the Government that the twenty-one years' operation of the Sanitary Laws had not been altogether satisfactory in its results, and a Royal Commission was appointed to inquire into their administration. It also occurred to the "Local Surveyor" that he had something to say in the matter.* In February, 1871, the Editor ventured to issue a circular † to his colleagues. The result was simply astounding. ‡ Various meetings were held, and ultimately an Association formed with the determination of improving and maintaining the professional position of the "Town Surveyor" and promoting sanitary work. Town clerks, Medical officers, and even the Municipal corporations, have their Associations; last of all, in 1873, came the "Association of Municipal and Sanitary Engineers and Surveyors." Scattered as its Members are throughout the country, no two living in the same town, the experiment was a bold one, and the following volume—the first of the "Proceedings"—is the result.

TOWN HALL, STRATFORD, LONDON.

* See Correspondence, p. 227, Appendix.
† See p. 230, Appendix.
‡ See Evidence, p. 244, Appendix.

CONTENTS.

ASSOCIATION OF MUNICIPAL AND SANITARY ENGINEERS AND SURVEYORS.

LIST OF OFFICERS, 1873–4–5.

COUNCIL.

President.

LEWIS ANGELL, M. INST. C.E., F.R.I.B.A., LONDON.

Vice-President.

JAMES LEMON, ASSOC. INST. C.E., F.R.I.B.A., SOUTHAMPTON.

Ordinary Members of Council.

F. ASHMEAD, M. INST. C.E., BRISTOL.
P. B. COGHLAN, C.E., SHEFFIELD.
G. F. DEACON, M. INST. C.E., LIVERPOOL.
C. DUNSCOMBE, M.A., C.E., KINGSTON-ON-THAMES.
A. M. FOWLER, M. INST. C.E., SALFORD.
J. E. GREATOREX, C.E., PORTSMOUTH.
T. W. GRINDLE, ASSOC. INST. C.E., HERTFORD.
S. HARPUR, ASSOC. INST. C.E., MERTHYR TYDVIL.
J. H. C. B. HORNIBROOK, C.E., REIGATE.
A. JACOB, B.A., ASSOC. INST. C.E., BARROW-IN-FURNESS.
P. C. LOCKWOOD, ASSOC. INST. C.E., BRIGHTON.
W. G. LYNDE, M. INST. C.E., MANCHESTER.
A. W. MORANT, ASSOC. INST. C.E., F.S.A., F.G.S., LEEDS.
J. FOX SHARP, ASSOC. INST. C.E., HULL.
E. L. STEPHENS, C.E., LEICESTER.
G. THOMPSON, C.E., DERBY.
T. C. THORBURN, C.E., BIRKENHEAD.
C. THWAITES, ASSOC. INST. C.E., NORWICH.
W. H. WHEELER, M. INST. C.E., BOSTON.

Honorary Secretary.

C. JONES, ASSOC. INST. C.E., EALING.

Hon. Secretaries of District Committees.

H. ALTY, C.E., KEIGHLY, YORKSHIRE DISTRICT.
E. B. ELLICE-CLARK, ASSOC. INST. C.E., RAMSGATE, HOME COUNTIES DISTRICT.
E. PRITCHARD, ASSOC. INST. C.E., WARWICK, MIDLAND COUNTIES DISTRICT.
R. VAWSER, M. INST. C.E., WARRINGTON, LANCASHIRE AND CHESHIRE DISTRICTS.

The Hon. Secretaries are also Members of Council.

Treasurers and Bankers.

THE LONDON AND COUNTY BANKING COMPANY.

HONORARY MEMBERS.

BAZALGETTE, SIR JOSEPH, C.B.,   Metropolitan Board of Works.
    M. Inst. C.E.
COX, COLONEL PONSONBY, R.E. .. ..   Local Government Board, Whitehall.
HARRISON, J. T., M. Inst. C.E. .. ..   Local Government Board, Whitehall.
HAYWOOD, W., M. Inst. C.E.   ..   Guildhall, City of London.
RAWLINSON, R., C.B., M. Inst. C.E. ..   Local Government Board, Whitehall.
TULLOCH, MAJOR H., R.E., Assoc. Inst.   Local Government Board, Whitehall.
    C.E.

MEMBERS.

ALLEN, T. T.   .. .. ..   Town Surveyor, Stratford-on-Avon.
ALLISSON, J. ..   ..   Town Surveyor, Bradford.
ALTY, H.   .. .. ..   Surveyor to the Local Board, Keighly.
ANGELL, L., M. Inst. C.E.   Westminster and West Ham.
    (President.)
ARMYTAGE, J.   .. .. ..   Borough Surveyor, Preston.
ASHMEAD, F., M. Inst. C.E. ..   Borough Surveyor, Bristol.
    (Member of Council.)
ASPINWALL, H. S. .. .. ..   Borough Surveyor, Macclesfield.

BAKER, B.   .. ..   Surveyor to the Local Board, Willenhall.
BANKS, J.   .. ..   Borough Surveyor, Kendall.
BATTEN, W., Assoc. Inst. C.E.   Surveyor to the Local Board, Manor-of-Aston, Warwick.
BAYLIS, T. W.   .. .. ..   Surveyor to the Local Board, Redditch.
BEAUMONT, J.   .. .. ..   Borough Surveyor, Beverley.
BELLAMY, P. ..   ..   City Surveyor, Lincoln.
BETTRIDGE, E.   Surveyor to the Local Board, Balsall Heath, Worcester.
BIDDLE, G.   .. .. ..   Town Surveyor, Dewsbury.
BLACKSHAW, W.   .. .. ..   Borough Surveyor, Congleton, Cheshire.
BOYS, W. J. ..   ..   Borough Surveyor, Walsall.
BRESSEY, J. T.   .. .. ..   Surveyor to the Local Board, Wanstead.
BRIERLY, R. ..   ..   Town Surveyor, Newton-in-Makerfield.
BRYAN, W. B.   .. .. ..   Borough Surveyor, Burnley.
BUCKHAM, E., Assoc. Inst. C.E.   Borough Surveyor, Ipswich.
BURNHAM, F. W. .. .. ..   Borough Surveyor, and Surveyor to the Local Board, for the Parish of High Wycombe, Bucks.
BUTLER, G. J.   .. .. ..   Borough Surveyor, Shrewsbury.

CARTWRIGHT, J.   .. .. ..   Surveyor to the Local Board, Duckinfield, Cheshire.
CLARKE, H. F.   .. .. ..   Surveyor to the Local Board, Briton Ferry, Glamorgan.

CLAVEY, E. ..	Town Surveyor, Burton-on-Trent.
CLEMENTS, J. A. ..	Surveyor to the Local Board, Tottenham.
CLEMMEY, W. H.	Borough Surveyor, Bootle-cum-Linacre.
COGHLAN, P. B.	Borough Surveyor, Sheffield.
(Member of Council.)	
COLE, G.	City Surveyor, Hereford.
COMBER, A. ..	Borough Surveyor, Kidderminster.
CRABTREE, W.	Borough Surveyor, Southport.
CREGEEN, H. S.	Surveyor to the Local Board, Bromley, Kent.
CRUSE, T.	Surveyor to the Local Board, Warminster.
DAVEY, E. ..	Borough Surveyor, Maidenhead.
DAVIDSON, R.	Surveyor to the Local Board, Leamington.
DEACON, G. F., M. Inst. C.E.	Borough Surveyor, Liverpool.
(Member of Council.)	
DEVIS, J.	Surveyor to the Local Board, Oldbury.
DEWEY, L. ..	Town Surveyor, Cheshunt.
DICKENSON, G.	Surveyor to the Local Board, Pennington, Lancashire.
DUNSCOMBE, C., M.A.	Borough Surveyor, Kingston-on-Thames.
(Member of Council.)	
ELLICE-CLARK, E. B., Assoc. Inst. C.E.*(Member of Council.)*	Town Surveyor, Ramsgate.
ESCOTT, E. R. S.	Borough Surveyor, Halifax.
FARRAR, J., Assoc. Inst. C.E.	Borough Surveyor, Bury, Lancashire.
FEREDAY, J. W.	Surveyor to the Local Board, Wednesbury.
FOWLER, A. M., M. Inst. C.E.	Borough Surveyor, Salford.
(Member of Council.)	
FOX, W. H., Assoc. Inst. C.E.	Town Surveyor, Dalton.
FROST, J.	Town Surveyor, Leek, Staffordshire.
GALSWORTHY, J. ..	Surveyor to the Local Board, Aldershot.
GOLDSWORTH, W.	Surveyor to the Local Board, Prescot.
GOODCHILD, T.	Surveyor to the Local Board, Teddington.
GORST, R.	Town Surveyor, Blackpool.
GOTT, C., M. Inst. C.E. ..	Borough Surveyor, Bradford.
GREATOREX, J. E.	Borough Surveyor, Portsmouth.
(Member of Council.)	
GRINDLE, T. W., Assoc. Inst. C.E. *(Member of Council.)*	Borough Surveyor, Hertford.
HALES, R.	Surveyor to the Local Board of Burslem, and Tunstall, Staffordshire.
HALL, H.	Surveyor to the Local Board, Waterloo, Liverpool.
HALL, J. A. ..	Surveyor to the Local Board, Toxteth Park, Liverpool.
HALL, J. G. ..	City Surveyor, Canterbury.
HALL, M. ..	Surveyor to the Local Board, South Shields.
HARDING, J. R.	Surveyor to the Local Board, Epsom.
HARPUR, S., Assoc. Inst. C.E.	Surveyor to the Local Board, Merthyr Tydvil.
(Member of Council.)	
HARTLEY, J.	Borough Surveyor, Lancaster.
HIGGINBOTTOM, J. W. ..	Town Surveyor, Fenton, Staffordshire.
HILDRED, J.	Borough Surveyor, Batley, Yorkshire.
HODGE, R.	Borough Surveyor, Plymouth.
HODSON, G., Assoc. Inst. C.E.	Surveyor to the Local Board, Loughborough.
HOLLAND, J. ..	Surveyor to the Local Board, Witton-cum-Twam-brookes, Cheshire.
HOLT, J. C. ..	Surveyor to the Townships of Ardwick and Beswick.

HORNIBROOK, J. H. C. B. .. Borough Surveyor, Reigate.
   (*Member of Council.*)
HUME, JNO. .. .. Borough Surveyor, Derby.
HUMPHRIS, D. J. .. Town Surveyor, Cheltenham.

JACKSON, J. .. .. Borough Surveyor, Stockport.
JACOB, A., B.A., Assoc. Inst. Borough Surveyor, Barrow-in-Furness.
   C.E. (*Member of Council.*)
JAMES, W. P. .. .. .. Surveyor to the Local Board, Canton, Glamorgan-
   shire.
JEPSON, W. .. .. Surveyor to the Local Board, Heaton Norris,
   Stockport.
JOHNSON, T. L., Assoc. Inst. Borough Surveyor, Cardiff.
   C.E.
JONES, C. Assoc. Inst. C.E. *Hon. Secretary,* Surveyor to the Local Board,
   (*Member of Council.*)   Ealing.
JONES, J. .. Surveyor to the Local Board, Builth, Brecon.
JONES, J. M. .. City Surveyor, Chester.

KELSALL, S. .. .. Surveyor to the Local Board, Stretford.
KENWORTHY, E. .. .. Borough Surveyor, Barnsley.

LATHAM, E. D. .. Borough Surveyor, Middlesbrough.
LEA, J. T. .. .. Surveyor to the Local Board, Wallasey, Cheshire.
LEMON, J., Assoc. Inst. C.E. *Vice-President,* Borough Surveyor, Southampton.
   (*Member of Council.*)
LITTLE, J. .. .. Surveyor to the Local Board, Torquay.
LIVESAY, J. G., Assoc. Inst.C.E. Town Surveyor, Ventnor.
LIVINGSTONE, G.,Assoc.Inst.C.E. Borough Surveyor, Maidstone.
LOBLEY, J., Assoc. Inst. C.E. Borough Surveyor, Hanley.
LOCKWOOD, P. C., Assoc. Inst. Borough Surveyor, Brighton.
   C.E. (*Member of Council.*)
LOVEJOY, C. C. .. Surveyor to the Local Board, Watford.
LUND, J. Surveyor to the Local Board, Worthing.
LYNAM, C. .. .. Borough Surveyor, Stoke-on-Trent.
LYNDE, J. G., M. Inst. C.E. City Surveyor, Manchester.
   (*Member of Council.*)

McBEATH, A. G. .. .. .. Surveyor to the Local Board, Sale, Cheshire.
MARKS, T. T., Assoc. Inst. C.E. Town Surveyor, Lowestoff,
MARTIN, J. .. .. Surveyor to the Local Board, Radford, Notts.
MAUGHAN, J. .. .. Borough Surveyor, Great Grimsby.
MITCHALL, J. .. Surveyor to the Local Board, Hyde, Manchester.
MITCHESON, W. S. .. .. .. Borough Surveyor, Longton, Staffordshire.
MONSON, E., Assoc. Inst. C.E. Surveyor to the Local Board, Acton, London.
MOORE, J. H. .. .. .. Borough Surveyor, Basingstoke.
MORANT, A. W., Assoc. Inst. Borough Surveyor, Leeds.
   C.E. (*Member of Council.*)
MUDD, E. .. .. Town Surveyor, Sittingbourne.
MUMFORD, C., Assoc.Inst.C.E. Borough Surveyor, Wisbech.

NEWEY, W. .. .. Surveyor to the Local Board, Harborne, Stafford-
   shire.
NEWTON, J. .. .. Surveyor to the Local Board, Bowden.
NICHOLSON, H. Sanitary Authority, Axbridge.
NOOT, W. Surveyor to the Local Board, Tunbridge.

PALMER, J. E. .. .. .. Surveyor to the Local Board, Malvern.
PARRY, A.W.,Assoc. Inst.C.E. Borough Surveyor, Reading.
PETCH, J. .. .. Borough Surveyor, Scarborough.
PIDCOCK, J. H. .. .. .. Borough Surveyor, Northampton.
PINKERTON, E. J. .. .. Town Surveyor, Richmond, Surrey.
PLACE, G. .. .. Borough Surveyor, Wakefield.
POLLARD, H. S. .. .. .. Surveyor to the Local Board, Sheerness.
POWELL, G. G. .. .. .. Town Surveyor, Penryn.
PRITCHARD, E., Assoc. Inst. Borough Surveyor, Warwick; Hon. Secretary, Mid-
C.E. (Member of Council.) land District.
PROCTOR, J. .. .. .. Borough Surveyor, Bolton.
PURNELL, E. J. .. .. .. City Surveyor, Coventry.

RAMSAY, H. M. .. .. .. Surveyor to the Local Board, Twickenham,
London.
RICHARDSON, W. A. .. .. Surveyor to the Local Board, Tranmere.
ROBINSON, J. .. .. Borough Surveyor, Ashton-under-Lyne.
ROBINSON, S. .. .. Borough Surveyor, Maldon.
RODGERS, S. .. .. Town Surveyor, Wath-upon-Dearne, Yorkshire.
ROGERS, J. R. .. .. .. Surveyor to the Local Board, Hornsey, London.
ROSEVEAR, J. .. .. Town Surveyor, Fareham.
ROYLE, H. .. .. Town Hall, Hulme, Manchester.

SARGENT, B. .. .. Borough Surveyor, Newbury, Berks.
SANDOE, W. D. .. .. ..
SHARMAN, E. .. .. Surveyor to the Local Board, Willingborough.
SHARP, J. Fox, Assoc. Inst. Borough Surveyor, Hull.
C.E.
SHUTTLEWORTH, F. H. .. Surveyor to the Local Board, Littleborough.
SIDDONS, G. .. .. Town Surveyor, Oundle, Northamptonshire.
SIMPSON, J. D. .. .. .. Surveyor to the Local Board, Buxton.
SMITH, E. B. .. .. Surveyor to the Local Board, Oswestry.
SMITH, F., Assoc. Inst. C.E. Borough Surveyor, Blackburn.
SMITH, J. .. .. Surveyor to the Local Board, Taunton.
SMITHURST, J. H. .. .. .. Surveyor to the Local Board, Sowerby Bridge.
SPENCER, J. P. .. .. .. Borough Surveyor, Tynemouth.
SPRINGALL, W. E. .. .. Town Surveyor, Folkestone.
STANDING, J. .. .. Surveyor to the Local Board, Garston, Liverpool.
STAYTON, G. H. .. .. .. Borough Surveyor, Ryde.
STEPHENS, E. L. .. .. .. Borough Surveyor, Leicester.
(Member of Council.)
STEPHENSON, G. W. .. .. Town Surveyor, Cambridge.

THOMPSON, G. .. .. .. Borough Surveyor, Derby.
(Member of Council.)
THORBURN, T. C. .. .. .. Town Surveyor, Birkenhead.
(Member of Council.)
THWAITES, C., Assoc. Inst. City Surveyor, Norwich.
C.E. (Member of Council.)
TILL, W. S. .. .. Borough Surveyor, Birmingham.
(Member of Council.)
TRAPP, S. C. .. .. Surveyor to the Local Board, Prestwich, Lanca-
shire.

VALLE, B. H. .. .. .. Surveyor to the Local Board, Stow-on-the-Wold,
Gloucester.
VAWSER, R., M. Inst. C.E. .. Borough Surveyor, Warrington; Hon. Secretary,
(Member of Council.) Lancashire District.

WALKER, H. .. ..   Surveyor to the Local Board, Basford, Notts.
WALKER, T., Assoc. Inst. C.E.   Surveyor to the Local Board, Croydon.
WARE, C. E., Assoc. Inst. C.E. City Surveyor, Exeter.
WARING, T., M. Inst. C.E. ..   Borough Surveyor, Cardiff.
WATSON, G. .. ..   Surveyor to the Local Board, Crewe.
WHEELER, W. H., M. Inst.   Borough Surveyor, Boston.
  C.E. (*Member of Council.*)
WHITE, W. H., Assoc. Inst.   City Surveyor, Oxford.
  C.E.
WHITEHOUSE, J. .. .. ..   Surveyor to the Local Board, Eton.
WILLIAMS, H. .. .. ..   Surveyor to the Local Board, Pemberton; and
                             West Houghton, Lancashire.
WILSON, J. .. ..   Surveyor to the Local Board, Bacup, Lancashire.
WOOD, J. .. ..   Town Surveyor, Dorchester.
WOOD, JOSEPH .. .. ..   Town Surveyor, Manchester.

TOWNS AND DISTRICTS REPRESENTED BY MEMBERS
OF THE ASSOCIATION.

ACTON	E. Monson.
ALDERSHOT	J. Galsworthy.
ARDWICK	J. C. Holt.
ASHTON-UNDER-LYNE	J. Robinson.
AXBRIDGE	H. Nicholson.
BACUP	J. Wilson.
BALSALL HEATH	E. Bettridge.
BARNSLEY	L. Kenworthy.
BARROW-IN-FURNESS	A. Jacob.
BASFORD	H. Walker.
BASINGSTOKE	J. H. Moore.
BATLEY	J. Hildred.
BEDFORD, LANCASHIRE	G. Dickenson.
BEVERLEY	J. Beaumont.
BIRKENHEAD	T. C. Thorburn.
BIRMINGHAM	W. S. Till.
BLACKBURN	E. Smith.
BLACKPOOL	R. Gorst.
BOLTON	J. Proctor.
BOOTLE-CUM-LINACRE	W. H. Clemmey.
BOSTON	W. H. Wheeler.
BRADFORD	C. Gott (late).
DITTO	J. Allison.
BRIGHTON	P. C. Lockwood.
BRISTOL	F. Ashmead.
BRITON FERRY	H. F. Clarke.
BROMLEY	H. S. Cregeen.
BUILTH	J. Jones.
BURNLEY	W. B. Bryan.
BURSLEM	R. Hales.
BURTON-ON-TRENT	E. Clavey.
BURY	J. Farrar.
BUXTON	J. D. Simpson.
CAMBRIDGE	G. W. Stephenson.
CANTERBURY	J. G. Hall.
CANTON	W. P. James.
CARDIFF	T. L. Johnson.
CHELTENHAM	D. J. Humphris.
CHESHUNT	L. Dewey.
CHESTER	J. M. Jones.
CONGLETON	W. Blackshaw.
COVENTRY	E. J. Purnell.
CREWE	G. Watson.
CROYDON	T. Walker.
DALTON	W. H. Fox.
DERBY	J. Hume.
DITTO	C. Thompson.
DEWSBURY	G. Biddle.
DORCHESTER	J. Wood.
DUCKINFIELD	J. Cartwright.

EALING .. .. C. Jones (*Hon. Sec.*).
EPSOM .. .. J. R. Harding.
ETON .. .. J. Whitehouse.
EXETER .. .. C. E. Ware.

FAREHAM .. .. J. Rosevear.
FENTON .. .. J. W. Higginbottom.
FOLKESTONE .. .. W. E. Springall.

GARSTON .. .. J. Standing.
GREAT GRIMSBY .. .. J. Maughan.

HALIFAX .. .. E. R. S. Escott.
HANLEY .. .. J. Lobley.
HARBORNE .. .. W. Newey.
HEATON NORRIS .. .. W. Jepson.
HEREFORD .. .. G. Cole.
HERTFORD .. .. T. W. Grindle.
HIGH WYCOMBE .. .. F. W. Burnham.
HORNSEY .. .. J. R. Rodgers.
HULL .. .. J. Fox Sharp.
HULME .. .. H. Royle.
HYDE .. .. J. Mitchall.

IPSWICH .. .. E. Buckham.

KEIGHLY .. .. H. Alty.
KENDALL .. .. J. Banks.
KIDDERMINSTER .. .. A. Comber.
KINGSTON-ON-THAMES .. .. C. Dunscombe.

LANCASTER .. .. J. Hartley.
LEAMINGTON .. .. R. Davidson.
LEEDS .. .. A. W. Morant.
LEEK .. .. J. Frost.
LEICESTER .. .. E. L. Stephens.
LINCOLN .. .. P. Bellamy.
LITTLEBOROUGH .. .. F. H. Shuttleworth.
LIVERPOOL .. .. G. F. Deacon.
LONGTON .. .. W. S. Mitcheson.
LOWESTOFT .. .. T. T. Marks.

MACCLESFIELD .. .. H. S. Aspinwall.
MAIDENHEAD .. .. E. Davey.
MAIDSTONE .. .. G. Livingstone.
MALDON .. .. S. Robinson.
MALVERN .. .. W. D. Sandoe (late).
     DITTO .. .. J. E. Palmer (present).
MANCHESTER, CITY .. .. .. J. G. Lynde.
     DITTO, TOWNSHIP .. .. .. J. Wood.
MANOR-OF-ASTON .. .. .. W. Batten.
MERTHYR TYDVIL .. .. S. Harpur.
MIDDLESBROUGH .. .. E. D. Latham.

NEWBURY .. .. B. Sargent.
NEWTON-IN-MAKERFIELD .. .. R. Brierly.
NORTHAMPTON .. .. J. H. Pidcock.
NORWICH .. .. C. Thwaites.

OLDBURY .. .. J. Devis.
OSWESTRY .. .. E. B. Smith.
OUNDLE .. .. G. Siddons.
OXFORD .. .. W. H. White.

PEMBERTON .. .. H. Williams.
PENRYN .. .. G. G. Powell.
PLYMOUTH .. .. R. Hodge.
PORTSMOUTH .. .. J. E. Greatorex..
PRESCOT .. .. W. Goldsworthy.
PRESTON .. .. J. Armytage.
PRESTWICH .. .. S. C. Trapp.

RADFORD .. .. J. Martin.
RAMSGATE .. .. E. B. Ellice-Clark.
READING .. .. A. W. Parry.
REDDITCH .. .. T. W. Baylis.
REIGATE .. .. J. H. C. B. Hornibrook.
RICHMOND .. .. E. J. Pinkerton.
RUGBY .. .. J. E. Palmer (late).
RYDE .. .. G. H. Stayton.

SALE .. .. A. G. McBeath.
SALFORD .. .. A. M. Fowler.
SCARBOROUGH .. .. J. Petch.
SHEERNESS .. .. H. S. Pollard.
SHEFFIELD .. .. P. B. Coghlan.
SHREWSBURY .. .. G. J. Butler.
SOUTHAMPTON .. .. J. Lemon (*Vice-President*).
SOUTHPORT .. .. W. Crabtree.
SOUTH SHIELDS .. .. M. Hall.
SOWERBY BRIDGE .. .. J. H. Smithurst.
STOCKPORT .. .. J. Jackson.
STOKE-ON-TRENT .. .. C. Lynam.
STOW-ON-THE-WOLD .. .. .. B. H. Valle.
STRATFORD-ON-AVON .. .. .. T. T. Allen.
STRETFORD .. .. S. Kelsall.

TAUNTON .. .. T. Smith.
TEDDINGTON .. .. T. Goodchild.
TORQUAY .. .. J. Little.
TOTTENHAM.. .. .. J. A. Clements. ·
TOXTETH PARK, LIVERPOOL .. J. A. Hall.
TRANMERE .. .. W. A. Richardson.
TUNBRIDGE .. .. W. Noot.
TUNSTALL .. .. R. Hales.
TWICKENHAM .. .. H. M. Ramsay.
TYNEMOUTH .. .. J. P. Spencer.

VENTNOR .. .. J. C. Livesay.

WAKEFIELD.. .. .. G. Place.
WALLASEY . .. . J. T. Lea.
WALSALL .. .. W. J. Boys.
WANSTEAD .. .. J. T. Bressey.
WARMINSTER .. .. T. Cruse.
WARRINGTON .. .. R. Vawser.
WARWICK .. .. E. Pritchard.
WATERLOO, LIVERPOOL .. .. H. Hall.
WATFORD .. .. G. E. Lovejoy.
WATH-UPON-DEARNE .. .. .. S. Rodgers.
WEDNESBURY .. .. J. W. Fereday.
WELLINGBOROUGH .. .. .. E. Sharman.
WEST HAM, LONDON .. .. L. Angell (*President*).
WESTLEIGH AND PEMBERTON .. G. Dickenson.
WILLENHALL .. .. B. Baker.
WISBECH .. .. C. Mumford.
WITTON-CUM-TWAMBROOKES .. .. J. Holland.
WORTHING .. .. J. Lund.

RULES OF THE ASSOCIATION.

I.—That the Society be named the "ASSOCIATION OF MUNICIPAL AND SANITARY ENGINEERS AND SURVEYORS."

II.—That the objects of the Association be—

    a. The promotion and interchange among its Members of that species of knowledge and practice which falls within the department of an Engineer or Surveyor engaged in the discharge of the duties imposed by the Public Health, Local Government, and other Sanitary Acts.

    b. The promotion of the professional interests of the Members.

    c. The general promotion of the objects of Sanitary Science.

III.—That the Association consist of Civil Engineers and Surveyors holding permanent appointments under the various Urban and Rural Sanitary Authorities within the control of the Local Government Board.

IV.—That the Affairs of the Association be governed by a President, Vice-President, and Council, to be elected by the Members.

V.—That the Association be formed into District Committees which shall include the whole of the Members. Such Committees shall meet from time to time, in convenient centres, for the discussion of matters of local and general interest connected with the Association. Each District Committee shall appoint a Local Secretary, who will keep records of local proceedings, and communicate with the Council. No District Committee or Local Secretary shall be entitled either to represent or act on behalf of the Association.

VI.—That a General Meeting and Conference of the Association shall be held annually in such Towns, in rotation, as may afford convenient centres for assembling the Members.

VII.—That an entrance-fee of One Guinea, and a subscription of One Guinea per annum, from Civil Engineers and Surveyors under Rule III., shall constitute Membership of the Association.

SUBSCRIPTION ACCOUNT.

	£	s.	d.		£	s.	d.
Subscriptions due from Members ..	156	9	0	Received for Subscriptions ..	147	0	0
Admission Fees	15	15	0	„ Admission Fees ..	15	15	0
Subscriptions in advance for 1874-5	11	11	0	„ Subscriptions in advance ..	11	11	0
Admission Fee	1	1	0	„ Admission Fee ..	1	1	0
				Balance—Arrears due ..	9	9	0
	£184	**16**	**0**		**£184**	**16**	**0**

CASH ACCOUNT.

RECEIPTS.

	£	s.	d.
Preliminary Contributions ..	25	7	9
Subscriptions	147	0	0
„ in advance ..	11	11	0
Admission Fees ..	15	15	0
„ Fee in advance ..	1	1	0
	£200	**14**	**9**

EXPENDITURE.

	£	s.	d.	£	s.	d.
Preliminary Expenses incurred in forming Association				35	13	2
Home Counties District—Printing and Postages				0	19	6
Midland District—Printing and Postages ..	6	8	11			
Expenses of Room for Meeting ..	1	15	0	8	3	11
Lancashire and Cheshire District—						
Printing and Postages ..	8	7	6			
Rent of Room	0	5	0			
Reporter at Liverpool Meeting	2	2	0	10	14	6
Yorkshire District—Printing and Postages				1	6	8
General Expenses—						
Printing and Stationery ..	40	12	1			
Advertisements ..	3	6	9			
Expenses of Meetings ..	4	13	0			
Stamps	4	14	6			
Sundries	2	3	0	55	9	4
Balance carried forward				88	7	8
				£200	**14**	**9**

I have examined the above Accounts and compared them with the vouchers and receipt books, and certify them to be correct, and that the balance in hand at the close of the Subscription year 1874 is £88 7s. 8d., and that the amount of arrears due is £9 9s.

Dated 18th March, 1875.

(Signed)   EDWARD MONSON, Auditor.

ADVERTISEMENT.

ASSOCIATION OF MUNICIPAL AND SANITARY ENGINEERS AND SURVEYORS.

PRELIMINARY PROCEEDINGS.

THE first Meeting in connection with the formation of the Association was held in Mr. ANGELL's office, Town Hall, Stratford, London, March 11, 1871. A few only were invited to discuss the matter, and Mr. ANGELL, West Ham; Mr. GREATOREX, Portsmouth; Mr. JACOB, Bromley; Mr. JONES, Ealing; and Mr. MONSON, Acton; attended the meeting. The feeling was unanimously in favour of concerted action on the part of the Local Surveyors of the country.

On the 29th of April, 1871, a Conference of Borough Engineers, Town and Local Board Surveyors, was held at the Institution of Civil Engineers, Westminster, when the various matters connected with the position of Local Surveyors, sanitary legislation, and an Association, were discussed. A committee was formed, with power to act, consisting of Messrs. ANGELL, West Ham; GREATOREX, Portsmouth; HANVEY, Dover; MARSHALL, Tottenham; JACOB, Bromley; BRESSEY, Wanstead; and JONES, Ealing.

A General Meeting was called at the Institution of Civil Engineers, February 8, 1872, to submit, by appointment, the following Memorial to the Local Government Board:

THE MEMORIAL of the hereinafter-named CIVIL ENGINEERS and SURVEYORS holding office under the various LOCAL SANITARY AUTHORITIES in England and Wales.

SHEWETH—

That your Memorialists are the executive officers under the Local Sanitary Authorities, charged with the initiation and execution of sanitary works of the utmost importance in connection with the life, health, and comfort of the people.

That the matters upon which your Memorialists have to report and advise, and the works which they are called upon to execute or enforce, are such as bring them into frequent antagonism with the prejudices and pecuniary interests of large sections of the ratepayers and small property owners who have great influence with the "Local Authority" upon whom your Memorialists are dependent as public officers.

That your Memorialists suffer from a condition of things recognized in the Report of the Royal Sanitary Commission, viz. that while persons of intelligence and social position abstain from the administration of local affairs, there exists a "number of persons interested in offending against sanitary laws even amongst those who must constitute chiefly the local authorities."

That nearly the entire expenditure of local rates, as well as the expenditure of property owners upon compulsory works, is under the direction of the "Local Surveyor," who becomes, therefore, especially the subject of private and personal attack.

That your Memorialists, as the executive officers of the "Local Authority," respectfully submit that they cannot render active assistance to a protected medical officer of health in ascertaining local sanitary defects, or give cordial co-operation in removing them, so long as your Memorialists are conscious that such activity or co-operation may be distasteful to the "Local Authority" upon whom they are dependent for office.

That the general experience of your Memorialists has taught them, that it is impossible to discharge their duties efficiently and impartially, in accordance with the true spirit of sanitary legislation, while they continue to be entirely dependent upon local feeling, which is so often influenced by prejudice and personal interest.

That although your Memorialists were not represented in the inquiry before the Royal Sanitary Commission, they are prepared to submit evidence * in proof of the facts herein stated.

That as the administration of the Sanitary Laws and of the Poor Laws has been united under one department in the recently constituted "Local Government Board," your Memorialists most respectfully submit that such protection as to office, emolument, and superannuation as is at present enjoyed by the Poor Law officers should be extended to your Memorialists, so that they may be protected from unjust attack and enabled to discharge their responsible duties honestly, impartially, and, to quote the words of the Royal Sanitary Commissioners with regard to the medical officers, "without fear of personal loss."

Your Memorialists therefore earnestly pray that their office may be recognized by the Government, and in the proposed legislation such provision shall be made as will enable them individually, and in co-

* See p. 244, Appendix.

operation with the medical officers, to render active and efficient assistance in promoting sanitary progress throughout the country.

And your Memorialists, as in duty bound, will ever pray.

The names of one hundred and thirty-three Civil Engineers and Surveyors were appended to this Memorial, including most of the chief appointments in the country.

The Deputation proceeded to the Local Government Office, and was received with the greatest courtesy by Mr. STANSFELD, M.P., President of the Local Government Board, Mr. HIBBERT, M.P., the Parliamentary Secretary, and other officials.

After hearing the Memorial and the statements of various Members of the Deputation,

Mr. STANSFELD expressed his sympathy with the position and drawbacks of local officers, but reasons of policy, and his respect for the principles of local government, precluded the introduction of the protection asked in the Bill then pending before Parliament : such clauses would, he feared, imperil the Bill. Mr. Stansfeld hoped that an improved condition of the sanitary laws, and the greater interest which he hoped the public would take in sanitary progress, also an improved constitution of the local boards, would accomplish all the officers desired, without any interference with the liberty of action of local authorities. He had too much faith in local government to believe it capable of such abuse as submitted by the Deputation. He could not imperil his Bill by the introduction of features which might provoke the opposition of local authorities, but intimated that if the officers required protection, it might be introduced into the Bill by independent Members of the House. In short, Mr. Stansfeld took a theoretical view of the subject, rather than the practical one which experience had forced upon the officers represented by the Deputation.

FORMATION OF THE ASSOCIATION.

On the 15th of February, 1873, a General Meeting of Local Surveyors was held at the Institution of Civil Engineers, for the formation of an Association. The matter was fully discussed, and the following resolution, proposed by Mr. ANGELL (West Ham), and seconded by Mr. LEMON (Southampton), was unanimously adopted :

"That this Meeting of Civil Engineers and Surveyors, holding appointments under the various sanitary authorities, called together at the Institution of Civil Engineers by public advertisements in the *Builder, Engineer,* and *Building News,* hereby resolves to form an Association for the promotion of the professional interests of its Members and of that branch of sanitary science which falls within their official duties."

Draught rules were submitted, and, with certain amendments, adopted. Those attending the meeting were declared to be an Executive Committee. Mr. ANGELL was appointed Chairman of the Association, *pro tem.*; and it was resolved that the Inaugural Meeting, for the confirmation of the present proceedings and appointment of officers, should be held in London in the first week in May.

A Meeting of Local Surveyors in the Midland District was subsequently held in Birmingham, April 19, 1873, when the proceedings of the Meeting in London, February 15, were approved and adopted.

INAUGURAL MEETING.

HELD AT THE INSTITUTION OF CIVIL ENGINEERS, WESTMINSTER,

May 2, 1873.

THE Inaugural Meeting of the Association of Municipal and Sanitary Engineers and Surveyors was held on Friday, May 2, at 2 P.M., at the Institution of Civil Engineers, Great George Street, Westminster. The attendance was large, and included the follow-- · ing Members:—LEWIS ANGELL, of Westminster, Engineer to the West Ham Local Board, &c., Chairman *pro tem.* of the Association; Messrs. J. LEMON, Borough Engineer, Southampton; C. JONES, Local Board Surveyor, Ealing; T. W. GRINDLE, Borough Engineer, Hertford; J. E. GREATOREX, Borough Engineer, Portsmouth; F. ASHMEAD, Borough Engineer, Bristol; C. DUNSCOMBE, Borough Engineer, Kingston-on-Thames; J. R. ROGERS, Local Board Surveyor, Hornsey; JOSEPH DEVIS, Town Surveyor, Oldbury; W. RICHARDSON, Local Board Surveyor, Tranmere; EDWARD PRITCHARD, Borough Engineer, Warwick; R. DAVIDSON, Town Surveyor, Leamington; E. DAVEY, Borough Surveyor, Maidenhead; W. H. WHEELER, Borough Surveyor, Boston; H. S. POLLARD, Local Board Surveyor, Sheerness; T. C. THORBURN, Town Surveyor, Birkenhead; J. HARTLEY, Borough Surveyor, Lancaster; E. SHARMAN, Local Board Surveyor, Wellingborough; P. P. MARSHALL, Local Board Engineer, Tottenham; H. WALKER, Local Board Surveyor, Basford, Notts; G. HODSON, Local Board Surveyor, Loughborough; W. BLACKSHAW, Local Board Surveyor, Congleton; J. WHITEHOUSE, Local Board Surveyor, Eton, Bucks; T. L. JOHNSON, Town Surveyor, Barnsley; G. LIVINGSTONE, Borough Surveyor, Maidstone; J. LOBLEY, Borough Surveyor, Hanley; H. G. CREGEEN, Local Board Surveyor, Bromley; H. S. ASPINWALL, Borough Surveyor, Macclesfield; J. JACKSON, Borough Surveyor, Stockport; LEWIS DEVEY, Town Surveyor, Cheshunt; G. COLE, City Engineer, Hereford; E. B. ELLICE-CLARK, Town Surveyor, Ramsgate; J. BARNETT, Local Board Surveyor, Woolwich; J. H. C. B. HORNIBROOK, Borough Surveyor, Reigate, &c.

· Letters were read from Engineers and Surveyors of the following towns, who were unable to attend :—MANCHESTER, SALFORD, BLACKPOOL, STRATFORD-ON-AVON, COVENTRY, BEVERLEY, LEICESTER, READING, CANTERBURY, RYDE, SOUTHPORT, WILLENHALL, ASTON, EXETER, BURTON-ON-TRENT, CHELTENHAM, LEIGH, NEWTON-IN-MACKERFIELD, WEDNESBURY, WATFORD, TWICKENHAM, BARROW-IN-FURNESS, SALE, LOWESTOFT, CAMBRIDGE, NEWBURY, BOLTON, HIGH WYCOMBE, WALSALL, PLYMOUTH, FAREHAM, STOW-ON-THE-WOLD, BISHOP'S STORTFORD, HALSTEAD, IPSWICH, &c.

Mr. ANGELL occupied the chair, and briefly narrated the history of the Association. He stated that some few years ago, a movement in favour of consolidating and improving the sanitary legislation of the country took place, and a Royal Sanitary Commission was appointed. He then felt the importance of Engineers and Surveyors to Local Boards doing something to make themselves heard and felt, and he took the liberty of entering into a correspondence * with the Government authorities on behalf of local officers; he also sent a circular † to some of his professional friends, suggesting the necessity of organization. Subsequently a meeting was held at his office; and sometime afterwards a conference was held at the Institution of Civil Engineers. The result of that conference was, a committee appointed to watch sanitary legislation, and to strive to obtain clauses in the then pending Sanitary Bills for the protection of the Surveyor. A memorial was submitted, Feb. 8, 1872, to the President of the Local Government Board, Mr. Stansfeld, signed by 133 Civil Engineers and Surveyors holding sanitary appointments throughout the country. The deputation evidently impressed Mr. Stansfeld with the need for some consideration to the case submitted, but failed, from political considerations rather than on the merits, in obtaining the protection asked, although such protection *was* extended to Medical Officers and Inspectors of Nuisances. The Committee met several times afterwards, and put themselves in communication with various members of Parliament, also other societies. He (the Chairman) wrote to the British Medical and Social-Science Associations on the subject, and they did him the honour of electing him on their joint Committee. He induced that Committee to include in their petitions to Parliament a clause asking for protection for Engineers and Surveyors, as well as Medical Officers. He also induced Mr. Andrew Johnston, M.P. for South Essex, to introduce a protective clause, and obtained the promise of several Members of Parliament

* See p. 227, Appendix. † See p. 230, Appendix.

to support it; but the Bill was hurried through the Houses of Parliament without discussion, and the various amendments dropped. That brought him to remark how disunited and unrepresented they had hitherto been as a class, and he also felt impressed more than ever with the necessity of forming an Association. Of course he need not dwell upon the advantages of the Association. Their previous discussions and the correspondence he had printed sufficiently showed its necessity, and the number who had joined, and the large attendance that day, testified to the value they attached to it. They must have organization, not in an aggressive spirit, but for the promotion of their professional interests and of sanitary progress. Other public officers were combined; there were the associations of Town Clerks, of Clerks to Local Boards, of Medical Officers, and of their masters the "Municipal Corporations Association," therefore the Engineers and Surveyors were not setting the example, they were only following the precedent of other public officers, by coming together, although late in the day, and forming an Association among themselves.

The minutes of the meeting held on February 15, 1873, in London, forming the Association, and one held at Birmingham, April 19, confirming the same, were then read.

Mr. LEMON (Southampton) moved that the proceedings up to the present time be confirmed. The CHAIRMAN had gone fully into the objects of the meeting, and he would not therefore take up their time by dwelling on the advantages of such an Association. He would simply move that the proceedings up to the present time be confirmed.

Mr. T. C. THORBURN (Birkenhead) seconded the proposition, and the minutes of previous proceedings were confirmed.

The following report of the Executive Committee was then read:

"Report of the Executive Committee (pro tem.) of the Association of Municipal and Sanitary Engineers and Surveyors, appointed February 15th, 1873.

"The Committee have met on three occasions, and beg to submit the following report:

"That they have examined and certified the accounts of printing, &c., in connection with the previous movement in 1872, amounting to 35l. 13s. 2d., being an excess of expenditure over receipts of 6l. 0s. 1d., which sum they have authorized to be repaid to Mr. Angell out of the funds of the Association.

"The Committee recommend that those who contributed to the

previous expenses be credited with such contribution as part of
their first annual subscription to the Association.

"The Committee resolved, that as Saturday would be an inconvenient day for Members from a distance to attend in London,
Friday, May 2, be substituted as the day of the Inaugural Meeting.

"The Committee recommend that the Council of the Association
consist of thirty members, twelve of whom shall reside within
convenient distance of London; also, the Local Secretaries of the
District Committees, and that the remainder of the Council consist of Engineers and Surveyors of chief towns.

"The Committee recommend the following Members of the
Association as Members of Council:

Mr. ANGELL, West Ham, London.	Mr. JONES, Ealing.
„ ASHMEAD, Bristol.	„ LEMON, Southampton.
„ DUNSCOMBE, Kingston-on-Thames.	„ LOCKWOOD, Brighton.
„ ELLICE-CLARK, Ramsgate.	„ LYNDE, Manchester.
„ FOWLER, Salford.	„ MORANT, Leeds.
„ GREATOREX, Portsmouth.	„ STEPHENS, Leicester.
„ GRINDLE, Hertford.	„ THOMPSON, Derby.
„ HORNIBROOK, Reigate.	„ THORBURN, Birkenhead.
„ JACOB, Barrow-in-Furness.	

"The Secretaries of District Committees will be added as elected
in the country.

"The remaining vacancies to be filled by the Council.

"The Committee recommend that the District Committees meet
at least once a quarter, for the purpose of reading and discussing
papers of professional interest, and for general business.

"The Committee recommend that the London and County Banking Company be appointed Treasurers, and that cheques upon the
funds of the Association be signed by two Members of the Council,
one of whom must be the President or Vice-President, and the
Secretary.

"Mr. Jones, of Ealing, having kindly consented to act as Hon.
Secretary to the Association, the Committee recommend that
Mr. Jones be so appointed.

"The Committee have pleasure in reporting that more than 100
Engineers and Surveyors of various towns, from the largest to the
smallest, have up to the present time joined the Association, and
the Committee earnestly hope that the present interest will be
maintained.

                    "Signed on behalf of the Committee,
                                        "LEWIS ANGELL,
"May 2, 1873."   "Chairman (pro tem.)."

Mr. THORBURN (Birkenhead) thought the number proposed for the Council was too large. When so large a body was elected it might be, as it had been in other societies, that one depended upon others to be present, and frequently there would only be small meetings. He did not object to the number proposed from the neighbourhood of London, but thought the number should be more equally divided. They wanted the representation of districts more than the representation of towns. He would propose that the number be reduced to twenty-one.

Mr. MARSHALL (Tottenham) seconded the amendment.

Mr. LEMON (Southampton) supported the amendment. They might have a President in succeeding years who might reside in Liverpool, Manchester, Leeds, or other places, and then it would not be so convenient that the Council should meet in London.

The CHAIRMAN replied to the effect, that he always contended from the first against introducing into the Association what might be termed the "Cockney" influence, but still he thought their Council must meet in London. The Town Clerks' and other Associations had their head-quarters in London, Engineers and Surveyors were frequently in London during the Parliamentary Session, and at their previous meetings, both in London and Birmingham, it had been agreed that their head-quarters should be in London. Really it was not introducing London men into the Council, for he (the Chairman) would be the only London man upon the Council; the others would come from Reigate, Ramsgate, Ealing, Hertford, Kingston-upon-Thames, Southampton, Portsmouth, and Brighton, to form the nucleus of a Council within reach of London, but there would be no undue influence.

In reply to Mr. GRINDLE (Hertford) about the formation of districts, the CHAIRMAN said that under Rule 5, the idea was that they would have some six or eight central towns, of which Birmingham, for instance, would be one. Every member of the Association would be a member of his own District Committee, and such Committees would always act in concert with the Council in London. No Committee would act independently; every important matter would go through the Council. To the nine names suggested as within convenient distances of London, he would like to add the name of the Surveyor of Tottenham. They would be able to add representatives from such large towns as Manchester, Salford, Leeds, Birkenhead, Derby, and Barrow-in-Furness; there would also be, in addition, the Local Secretaries of District Committees when they were appointed.

In the discussion which ensued, Messrs. RICHARDSON (Tranmere) and WHEELER (Boston) supported the recommendations by the Executive Committee, and on being put to the vote only two voted for the amendment (that the number of the Executive Council be twenty-one), while the recommendation by the Committee (that the number be thirty) was carried without opposition, the names of Messrs. MARSHALL (Tottenham) and WHEELER (Boston) being added to the names proposed by the Committee as Members of Council.

EXTENSION OF THE ASSOCIATION.

In reply to Mr. MARSHALL (Tottenham), the CHAIRMAN said he would like the Association to take in Town Surveyors of Scotland and Ireland, if they desired to join.

RETIREMENT OF COUNCIL.

A discussion as to the election and retirement of Council resulted in a proposition by Mr. RICHARDSON, (Tranmere) seconded by Mr. ELLICE-CLARK (Ramsgate) being passed, to the effect "that one-third of the Council shall retire annually ; that it be decided at the Annual Meeting, by ballot, who shall retire and also who should be elected; and that Members of the Council be eligible for re-election."

TREASURER.

The London and County Banking Company were appointed Treasurers of the Association.

SECRETARY.

Mr. JONES, Surveyor to the Ealing Local Board, London, was, on the proposition of the CHAIRMAN, unanimously elected to fill the office of Honorary Secretary.

ASSISTANT SURVEYORS.

Mr. LIVINGSTONE (Maidstone) asked whether Assistant Surveyors would be eligible for membership. Some whom he knew were anxious to join.

The CHAIRMAN said that the matter had been discussed both in Committee and at previous meetings, and it was thought that they hardly came within the intentions of the Association. It was thought that they had better confine the membership of the Association to those who held chief appointments under Local Authorities.

ELECTION OF PRESIDENT.

Mr. LEMON : We have now arrived at a very important stage in our proceedings. It is our duty to elect a gentleman to preside over this Association for the ensuing year. We all know the vast amount of attention our present Chairman has paid to the Association, and I think I may fairly say that the formation of the Association is due to his untiring industry and energy. Therefore I do not think that under these circumstances we can do otherwise than place him in the same position as President that he now occupies as Chairman. I think it is a position he is fairly and honestly entitled to. We want a man for President who has the interest of the Association at heart, and I am sure Mr. Angell has. I propose him, therefore, as President.

Mr. THORBURN said he would second the proposition. Any one hearing the account of the work carried on by the Chairman during the past two and a half years, for the purpose of forming some organization of that kind, would see the advantage of having him as President. He felt sure that Mr. Angell would not disappoint them at the end of the presidency.

Mr. RICHARDSON supported the proposition. There had been a serious grievance felt by Local Board Surveyors. The protection given them under the Public Health Act, 1848, was taken away in 1858. Personally he felt a deep obligation to Mr. Angell, and he felt that the same feeling was experienced by Surveyors who had considered the matter throughout England generally. Mr. Angell had had hard work, and if there was any honour that could be conferred upon him he richly deserved it.

Mr. LEMON put the proposition, which was carried amid cheers.

Mr. ANGELL, in reply, said : Mr. Lemon and Gentlemen,—I thank you very much indeed for the honour which you have done me. When first I thought of the Association, and when first I commenced my work in connection with it, I little dreamt I should come to the proud position of being its first President. However, as you have done me the honour to make me your President, it will be my endeavour to bring honour to the Association, and when I vacate this post you will, I trust, have no reason to regret my appointment. I hope this is only the commencement of successful organization on our part.

On the proposition of Mr. RICHARDSON, seconded by Mr.

WHEELER, a special vote of thanks was unanimously passed to Mr. ANGELL for his work in the past.

VICE-PRESIDENT.

Mr. PRITCHARD (Warwick) said he had much pleasure in submitting a name for the office of Vice-President, and hoped it would meet with support. He referred to Mr. Lemon, Borough Engineer, Southampton, a gentleman who had been a member of the Committee from the onset, and had come a great distance on almost every occasion that the formation of the Association was considered. Mr. Lemon would no doubt prove himself a valuable officer, and supporter of the President. Feeling this, without making any further remarks, he would propose that Mr. Lemon, of Southampton, be Vice-President of the Association for the ensuing year.

Mr. THORBURN seconded the proposition, and Mr. Lemon was unanimously elected.

Mr. LEMON thanked the gentlemen present for electing him as Vice-President. He assured them he should do everything he could to support the President. He saw no reason why they should not hold a sanitary congress every year, in some of the most important towns of the kingdom. He (Mr. Lemon) was quite sure that if they united together they would, by the intercommunication of thought, be enabled to show to the public generally, they could do good, and that they were not merely a trades' union, but a scientific society, formed for the benefit of the community at large. (Hear, hear.)

HONORARY MEMBERS.

The PRESIDENT. Although we confine our Association to those who are officers under local authorities, I think it will be quite competent for us to elect Honorary Members. I have the pleasure of proposing Robert Rawlinson, Esq., C.B., C.E., Chief Engineer of the Local Government Board; and J. T. Harrison, Esq., C.E., also Engineer of the Local Government Board. I have received their consent in very flattering letters approving of the objects of our Association.

Mr. J. E. GREATOREX (Portsmouth) seconded the proposition, and those gentlemen were unanimously elected.

REPORTS OF THE ASSOCIATION.

Mr. PRITCHARD proposed that the minutes of the proceedings be printed and circulated among the Members of the Association. He thought much good would accrue from doing so, and it would be very interesting to have a record of the business transacted.

The PRESIDENT suggested that it be a rule of the Association to publish the proceedings.

Mr. DEVIS (Oldbury) seconded the proposition of Mr. Pritchard, which was adopted.

THE NEXT ANNUAL MEETING.

The PRESIDENT alluded, in complimentary terms, to the activity of Mr. Pritchard, of Warwick, in promoting the Association in the Midland Counties, and in recognition of such services proposed that the next annual meeting should be held in Birmingham, in May, 1874.

Mr. LEMON, Vice-President, seconded the proposition, which was adopted.

It was also understood that such annual meetings form a sanitary congress, lasting over one or more days.

PRESIDENT'S INAUGURAL ADDRESS.

The PRESIDENT then read an Inaugural Address.*

Upon the proposition of Mr. LEMON, Vice-President,

It was resolved that the address of the President be printed and circulated among the Members.

The Meeting then terminated, and the Members of the Association adjourned to the London Tavern to dine, in celebration of the event.

* See p. 17.

INAUGURAL DINNER.

THE Chair (London Tavern, May 2, 1874) was occupied by the President of the Association, Mr. LEWIS ANGELL, and the Vice-Chair by Mr. JAMES LEMON, the Vice-President.

Upon the removal of the cloth,

The PRESIDENT said: Mr. Vice-President and Gentlemen, the first duty which occurs to every Englishman on festive occasions like the present is to propose " The Health of Her Most Gracious Majesty the Queen." With the exception of a few—and I hope they are very few—honest, philosophical theorists, and a few dishonest agitators, Englishmen are loyal to the backbone, and none more so than the Association of Municipal and Sanitary Engineers and Surveyors, whose inauguration we this night celebrate. (Cheers.)

The National Anthem having been sung,

The PRESIDENT, in proposing " The Health of the Prince and Princess of Wales, and the rest of the Royal Family," said: If we are loyal to the Throne we must also be loyal to the succession ; and whether we refer to the past history of our own country or look abroad among other nations, we have every reason to be satisfied with our present Royal Family; they are devoted to the ways of peace and not of intrigue. At the present moment the Prince of Wales is at the Vienna Exhibition in the interests of the world's progress.

The PRESIDENT, in proposing the toast of " The Navy, Army, and Reserve Forces," said the art of war had become an engineering art, and he was sure there were none who could more than the Civil Engineers fully appreciate scientific weapons and the iron ships which had taken the place of the old wooden walls of England. The Sanitary Engineers were not warlike. Their object was to preserve life and to prevent disease. It was a statistical fact that there had been more lives lost by pestilence, plagues, and preventible disease than by the whole of the wars in the world's history. Notwithstanding, if it were necessary to protect the hearths and homes of England, he could say, as one of the earliest of the volunteers, that Engineers and Surveyors would be among the first to come forward. (Cheers.) He coupled with the toast the name of Captain Thorburn, of the Cheshire Volunteer Engineers.

Captain THORBURN suitably responded.

The PRESIDENT then proposed " The Health of the President of the Local Government Board, the Right Hon. James Stansfeld, M.P." Mr. Stansfeld, he said, is our chief in connection with all sanitary matters, and when he (the President) had appeared before him, which had been on several occasions, he had formed the opinion that Mr. Stansfeld was an earnest, large-minded, and particularly courteous statesman, whose sympathies were with us, although political and sentimental considerations may have prevented him from extending to us that measure of justice and recognition to which we believe we are entitled.

D. W. YOUNG, Esq., visitor, proposed the next toast, " Success to the Association of Municipal and Sanitary Engineers and Surveyors." This (said Mr. Young) was the toast of the evening, and it gave him very great pleasure in proposing it, because in former times he held the position of surveyor of one of the largest metropolitan districts, where he felt how desirable such an association was. He regretted to say that the Metropolitan Association with which he had been then connected was *non est*, but with a President like Mr. Angell, whom he had the pleasure of claiming as an old friend, he was confident that such a fate would not befall the present Association. Mr. Angell deserved their gratitude for the way in which he had worked and brought so many gentlemen together from all parts of the country, and he understood there were Members present from a radius of two hundred miles, a fact which showed the interest taken in the Association ; he had therefore much pleasure in proposing its success.

The PRESIDENT briefly responded.

Mr. J. E. GREATOREX, Borough Engineer, Portsmouth, proposed " The Health of Mr. Angell, their first President," in highly flattering and eulogistic terms. They had, he said, put the right man in the right place, and the Association was fortunate in having a President with so much energy as Mr. Angell had shown.

The toast was drunk upstanding, with cheers and musical honours.

The PRESIDENT, in responding, said he found it very much easier to propose a toast than to respond. He thanked them very much for the kind and enthusiastic manner in which they had received his name, and he thanked the Members of the Association for all the assistance they had given him, especially for the honour they had done him that day by placing him in the position of President. When he first took the matter in hand he little expected to found such an Association, or that he would stand in the position he did that night. It would be his constant endeavour to do honour to, and promote the interests of, the Association. His friend, Mr. Young, had referred to a defunct Association in the Metropolis. He (the President) did not anticipate any such fate for their own Association. He would not identify himself with a failure, but, with their assistance, the Association should be a success. (Cheers.) The Association is not aggressive. Every body of officials has formed associations, and we are the last, but perhaps not the least. Sir Joseph Heron, at the meeting of Town Clerks in this very building recently, said that the newly-formed Municipal Corporation Association was an "organization against which no Government could stand if once its powers were exercised." We are more modest; we neither threaten the Government nor our more immediate masters, the Corporations and Local Boards. In promoting our own professional interests we seek also to promote good work and sanitary progress. Gentlemen, I thank you for the honour you have done me on this occasion.

Mr. T. W. GRINDLE, Borough Engineer, of Hertford, in a humorous speech, proposed "The Health of the Vice-President."

Mr. LEMON returned thanks.

Mr. LOBLEY, Borough Surveyor of Hanley, proposed ".The Council," to which Mr. THOMPSON, Borough Surveyor, Derby, responded.

Mr. THORBURN, Town Surveyor of Birkenhead, proposed "The Health of the Hon. Secretary of the Association, Mr. Jones," and of "Mr. Pritchard, Local Secretary of the Birmingham District," to which Mr. JONES and Mr. PRITCHARD respectively returned thanks.

Mr. JONES, the Hon. Secretary, in an effective speech, proposed "The Visitors," to which D. W. YOUNG, Esq. of Westminster, responded.

Mr. POLLARD, Town Surveyor, Sheerness, proposed "The Ladies," which was responded to by Mr. ELLICE-CLARK, Town Surveyor, Ramsgate, in a very neat and amusing speech.

The musical arrangements were conducted by Mr. Frank Elmore.

INAUGURAL ADDRESS

Of Mr. LEWIS ANGELL,

First President of the Association.

(Read at the Institution of Civil Engineers, May 2, 1873.)

In taking the first Presidential Chair of the Association of Municipal and Sanitary Engineers and Surveyors, I propose to follow the precedent of our older scientific societies, and submit a few remarks by way of an Inaugural Address.

Although the Association has done me the honour of recognizing my efforts for its establishment by placing me in this Chair, I do not assume the credit of originating the idea. I have long thought such a society desirable, and others have made similar suggestions, but hitherto the matter has not been taken up with vigour, and I only now take to myself the credit of having, with your assistance, pushed to a successful issue an object long desired by many. I therefore congratulate you upon the Association being an accomplished fact, and that henceforth it takes its place among the societies of the day.

The first question which naturally will be asked of us is, what are our aims and our objects? Our answer is, they are twofold: they are sanitary, and they are professional.

The objects of our Association, as defined by Rule II., are—" the promotion and interchange among its Members of that species of knowledge and practice which falls within the department of an Engineer and Surveyor engaged in the discharge of the duties imposed by the Public Health, Local Government, and other Sanitary Acts; the promotion of the professional interests of the Members; and, the general promotion of the objects of sanitary science."

Our society may be said to be national, for our Members are scattered over the face of the country, from the largest borough to the smallest township. Wherever there is a centre of population there is the " Town Surveyor," and where the population is more scattered there also is our representative, engaged in sanitary work under the rural authority. Our official existence dates back a quarter of a century. During that period how much we have advanced in sanitary knowledge, and how much has been accomplished in sanitary work; but yet, relatively, how little! We look back with satisfaction upon the extinction of the plagues of the middle ages, and the mitigation of modern visitations. We have banished or repressed the grosser forms of filth and unsavouriness such as abounded in this country of old, and are still to be found in Continental towns. We have established a general respect for outward decencies and municipal cleanliness; any one suspecting an odour "betwixt the wind and his nobility," may now call a nuisance inspector, or appeal to a sanitary board. The nose of the English citizen has been "educated." But such sanitary refinement can only be acquired under certain conditions. Municipal life demands sanitary precautions, public works, and official supervision; in other words, municipal life involves those bug-bears of the ratepayer—taxation and officials—and we, the officials, are here to-day in Association assembled.

The Legislature, in its wisdom, established our office under the Towns Improvement Act of 1847, and the Public Health Act of 1848, and I here propose to review the qualifications, duties, remuneration, position, and prospects of the office. In so doing, I shall speak most unreservedly, with an official experience of twenty years, but no word from this Chair shall be prompted by either personal feeling or political considerations. I shall endeavour to discuss each point upon its merits, and I may do so the more unreservedly because I happen, for the moment, to be without an official grievance.

The office of a "Town Surveyor" of the present day is no sinecure. The qualifications and duties may best be described in the technical language of one of those very long advertisements of Mr. Town Clerk which so frequently attract attention in the columns of our professional papers, headed—

"To CIVIL ENGINEERS AND—*others*.

"The Corporation of Mudborough require the services of an "experienced ' person ' to fill the office of Borough Engineer and "Surveyor. He must be a man of good education and able to keep "accounts. He must be competent to take charge of workmen "and the direction of works. He must be acquainted with the "value of building materials, and able to take out quantities, make

" estimates, specifications, and measure up works. He must have
" a practical knowledge of road-making and paving work in all its
" branches, and must superintend the lighting and cleansing of the
" public highways, and perhaps take charge of the Fire Brigade.
" He must be competent to make surveys, take levels, and be a
" good draughtsman. He must be able to design and superintend
" the erection of public and private buildings, perhaps a Gaol or a
" Town Hall, and to enforce the Building Bye-Laws. He must
" have both general knowledge and practical experience of en-
" gineering works, and be able to design and carry into execution
" works of house and town drainage, and advise the Corporation
" upon the best means of disposing of or utilizing sewage. He
" may also have to act as Engineer and Manager of the Water-
" works. He must prepare the necessary plans for promoting or
" opposing schemes in Parliament, and generally advise the Cor-
" poration upon any works which may come under their notice.
" He must be conversant with the requirements of the Public
" Health, Local Government, Nuisances Removal, and various other
" Acts (which Mr. Justice Blackburn recently declared to be the
" greatest muddle out). He must produce testimonials of the
" highest character, find sureties, and be not more than 40 years
" of age."

This is no exaggeration of recent advertisements, and if our
" Town Surveyor" be not equal to all this, and such further
duties as may be required of him, he is not equal to the post.

In return for such duties, qualifications, and responsibilities, and
perhaps his entire service and the keep of a horse, he will obtain
that amount of remuneration, consideration, public gratitude, and
peace of mind which we have all experienced, particularly in the
smaller towns where the public have the more leisure to observe
and appreciate their officers.

Upon the mode of selecting candidates, and testing their qualifications, I will not now enter; it is sufficient to remark that the
formidable advertisement does not deter "persons" innocent of
levels, and whose knowledge of surveying does not extend beyond
a foot rule, from soliciting the responsibilities of the office. Many
candidates present themselves who know as much about sanitary
work and hydraulics as of Hindustani, perhaps less, nevertheless they
will undertake to drain a town, and may indeed succeed, but not in
an engineering sense; in short, the election of a Town Surveyor is
generally a free fight, and too frequently a farce.

c 2

I have said the Acts of 1847 and 1848 established our office ; those Acts also protected us. But recent legislation has entirely ignored our existence. The protection of the Public Health Act was first removed, and now a new class of officers has been established without any attempt to utilize the old. The Medical Officer of Health, with his satellite the Inspector of Nuisances, is in the ascendant, recognized, paid, and protected by Government. If we, the pioneers of sanitary work, have been found wanting in efficiency, surely it has been from no fault of our own, but of the position in which we have been placed. The Town Surveyor, according to his opportunities, has done the country good service, but surrounded as we have been with obstructions and difficulties, cramped and restricted by popular prejudices and private interests, subject to clamour and attack, without protection and without appeal, it is indeed surprising that we have accomplished so much. Had such officers been from the first judiciously selected, adequately remunerated, properly supported, and duly protected, our influence upon sanitary progress would have been more conspicuous, and our office better appreciated.

As Engineers, we do not pretend to a knowledge of medical science, but it is equally within the knowledge of the average Sanitary Engineer as of a Medical Officer of Health, that pure air, pure water, properly constructed houses, and an unpolluted soil are the cardinal conditions of health. These are mere sanitary axioms. The means by which such conditions are attained are drainage, ventilation, water supply, and other matters entirely within the functions of the Engineer. It is the function of the Sanitary Engineer to prevent that which the Medical Officer is called upon to detect. The laws and conditions of health and the practice of medicine are totally distinct matters, and I protest against the recent official exaggeration of the Medical Office to the depreciation of the more practical department of the Sanitary Engineer. I do protest, from a social, a professional, and an equitable point of view, against the one being recognized, paid, and protected by Government, while his colleague, the Surveyor, is entirely ignored. It is due, however, to the medical profession to state that the Parliamentary Sub-Committee of the British Medical and Social Science Associations, of which I have the honour of being a member, have recommended protection to the Engineer conjointly with the Medical Officer.

The results of the Medical Officers' recommendations must

depend, to a very great extent, upon the zeal and efficiency of the Surveyor's department; it is through this department that the Medical Officer derives much of his information. In many cases the unprotected Surveyor may be required to report, to a protected Medical Officer, the negligence of his own employers. No local Surveyor or Engineer can be expected to give cordial and active assistance in compulsory sanitary work when he is conscious that his action would be opposed to the views or the interests of his employers, the public, upon whom he is dependent. The existence of such a distinction between the Medical Officer and Surveyor, under the same Board, will produce a want of harmony in interest, and must lead to a divergence of action between the two departments.

I do not desire to provoke any class feeling; far be it from me, from the Presidential Chair of this Association, to depreciate hygienic science, or to undervalue the functions of the Medical Officer of Health. The nation owes the medical profession a debt of gratitude; a more scientific, devoted, self-denying, or philanthropic profession does not exist, and it is unquestionably convenient and desirable that in sanitary work there should be a division of labour, application of special qualifications, and authoritative enunciation of principles. It is also desirable that the Medical Officer should be recognized, remunerated, and protected; but I as emphatically maintain that it is no less equitable and desirable that similar conditions should apply to the Engineer, without whose practical knowledge and cordial co-operation Medical Officers, and their protectors the Local Government Board, would be helpless, and their recommendations without practical effect.

As a result of this special Government patronage we have recently seen, almost daily, in one column of a newspaper an advertisement for a Medical Officer at a salary of 800*l.* per annum, half of which is paid by the nation; and in another column an advertisement for a Surveyor, at 150*l.* per annum, the whole of which is grudgingly paid out of local rates. I am not referring to mere nuisance inspectors, whose pay, under the new system, is frequently equal to that of a professional Surveyor. Such advertisements lead the public to infer an inferior social status and qualification of a profession which can produce an unlimited supply of pseudo Surveyors.

It is true our profession is a free and open one—indeed, a new profession, lacking the protective advantages of the old Faculties. We are not hedged round by enactments, charters, diplomas, and

22   THE PRESIDENT'S INAUGURAL ADDRESS.

registration; nevertheless, the modern Engineer has done more for
the material prosperity of the world and the advance of civilization
than any other single profession at any period of the world's
history.   If status be judged by results, we may fairly hold our
own, and class unqualified Sanitary Surveyors with unregistered
medical quacks.   The abilities of a certain class of adventurers
are amply repaid by small salaries; it is no reflection upon our
profession, but upon those authorities who offer such miserable
inducements, and, as a consequence, fail in obtaining good service.
    Nor, on the other hand, is the question of pay a measure of
ability; in a crowded country like ours we cannot all gain prizes;
a man must follow his profession in whatever channel the accidents
of his position may have placed him; where there is competition
many deserving men must go to the wall, and the "overburdened
ratepayer" does not fail to avail himself of this circumstance to buy
engineering ability at but little above the price of the brute labour
which it directs; consequently the public either obtains an inferior
article, or loses its bargain with the first turn of fortune's wheel.
Nor does it follow that because men with more or less qualification—frequently less—accept public offices at ridiculously low
salaries that the public has the advantage, or that they have put
"the right man in the right place." True economy means efficiency,
not parsimony.   If we were to advertise any office in State, from
the Archbishop of Canterbury downwards, there would be legions
of candidates ready to undertake the duties at 75 per cent. less
salary than the present illustrious incumbents receive.
    Not only is it false economy to underpay a responsible officer,
but there is not even the actual saving which the ratepayer
imagines; the difference between fair pay and a pittance is inap-
preciable upon the rates.   While thousands are expended upon
necessary works, and in the repayment of debts and interest spread
over a whole generation, what is the object of an odd 50l. or 100l.
per annum where it is justly due? with the advantage of securing
a zealous and contented officer who values his position, instead of a
discontented and necessarily a careless one.   Ratepayers cannot
escape their legal obligations; roads must be maintained, streets
lighted and cleansed, sewers constructed, and debts paid; these are
the great items of town expenditure which cannot be reduced; but
the ubiquitous "reformer" is sent to your Board pledged to do
something, therefore it is upon official salaries that the great economical demonstration is made, to catch the popular ear, and serve

election purposes; your reformer may, perhaps, save a farthing or two in the pound out of salaries, and the public will lose as many pence through the inefficiency of unqualified or dissatisfied officers.

Referring again to the work of the Town Surveyor, previously summarized—any one section of his duties would, under commercial circumstances, command fair pay according to its importance; but where cumulative duties are included in the same office they demand constant attention, special knowledge, professional experience, and administrative ability; to which is added the anxiety which the responsibilities of public office always involve. Such a position in a commercial concern would receive high remuneration in proportion to the extent of the undertaking, but unfortunately our work does not pay a dividend; it is all expenditure from which the town derives no return excepting in health and comfort, matters which are neither fairly assessed nor duly appreciated, consequently the Municipal Engineer is paid less for his professional knowledge than the contractor's agent whose works he directs.

So long as the Town Surveyor is paid out of local rates I fear he must be content with small pay or seek some other market for his services, and a good man, in any calling, will not sell his services below the market value. The British ratepayer will willingly tax himself for beer, spirits, tobacco, and other health-destroying agents he will even pay his doctor—but he will not, willingly, be taxed for preventive sanitary measures.

In the great question of local taxation, it is worthy of consideration, as matter of detail, whether a portion of local officers' salaries should not come from some source other than local rates. I would, for example, suggest fees as one source of professional income, as in the case of the Metropolitan Building Surveyors, and many other public offices.

A large portion of the duties of a Town Surveyor consists of the supervision of new buildings, estates, roads, drainage, and other matters of private enterprise undertaken for private gain. The entire cost of the official supervision of such works is at present thrown upon local rates. Builders, property owners, and speculators, whose works require supervision in the public interest, should pay the cost of such supervision. In many towns such fees would pay the entire cost of the office and staff; the fee in each case would be relatively small, but the income in the aggregate appreciable, the ratepayer would be better satisfied, and the office better served.

In no case where a town cannot, or will not, pay a liberal salary, has it a right to demand the entire services of an officer.   When a man gives his whole time to a salaried office, he is the more dependent upon his employers, and if he be deprived of office after the best years of his life have been devoted to the public service, he has nothing to fall back upon, not even a pension, and if in middle life he will, notwithstanding his experience, be ineligible for similar office elsewhere, by reason of the limit of age imposed upon candidates.   If the Town Surveyor be a necessary officer, it is equally necessary that he be qualified and efficient, be the town large or small, but efficiency cannot be secured without adequate remuneration; it is, therefore, better to have the partial services of an efficient man than the whole services of an inefficient one.   The more opportunities a Surveyor has for the exercise of his profession, the more valuable is he to his clients, be they public or private.

I have thus enlarged upon the question of official remuneration because it has hitherto constituted the great injustice of our position and lessened our influence; because the subject has been unpleasantly forced on our notice by recent legislative action in connection with the Medical Officer, and because our profession is almost daily insulted by advertisements requiring the knowledge of an Engineer, and the administrative ability of a Manager, for the pay of a mechanic.   There are exceptions, in some of our larger towns, to which these remarks do not apply; and especially has there been an improvement of late; but even some of our large towns fail to appreciate the services of their officers, many of whom are still hedged by restrictions, and niggardly paid.   Eliminate the largest towns, and the position of the Surveyor is one demanding the serious consideration of this Association, and calling for all the sympathy and co-operation which those of our number who are more favourably circumstanced can render them.

Next to the subject of remuneration, that of protection demands our consideration.   This also is a matter which may less affect the officers of our large towns, where there is less opportunity for petty tyranny and local intrigue, but experience has taught me that even in populations of considerable magnitude the Surveyor needs a power of appeal.   Large towns are frequently governed by a clique, or rather two cliques, one in office and the other out, between which the Surveyor is a shuttlecock.   Corporations proverbially have neither a conscience to appeal to nor a body to be kicked; but an officer, particularly the Surveyor, who spends all the money, becomes a convenient scapegoat, and unquestionably receives more "kicks than halfpence." The general nature of his duties, especially in connection with sanitary works and private improvements, are such as, if actively and impartially performed, bring his office into antagonism with popular prejudices and pecuniary interests, and sometimes even with his immediate masters. The Report of the Royal Sanitary Commission refers to "the number of persons interested in offending against sanitary laws, even amongst those who must constitute chiefly the local authorities."

Again, there are many conflicting commercial interests in a town—a gas interest, a water interest, a railway or a tramway interest, &c., various such directors have seats in the local authority. It is, therefore, almost impossible for the local Surveyor to discharge his duties faithfully and impartially without giving offence to interested parties, hence he is peculiarly liable to harassing attacks, from which he has no protection. Boards are constantly changing in constitution and varying in tactics; one party is sent to reverse the work of another; a dependent officer is, therefore, tempted by self-interest to discharge his duties from motives of policy and time-serving rather than of consistent principle. The very large number of letters I have received from Surveyors on this point,* detail an amount of personal injustice, evasion of the law, and wrong doing, which can hardly be conceived. We have endured these things for five-and-twenty years, but it is our new colleagues, the Medical Officer and Inspector, who are now to be protected, in order, to use the words of the Royal Sanitary Commission, that "they may be able to discharge their duties without fear of personal loss." In my humble opinion the "fear of personal loss" is a matter as important to the Sanitary Surveyor as it is to the Medical Officer.

It may be said that many local authorities will not avail themselves of Government aid, in order that they may retain complete control over their officers. I reply that the Government has established a principle which will probably prevail in the end. In fact, many such appointments have already been made. I contend only for the principle, and that the same principle which the Government has applied to one class of officers should be extended to another equally entitled to their consideration.

Surveyors appointed under the Towns Improvement Clauses Act were protected. During the existence of the General Board of

* *Vide* "Evidence," page 244.

Health we were protected. Sir C. Adderley's Public Health and
Local Government Bill of 1872 proposed similar protection.
Officers employed under the Poor Laws are fully protected as to
position, emoluments, and superannuation; the administration
of the Poor Laws and the Public Health Acts is now united in
one department under the newly established Local Government
Board; it is therefore, in my opinion, equally due to Local Board
officers that they also should be recognized and protected. Without
such protection sanitary legislation cannot, in the words of the
Royal Sanitary Commission, be "active and effective," because local
officers are "too dependent on their immediate employers to be
thoroughly efficient."

In advocating protection let me not be misunderstood. I do not
mean centralization, or the removal of that proper control which
every local authority should maintain over its own officers. I
would maintain intact the great principle of local government
which has ever been the bulwark of our social and political freedom. But local government may degenerate, and in small towns
deteriorate into littleness; local affairs are too frequently avoided
by those who are most fitted by intelligence and social standing to
take part therein. I would simply control, in the most constitutional manner, the short-comings or excesses of local government,
as is already done in various other departments. I would require
that local officers should be properly qualified and adequately
remunerated; that in the honest discharge of their duties, and
during good behaviour, they should be protected from the effects of
ignorance, narrow prejudices, and interested clamour; and that
they should have an appeal to a disinterested and judicial body
superior to local feeling. The demand is reasonable, I ask no
more.

I now leave the personal question which has moved us to
associate, to speak briefly on the more general objects of our
Association.

One of the greatest difficulties we have to contend with, as
Sanitary Engineers, is to induce people to appreciate sanitary
principles, a difficulty by no means confined to the illiterate or the
penurious. The elements of sanitary science—by which I mean
those general laws and conditions of health, affected by the action
of physical agents and local circumstances, sufficiently within control to enable us to promote comfort, prevent disease, and prolong
life—should be generally known and taught from the lowest grade

school to the University. One of the objects of our Association will
be to promote such knowledge, so that our work may be better
appreciated, our office better supported, and the public correspond-
ingly benefited.

The conditions of society have changed. Five hundred years ago
the population of the kingdom was only equal to the present population of the Metropolis. When the first census was taken in 1801,
the population of England and Wales was less than 9,000,000; it
has now reached nearly 23,000,000. We crowd together as we
never crowded before; our pursuits are more sedentary, our habits
more luxurious; houses grow apace; land is more valuable, the
green fields more remote; our children are reared among bricks and
paving-stones; the public health can only be maintained by special
sanitary appliances and precautions.

I have already said that, in this country, we have banished the
grosser forms of sanitary defects. We have " cleaned the outside of
the cup and the platter," but we have yet to deal with dangerous
refinements. We have improved away the open cesspool from our
premises only, in too many cases, to establish an " elongated cesspool" in our streets, a subterranean "retort," from which poison-gas
is "laid on " by " services " to every house. We have ceased to
pollute wells, but ventilate drains through our household cisterns.
We have filled up cesspools in detail, and poisoned rivers wholesale.
We have striven on every hand to hide, to bury, and to forget, but
the obnoxious and irrepressible thing will come to the surface, not
infrequently to strike down our loved ones, from the prince to the
peasant, with its concentrated and fatal poison.

There is yet much to be done, or we must pay the penalty of
herding together and the neglect of sanitary laws. We have yet to
remedy defects which are everywhere apparent, not only in the
mansions of the rich and the villas of the middle class, who can
help themselves, but more especially in the homes of the poor, who
are dependent on others and consequently most need our protection. We have yet to establish and promote general principles
of sanitary economy in connection with the drainage, ventilation,
and warming of our dwellings.

Again, there is the great question of utilization, or at least the
disposal, of our sewage, upon which I dare not now enter. If our
Association can solve this troublesome problem it will accomplish
that which Royal Commissions and chemists have failed to do.

These are matters for the earnest consideration of our Association, questions in which our experience, our influence, and our intimate knowledge of local details, may be of some value to the country. By an interchange of experience, by unity of action, by zealous co-operation with other departments, we may materially assist sanitary progress, and promote useful legislation. It is a remarkable fact, that among the various officials who gave evidence before the Royal Sanitary Commission upon the practical working of the existing Acts, not one Surveyor holding office under a local authority was called, although several hundreds of such officers are actively engaged throughout the country who have great experience in the details and the defects of existing arrangements.

Our organization will give us weight, and gain for us attention. We may hope in the future that our discussions and united action in aid of sanitary progress will obtain for us, individually and collectively, some better recognition, and that the country will also share in the advantages of our Association.

ANNUAL MEETING OF THE ASSOCIATION OF MUNICIPAL AND SANITARY ENGINEERS AND SURVEYORS.

HELD IN THE COUNCIL CHAMBER, MOOR STREET, BIRMINGHAM, MAY, 1874.

FIRST DAY'S PROCEEDINGS.

THURSDAY, MAY 28, 1874.

MR. LEWIS ANGELL, C.E., West Ham, London, President of the Association, occupied the chair. There were also present: Messrs. J. LEMON, Southampton, Vice-President; C. JONES, Ealing, Hon. Secretary; J. W. GRINDLE, Hertford; E. PRITCHARD, Warwick, Hon. Secretary for the Midland Counties; T. C. THORBURN, Birkenhead; R. VAWSER, Warrington, District Secretary for Lancashire and Cheshire; W. S. TILL, Birmingham; E. ELLICE-CLARK, Ramsgate, Hon. Secretary for the Home Counties; A. M. FOWLER, Salford; E. L. STEPHENS, Leicester; W. NEWEY, Harborne; E. BUCKHAM, Ipswich; G. COLE, Hereford; J. BANKS, Kendal; E. SHARMAN, Wellingborough; J. MAUGHAM, Great Grimsby; J. LOBLEY, Hanley; E. BETTERIDGE, Balsall Heath; T. W. BAYLIS, Redditch; T. T. ALLEN, Stratford-on-Avon; E. R. S. ESCOTT, Halifax; B. H. VALLE, Stow-on-the-Wold; G. H. STAYTON, Ryde; R. DAVIDSON, Leamington; J. CARTWRIGHT, Dukinfield; J. DEVIS, Oldbury; J. STANDING, Garston; E. DAVEY, Maidenhead; J. E. PALMER, Great Malvern; H. HALL, Liverpool; G. WATSON, Crewe; W. A. RICHARDSON, Tranmere; W. J. BOYS, Walsall; E. MONSON, Acton, London; J. WOOD, Sidmouth; B. BAKER, Willenhall; W. 'BATTEN, Aston; A. COMBER, Kidderminster; J. ROBINSON, Ashton-under-Lyne; and A. JACOB, Barrow-in-Furness.

The following gentlemen were present as visitors: His Worship the Mayor, Mr. Alderman CHAMBERLAIN; and Mr. Alderman SADLER; Messrs. W. H. GREENING, T. A. SKELTON, London; Dr. WILSON, Medical Officer of Health for Warwickshire; J. WILKINSON, Birmingham Sewerage Works; J. MITCHELL, Ryde.

REPORT OF THE COUNCIL TO THE GENERAL MEETING HELD AT BIRMINGHAM, THURSDAY, MAY 28, 1874.

It is with a feeling of satisfaction that the Council and Officers of the Association of Municipal and Sanitary Engineers and Surveyors report the proceedings which have taken place during the past year, and congratulate the Members upon the success which has attended their efforts, a success which has surpassed all expectations.

Although the Association proper has been in existence only one year, the Council cannot but remind the Members that the work has really been in hand since February, 1871, when the President addressed a letter to the officers of local boards, calling their attention to the importance of co-operation. From that date till February 15, 1873, quietly but surely the work was progressing. On that day a meeting was held at the room of the Institution of Civil Engineers, when the Association was practically formed, the inaugural meeting being held May 2, 1873.

In reporting the proceedings of the past year the Council cannot but refer to that feature of the Association which we may almost call a speciality in its organization, viz. the division of the country into districts or centres, each worked by its own appointed secretary and sub-committee of management, the success of the arrangement is so evident that the Council are most desirous of seeing the remaining portion of England and Wales not yet occupied taken up and apportioned, so that the Association may point to the map of England and Wales and say that it covers the land.

The first district brought into operation was the Midland Counties, with Birmingham as a centre, and taking Warwickshire, Leicestershire, Staffordshire, and a radius of forty miles; and so prompt was the action in this district that a meeting was held on the 15th of March, just one month after the Association was formed, when all the necessary preliminaries were arranged, a sub-committee formed, and Mr. E. Pritchard, of Warwick, appointed District Secretary for the Midland Counties.

On the 19th of April a second meeting was held at Birmingham, when the President was in the chair, and important business was transacted.

On the 18th of October a third meeting was held, at Leamington, the President in the chair. During the day the Members visited the Warwick and the Leamington Sewage Pumping Stations and sewage farms; after which papers were read by Mr. Betteridge, of Balsall Heath; Mr. Allen, of Stratford-on-Avon; and Mr. Monson, of Acton. And on the 14th of March the fourth and last meeting of the year for the Midland District was held at Leicester, when a most interesting and instructive visit was paid to the Leicester Water-Works, and the Sewage Works, and a paper was read by Mr. Stephens, of Leicester.

The second district in date of formation was that of Lancashire and Cheshire, with its centre in Warrington. On the 15th July a preliminary meeting was held at Warrington, when business arrangéments for the management of the district were made. Mr. R. Vawser, Borough Surveyor of Warrington, was appointed District Secretary; and a sub-committee, consisting of the Surveyors of Manchester, Salford, and Birkenhead, was appointed to confer with and assist the Secretary.

A second meeting was held at Manchester on the 4th of October, Mr. J. G. Lynde, of Manchester, in the chair; when a considerable number of Surveyors were present, representing towns with some 1½ million of inhabitants. Visits were paid to the Manchester sanitary manufacturing depot, the fire and police stations, the abattoir, the new Town Hall, and the Salford main intercepting sewer-works.

On the 3rd of January, 1874, a third meeting was held at the Town Hall, Liverpool; Mr. J. Lemon, Vice-President, in the chair. Various places of interest were visited, including the new Central Station, the docks, and new river approach. The Resident Engineer also attended and explained the proposed work for a new tunnel under the Mersey. Papers were likewise read by Messrs. G. F. Deacon, A. M. Fowler, J. A. Hall, and T. C. Thorburn. Mr. Deacon likewise exhibited and explained a water meter or water detector, invented and adopted by him.

The fourth and last meeting of the year for the Lancashire and Cheshire District was held in the committee room of the Town Hall, Chester, on the 10th of April; Mr. Thorburn in the chair; when the important sewage-works now being carried out under the superintendence of Mr. G. A. Bell, were visited—Mr. Bell kindly reading a paper descriptive of the same. A paper was also read by Mr. Fowler.

A third district is now in course of formation for the important county of York. A meeting was held in the Town Hall, Leeds; Mr. A. W. Morant in the chair; when Mr. Henry Alty,

of Keighly, was appointed District Secretary. Resolutions as to
the transaction of business in the district were agreed to.

The district last formed, although "not the least," is the Home
Counties District: it includes, as well as the Home Counties, Hamp-
shire, Sussex, Berkshire, and Hertford, with London as its centre,
and, till other arrangements for districts can be made, Cambridge,
Suffolk, Bedford, Buckingham, Oxford, and the Southern Counties
not yet affiliated to a district. The first meeting was held at the
Town Hall, Stratford, on Friday, April 24; the President in the
chair; when Mr. Ellice-Clark, of Ramsgate, was appointed District
Secretary, with Mr. Grindle (Hertford), Mr. Parry (Reading),
and Mr. Hall (Canterbury), as a sub-committee to assist the
Secretary. The programme of the day's work included visits to
the metropolitan pumping station, the West Ham sewage works,
and the Lodge Farm and Phosphate Company's works at Barking.
The District Secretary, in referring to this district, says, "The
large number of works being carried on in the Home Counties
District will afford the Members interesting and instructive labour.
Two of the greatest sanitary wants of the country come within
their boundary, viz. the drainage of the towns in the Thames and
Lea valley, the whole of the said towns being represented by
Members of the Association. Thus it will be seen that there is an
immense and increasing area for their labour, and this section of
the Association will doubtless from these causes have a large influence upon the sanitary legislation of the south of England."
Doubtless the remarks which have thus found utterance through
the Secretary of the Home Counties District will be echoed by the
Secretaries of every district, for throughout the length and breadth
of the land the need of practical sanitary work is more and more
felt.

During the present month your Council have communicated
with the officer of every local board throughout England and
Wales, and doubtless the result will be that a large accession of
Members will be brought. The meetings which have been held
in various parts of the country, and which have been so fully and
so faithfully reported by the local press of the various districts, all
tell a tale of progress. At the present moment the Association
numbers 160 Members, including, with two or three exceptions,
the municipal Engineers and Local Board Surveyors of every
important town in the country.

At their last meeting the Council, in virtue of the power vested in them, elected as Members of Council: Mr. DEACON, Liverpool; Mr. FOX SHARP, Hull; Mr. THWAITES, Norwich; Mr. COGHLAN, Sheffield; and Mr. HARPER, Merthyr Tydvil; and as Honorary Members, Sir J. W. BAZALGETTE, C.B., Engineer to the Metropolitan Board of Works; and J. W. HAYWOOD, Esq., Engineer to the City of London. Upon the question of re-election of officers, the Council, after mature deliberation and taking into consideration the various points as to advantage or disadvantage likely to ensue by change of officers in the present early stage of the Association's history, unanimously resolved to recommend to the annual meeting the re-election of the President, Vice-President, Council, and Officers as at present, with the addition of the new names above referred to.

The accounts, as audited, will be published with proceedings of the Association.* The balance at the banker's at the present time is 88*l.* 7*s.* 8*d.*

On the motion of Mr. DAVIDSON, seconded by Mr. ESCOTT, the Report was adopted.

Mr. MONSON moved, and Mr. DAVEY seconded, the re-election for the ensuing year of the President and Council.

Mr. THORBURN moved an amendment to the effect that a second Vice-President be elected. Seeing the extent of the society, he thought the business was too much for one such officer.

A further amendment, that there should be three Vice-Presidents of the Association, was moved, but not seconded.

The original resolution was carried; after which, on the motion of the VICE-PRESIDENT, it was decided to hold the next annual meeting at Manchester.

* See page xvii.

THE PRESIDENT'S ADDRESS.

The PRESIDENT (Mr. Lewis Angell) then delivered the following address. After thanking the Members for the honour they had done him in re-electing him to the Chair, and congratulating those present upon the success which had attended their efforts to establish the Association, he said they had united the scattered members of a special branch of their profession, and created an *esprit de corps*: already they had a history and an influence. He would briefly review some of the subjects to which the Association might with advantage be directed during the ensuing year. The position of local officers, he regretted to say, was not satisfactory. They still lacked that support and protection which, after twenty-one years' experience, he emphatically declared would alone render them efficient officers, superior to local influence and interested or ignorant obstruction and attack. There had been a marked improvement during the year in the inducements offered to their profession to accept municipal employment, which he hoped was partly due to a better appreciation of sanitary services and requirements. With regard to the work of Members, first and foremost stood that most troublesome and vexatious of all subjects with which they had to deal with—the sewage question. Was sewage a "mine of wealth" or a "Slough of Despond"? As that subject would be discussed on the following day he would not enter into the technical part of the question. He must remark that the present legislative aspect of the question was most unsatisfactory, and that municipal authorities and their official advisers had been placed in a most difficult position by the uncertain action of the Government. Upon sanitary matters there had been over-legislation as well as too little legislation: if he might use the expression, there was too much law and not enough of gospel. Sanitary enactments had overreached practical facts. If some of the official energy which had been directed to the detection and prosecution of unfortunate towns were directed to the discovery of the remedy; if there were some declaration or authority of what might be accomplished, and what was satisfactory

under certain given conditions, the Government would render a
real service to the country; instead of which they were without
guidance, and referred to the unmeaning formula, "The best
known practicable process." Government inquiries were held all
over the country at great cost, deputations went from town to
town inspecting and reporting, the same evidence and the same
facts were repeated over and over again before Government inspectors and Parliamentary committees—in all this there was
waste of money, energy, and time. A Government commission
might establish, as far as could be ascertained, some standard
method applicable to varying circumstances of meeting their own
standard of purity. It surely ought to be well known whether the
intermittent scheme of filtration at Merthyr Tydvil was or was
not a success, and how far it might be applied elsewhere under
similar or different conditions; whether or not irrigation farms
were successful; wherein they failed, or under what conditions
they should be undertaken. If from local circumstances any one
of such systems was inapplicable, it should be known what other
processes, chemical or mechanical, would meet the varying circumstances of the case. Surely there was work for a Royal Commission.
On the one hand, they had been told, with all the weight of official
authority, that in sewage there was a mine of wealth, and that its
waste was a "stupid crime." Whilst, on the other hand, specula-
tive enthusiasts had lost a "mine of wealth" in search of this
El Dorado. For twenty years past Parliamentary Committees
and Royal Commissions had inquired, experimented, and reported;
but they had lived to see the reporters repudiate their own recommendations. Such results as Birmingham and West Ham did not
encourage Engineers to delve for the mine of wealth, or attach
much practical value to official inquiries. There had been volume
upon volume on irrigation, and town after town had been
refused irrigation. A Government inspector had reported un-
favourably upon the financial results of sewage farming, and
declared that nothing short of "absolute necessity" would justify a
town in undertaking a large irrigation scheme. Chemical systems
had been tried and had failed, and the Royal Commissioners reported that chemistry held out no hope. Could a greater dilemma
for the ratepayers be imagined? Instead of thus remaining
floundering in the mire, and having no "policy of sewage," it would
be better that the Imperial Exchequer should expend a few thousands in crucial experiments for the guidance of the nation, than

that town after town should be harassed by injunctions and
penalties, in addition to the waste of thousands in partial, imperfect,
and altogether unsatisfactory attempts to solve the vexed question.
At present Engineers could not advise, and towns would not act.
They were at the mercy of Government inspectors, who changed
their opinions and differed among themselves. It was full time
that some definite legislative action should be taken.

The subject of sewage pollution and purification suggested that of
water supply. The insufficiency of water, the waste of water, and
the purity of water, were important questions for the Engineer
and the sanitarian. The insufficiency of the water supply in many
towns was a fact which was forced upon the attention of every
traveller. Concurrently with insufficiency they found absolute
waste, due to carelessness and defective pipes and fittings. There
was great waste in the purification of water not required for
domestic purposes. Out of the thirty or forty gallons per head of
water supplied to the population, less than one-fourth was used for
domestic or drinking purposes, the remainder being used for street
watering, fire extinguishing, sewer flushing, and other processes
which did not demand any degree of purity. The necessity for
purification of water was confined to the five and six gallons per
head required absolutely for domestic purposes. Such a distinction
of supply would of course involve a dual system in every house.
Town wells would then be safely available for ordinary purposes.
The reduction of the purified domestic supply within reasonable
limits would, he thought, greatly assist in the settlement of the
sewage question by reducing the demands upon water companies,
and bringing the standard of sewerage purification within easily-
obtainable limits. Rivers were the natural channels of drainage.
The stream which flowed through a cultivated country or populous
towns must necessarily be highly charged with organic matters
apart from sewage, and largely polluted with street washings, trade
refuse, and matter from various sources. Such being the case, was
it right that people should derive their water from a polluted source
instead of from the pure water-bearing strata, or from the fountain-
head, as Sir Hugh Myddleton supplied London two and a half cen-
turies ago, and as recently it had been proposed to supply London
and other large towns from the great lakes and watershed districts?
If people must needs drink town washings, should not the water
companies, who make large profits, intercept and purify town
drainage at their own cost, or bear a share thereof? Or should

such burdens be thrown on the public, and standards of purity recommended by Royal Commissioners and adopted by river conservancies be maintained by exorbitant rates? This was a subject worthy of discussion. The subject of road watering was open to very much improvement in practice. The present method was slow, cumbersome, and costly. A system had recently been exhibited in London, Brighton, and elsewhere, which might be described as an elongated water-cart distributor, connected with the water mains, and laid longitudinally along the kerb, from which the water was projected laterally over the roadway. By these means a whole town might be watered simultaneously with very little labour by the ordinary road-men, and the entire heavy cost of horses, carts, and hydrants would be saved. Allowing for the repayment of capital, watering a town this way would not cost annually more than one-third that of the present cumbrous and inefficient system. Some improved system must ultimately displace the water-cart.

On the subject of building irregularities, he thought nothing short of general building regulations applicable to the whole country would obviate the difficulty. Outside the Metropolis builders do very much as they like, and frequently, directly or indirectly, rule the local board as well as the Surveyor. In such matters officers should be unassailable, and subject only to a higher power. He especially denounced the common practice of excavating for sale the gravel from building sites, which were afterwards filled in with any rubbish, generally the town refuse, containing putrescible matter, upon or adjoining which houses are afterwards built. Such houses form the sick homes of family after family, who are unaware of the condition of the soil upon which the attractive cottage stands.

Since their last meeting the practice of cremation had been advocated by so eminent a surgeon as Sir H. Thompson, and societies had been formed in London and New York to promote its practice. No proposition was considered too alarming for the present day; the age of prejudice was passing away, and many proposals which at first shocked our senses ultimately obtained approval. The practice of cremation might shock English feelings and Christian traditions, but he was not prepared to say that it might not ultimately commend itself to the sanitarian.

The subject of sewer ventilation was one which would occupy their attention. He would only observe that, in his opinion and experience, the best means of preventing foul sewers was the freest admission of fresh air at all points, and the prevention of stagnation by a continuous waterflow. All drains should have free communication with the air. Attention to these points would be more effective than all the cunningly-devised patents and disinfectants. The dispersion of vapours into the air, the discharge of factories' refuse into the sewers, were, in his experience, matters calling for the active interference of both the medical officer and the Engineer.

The Members of the Association had an ample field for labour, and he thought that their influence upon sanitary progress and town improvement might be great. With qualified officers, intelligent and disinterested boards, and a public educated in sanitary principles, their efforts would be appreciated. He trusted that such expectations were not Utopian, but until such a time arrived they would have " to labour and to wait."

The thanks of the Association were accorded to the President for his address.

BUILDING AND SANITARY BYE-LAWS.

By Mr. JAMES LEMON, Borough Engineer, Southampton, Vice-President of the Association.

The want of a better and more uniform code of bye-laws throughout the kingdom must be my excuse for placing these few remarks before this Association.

The difficulty of passing bye-laws through the town councils against vested interests is one of the reasons of their incompleteness and in many instances their inefficiency. Under Section 34 of the Local Government Act, 1858, every local board *may* make bye-laws with respect to the following matters, viz. :

New Streets — Construction of Buildings, Space and Ventilation — and as to 'Drainage, Water-Closets, Privies, Ash-Pits, and Buildings unfit for Human Habitation.

But how few local boards have availed themselves of this opportunity for sanitary improvement and made efficient bye-laws is well know to most of my hearers. The questions I wish to put before this Association are : Should this power remain as it is, permissive? Should it be made compulsory? or should the present regulations by bye-laws be included in a general Act of Parliament ?

To the first, I say most emphatically, No. To the second, An improvement; and to the third, Yes.

I shall be told, no doubt, that some large towns have *local* Acts of Parliament embracing all they require.

To this I say that the efficient local Acts should not be repealed, and the proposed new Sanitary Act would only give them additional powers.

Some of my hearers may say, " But we want liberty of action, and what will apply to one town will not apply to another, and all this proposed uniformity would be impracticable."

To this I reply by 'taking the ordinary bye-laws seriatim, and discussing them in detail.

New Streets.

Their Width.—Every local board in framing its bye-laws has adopted a certain minimum width according to the individual views of the promoters. In some towns it is 36 feet, in some 40 feet, and so on; but as this provision is only a minimum one, and the object is to secure sufficient light and air, I really cannot see why this width should not be uniform. A good wide street is one of the safeguards of health, and no new street in my opinion should be less than 40 feet wide, and no paved way not being a carriage road less than 20 feet wide, and more than 100 feet in length. If that length be exceeded, then it should be of the minimum width of a carriage road, viz. 40 feet.

The proposed level, inclination, materials and size, depth, inclination, and construction of the sewers, drains, and gullies to be determined by the Borough Surveyor, and set out as a standing or special instructional order for the guidance of persons constructing new streets. The apportionment of the cost of a new street to the various owners fronting and abutting thereon is one of those difficulties which we all feel, more especially as regards corner lots. Some alteration in the law is necessary, to remove the present injustice to the owners of corner frontages, and I think some expression of opinion should be given by this Association on this very important question. I would throw out a suggestion that the owner be charged only half the *side* frontage, and that the cost of the other half be spread over the frontages to the said street.

The "height of buildings" in new streets is one of importance, and calls for consideration. In the Southampton bye-laws, no building can be erected in a new street which shall exceed in height the width of the street. The effect of this law is, persons wishing to erect lofty buildings must either set them back, or increase the width of the street to the height of the proposed highest building.

Construction of Buildings.

These regulations mostly have reference to the prevention of fire and the stability of walls, and as the same laws will apply to every house in the kingdom, the Metropolitan Building Act might with advantage be extended to every town where there is a corporation or local board.

I recommended my board to adopt the clauses bearing on this subject, and they did so, and find them work very well. There is now a Bill before the House of Commons, introducing some important amendments, the principal of which are:

The clauses in reference to large warehouses.   Under these clauses it is proposed to limit the size of warehouses to 300,000 cubic feet, and all buildings exceeding this will have to be vertically separated into divisions by party walls.   (Unless the board otherwise allow.)

This is a very important provision as regards a town like Manchester, and would certainly have the effect of preventing large fires.

Communications by fire-proof doors are to be allowed under certain conditions; but I would go farther than this, and prohibit all *internal* communications whatever, and compel the construction of *outside* galleries in lieu thereof.

Amongst the many provisions under this head, are those in reference to party walls.

Some Members of the Association are opposed to their being taken through the roof, but I have always advocated the contrary course, as I am strongly of opinion that the mere stopping of a party wall under the slates is a delusion and does not prevent the spread of fire through the roofs.

I find no difficulty in keeping the water out by putting a double slate course in the walls above the roof and slate hanging the walls below.

Timber in Party Walls.—No timber should be allowed nearer than 4½ inches from the centre of a party wall. This, of course, will always give 9 inches between timbers.

Sufficiency of Space about Buildings, and Ventilation.

Under this head we have the all-important question as to yard space.   150 feet super is the minimum space provided for by most local boards, and I think this is little enough.   Under the Metropolitan Building Act it is only 100 feet, but this is proposed to be increased to 150 feet.

We have then the vexed question as to the space not being afterwards built over without the sanction of the local board.   We know the difficulties of our works committee in this matter.   Toolhouses, summer-houses, and many other like constructions have been condemned, and a good deal of ill feeling engendered between local boards and their constituents.

These differences might be removed if the clause was more

clearly defined, and the restriction made to apply only to the space of 150 feet super, and then only to buildings exceeding seven feet in height.

Ventilation.—The ventilation of buildings, whether public or private, does not appear to receive that amount of attention which it demands. It is as necessary to provide for the exit of the vitiated air from a room as the smoke from the fireplace, yet in the majority of cases, even in good houses, the ventilation is never thought of in the construction of the building; and after it is occupied, abortive attempts are made to remedy the evil.

The ventilation of an ordinary building is a simple matter and not costly; but it must be done during the construction of the building, and cannot be done effectually afterwards; therefore I say the ventilation of every new house should be made compulsory either by bye-law or by Act of Parliament.

Ignorant builders would no doubt consider this harassing legislation, and oppose it strongly; but time would soon remove the objections, the public would seek the ventilated houses, and ventilating shafts would ultimately become as common as smoke-flues in every dwelling.

Provision is made in many bye-laws for the ventilation of small rooms without fireplaces and of less area than 100 feet super, and also for public buildings, schools, workshops and factories; but why dwelling-houses should be omitted is not very clear.

The ventilation of the space under floors is also a necessary provision, and should be enforced in every case. In the Southampton bye-laws a clear space of nine inches at the least is specified, connected with the external air by iron gratings or otherwise.

The Drainage of Buildings, Water-Closets, Privies, Ashpits, Cesspools, and the closing of Buildings unfit for Human Habitation.

House drainage is provided for in most bye-laws, but I doubt whether it receives that amount of supervision which it demands. Builders are told they must lay their drains in a certain manner, and to the approval of the Borough Surveyor; but this overworked official cannot possibly see every pipe laid, and parsimonious boards do not give him the necessary assistance to ensure a rigid inspection by deputy.

House drainage, the ventilation of soil pipes, the disposal and removal of excrementitious matters, and the drainage of the subsoil next basements, are all sanitary questions of the highest importance, and more or less dealt with in bye-laws of local boards; but there is a certain blindness amongst sanitarians, local boards, and Government officials which does not augur well for the advancement of sanitary science in this particular.

We live in an age of superficial sanitary patching. Appoint your medical officer and inspectors of nuisances, say the central Board, and down goes your death-rate; but as " prevention is better than cure," I say appoint your Civil Engineer also, and, if appointed, strengthen his hands. Let your dwellings be constructed on the best known sanitary principles, the house drainage well laid, properly ventilated, and the construction inspected day by day, the sewers well designed and constructed, the water supply good and plentiful, and the house refuse regularly removed, and the office of our friend, the medical officer, will be a sinecure.

But as very little has been done by our forefathers to get properly constructed dwellings, the time of the medical officer must necessarily be fully employed in removing the existing evils; amongst these I wish to draw special attention to overcrowding and " houses unfit for human habitation."

These sources of high death-rate should receive special attention, and greater powers should be given to local authorities for the prevention of overcrowding and the removal of unwholesome houses. At the present time any overcrowding may be perpetrated by a *single family*, the law only applies to houses where there are more than one family—except you can deal with it as a nuisance under the Sanitary Act, 1866—so that the Legislature really sanctions the husband, wife, and grown-up family sleeping in one room.

Then as regards houses unfit for human habitation, the local authority may order the house to be closed, but when the owner patches it up and limewhites it, the order is invariably revoked, and the same state of things very soon recurs.

What is wanted is power to order the demolition of such houses, and so to bring about a better sanitary condition of the locality.

In offering these few, and I fear crude, thoughts, I have been actuated with a desire to bring about better sanitary construction in our houses and streets, and so to relieve the medical officer from the onerous duties he now very often performs in searching out the causes of bad smells and the escape of sewage gases, which ought not and could not exist under more rigid sanitary constructional inspection.

Discussion.

The discussion was opened by Mr. MONSON and Mr. LOBLEY.

Mr. JACOB, B.A. (Barrow-in-Furness), said a code of proposed universal bye-laws was already in print, prepared by Mr. Geo. Frederick Chambers, at present attached to the Local Government Board. He (Mr. Jacob) had suggested at the time certain difficulties in establishing a universal code, and he was sure they could not be adopted by every borough in their integrity. It introduced many provisions which would not meet with the approval of Town Councils or of Surveyors. A great many new matters were introduced into the code, and many valuable suggestions were made. Many of the instructions of the Local Government Board were *ultra vires,* and involved corporations in litigation that they were not able to get out of satisfactorily to themselves.

Mr. STAYTON (Ryde) said that Mr. Lemon referred to the difficulty of getting efficient bye-laws passed by the council. He found the same thing in Ryde, when he was appointed some years ago. The bye-laws were old-fashioned, signed by five members of the local board; and the gentleman who was the first to sign these laws was the first to break them. For endeavouring to get better bye-laws, he was cartooned in a local paper called the *Earwig,* and persecuted much in that way.

Mr. FOWLER (Salford) was of opinion that there should be no bye-laws; that the members of the council should have no discretionary power, but that a general Act should apply to the whole country.

Mr. MONSON (Acton) said that local bye-laws hampered Surveyors and inspectors of nuisances, and had better be abolished for general enactments.

Mr. LOBLEY (Hanley) thought that some modification of the Public Health Acts was necessary, especially with regard to lines of frontage.

Mr. THORBURN (Birkenhead) thought they were pretty well agreed that the bye-laws should be swept away, and their proceedings would be very much simplified if they could get a universal Building Act; but, at the present, he must confess that he did not see any way to work out a code of building regulations to be included in any Act of Parliament that would be likely to be completely and successfully applied to all towns. What they wanted more particularly was some general rules laid down by Parliament.

There might be a difficulty in small towns of getting laws put into operation ; but they ought to be compulsory, and not optional. ·

Mr. CHARLES JONES (Ealing) said he would rather have an absolute and compulsory Act of Parliament than a permissive one, and suggested that the Association should form a committee and draw up a code of bye-laws which they thought would be satisfactory to urban and rural districts, towns and villages, that their experience showed could be carried out. Probably they would be accepted by the Local Government Board, who would look upon it as the emanation from the minds of practical men, and might be considered better than even what Mr. Chambers could produce.

The PRESIDENT thought Mr. Lemon struck at the root of the thing when he said that the difficulty was to deal with vested interests. The remedy was to make the duties of Surveyors directory, without having continually to report minor details to a local board, who decided things differently at different times, in accordance with their humour, or perhaps of their personal interests or that of their friends. In the Metropolis the District Surveyors carried out the Act of Parliament. If they found an infraction, they went direct to the magistrates and insisted on the law being carried out without the intervention of boards. He could not see why a general Act should not be applied to the country, with certain modifications for rural and urban districts.

Mr. LEMON having briefly replied, a vote of thanks was passed to him for his paper.

SANITARY LEGISLATION, AND ITS PRACTICAL EXPONENTS.

MR. C. JONES (Hon. Sec. of the Association) was announced to read a paper on this subject, but, owing to the advanced hour of the afternoon, he contented himself with making a short oral explanation. He said the subject of sanitary legislation had occupied the attention of their legislators; bill after bill had been brought before the House of Commons, commission after commission had been appointed, and tens of thousands of pounds thrown away. They had had to carry out Acts of Parliament bearing upon sanitary measures, and it was now twenty years ago since men like Dr. Lyon Playfair and Mr. Chadwick took up the question, and reported upon the position of towns in Lancashire and other places, and legislative measures, based on the recommendations of these reports, were passed. And so it went on from time to time, and they had been looking for something which would prove a panacea of all the sanitary wants of the nation. That came at last, and in the year 1872 an important Act was passed, which they hoped would have been the great remedy for all their necessities. The evidence of those who knew everything, and those who knew nothing about sanitary measures was taken into account, with the exception of the men who had to carry out the matter. It was an extraordinary circumstance that not one officer, not one of the Engineers or Local Board Surveyors throughout England, was called upon to give evidence in connection with that important measure. It was founded upon the evidence of medical officers—all respect to them in their department—town clerks, chairmen of boards, and everyone else who had anything to do with the matter; but not the men who had to carry out the minutiæ of the affair, and who understood the working of it. The mountain was in labour, and it brought forth not a mouse, but an inspector of nuisances, one of the most extraordinary developments of legislative enactment. He believed that nothing had occurred in connection with the legislation of the last 25 or 30 years which had had such a baneful effect on the sanitary condition of the country as that production.

The inspector of nuisances under any rural sanitary authority or
board of guardians was not a Surveyor, and he was not an
Engineer. He was a man to do what the board told him, and he
was not to poke his nose into everybody's affairs. It was a matter
of false economy, of putting down everything likely to increase the
rates. To illustrate the point which he was anxious to take up, he had
cut out some advertisements for inspectors from the *Local Government Chronicle*. One offered a salary of 75*l.* per annum, payable
quarterly, for an inspector to look after thirty-five parishes, something like 2*l.* 3*s.* per parish per annum, and he had to undertake
the sanitary measures in connection with all these parishes under
the enormous power of an Act of Parliament. He had to make a
sanitary inspection of the whole district, looking after their sewage
and water arrangements, and in many cases 25 or 30 miles of road.
Here was another case. For 19,090 acres an inspector was offered
75*l.* per annum. He had also one in which they advertised for
an inspector for 69,000 acres, and the parishes included in it,
and they offered a salary of 2*l.* 2*s.* a week. In another case, where
there were thirty parishes in the union, where the duties to be
performed were those prescribed by the Public Health Act of 1872,
80*l.* was offered, and the officer had to provide all necessary
expenses, travelling and keeping a horse at his own cost. If he did
not pity the inspector, he pitied the poor horse. He had another
case of thirty-five parishes, at 75*l.* per annum. He would like to
hang the man who put that advertisement out first, because it had
been so extensively copied. He had a curious case of thirty-five
parishes, with 40,000 acres, and a salary of 75*l.*, to commence from
the date of confirmation, to include all travelling and other
expenses, except the books; the appointment was to be for one
year only, and the officer was to do no other work. At the bottom
of that was an advertisement for a porter at a workhouse, where
there was a salary of 30*l.* per annum, and everything found, with
some perquisites in the way of 5*l.* 10*s.* for shaving. There was
another case, with an area of 103,426 acres, and there was 50*l.* per
annum, which would include travelling and other expenses. There
was, however, a saving clause; the inspector would not be required
to devote his whole time to attend to the duties of his office. He
also knew a case in which an inspector of nuisances, in one of the
dirtiest places under the sun, kept a beershop, and yet he had been
appointed with the approval of the Local Government Board as a
" practical exponent of an Act of Parliament." He trusted the

time was not far distant when this institution would make its voice heard, and when these monstrosities would be thrown upon the public no longer.

Mr. THORBURN (Birkenhead), to bring the question to a practical issue, moved that a memorial be presented to the Local Government Board, protesting against these absurd appointments.

The motion was seconded.

Mr. MONKS (a member of the Town Council of Warrington) said he was not an Engineer but came as a visitor: he would like to know whether, if all the town councils and local government boards paid their officers good salaries, they could find a supply of competent men? He hoped they would have patience in that matter, considering that they were on the threshold of sanitary legislation. They might trust to the good common sense and kindly feeling of local boards that when they had efficient men they would pay a good salary.

The PRESIDENT replied that if officers were properly paid there would be no lack of competent men; but at present he had seen very little disposition on the part of town councils to recognize competent services. The President suggested that the resolution should be altered to, " That the subject be referred to the Council, with the view of memorializing the Local Government Board," which was carried unanimously.

VENTILATION OF SEWERS.

By Mr. E. B. ELLICE-CLARK, Town Surveyor, Ramsgate.

The question of ventilating our sewers is one that has largely occupied the attention of Sanitary Engineers, and as a body of practical men, you will agree with me it is a subject of vast importance, and one which we cannot too freely discuss until we find out a perfect system of ventilation, which, I fear, we are far from having done at present.

Of the thorough necessity of ventilating sewers there now remains no doubt whatever; experience of forty years has taught us that a system of sewers without ventilation of some description is little better than the old cesspool system—indeed, in some favourably-situated small towns, and under certain conditions, I would prefer having impervious cesspools ventilated than sewers unventilated. Important, however, as the subject is, forming as it does an integral and inseparable part of successful drainage, the evidence I have obtained from nearly a hundred towns shows a deplorably backward state of things as regards the actual ventilation of sewers. Having thus had forced on us that in every extensive system of sewers there is a compound gas formed which contains that which is likely not only to bring about cases of individual sickness, but threatens to bring wholesale pestilence on us, I have endeavoured to find out from the various towns what was the nature of the gases given off, and the velocity of the currents of sewer air; it must be apparent that both vary considerably; for instance, the gas generated in the sewers of Burton-on-Trent, Leeds, and Ramsgate, must be of very different constituents, while the levels of the same towns vary likewise. I, therefore, asked the question in my inquiries, " Have any experiments been made by you to obtain the velocity of air in sewers, and the nature of the gases?" Out of forty-three towns whose answers I have tabulated,* in twenty-eight towns no experiments of any description whatever have been made to determine

* See Appendix, p. 252.

these facts. This is much to be regretted, as I am convinced it is only by such experiments we shall ever determine the best mode of ventilating the various sewers of these towns; while, however, we have twenty-three answering "No," we have several Engineers giving us most valuable information on the subject; by far the most important communication received was from Mr. J. J. Nicholson, of Sunderland; and as these experiments are likely to be made in other parts of the country, I extract from his paper the mode of obtaining the sewer gas for analysis. He says: "I made an examination at the end of September, 1871, obtaining the air by fixing a bell-mouthed pipe of about 10 inches diameter into the wall of one of the main sewers at its upper end; from this I carried up a small pipe into a temporary house erected near the spot, and drew the air out with an air respirator, taking care to have every joint air-tight, and to draw out a few thousand cubic inches every time before commencing.

"This sewer drains a considerable section of the town, and was selected for examination because it was considered more thoroughly trapped than any other, and has its outlet into the river, under water, at all times, except the low-water spring tides." Mr. Nicholson found the composition of the sewer air to be, nitrogen, 81·1; oxygen, 18·4; carbonic acid, 0·5, with traces of sulphuretted hydrogen and ammonia. Comparing this with the analysis of other sewers shows conclusively how the gases vary in their composition. Dr. Letheby gives the following figures of the result of his experiments in London. Nitrogen, 79·96; oxygen, 19·51; carbonic acid, 0·53, with traces of sulphuretted hydrogen. I have tabulated some of the analyses, they are:

	Nitrogen.	Oxygen.	Carbonic Acid.	Sulph. Hydrogen.	Ammonia.
Letheby, London, 1858	79·96	19·51	0·53	traces	
Paris	78·8	17·93	2·29	0·92	
„ Cesspool	79·02	18·14	1·93	0·01	
Sunderland, 1873	80·35	19·37	0·23	none	traces
„ 1871	81·10	18·44	0·55	traces	
Sewer, London	78·81	20·79	0·40		
Drain at 45, Upper Hamilton Terrace	78·79	20·70	0·51	traces	

In the Ramsgate sewers we have discovered nitrogen (in excessive quantity), oxygen, carbonic acid, sulphuretted hydrogen, and ammonia, but no quantitative analysis has been made. With regard to the danger of these gases entering our houses, there is little doubt the most poisonous of these is sulphuretted hydrogen, which is fortunately found to be present in very small quantities; it is a gas that can be instantly detected by its most singular fetid smell, and can be traced even if mixed with 10,000 times its bulk of atmospheric air. Water at freezing point, Fahrenheit, dissolves 4·37 its volume of the gas, and 2·9 at 52° (the average heat of sewers at ordinary depths); it has immense powers of diffusion. Carbonic acid, found to exist in sewers from very slight and almost imperceptible traces to 2·3, is half as heavy again as atmospheric air; it will not support combustion, and has large powers of diffusion. These two are gases which are present in much larger quantities than above stated in the old sewers of deposit in London and elsewhere; and it is for this reason that open ventilation is attended with greater danger to public health than flushing and no ventilation at all, as these gases are carried up by the light specific gravity of the whole compound of sewer gas into our streets. By far the greater part, as we have seen, nearly 79·00 of sewer gas, is composed of nitrogen, which is lighter than atmospheric air, density 14. By comparing the quantity of nitrogen and oxygen found in sewer gas and atmospheric air we can see at a glance the effect of the decomposition in sewers.

Air	$\begin{cases} 20\cdot9 \text{ oxygen.} \\ 79\cdot1 \text{ nitrogen.} \end{cases}$
Sewers (mean of seven analyses)	$\begin{cases} 19\cdot26 \text{ oxygen.} \\ 78\cdot12 \text{ nitrogen.} \end{cases}$

But this large amount of nitrogen need not alarm us: on the contrary, it is one of the most unfortunate things that the decomposition in sewers adds nitrogen instead of dangerous gases; its large presence in a sewer cannot be ascertained by smell, as it is perfectly inodorous and tasteless; its specific gravity is 0·972; it neither supports combustion nor animal life; it has, however, no poisonous properties, and, practically, may be considered as harmless in the sewers: it is remarkable that there should be such a diminution in the quantity of oxygen and an excess of nitrogen; for when we remember that these two bodies never vary under any circumstances in atmospheric air, it is difficult to assign a reason why such should be the case, unless it is from the absorption of the oxygen to form carbonic acid gas; to these gases must be added fetid organic vapour and marsh gas. We have thus clearly proved

E 2

to us that certain sewers contain a number of gases, the whole
forming one body, which we know as sewer gas—a homogeneous
mixture of light specific gravity, with immense diffusive power,
acting as a distinct body, with its own individual characteristics.
The mean specific gravity of the Sunderland sewer gas was
1001·5. This is exceptional and very close to the diffusive power
of atmospheric air. I am one of those whose opinion is that a
vast amount of evil is laid to the door of sewer gas that springs
from other causes, and that in the majority of cases it is not
of that deadly nature popularly supposed; this depends, however,
much upon the nature of the sewer. The sewers, the analysis of
which I cite, are by no means likely to contain such a large
quantity of poisonous gases as in manufacturing towns, where
various chemicals are constantly thrown into the sewers; as, for
instance, St. Helen's, Leeds, Bradford, and other places; nor are
the poisonous gases likely to be generated in the London sewers
analyzed, as they are in other towns where the temperature of the
sewers fluctuates to a greater degree, this being one of the main
causes of the presence of the actually poisonous properties in
sewer gas. In Liverpool, Mr. Deacon, without analyzing the
sewer air, considers the heating of the sewer by steam jets and the
discharge of hot water as one of the great difficulties he has to
contend with in proposing open ventilation; indeed, to such an
extent does this hot-water discharge raise the temperature of the
Liverpool sewers, that the Engineer says: "The most important
exceptions to the street (open?) ventilating system will be those
portions of sewers into which hot water is ejected." The mean
temperature of the air of the Avenue Road, London, sewer, on
certain days in the months of April and May, was found to be 50·8°,
that of the outer air being 45·8°; in May, June, July, and October,
the mean temperature was 56·2°, while the outer air was 54·2°;
there was thus a difference of 5° in April and May, and 2° in the
other period. This difference is a very small one, and would speak
favourably for the sewer so far as its being easily ventilated and
non-likelihood of producing decomposition. Mr. Haywood, the
City of London Engineer, states, from experiments extending over
a year, the mean temperature of the sewers to be 55·35°, the outer
atmosphere being 5·11° below that. Mr. Baldwin Latham states
the Croydon sewers to be pretty nearly uniform during the whole
year, on 220 days being lower than that of the outer air. The
temperature of the Ramsgate sewers averages about 5° higher than

the outside atmosphere, but there are several sewers where the temperature is always higher; in one instance, while the atmosphere was 60°, the sewer was as high as 72°: this is a sewer of which I shall speak hereafter as having been ventilated by charcoal ventilators. The Queen Street sewer averages 1° below the temperature of the outside air in summer, and 10° above in winter, never falling below 45° in winter. We have in sewers, the temperature of which rises from 45° to 70°, this great cause of gases, independent of other causes, which tends materially to the generation of them, and without which indeed they could not exist, and it is very doubtful whether baneful gases exist at all in sewers where the temperature is kept down by constant flushing. On the other hand, there cannot be the shadow of a doubt that there are miles of sewers, the construction of which is either so defective, or the peculiar nature of the sewage is such, as to give off a large amount of highly dangerous gas. To get rid of this gas, it would be simply impossible to lay down a rule; almost every mile of sewer in England differs in its conditions, and therefore different methods must be adopted to suit different cases. How are we to get rid of sewage gas? It appears to me that we must first consider how we are to prevent gas being engendered in the sewers. It is an impossible thing to prevent some noxious gas being formed, but I am strongly of opinion that careful attention as to the flushing of sewers—even though they may be badly constructed and ventilated—will effect a large diminution in the volume of dangerous gases in such sewers. Sewer gas I have proved, by a very rough test, to be soluble in water to such a degree, that, having been in a sewer of constant flow, where the stink was such as would preclude a man working in it for any length of time before flushing, after discharging a large volume of water, the sewer running seven-eighths of full bore, very slight smell was perceptible, and the temperature lowered 4°. To obtain ventilation in sewers a current of air at a certain rate must be established. Mr. Bazalgette, when before the Committee of the House of Commons, and being examined on the production of a current of air by furnaces, said that 6 feet a minute was stagnation, and not ventilation; and that there existed in sewers, from various causes, a current amounting to 100 feet per minute and upwards. On the 6th of this month the air in the Queen Street sewer, Ramsgate, had a current opposite to the water flow of 1 mile 110 yards in an hour; the sewer was in a condition that sewer gases could be evolved, as there was an amount of deposit in it, and the temperature of it stood at 60°, while the outside atmosphere stood at 54°: the outlet was tide-locked. It is ventilated by several open ventilators at its upper end, which doubtless caused a current of air to pass up the sewer. Could a current of this rapidity be kept up, no doubt the diffusion and dilution of sewer gas would be complete. Indeed, I consider a quarter of a mile an hour would give ample ventilation, and prevent the gases accumulating in such a degree as to become dangerous. It would be out of the question in a paper of this description to enter into the various methods by which Engineers and chemists have proposed to ventilate sewers. The furnace idea I think exploded after the evidence of Messrs. Haywood and Bazalgette. As I believe a solution of this question is more likely to come from practical men who have the care and management of the sewers, the evidence I have gathered I consider to be most important and valuable, and I will as briefly as possible summarize it. The earliest ventilators were the gully gratings; but these were trapped, as the gas was annoying and dangerous to foot passengers; since then various measures have been adopted; but so far as I can learn, none so successful as that of open ventilation in the centre of the street. With a view of destroying the gases, charcoal has been used to a large extent, and it is to keep this dry and free from dust that many men have turned their attention, but the experience of years has proved charcoal to be successful only in exceptional cases.

However great the absorbent powers of charcoal may be—and they are very large, and have been proved so to be, especially in the case of sewer gas—my own experiments and the evidence I have obtained are opposed to its use. The questions I put to various Engineers were: "Are your sewers ventilated; if so, what description of ventilator?" "Have you used charcoal in any form, and with what result?" One Engineer says: "Yes; no good" (brief, but to the purpose). The other answers are: "The basket containing the charcoal must be constructed so as to prevent it becoming consolidated by the tremulous motion of the traffic." The same Town Surveyor (Bacup) says: "A sewer 480 yards long, 3′ × 2′, and 520 yards, 30″ × 20″, gradient 81·75, has been ventilated with Latham's charcoal ventilators, and the sewer is comparatively free from gas ;" but we are not informed of the nature of the houses and factories connected, or the flow of the sewage, or whether gas had been previously found in the sewers. In Bury, ventilation is by means of the gully gratings, few traps being used. In Bradford, "the sewers are ventilated by vertical pipe-shafts and open grates at the street surface, by untrapped gratings, and in one case by a shaft 50 feet high." In Birkenhead, the ventilators are filled with charcoal, and described by Mr. Thorburn as very satisfactory, being placed from 60 to 120 yards apart. In Blackburn, " the fall of the sewer is very great, the velocity of the sewage carries all with it." The Engineer does not see the necessity of artificial ventilation, but continues, " the end of each tributary main is connected with the street by an open grate, all other mains have an open connection with each manhole, by which there is obtained a complete current of air." In Barnsley, the ventilators used are Brooks's patent, placed about every hundred yards in highest levels; the gases remaining in the sewer, *if any*, are very slight.

Bolton sewers were being ventilated, at the time of my inquiries, by open gratings about 100 yards apart. At Barrow-in-Furness Mr. Jacobs used his own gratings with charcoal, at distances vary-ing from 100 to 150 yards apart. In this great centre of industry, Birmingham, the ventilation is by means of open shafts, and in some instances down-spouts are used. Colchester rejects ventila-tion in any form whatever. Mr. Purnell, of Coventry, ventilates the sewers by "seventeen engine stacks,' and 1230 down-spouts from houses."

At Chatham, the system used to be open ventilation; the Sur-veyor adds: " *which became very objectionable, and I have done away with them in most cases.*" Chelmsford uses the rain-water down-spouts; and at Ealing the same, "where down-spouts can be used," also by "charcoal in baskets, ten to the mile." In Eastbourne, the gratings are made to receive charcoal, but " none is at present used." The Surveyor makes this significant remark as to the use of charcoal: " We have used charcoal, but find, after it has been placed in the boxes a few hours, it becomes useless." In Folkestone, the dual system is in vogue, charcoal being used both in the centre of the streets and in the gullies for the purpose of neutralizing the gases: these are never more than 100 yards apart: they are placed according to circumstances. In Huddersfield, in all the new works, Brooks's charcoal ventilator is used, " and it answers very well ; " the Surveyor continues: " The use of charcoal has produced beneficial results; but my notion is that any method of ventilation which requires looking after is bad, and that the best is by tall pipes or chimney-stacks wherever practicable." Hartlepool ventilates by rain-water pipes. In Ipswich, the sewers "are not ventilated by any properly-designed means." The Surveyor is partial to the use of chimney-shafts where practicable. Latham's spiral ventilators are used at Kingston-on-Thames. No ventilation of any kind is in operation at Lowestoft.

In Leeds, the old-fashioned system of ventilating through the gully grates is in operation, 10,000 being in use. In Leicester, open gratings in the centre of the road are used, and shafts of boiler-houses; also the summit ends of the sewers are "furnished with charcoal tray ventilators," these also acting as a flushing box. In Leamington, by manhole covers at irregular distances, charcoal has been used, and "gets clogged" where the traffic is heavy: where the traffic is light it remains good for six months. In Nottingham, the ordinary manholes, about 80 yards apart, have an opening 18″ square at the side, which acts as a ventilator; charcoal has been used, "but as it impedes ventilation, we have abandoned it." Many of the old sewers of Nottingham are not ventilated, others are so by open gratings; "charcoal cages are provided, but for ordinary use, as the charcoal impedes free vent, we do not use it." In Oxford, the ventilators will be open in the centre of the road when the works now in hand are completed.

The remarks from Plymouth are especially worthy of our attention : " The sewers are ventilated by chimneys or shafts into house chimneys, no regular distances being observed, and very few persons know where they are, to prevent prejudice or imagination from being injurious to the residential property."

In Portsmouth, charcoal 'is used in baskets at the side of the manholes, and found to be quite satisfactory if removed when requisite. (How often?) At Rugby, Latham's charcoal ventilators are found to answer "with good results, provided the charcoal is carefully placed in the baskets; if not, the gases are obstructed." In Southport, "there are four ventilators to engine chimneys, 6″ diameter and 25″ × 4″ pipes to high gables, and all the houses since 1871 have a 2″ pipe to the highest part of the roof." In Sheffield, the manholes and street grates are the ventilators. In Stockton-on-Tees, the sewers are not ventilated "uniformly, but chiefly by down-pipes." The Surveyor adds: " I have no faith in charcoal; it is complicated; plain shafts under a regular system would be ample." In Salford, the London system in the centre of the road is in vogue. In St. Helen's, large chimneys of engine-houses are used, and open grids " sufficiently distant from windows and doors of dwelling-houses." At Stockport, special ventilators are constructed, " and all down-pipes for rain-water connected direct to the sewer; eight Archimedean screw ventilators have been erected, and answer very well." In Warwick, " the sewers are only ventilated at the outfall; charcoal has been used, but the Engineer considers it loses its qualities." The sewers of Sunderland are ventilated by manholes, street-grates, lamp-holes, and special ventilators on the surface, 100 yards apart. In Warrington, open grids are used at varying distances of 80 to 100 yards.

These, then, are the opinions of the professional men under whom the various modes of dealing with sewer gas by charcoal deodorizing or otherwise, are at work; and if the opinion against the use of that disinfectant is not unanimous, it is nearly so: it is to me quite overwhelming. The great proof of these theories is in their application, and as our President told us at our inaugural meeting, one grain of practice is worth a bushel of theory. It cannot be denied that charcoal will effectually absorb and render harmless sewer gas, but the difficulties attending its application are evinced by the evidence I have read to you; and the expense attending its use is such as, to my mind, entirely precludes its being used on a large scale.

My own experience is based on having ventilated a sewer with Latham's ventilators, the gradients varying from 1 in 400 to 1 in 15, the pipes being 18″, 15″, and 12″. Although great care was taken in fixing the ventilators, especially in the steep gradients, after every heavy shower of rain I found the charcoal completely saturated, and several times covered with mud in wet weather; in dry weather the charcoal became consolidated by the traffic, and covered with fine dust. I attribute the latter to an intake of air, from the lower levels to the higher. A month's use of the ventilators, and the sewer became as foul as before. Without mentioning the subject, I had the charcoal trays removed; the effect has been that not a single complaint has been made, and the sewer is now ventilated by these open gratings without causing any annoyance, where formerly complaints were almost daily in the summer months. These ventilators are placed respectively from the lower end of the sewer—which is 1 in 16—at 125, 160, and 200 feet apart; on the next portion, 1 in 60, two gratings are fixed 300 feet from each other, and the end of the sewer is connected by a 9-inch pipe with a furnace shaft 200 feet high. This has produced the best results. As there are still a few who believe in the theory of ventilating the sewers as mines are ventilated, I will give my experience of this furnace. The sewer is a 12″ pipe, being the last length of the sewer quoted before; it has a gradient of 1 in 60; is running nearly half full bore during nine hours of the day; its temperature has been 72° when the atmosphere has been 65°. From the nature of the sewer a large amount of gas is evolved, and complaints from residents were numerous before it was ventilated. The draft of the furnace, which is always alight, produced a current of air at the rate of 4 miles an hour, close to the junction with the shaft, but 100 yards down the sewer the draft was reduced to 300 yards per hour. Close to and above the open grating the draft was up into the street, and reversed to the draft of the shaft. The words of Mr. Haywood, therefore, as to this mode of ventilation, appear to me to be true to the letter. "You may do it, there is no doubt, if expense be a matter of no moment whatever;" but, as he further said, "the expense would be enormous;" and, to quote Mr. Thorburn, it would be "local, intermittent, and dangerous." I can therefore come to no other conclusion than that charcoal and other disinfectants for the purpose of deodorizing the gases, and furnaces for extracting the air, are impracticable.

By far the most effective system yet adopted is the simple one of open gratings in the centre of the street. Crude it may be, yet it has well answered its purpose: it possesses many advantages over any system that attempts to deodorize the gases, being self-acting, no expense after the first cost, not liable to get out of order, from its entire simplicity, and is unquestionably superior to any other mode in diluting and dispersing the gas. With modification, I believe it to be the only sound way of ventilating our sewers. The principal objections to open ventilation are, first, that the gas finds its way directly from the sewers to the passengers and house occupiers; that under certain conditions, when the gas contains a large amount of carbonic acid and will not rise, or do so very slowly, the street, especially at night and early morning, is filled with this pestiferous odour. Some objectors to open gratings have urged that the sewer thus becomes practically an open one, almost

like the old open ditch, removed from us only by a few cubic feet
of earth. This appears to have been the view taken in Chatham,
where the open gratings were closed. This is a plausible idea
at first blush, but, on a little consideration, will not hold water. In
the first place, if the old sewer ditch familiar to us all twenty years
ago in the suburbs of large towns, and too frequently met with now,
had had an impervious lining, the stink would have been slight. It
was not the water that stank, it was the residue left on the banks
that became putrid. So it is with sewers. The maximum flow in
most sewers is from 10.30 A.M. to 2.30 P.M., after which time, as
you know, the sewage subsides, leaving the wetted perimeter
covered with fine particles of excreta and other solids. These are
the actual producers of sewage gas ; and if, while that gas is being
given off slowly, the air can be constantly changed and the noxious
gases largely diluted, you have succeeded in a great measure in accomplishing sewer ventilation, your next object is, that when this gas
rises to the surface, it will be harmless to the health of the people.
There are many advocates for carrying pipes up the houses directly
from the sewers, but we must not forget that sewer gas will not
climb a tortuous and small passage without much pressure, but will
prefer to rush out of the numerous large and open connections with
which nearly all sewers abound. When such pipes are carried up
they should be as large as possible and vertical, otherwise they only
act as relievers of pressure ; and these tall shafts will rarely if ever
act as downcast shafts : that they take the gas beyond the area of
the air immediately used for vital purposes is a great thing, but
they may be made to accomplish much more than this by making
them *downcast* shafts.

In the investigation of this subject I have been struck with the
fact that few attempts have been made to force fresh air into the
sewers, leaving that quite at the mercy of untrapped gratings and
other openings : nearly all efforts at ventilation have been in
dealing with the gas *coming from the sewer*. I believe the solution
of the problem to be by the *introduction of atmospheric air into
the sewers ;* and to obtain this I have for sometime past been turning
my attention. The artificial current created by a furnace having
to my mind exploded, I have endeavoured to suggest a means which
would be cheap, self-acting, easily fixed, and at the same time
perform its duty. To this end I have constructed a cowl-head to be
placed on the top of a tall pipe communicating with the sewer ; this

head, unlike the cowl on the ordinary chimneypot, always presents its opening to the wind, thereby carrying down to the sewer a large amount of atmospheric air, for the pressure of the wind would nearly always overcome the sewer gas. This head would be placed at a height of 20 feet, or above the eaves of the houses; these being placed between two open gratings, terminating at the street level.

Let there be two openings into a sewer, with a difference in height between the two of 30 feet, and let the shaft communicating with the higher aperture be 1 foot square, and the temperature of the air in the sewer and shaft be 15° higher than the temperature of the outer air. Then the current in the shaft would have an ascending force of about 1 oz.; for each cubic foot of air in the shaft would be less in weight than an equal volume of outer air by $1 \cdot 097$ grains for each degree of difference in temperature, and

$$1 \cdot 097 \text{ grains} \times 15° \times 30 \text{ feet} \quad 493 \cdot 650 \text{ grains}$$
$$= \text{a little over 1 oz.}$$

If the difference between the openings were 60 feet, the force would be 2 oz., and so on.

If the temperature of the air in the sewer and shaft were lower than that of the outer air, the air in the shaft would sink by its superior gravity, until it arrived at the same level as the lower opening, and would remain stationary. The shaft would become filled from the cowl-top with air of the same temperature, and therefore of the same specific gravity as the outer air, and create a current to the lower opening.

The greatest amount of pressure yet registered from sewer gas has been $0 \cdot 10$ of an ounce to the square foot. From the meteorological returns of the pressure of wind, as deduced from the anemometer, I find it is rare, excepting indeed on very calm days, that the pressure of the wind is so small as not to create a draught down the tall or inlet pipe, and out of the outlet pipe terminating at the street level; this current of air would be kept up in the sewer, and by this means be constantly changed. The gas that now issues from the open street gratings of London would be so diluted by atmospheric air as to render it quite harmless. Supposing we take a day in August, the calmest month in the year, I find that in August, 1873, the following is the return of the pressure of wind:

As deduced from Anemometers.					
Osler's.					Robinson's.
General Directions.		Pressure on Square Foot.			Amount of Horizontal Movement of Air each day.
A.M.	P.M.	Greatest.	Least.	Mean of 24 abs.	
		lb.	lb.	lb.	miles.
ESE. and E.	E.	2·2	0·0	0·1	216
E., WSW., and SSE.	ESE. and SE.	0·7	0·0	0·0	152
SSE. and SSW. ..	SSW. and SW.	11·4	0·0	0·4	324
SSW.	SW. and SSW.	3·7	0·0	0·3	320
SW.	SW. and WSW.	19·6	0·0	0·9	510
W. and WSW. ..	W. and WSW.	4·6	0·0	0·6	458
WSW.	W. and WSW.	1·8	0·0	0·2	275
SW.		..	..	..	Sum 2255

By this it will be seen that, except on one day, the pressure of the wind, with a deduction for friction, would create a considerable draught in the sewer. I make no observation with regard to the horizontal movement of air, a proportion of which was not appreciable to pressure on the anemometer, averaging, as it did in the above week, 322 miles per day; but it is just possible that with a number of open ventilators we should get a current from this cause, slight though it might be.

In connection with this system of ventilation, I propose in constructing new roads and sewers to form the channel of the roadway in the centre, which would afford us an opportunity of fixing the downcast shafts without impeding the traffic, as the section of the road would be a retiring obtuse angle instead of an elliptical projection as at present. This is a subject, however, which, with your permission, I shall bring forward at an early date, with a view of constructing a cheaper and better section of roadway to suit this system, which I believe to be a practical solution of the question of the ventilation of sewers.

Some discussion followed, and the plan advocated by Mr. Ellice-Clark was generally approved of.

THE SEWAGE DIFFICULTY.

By Mr. E. MONSON, Surveyor to the Acton Local Board, London.

The subject of sewage disposal has been with me a matter of special study. My object in writing this paper was to bring our knowledge of the sewage question down to the present date; to determine the best method of purifying sewage so as to render the water again fit for use; to settle the value of sewage; and to ascertain if it could be utilized, at a profit, in increasing the fertility of the soil. I have gladly availed myself of the opportunities afforded by this Association for visiting various sewage farms and sewage works, and exchanging ideas with my brother Members of the Association; and I have consulted such books upon the subject as were within my reach.

The sewage difficulty is emphatically the great question of the day, and it concerns everybody. From east, west, north, and south—from the city and town, and from the village and hamlet—comes the question: How shall we dispose of our sewage? The sewage difficulty arises from three causes: From the introduction of the water-closet; from a new method of removing town refuse; and from a new style of farming. And it involves the question of the best method of collecting town refuse as well as the best method of sewage disposal.

Previously to the adoption of the water-closet, and before this country was so thickly populated, the excreta was received into a pit made under the privy seat, the liquid being allowed to drain away, and when the pit became full it was emptied. A modification of this system is the ash-closet, which is arranged so that the night soil is discharged amongst the ashes into a movable receptacle. One advantage of this system is that the excreta being saved can be disposed of for agricultural purposes, and in some cases this will pay the cost of removal and yield a profit. Earth-closets accomplish the same result in a more expensive way. But it having been found that decaying animal and vegetable matter in the proximity of dwellings contaminated the water supply obtained from wells, and gave off noxious gases which polluted the air, the Legislature interfered in the interests of the inhabitants of towns, and cast upon sewer authorities the duty and responsibility of periodically and frequently removing excrementitious matters and all waste and refuse that will decompose and pollute the atmosphere. It is stated in the minutes of information collected by the General Board of Health, 1852, "In no mode can the refuse be so well received, so completely preserved, and so productively applied, as by suspension in water."

As the farmer formerly utilized town manure for increasing the fertility of the soil, it was naturally thought that he would employ town sewage for the same purpose; but this is not found to be the case; for there is no demand for sewage in its present form, and it is not sought after by farmers. The introduction of artificial manures has hitherto caused the loss of human excreta to be little felt; but a time may come when we shall be compelled to return to our soils the elements of fertility taken from them.

If untreated sewage be turned into our rivers and streams it kills the fish; and, converting the babbling brook and limpid stream into a dark and loathsome sewer, is a nuisance and injurious to health; it pollutes the air, poisons the water supply of persons residing lower down the stream, and spreads disease. For these reasons sewer authorities are cut off from that means of disposal, and it is rendered unlawful to turn untreated sewage into streams.

The Water-Closet.—All points considered, there is no method so convenient and so expeditious as water carriage for removing excreta from dwelling-houses, and its introduction into closely-populated towns has been a great gain to the public health; but it is not an unmixed blessing, for it sometimes brings noxious gases into our dwellings, and pollutes the air we breathe; and *this new method of removing human excrement by suspension in water is the chief cause of the sewage difficulty.* The water-closet system is thought to be imperfect, because it wastes the valuable products of town refuse, which might and ought to be employed to give fertility to the soil, increase our food supplies, and reduce our rates. The loss of this manure to the country is a great loss of national wealth, and efforts have been made to collect it in a portable and marketable form, but these efforts have not been very successful.

In the minutes of the Select Committee on Sewage, 1864, it was stated in evidence (p. 88) that pipe-clay could be most cheaply conveyed to a distance by suspension in water, and after lifting it

to the required height by pumping, to allow it to flow through
pipes to its destination; and from this it was inferred that human
excrement could be most conveniently removed in the same manner.
But in comparing human excreta to pipe-clay, it seems to have
been overlooked that pipe-clay is inodorous and insoluble, and when
it has arrived at its destination can be easily separated from the water
used in its conveyance; whilst sewage, on the other hand, not only
consists of inorganic elements which can be removed by subsidence
and filtration, but of organic elements (derived from the excreta of
man and animals, and from the decomposition of vegetable substances) which cannot be rendered insoluble by any known chemical
agent available for that purpose, and cannot therefore be removed
by filtration.

Various plans have been proposed, and large sums of money
spent in trying experiments to purify sewage, and the conclusion
come to is, that if human excrement is removed by water, there is
no way of purifying the water fit for domestic use except by passing it through the soil. Now it unfortunately happens that in the
neighbourhood of large towns land is of such enormous value that
it cannot be obtained for sewage purification except at a great price.

The Use and Value of Sewage.

It is very necessary that the value of sewage should be settled;
because if sewage is a valuable manure, as some assert it is, it will
pay to lay out large farms and avail ourselves of its fertilizing properties. But if it is of *no value*, we shall just go to such expense
as is necessary for purification only, and simply take as much land
as is sufficient for that purpose, and get rid of the sewage in the
cheapest way.

Agricultural chemistry has made great progress during the last
few years, and this, with the introduction of artificial manure, has
completely revolutionized the system of farming.

I had been taught to believe that sewage was of the utmost
importance and of immense value to agriculturists, and I wondered
greatly that they could not appreciate its virtues and develop its
latent qualities. I knew that the farmer was deprived of his
supply of potash from the burning of coal instead of wood, and
from the using of soda for washing instead of potash; that his
pastures were ploughed up, and his cows gone that used to supply
him with manure—only two cows being now kept at farms where
there were formerly forty; that his supply of manure from towns

ran short in consequence of the new method of removing town refuse by suspension in water: and yet the farmer was not ruined, nor was his land impoverished. I set myself to inquire how this could be, and how he could possibly do without sewage, and I found that the introduction of artificial manure had rendered him independent of it; that on account of its bulk he could not use it at a profit, and would rather be without it.

The fact is, sewage has a great theoretical but not a commercial value. If not, why is the sewage of London, said to be of the enormous value of upwards of one million pounds sterling per annum, allowed to run to waste? Where are the applicants for the sewage of our large towns? Why are our farmers spending thousands of pounds in guano and other artificial manures, whilst the worth of millions of pounds sterling of sewage is running to waste? How is it that capitalists do not invest their money in sewage farms and sewage works? Have the people of England no enterprise; or are they blind, and do not perceive this mine of wealth? How is it that neither farmer, chemist, nor engineer can get a value out of it; and why are sanitary authorities obliged to take land compulsorily for the disposal of it? These questions admit of but one answer, which is, that the sewage is of so little value as a manure that it cannot be utilized at a profit. The proper use for sewage is to grow root crops and to increase the quantity of green food for cattle, but for this latter purpose it is found to be little better than water which has passed over fertile soils—such as is ordinarily used for irrigation.

The following extract is from *The Builder*, Oct. 19, 1872 :

" The highest returns claimed from the use of sewage manure have been at the rate of from 32*l.* to 40*l.* per acre. We find that the growth of Italian rye-grass amounting to 7 tons an acre is stated to have been produced. If we took last year's price for hay this would give a higher value, but that may be considered as exceptional ; 31*l.* 10*s.* would be the return for the hay at 4*l.* 10*s.* per ton. In water meadows, without manure, or with an occasional top dressing of bone dust, that will not amount to more than 14*s.* per acre per annum, crops of 5 tons per acre, including that which is eaten on the ground, are about the maximum. There is little doubt that these may be materially augmented by such a disposal of the irrigation as should avoid the present wasted area of innumerable water carriers. But it is possible this may cut both ways, so that we take the difference of yield between the ordinary water meadow

F

and the sewage farm at 2 tons of hay, say 9*l.* per annum. This is therefore the total produce of the application of a quantity of sewage averaging in the value hitherto nominally attributed to it at from 6*l.* 10*s.* to 312*l.* (at Merthyr the sewage from 1100 souls is applied to an acre of ground, and the fertilizing elements according to theory are of the value of 312*l.*). That the effluent water from sewage must go through the ground to be purified we take to be an undoubted maxim in the present state of sanitary science. But we complicate this problem, in itself not a simple one, by attempting to derive from the sewage materials fitted for food of plants which do not exist in it in a state in which plants can assimilate it, and which we cannot convert into such a state. We go in the wrong direction."

Sewage cannot supersede farm-yard manure, for it cakes the ground, and, binding it down, seals up its pores and *prevents* the air from getting to the roots of the crop. Farm-yard manure, applied in a state of decomposition and fermentation, gives off gases which, acting upon various bases, liberate elements already in the ground, and lightening up the soil, *let in air* to the roots of the crops. The former is chiefly available for growing root and green crops; the latter is applicable to any kind of crops; the one sinks at once into the ground, and its action upon the soil and crops is passing and transitory; the other decomposes slowly, and keeps up a chemical action which is constant and continuous. As compared with artificial manure, it is of enormous bulk (about 500 to 1), but the whole tendency of farming is to reduce the bulk by applying artificial manure in a very concentrated form. Sewage, like water, retards the ripening of the fruit and grain and develops the leaf; it is limited in its application to particular crops; and as a railway car can only run as far as the rails are laid, so sewage can only be applied to the land as far as the pipes are laid or the carriers constructed; and in the neighbourhood of the Metropolis and large towns there is a considerable amount of manure, suitable for any kind of crops, that can be had almost for the carting, and growers taking their produce to market load back with manure which is applicable to all sorts of crops, can be applied to a farm not specially laid out, and can be conveyed in carts to any distance.

Seeing then that there is no demand for sewage; that there is so much difficulty in disposing of it; and that the result claimed for it might also be claimed for irrigation with water—I conclude that sewage cannot be utilized at a profit if it has to be pumped, but it may pay its expenses if utilized by gravitation; and the attention of town authorities should be directed to its purification by filtration or subsidence and utilization to a limited extent, which requires less land, and does not entail so much expense.

Purification and not Utilization being the main Object.—To perfectly utilize sewage one acre of land is required for twenty-five persons; but to purify sewage, only one acre of land is required for 1000 persons. The land is cropped in either case, whether it be for purification or for utilization.

Purification of sewage is simply a matter of expense, and there is no difficulty in rendering it sufficiently pure to be turned into any river or stream not used for drinking purposes. Purification may be most perfectly effected by dividing it into two stages.

The *first stage* deals with the *insoluble elements.* The sewage on arriving at the outfall is received into tanks constructed for the purpose, and passed through screens and filter-beds (some patterns filtering downwards, some upwards), which remove the insoluble matter. The floating matter is stopped by the screens, and the heavy matter sinks to the bottom. The result of filtration is to completely defecate the sewage, or, in other words, to remove all floculent matter, and this is assisted by the lime and various other processes, the details of which are not within the scope of this paper. In some cases the sewage is simply treated with lime and then left to subside.

The *second stage* of purification deals with the *soluble and organic matter.* Although the effluent water after filtration is clear to the eye, the soluble impurities are still present. To remove these it must be passed through the soil, which, exerting a chemical and galvanic action, resolves the organic matter into simple elements that combine with various bases in the soil; and "it is found," says Sutton, "that sewage passed through aerated porous soil contains very little organic carbon, organic nitrogen, or ammonia, but a large quantity of nitrates." And again, "All these substances are perfectly innocuous, but show by their presence that the water has been contaminated by animal matter." Sewage, after being thus treated and passed through the soil, is purified, and being again fitted for use, may be turned into any stream.

What is pure water? Purity is a question of degree, and purity as applied to water means fitness. In water absolutely pure fish cannot live; if taken into the stomach of man it is flat and disagreeable; and owing to the absence of dissolved atmospheric

F 2

air, it is positively injurious. *Rain-water* is not pure, as it is contaminated with ammonia and other impurities which it derives from the atmosphere as it falls from the clouds; and as soon as it touches the earth or any other surface, it derives further impurities therefrom. *Spring-water* is not pure, as it contains matter in suspension and in solution. *River-water* is not pure, for it is contaminated with organic and inorganic matter derived from the soil over which it has passed. If water be required for chemical purposes it must be distilled; if for drinking purposes, it requires to be free from organic matter; if required for manufacturing purposes, it requires to be free from elements which would be injurious to that manufacture. If sewage be turned into a tidal river it is sufficiently pure if the matter in suspension and so much of the matter in solution as would occasion a deposit in the river be removed. There are certain exceptional cases, and the treatment of sewage is like local government, a question of expediency—every case must be dealt with upon its own merits.

Sludge.—The insoluble matter removed by filtration is called sludge. According to present experience, sludge is of little or no value; and as it is a great nuisance at the sewage works, I propose to remove it from the works by pumping it along pipes and delivering it into railway trucks or barges, to be used as a manure; and if not required for that purpose, it can be shot to waste and used to fill up with. Sludge and sewage too require a great deal of leaving alone.

Another plan. I propose to bury or store the sludge. Dig out a trench six feet deep, ten feet wide, and of any length, and form a bank around it with the excavated earth. Fill the trench with sludge; when this is done, cover it with brushwood, and dig a fresh trench, placing the surplus earth from trench No. 2 upon the brushwood in trench No. 1; proceed in this manner until the ground is covered: then begin again. The sludge will be out of the way, and being covered with earth will not be a nuisance. At some future day it may be of value.

Various attempts have been made to extract a solid manure from sludge, but hitherto without success. Some processes for this purpose have had a run, but after a time have been given up, as farmers have found such manure to be comparatively valueless, and no wonder, for the most valuable part of sewage is ammonia, which being principally derived from urea and its allies, is in the liquid.

As urine contains the soluble portions of food, and the fæces the insoluble portion, the latter is not of value until it has been decomposed and rendered soluble.

Some persons have proposed to destroy the sludge by burning, but the objection to this is that it is a useless expense. There is, however, a close resemblance between combustion and oxidation, and the terms are almost synonymous ; the former being a rapid, and the latter a slow, chemical change—the one producing artificial light, the other being luminous in certain cases only ; as, for example, in those of phosphorus, decaying wood, and putrifying fish ; and the amount of heat generated by the slow process of oxidation is said to be exactly the same as that evolved during the most rapid combustion of the same substances. Combustion is decomposition by fire; oxidation is decomposition by chemical means, heat being evolved in both cases, and carbonic acid, water, and an oxide being formed. Oxygen, which is the most widely diffused body in nature, is estimated to form nearly half of our planet, and more than half of living plants. It exerts a mighty influence in the formation and dissolution of organic combinations ; it is the great purifier, and exposed to its continued action, no organic combination can maintain its permanence ; it decomposes the organic elements of sewage, which are gradually re-arranged into new compounds, containing at every step an increased quantity of oxygen, there being a continuous process of alternate combination and decomposition.

The Theory of Purification.

The theory of purification of sewage by passing it through aerated porous soil is as follows :

When sewage is fully exposed to the action of oxygen, the organic matter undergoes oxidation, which breaks up the various substances. The oxygen combines with the carbon, and forms carbonic acid. The hydrogen combines with oxygen and forms water, and with nitrogen forms ammonia, nitrous acid and nitric acid, and these last combine with the various bases in the soil to form nitrites and nitrates. The hydrogen also combines with the carbon, the phosphorus, and the sulphur, and forms carburetted, phosphuretted, and sulphuretted hydrogen gases, which occasion the nauseous smells of sewage. At the same time, the ammonia is also oxidized to nitric acid.

Farming consists in cultivating the ground so as to rear crops

of grain for the support of human life, and food for cattle destined
for the use of man. The soil is prepared by digging, ploughing,
harrowing, and rolling, which lighten it up and let in the air.

There is a great variety of plants; and we have marine plants,
which grow in salt'water; water plants, which grow in fresh water;
and land plants which require only a moderate quantity of water
for their subsistence. The water plants do not require much
consideration, but they are mentioned here for the purpose of
calling attention to the importance of drainage.

The condition of the soil is a matter of considerable importance,
and as you change it by cultivation, drainage, or other means, so it
will support a different kind of plant. If you embank a stream so
as to make the adjoining land always wet, water plants will spring
up and grow; or if the land is wet and swampy, and you put in
drains and lay it dry, the water plants will die from want of food.
The following curious facts were observed by the author whilst
surveying Pewit Island, in Essex: Nearest the water the ground
was soft mud, upon which persons could only walk with mud
splashers. At a higher level were little knots of moss; these would
bear the weight of a man without much danger of sinking. At a
still higher level the ground became firmer, and grew samphire;
and when still firmer, lamb's ears; and when yet firmer, grass;
and the state of dryness of the ground could always be told by
the growing plants. This island was afterwards enclosed, and
the salt water being kept off, grass and ordinary farm crops were
grown, and the plants that depended for life on sea-water died.
Fresh-water plants will die if watered with salt or brackish water,
as is experienced at Harwich, where if pot-flowers are to be kept
alive they must be watered with rain-water.

Cultivated plants are divided into three classes: *potash plants*,
which include beet, mangel - wurzel, turnip, and maize; *lime
plants*, which include clover, beans, and peas; *silica plants*, which
include wheat, oats, barley, and rye.

Every plant requires a special kind of food, and it is the business
of a farmer to supply this food in sufficient quantity and properly
prepared, so that it is easy for the plant to digest. For example,
granite is composed of silica, alumina, lime, and potash, which are
constituents of a fertile soil. The rock in its natural state will
only grow moss, stonecrop, and similar plants; but when decomposed it forms clay, which is suitable for cultivation; but although
the elements of food for plants were there previously in abundance,

they were not properly prepared for assimilation, and plants so situated would die, although the elements of food were within reach. The same may be said of the coprolite, which is of no use as food for plants until it has been reduced to powder, and rendered soluble by chemical treatment. The roots of plants have the power of absorbing from the soil the minerals and organic matter which have been rendered soluble, and of taking them up into the plant, and thence into the leaves.

Manure is any kind of animal, vegetable, or mineral substance used for the purpose of increasing the fertility of the soil, and may be either liquid or solid. The soil consists of organic matter from the decomposition of vegetables and mineral matter from the decay of rocks. Most of the elements required by the crop are, as a rule, abundant in the soil; but potash, phosphoric acid, and the nitrogenous elements exist in the soil fit for the food of plants only in limited quantities, and require to be replaced, or the soil will soon become unproductive. One of the objects of manuring land is to restore to the soil the elements which have been abstracted from it by the crops which have been grown. These elements were formerly obtained from farm-yard manure, which consists of decayed vegetable matter, such as straw used to litter the farm-yard, the stalks and leaves of plants, and the excrement of animals. It contains ammonia, phosphoric acid, potash, carbonic acid, and various saline and mineral ingredients in an assimilated form, and when applied to the soil in a state of decomposition it restores the elements taken therefrom by the crops, and so acts upon the soil as to fit it for vegetable growth. Potash was also formerly obtained from the ashes of wood, &c., which had been used for fuel. Town manure would at one time fetch from 5s. to 10s. per waggon load, and farmers who did not keep much stock depended very much upon this. But the introduction of the water-closet system having deprived them of this supply, they were thrown upon their own resources. Calling in the aid of science, they looked about for other supplies, and their efforts, being crowned with singular success, have given rise to the preparation and manufacture of artificial manures, which can now be obtained suitable for any crop in a cheap and concentrated form, and farmers are now to a large extent independent of town refuse as a manure, *and this is another cause of the sewage difficulty.*

With high rents and increasing expenses there must be high farming and increased production. By using artificial manures a

farmer saves in price, saves in cartage, saves in labour, and by
their aid he can put into the soil just the kind of food required
by the crop, or he can increase the fertility of his land by adding
to it one or two elements which are least abundant.

Chemists having determined the various constituents of plants,
and the true value of organic and inorganic manures, tables have
been published which show the exhaustion of the soil by the
most generally cultivated crops, and how the fertilizing elements
abstracted from the soil can be replaced.

Artificial Manures.

Phosphorus occurs in the state of phosphoric acid in union
with bases, chiefly lime and magnesia, in volcanic and other rocks.
It is a never-failing constituent of the plants used by man and the
domesticated animals as food, such as grain, peas, and beans, in
which it occurs both in the form of calcareous phosphates, and in
a peculiar state of combination with carbon, oxygen, hydrogen,
and nitrogen. It is an equally characteristic and important ingredient of animal structures. Their bony skeletons owe their
strength and rigidity to the phosphates of lime and magnesia,
whilst phosphorus exists in other states of combination in the
flesh, blood, brain, milk, and other tissues and secretions of animals.
Phosphoric acid for manure is obtained from the cheaper guanos,
the bones of animals, and from coprolites, which are found in
Suffolk, Cambridgeshire, and Bedfordshire, and are supposed to be
the petrified dung of animals and reptiles. It is also obtained
from phosphatic rocks and earths, and these substances, being
ground into powder and treated with sulphuric acid, are sold under
the name of superphosphates. The value of superphosphate manure
depends upon the quantity of phosphoric acid which it contains,
and whether it is soluble or insoluble. For land in good heart
superphosphate of lime is the only manure required. For a beet
crop and for poor land it should be used with sulphate of potash
and sulphate of ammonia. Corn plants cannot thrive without a
large supply of phosphate of magnesia and ammonia. Phosphatic
manures are not so quick in action as those containing nitrogen,
and the former accelerate whilst the latter retard the ripening
process.

Nitrogenous Manures.—Agriculturists attach great importance
to this class of manures. It was at one time contended, on high
authority, that plants could obtain all the necessary ammonia from

the air, and that only mineral constituents need be put into the soil; but this has been disproved by scientific men, and by the general practice of agriculturists. Some nitrogen they do derive from the air, but not all. Nitrogen constitutes four-fifths of the air by volume. It is present in nitrate of potash and nitrate of soda. It occurs also in coal and other minerals, and is a constant ingredient of plants and animals. The nitrogen of decaying animal and vegetable matters is discharged into the atmosphere in the form of ammonia, which is a most important source of food for plants. In the gaseous state ammonia readily unites with carbonic acid to form a volatile salt, the carbonate of ammonia. Ammonia and its compounds are extremely soluble in water, so that it is condensed by every shower of rain and conveyed to the soil. It is obtained from urine, and from the ammoniacal liquor of the gas-house. Amongst this class of manures may be mentioned guanos, nitrate of soda, sulphate of ammonia, and animal refuse. Sulphate of ammonia and guano, if applied in autumn and a wet winter follows, much of the nitrogen will be converted into nitrates, and be carried down into the ground and lost to the crops. Clover has the power of restoring nitrogenous matter to the soil.

Potash Manures.—Potassium occurs in nature abundantly, but solely in combination and chiefly as potash. It is found primarily in granite, trap, and other igneous rocks, associated with different bases in combination with silica. From these rocks, as they crumble down, it finds its way into soils which are uniformly barren if devoid of potash. Growing plants extract it from the soil, and when they are burned it forms a chief ingredient of their ashes. It occurs in small quantities also in animals, in natural waters, and in the sea. Potash, in the condition of a silicate, forms nearly one-sixth of felspar, a well-known constituent of granite. An average crop removes from the soil very large quantities of potash; but where the crops and straw are consumed on the ground and not sold off the farm, no potash is needed to compensate for the exhaustion of the soil produced by the crop. As a rule, potash may be applied with advantage to potatoes, clover, beet, and turnips. Potash manures are muriate and sulphate of potash and kainite. *Soda* is a much less fertilizing constituent than potash; and although the same class of manures may be used the one for the other, soda cannot replace potash in vegetable economy.

Lime is especially useful in reclaiming peat or bog land, where it decomposes the excess of vegetable matter, and renders the soil more open, while the lime becomes a carbonate. *Gypsum*, sulphate of lime, is the most generally usèful manure to apply to leguminous crops, at the rate of 4 or 5 cwt. per acre.

Carbon is the base of carbonic acid, and the most considerable elements of the solid parts of minerals and vegetables. The carbon of plants is principally obtained by the direct action of the leaves of the plants upon the atmosphere, and animal respiration and animal putrefaction furnish plants with a supply of carbonic acid.

Irrigation.

Irrigation is the application of water to the soil for the purpose of assisting the growth of plants, but as all waters are not equally applicable for the purpose, great care is required in their selection; and the chemical nature of the water is a matter of serious consideration. For example, the streams which flow from peat mosses, or those which contain hydrous oxide of iron, would be injurious to the soil; whilst water derived from decomposed granite rocks would be beneficial to some kinds of plants on account of the potash derived from the decomposed felspar; and water charged with lime is beneficial to another class of plants. Irrigation corrects natural defects in the soil, and what is suitable in one situation might be objectionable in another. Water passing over fertile soils always contains a large amount of fertilizing matter. It has been practised from the earliest ages in Assyria, India, China, Egypt, France, Spain, Italy, and in the south-western counties of England. The object, generally speaking, is to increase the quantity of green food for cattle, and hence it is commonly applied to meadows, either natural or artificial. "It has been found," says Burnell, "at all times and in all climates, that irrigation develops the growth of the leaves at the expense of the fruit or grain, and for this reason cereal crops are, as a rule, excluded from irrigated districts."

Sewage Farm.

A sewage farm is land laid out for the purpose of purifying and utilizing the sewage of towns by growing suitable crops. The sewage intended for irrigation should be filtered, or otherwise treated, as it is found in practice that if untreated sewage be applied to grass land the insoluble portions and undecomposed organic matter are deposited on the leaves of the plant. It is brought to the highest part of the ground to be irrigated by pipes fitted with sluice valves, and is then discharged by hydrants into the carriers

and distributed over the surface of the ground as required, and it
is of the utmost importance that it should be kept continually in
motion, no part being allowed to remain stagnant; for although
water is essential to vegetable life, an excess of moisture is injurious
to all but aquatic plants.

Good drainage is necessary to remove the water which has been
used, and good roads are necessary to remove the produce of the
farm.

There is some prejudice against sewage farms, but the people
who complain of them would also complain of manuring land in
the ordinary style of farming. The odour is never pleasant, and
manure is of little value unless it be decomposed. The land is
the proper place for town refuse; and if sewage be disagreeable to
the sense of smell, it is not a nuisance injurious to health when
upon the land, and can in no way be compared with the decomposition of animal and vegetable matter in the close neighbourhood
of towns.

The selection of a situation for a sewage farm is a matter of
great importance, for if it be situate at a higher level than the
outfall sewer the sewage must be pumped, and this will necessarily
entail considerable expense in the first instance for plant, and an
annual outlay for working expenses, which outlay will not be required if the farm be situate at a lower level than the outfall
sewer, so that the sewage can be utilized by gravitation; and this
will make all the difference as to whether a farm will pay or not.
The soil must be of a permeable character, with a gravelly or sandy
subsoil if possible; for if the soil be a stiff clay, for instance, the
sewage cannot enter it so as to become purified, and the clay will
not dry so as to be ready for another application. The surface of
a sewage farm requires to be levelled, so that the sewage may flow
equally; and it requires to be laid out with carriers having a
proper inclination and lined with earthenware, concrete, or clay, so
as to prevent the sewage sinking into the ground during its passage
along them.

THE BANQUET.

MAY 28, 1874.

In the evening the Members of the Association and their friends dined together in the Queen's Hotel. The chair was occupied by Mr. Alderman CHAMBERLAIN, Mayor of Birmingham. The Mayor was supported, right and left, by Mr. Angell, President of the Association; Major-General Scott, C.B.; Dr. Hill, Medical Officer of Health, Birmingham; Dr. Wilson, Medical Officer of Health, Warwickshire; Mr. Lawson Tait; Mr. Councillor Monk, Warrington, &c.

Upon the removal of the cloth,

The MAYOR, in proposing " The Health of the Queen," said : I think that on the present occasion it will not be out of place to say that Her Majesty had suffered as much, perhaps, as the poorest of her subjects by the neglect of those sanitary precautions and that special knowledge which it is the object of your Association to promote and spread amongst all classes. The late Prince Consort, as you are aware, lost his life by a disease which medical science tells us is preventible ; and the Prince of Wales very nearly fell a victim to what was simply gross carelessness in reference to what ought to be well known truths. (Applause.)

In proposing " The Health of the Royal Family," the MAYOR said : I have observed with very great pleasure in the papers during the last few days that the Prince of Wales has recently commenced the erection of cottages on his poorer estates, with all the latest sanitary improvements and appliances ; and certainly I hope such an example may be widely followed ; and I think there could be no better thankoffering on his part for his preservation. With respect to the other members of the Royal Family, I observed the other day that my Lord Mayor of London described the Princess of Wales and the Duchess of Edinburgh as " sweetness and light." I should be glad to endorse it, if it was not a little invidious as to which of them was sweetness and which of them was light. (Laughter.) It is a point on which I feel no loyal subject ought to venture to pronounce.

In proposing "The Army, Navy, and Reserve Forces," the MAYOR said : You belong to a profession which is perpetually waging war against death in the form of disease, and I think you will naturally sympathize with those who have to face death in other but not less serious forms. I think, further, that you will feel additional interest in the professions, which are every day becoming more and more scientific. We hear it said, with truth, I believe, that the latest wars in which we have been engaged are Engineers' wars ; and we are every day learning, in England at all events, to rely less upon brute force, and more upon the skill and knowledge with which we can control the forces of nature. This is true not only with regard to our military service, but also with regard to our naval service. Our ships of war are becoming huge factories and great machine shops ; and the British tar is disappearing from everything but poetry, and becoming a skilled mechanic. But I am sure, gentlemen, you will agree with me, that under whatever conditions—however altered the circumstances may be—we have reason to believe and know that the combined services will have a future as illustrious as the annals of their past. (Applause.) I am going to couple with this toast, the reserve forces—the Volunteers of this country. I do not believe that in our time we shall see that "battle of Dorking" which will allow us properly to appreciate our defenders. At the same time we must admire the perseverance and persistence which, in the absence of all stimulus, has maintained in efficiency this most important force, which for defensive purposes is generally acknowledged to be unsurpassable. I have much pleasure in coupling with the toast the name of General Scott, on behalf of the Army, and Capt. Thorburn, on behalf of the Reserve Forces. (Applause.)

Major-General SCOTT, C.B., in reply, said : It is always a matter of gratification to an officer to find that whenever Englishmen collect together for social purposes—whatever may be the immediate object of the gathering—the service of the body to which I belong is not forgotten. Not only do my own personal inclinations lead me to appreciate your labours, but there is a great likeness between the duties which you have to perform and those which belong to my own branch of the service, as the Mayor has pointed out.

Captain THORBURN briefly returned thanks for the Volunteers.

Mr. ANGELL, President of the Association, in proposing "The Municipal Institutions of the country," said : The kind of govern-

ment we have under the municipal institutions of the country is
undoubtedly the strength and backbone of our English liberties,
and as municipal officers we are bound to assist in its development.
I have to couple this toast with a most worthy representative on
the present occasion, the Worshipful the Mayor of Birmingham,
who has honoured us by presiding over this meeting. (Applause.)
I am sure you will consider his presence a graceful recognition of
municipal officers by the municipal authorities (hear, hear); and
therefore I ask you, in drinking the health of the municipal
institutions of the country, to associate with the toast the health
of our Chairman, the Worshipful the Mayor of Birmingham, wishing him long life, health, and prosperity. (Applause.)

The MAYOR, in replying, said : I feel that there would be something impertinent on my part if I were to criticise any action on
the part of my hosts. At the same time I should like to express
my own regret that the toast list is so complete a monopoly. I
would very much rather that the speech-making were more evenly
distributed amongst the gentlemen so eminently fitted for such a
task that I see around me. [After remarking that Mr. Angell and
he seemed to have almost all the speaking to do, he continued:]
There is no good you can say of municipal institutions that they
do not deserve. I admit there is a certain want of breadth sometimes about municipal corporations and local bodies which I very
much regret ; and especially do I regret that some members of
these bodies seem to think that their first aim in life is to save
money (hear); instead of which they are sent to their present
positions, not primarily in order to save money, but in order to
spend it wisely. (Applause.) Still, in spite of these defects, I do
not know how you could possibly obtain a system, in which most
important affairs are administered, with, on the whole, thorough
honesty, considerable cheapness, and, on the whole, great efficiency.
If there were any improvement possible, I should seek it in increasing our duties and in magnifying our offices. It seems to me that
there is a tendency to a mistake in modern legislation ; for the
Imperial Parliament first takes pains to create a thoroughly representative body, and then it seems to distrust its own creation, and
hampers and harasses it by all sorts of restrictive measures which
we find very embarrassing. (Hear, hear.) We have continually to
submit our decisions, come to after careful and sufficient consideration, to some committee of the House of Commons, or some central
office in London, which knows, after long inquiry, less about the

matter than we knew at the beginning. (Hear, hear.) I have been talking to my friend, Mr. Angell, who is an advocate for "home rule" in this respect (laughter), that local bodies should be supreme rulers within their own district, with respect to their own affairs and their own finances. I hold that opinion very strongly, and I believe that just in proportion as our importance is emphasized and our position assured by the Imperial Parliament, so you will find the character of our members raised.

The MAYOR next gave, "Success to the Association of Municipal and Sanitary Engineers and Surveyors." He said: I understand that this Association, which is still in the full heyday of its youth, is formed for a twofold object: in the first place, for the interchange of your special knowledge and acquired experience, and to spread sound views upon sanitary science; and in the second place, in the hope of improving the position, increasing the independence, and raising the status of your members. (Hear, hear.) Well now, gentlemen, it is certain that there is no more important profession than yours; and it appears to me clear that this country owes its present position as much, at all events, perhaps more, to Engineers as to any other class in the community. In almost every other branch of knowledge we are either equalled or surpassed by other nations. In chemistry, for instance, we derive very much from our neighbours and allies the Germans; in natural science, we are the debtors of half the Continent; and in mere mechanical ingenuity, I do not know that we are not surpassed by the Americans. I have heard it said that an American child has only been born a few minutes, when it looks round its cradle, invents itself a new one, and has a patent out and a company formed for working it before it is one year old. (Laughter.) Gentlemen, that is a precocity which I admit that we do not realize in this country. (Renewed laughter.) But in regard to general engineering, I think we can carry the palm from all the world. There is not a capital in Europe, there is not a corporation, or a great commercial undertaking throughout the world, which does not owe more or less to English skill and English experience; and many of the largest national undertakings have been planned and entirely executed by English Engineers. Of this very important profession yours is certainly not the least responsible or the least important branch. Corporations everywhere have to deal with growing, increasing difficulties—difficulties partly consequent upon the enormous aggregation of their constituencies, and partly the legacy

of past generations, from whose ignorance and neglect we have to
suffer; and with those gigantic difficulties we expect you to cope,
from them we expect you to relieve us; and therefore I am sure I
speak on behalf of the Birmingham Corporation, and I hope on
behalf of every enlightened corporation throughout the kingdom,
when I say we wish more power to your elbow, and we have hearty
sympathy with any movement that is calculated to increase your
influence and improve your position. (Hear, hear.) As regards
the second object of your Association, that is a matter of some
delicacy, on which it behoves me to speak with reserve. You desire,
as I understand, that the position of your Members should be
assimilated to that of Poor Law officers and medical officers of
health. You know better than I do where the shoe pinches, and
if you find it necessary in such a way to protect your independence,
you are the best judges. At the same time, you must be aware that
in all corporations there is very great jealousy of the central power,
and very considerable objections to anything in the nature of
Government interference. I think I may say for the Birmingham
Corporation, that since its existence, now for a matter of forty
years, no prominent officer has ever been dismissed by the Corporation. (Hear, hear.) I think that speaks well, of course, for
the officers themselves, for their fidelity and their ability; it speaks
well also for the Corporation, since it shows it is not easily moved
by gusts of prejudice and passion. (Hear, hear.) At the same
time, I think we may congratulate ourselves that our officers are as
independent as any in the kingdom. In fact, in the presence of
my friend, Mr. Till, our Borough Engineer, I am bound to say that
if I had to settle which was master, I am very much afraid—no,
not afraid, I am glad to say (cheers)—that I think the Corporation
is more dependent upon him than he is upon us. However, I
think in smaller towns difficulties may arise which I do not think
arise in great boroughs like Birmingham. There is one matter to
which you do not appear to have devoted your attention, much to
my surprise. An Association like this has, to my mind, always very
much the nature of a trades union, and I thought the object of
trades unions was to raise wages. (Laughter.) Now, in all
seriousness, I strongly advise you to direct your attention to that
branch of the question, because I certainly think that no officers
have more arduous, more responsible and important duties cast
upon them than Borough Surveyors and Sanitary Engineers; and I
think also that, on the average, they are quite insufficiently remu-

nerated. I have before now endeavoured to impress my view on this matter on persons whom it concerned, and I am not afraid publicly to avow my opinion on every occasion. I would like corporations and local boards to understand that they may get services for any price they please to name, but if the price is too low, they will not be worth having when they get them. Whether for these or any other matters that may come within your cognizance, it appears to me that the formation of such an Association is a distinct advance and an unmixed good. I have to couple with this toast the name of your President, Mr. Angell, whom I know to be the founder of this Association. (Applause.)

Mr. ANGELL, in reply, said: I have to thank you, Mr. Mayor, for the encouragement you have afforded our Association. Every great object is accomplished by unity and organization; but, sir, we are not like many of the organizations—aggressive. We have not yet, as you kindly suggest, sought a rise of wages. We are not a trades union; but the Municipal Engineers of the country united together to promote sanitary work, and every kind of town improvement. This is our first annual meeting, but we have every reason to be satisfied with our success, a success beyond our most sanguine expectations. We have been received, recognized, and entertained by the various authorities of the country; we have been reported by the local press and the professional journals; and even one of the London daily papers has said of us that we are an institution which bids fair to become a power in the country. Among our number there cannot fail to be many who have information to impart, and others who have errors to correct. This interchange of knowledge and comparison of experience must be of advantage to the public, and I most sincerely hope the public will appreciate it in the way our worthy Chairman has so generously indicated. I have to thank the Members of the Association very much for the position in which they have placed me, and also retained me in the coming year; and I have also to thank you, Mr. Mayor and gentlemen, for the kind manner in which you have associated my name with this toast. (Applause.)

Major-General SCOTT, C.B., proposed, "The Officers of the Association," and coupled with the toast the health of Mr. Lemon, the Vice-President.

Mr. LEMON, in reply, thanked the Association on behalf of the officers. They desired to assist and obtain protection for their less fortunate colleagues in their various appointments. His corpora-

tion approved of his connection with the Association, and he agreed
with the Mayor of Birmingham that local government should be
left in the hands of the corporations, who understood local details
much better than Parliament.

Mr. JACOB gave, "The Medical Officers;" to which Drs. HILL
and WILSON replied.

Mr. JONES proposed, "The Visitors;" to which Mr. LAWSON TAIT
and Councillor MONK responded.

Mr. TILL, Borough Engineer of Birmingham, proposed, "The
Local Secretaries." He said: Without the assistance and the
labours of the District Secretaries, the meeting would not have been
the success which all acknowledge it to have been.   (Hear, hear.)
I have therefore great pleasure in proposing to you the health of
the District Secretaries, coupled with the name of Mr. Pritchard,
District Secretary for the Midland Counties.   (Hear, hear.)

Mr. PRITCHARD, in reply, said: The proposer of the toast has
been pleased to speak in a very flattering manner of the exertions
made by the District Secretaries of this Association.   I can say, sir,
that it is with feelings of the greatest pleasure that we, the District
Secretaries, do all that we can to promote the interests of the
Association.   Without wishing to be egotistical, I will say that on
the District Secretaries a great deal depends as to the success of the
Association.   (Hear, hear.)   Our President and our most respected
and hardworking Secretary reside in the Metropolis; therefore, in
the provinces the District Secretaries must really do their share of
the work to ensure anything like success; and I may say that the
meeting we have this day had the pleasure of attending, and the
meeting this evening, have given us the greatest satisfaction we
could possibly expect to receive.   There are now four District
Committees of this Association, and I have the honour to be, sir,
without offering any offence to my brother Local Secretaries, the
Secretary of the one first formed.   It has been my great pleasure
to find in the Midland Counties great support; and it is really a
great gratification to me that the first annual meeting should have
been held in Birmingham, the metropolis of the Midlands.   We
commenced with the support of the local authorities; the Chairman
of the Local Board of Leamington first supported us.   We rose
in estimation, and at the Leicester district meeting we had the
presence of the Mayor.   Our success has culminated, sir, in what I
consider to be the very great honour of having you as our Chairman
this evening.   (Applause.)   When we look back to the difficulties

we had to labour under, and know that we have achieved so great a success, it gives us every encouragement for the future, and repays us for all our efforts. Mr. Till has spoken in kind terms of the Secretaries of the Association, and in return I can only say that we feel proud to number amongst our Members the name of Mr. Till, your Borough Engineer. (Applause.)

Mr. VAWSER proposed " The Ladies," and Mr. ELLICE-CLARK responded.

During the evening a quartette, consisting of Messrs. Fellows, Woodhall, Underwood, and Campion, sang appropriate glees.

ANNUAL MEETING OF THE ASSOCIATION OF
MUNICIPAL AND SANITARY ENGINEERS
AND SURVEYORS.

HELD IN THE COUNCIL CHAMBER, MOOR STREET, BIRMINGHAM,
MAY, 1874.

SECOND DAY'S PROCEEDINGS.

FRIDAY, MAY 29, 1874.

THE proceedings at the annual meeting of the Association of
Municipal and Sanitary Engineers and Surveyors were resumed on
Friday, May 29, 1874, in the Council Chamber, Moor Street,
Birmingham; Mr. LEWIS ANGELL, President of the Association,
occupied the chair; and there were also present, the Vice-President,
Mr. JAMES LEMON, Southampton; Mr. C. JONES, Ealing, Hon.
Sec. of the Association; Mr. E. PRITCHARD, Warwick, Hon. Sec.
for the Midlands; Mr. R. VAWSER, Warrington, Hon. Sec. for the
Lancashire and Cheshire District; Mr. E. B. ELLICE-CLARK,
Ramsgate, Hon. Sec. for Home Counties; and also Messrs. W. S.
TILL, Birmingham; C. DUNSCOMBE, Kingston-on-Thames; F. ASH-
MEAD, Bristol; A. M. FOWLER, Salford; T. W. GRINDLE, Hertford;
W. H. WHEELER, Boston; E. J. PURNELL, Coventry; EDWARD
BUCKHAM, Ipswich; EDWARD MONSON, Acton, London; J. N.
BAYLIS, Redditch; B. H. VALLE, Stow-on-the-Wold, Glouces-
tershire; GEORGE H. STAYTON, Ryde, Isle of Wight; E. DAVEY,
Maidenhead; JOHN ROBINSON, Ashton-under-Lyne; JOSHUA CART-
WRIGHT, Dukinfield; JOSEPH MITCHELL, Hyde; J. A. HALL,
Toxteth Park, Liverpool; A. COMBES, Kidderminster; JOHN
BANKS, Kendal; GEORGE COLE, Hereford; EDWARD SHARMAN,
Wellingborough; E. BETTRIDGE, Balsall Heath; WILLIAM NEWEY,
Harborne; JOSEPH LOBLEY, Hanley; JAMES STANDING, Garston;
JOHN WOOD, Sidmouth; JOHN MARTIN, Radford, Nottingham;
W. A. RICHARDSON, Tranmere; J. WATSON, Crewe; J. HILDRED,
Batley; H. CREGEEN, Bromley; GEORGE BIDDLE, Dewsbury;
R. DAVIDSON, Leamington; W. BATTEN, Aston Manor, &c.

The following Visitors were also present: Messrs. T. C. MELLISS, C.E., Kenilworth; CHARLES MARTIN, Leicester; Dr. ANDERSON, Coventry; T. S. SKELTON, London; W. WHITTHREAD, Edmonton; F. G. ORANGE, Liverpool; ROBERT MILLBURN, London; HENRY JACKSON, London; JOSEPH CARTER, Hereford; HENRY W. SCOTT, Ealing; Major-Gen. H. Y. D. SCOTT, C.B., Ealing; GILBERT R. REDGRAVE, Great George Street, Westminster; Alderman AVERY, Birmingham; Col. ALFRED JONES, V.C., Wrexham; J. WILKINSON, Sewage Works, Birmingham; Dr. WILSON, Medical Officer of Health, Warwickshire.

The PRESIDENT, in opening the proceedings, congratulated the meeting upon re-assembling after the interesting day, and the particularly pleasant evening they had spent under the presidency of the Mayor. That day would be specially devoted to the sewage question, in the discussion of which non-members were invited to take part. He proposed to read a short paper upon the general subject of sewage—running over the general question without advocating any special view, by way of opening the discussion. He thought it would be better to group the papers together and read them at once; and discuss the whole afterwards; otherwise, if they discussed each paper separately, they would have to go over the same ground several times. He therefore proposed that all the papers should be read, and the discussion upon them should follow.

The PRESIDENT proceeded to read the following paper.

ON THE TREATMENT OF SEWAGE.

By Mr. LEWIS ANGELL, President of the Association.

THE Association of Municipal and Sanitary Engineers and Surveyors, composed as it is of the Borough Engineers and Town Surveyors of England and Wales, cannot fail to take great interest in the sewage question: it is the one vexed and uncertain feature in our practice, a subject upon which we are constantly called to advise, although really more a question of chemistry and agriculture than of engineering.

It occurred to me that others, outside our number, might instruct us on this subject, or at all events give us,—the responsible advisers of the local authorities,—the advantage of their views on the special schemes they advocate—hence our invitation.

It has been my fortune, in my official capacity, to devote much attention to this subject, and I propose, by way of opening the discussion, briefly to submit the conclusions to which my experience has led me, without going into those details which will necessarily arise during the discussion.

The SEWAGE QUESTION presents itself under three aspects. The sanitary aspect, which is paramount; the municipal or financial aspect, which is important; and the agricultural aspect, which is subsidiary.

Under the sanitary aspect we are agreed that all excreta should be defecated or removed as soon as produced; that there shall be no retention of pollution about our dwellings; but we differ immediately we discuss the best methods of accomplishing our object.

The great difficulties into which we have been brought by the general introduction of the water-closet system induce many to desire to revert to the primitive cesspool, or the more modern midden or earth-closet system. Those who have experienced the advantages and cleanliness of water-closets will retain them at any cost. The mischief in this direction is irrevocable, and the probability is that the hydraulic system will, in the end, prevail over the earth system. Middens and earth-closets are simple and effective enough in theory, but they are costly, cumbersome, and inconvenient in practice, very suitable for country houses and small villages, for gaols, barracks, and workhouses, where there is rigid discipline and supervision; but in large towns the inconvenience and cost of cartage would be very great. Nor should we escape the cost of sewers; the earth system is not applicable to liquids; there must be a sewerage system; provision must be made for domestic drainage: some 20 or 30 gallons per head of polluted water, as well as the surface drainage containing organic matter, must go into the sewers. Sir J. W. Bazalgette stated, some years ago, that when Regent Street was paved with wood the surface became so saturated with ammonia and sulphurretted hydrogen from the road refuse that the exhalations tarnished the plate in the silversmiths' shops. At Birmingham comparatively few closets drain into the sewers, yet thousands of tons of most offensive matter, the bulk of which is road-drift, accumulates in the tanks, and subjected the corporation to legal proceedings. Town drainage, free from closets, needs purification as much as sewage, therefore I see very little advantage in excluding fecal matter from the sewers. The Rivers Pollution Commission suggest that if the houses of Manchester and Salford were removed, the site would be marked by 60,000 cesspools; and we know the sad tale of the death-rate of Salford. The Metropolitan Commissioners of Sewers abolished 30,000 cesspools, the Metropolitan Board completed the work, and London is now the healthiest city in the world.

But in avoiding Scylla have we not fallen into Charybdis? By filling up cesspools we have converted rivers into main sewers, and sparkling streams into "elongated cesspools." We have transferred the pollution from the land to the water. Granted, and I am inclined to think it better that such filth should be diluted and washed away, even in our rivers, than have our towns honeycombed with it.

I remarked yesterday, in my opening address, upon the question of river pollution and water supply. I do not think that potable water should be derived from rivers which flow through farmed lands and inhabited banks. If the small supply of pure water necessary for domestic purposes were derived from pure sources, the question of standard of purity would be very much simplified, and many towns relieved from impossible obligations.

I also had occasion to remark yesterday, that towns have been led to expect great things by enthusiastic sanitarians, but some of us have been taught by experience to estimate these matters at their true value. We think it more prudent to escape from our difficulties in the cheapest possible manner than to encourage hopes of gain, the sanitary element being always our first consideration.

At present the condition of the sewage question appears to be this: On the one hand, practical chemistry suggests artificial combinations and constituent changes by the action of certain agents, which are very effective but ruinously costly. On the other hand, Nature invites to her great laboratory, wherein she employs the simplest agents to effect all necessary combinations, conversions, and reproductions. The earth, the air, and vegetation quietly and economically effect all we require.

Laboratory experiments and chemical analyses have proved altogether unreliable in practice. We have seen heaps of unsaleable manure, and companies asking to be relieved from their obligations, but in no one case has chemistry shown even an approach to commercial success.

The value of sewage is well known, analytically, in comparison with guano as a standard manure. When diluted, as in the ordinary condition of town drainage, about 1250 tons of liquid sewage contains the value of one ton of guano; a liquid ton of sewage contains a fraction over two pennyworth of manurial constituents, $\frac{6}{7}$ths of which are in solution. Hence we have the problem, how to recover two pennyworth of ammoniacal salts from 225 gallons of water, or the $\frac{1}{113}$th part of a penny from a gallon. The chemist says, " Employ expensive agents, unite the feeble affinities, fix the few traces of nitrogen, fortify it, dry it with costly appliances, and invite the farmer to pay you handsomely for it."

In my district of West Ham, London, with a population of about 80,000, two of the modern sewage companies have informed us that the cost of treating the sewage by their processes will exceed 14,000l. per annum for chemicals alone; from which, we are told, we may realize double the value as a manure; but can any responsible official advise the ratepayers to speculate to such an extent? Would any representative board listen to such advice? Such companies can only prove their case by undertaking the processes at their own risk, and we have already seen the failure of some who have undertaken the task. We hear of fabulous values of manures; but where are the sales? This is the municipal and financial aspect.

The first of the long list of sewage patents dates from 1802, and it is now more than a quarter of a century since Mr. Wickstead expended nearly 50,000*l.* on the Leicester works, for the production of the celebrated " bricks," the result being a commercial failure. More recent companies have had their day on the Stock Exchange, but very little "wealth" has been made out of sewage; certainly not by the towns which have been favoured by their operations.

As Sanitary Engineers we do not depreciate the efforts of chemical science; we intervene no obstacle, we invite co-operation ; but we cannot be expected to advise our clients to expend money in a class of experiments which have hitherto failed, practically, in every form.

Where a high standard of purity is not an " absolute necessity," I cannot help expressing the opinion that the original lime process, with all its defects, still holds its own as practically sufficient and the cheapest. We find all the chemical processes resort to the assistance of lime. The analytical results of the lime deposit give a greater value than many of the other well-known processes. I have recently obtained a lime deposit, which Dr. Voelcker values at 2*l.* per ton, of dried powder,·as a " calcareous manure." Dr. Voelcker also valued the Leicester deposit at 15*s.* 5*d.* per ton, or an absolute gain of 11*s.* 5*d.* over the cost of the materials used; while upon the same basis of calculation the other processes either show no gain or an absolute loss. But such feeble manures are practically unsaleable : their adulteration or mixture with so much useless matter, and the bulk of material to be carted, destroys the theoretical value. It is true the lime process does not purify the effluent sewage water, but according to the Report of the Rivers Pollution Commission it removes a larger percentage of organic nitrogen than either the A B C or sulphate process; that is to say, that lime removes the most polluting properties of sewage in a greater degree than the other best-known processes investigated by the Commissioners.

The great difficulty of the lime process, in common with all tank processes, is in drying the deposit; it accumulates and becomes a nuisance if not disposed of. In open country it may be air-dried ; it may be mixed with ashes ; it may be mixed with shoddy or wool clippings ; it may be ploughed into the earth ; you may squeeze it in presses ; or you may dry it by artificial heat. Each one of these processes is attended with more or less cost. The great object is to get rid of it : its complete destruction would be cheaper than any manufacture.

With regard to the effluent water, I believe that if the volume of the stream into which it is discharged is large relatively to the volume of the sewage, and it is not used for drinking purposes, the lime process is sufficient. More than this I cannot say in its favour. But if we are to comply with the standards recently put forth and adopted by river conservancies, then, as I said yesterday, I think the law should also give some indication of the process which meets its requirements.

We have been officially told that sewage farming does not pay; and the Royal Commissioners have told us that chemistry holds out no hope. This is the dilemma in which the ratepayer finds himself. Can we wonder that he hesitates ?

Absolute purity can only be obtained from Nature's own defecator—the earth ; and more economically than by any known chemical or artificial system. The land will absorb, convert, and harmlessly store whatever value sewage may contain. If, therefore, I repeat, absolute purity be our aim, I believe that the earth, either by the process of intermittent filtration or by irrigation, to be the best and cheapest means of attaining it.

But our early dreams of profit were altogether illusory. Sewage farming has not been so profitable as was expected, but it has proved the cheapest and most satisfactory method of disposing of sewage ; and with more knowledge and greater care may be more satisfactory in its commercial results ; at all events, it is the most hopeful process.

With regard to the agricultural aspect, doubtless in the waste of sewage there is a great waste of manure, equivalent, Mr. Hope has told us, to the food of $5\frac{1}{2}$ millions during an entire year. But waste is a relative term ; no economic or theoretical views respecting the demands of the farmer are likely to influence the citizen unless it can be proved to be to his own advantage to expend municipal rates upon the production of food.

In these general observations I have simply stated the results of my own experience, without adding to your information. Of the sewage question it may be said, " What is true is not new, and what is new is not true."

WHITTHREAD PROCESS FOR THE THE TREATMENT OF SEWAGE.

By Mr. F. G. PRANGE.

I AM here to-day by the courteous invitation of your President, and with his permission will occupy a few moments of time in explaining the nature, and pointing out what we consider to be the advantages, of the WHITTHREAD PROCESSES for the purification and utilization of town sewage. These processes have only lately been brought before the public; but they have been the subject of investigation in various laboratories for two years, and of experiment, or rather working on a large scale, with sewage of varied conditions, for twelve months. I may, therefore, say that any statements I shall make are founded not less on scientific investigation than on practical experience.

In using the term sewage I mean the ordinary sewage of water-closet towns, not that I am here to advocate one method of disposing of excreta against the other, I merely accept the fact that the water-closet system, that of getting rid of these matters as quickly as possible, has generally superseded the cesspool system by which they were stored for certain periods of time. It is when they are poured down our sewers, mixed with the various refuse and the waste water of our towns, that the Sanitary Engineer has to deal with them in the great majority of instances.

Sanitary science is obliged to grapple with the sewage difficulty on account of its intimate connection with the health of the country, because the water supply must of necessity become tainted, if every brook and river in our populous districts runs black with dye-water, and foul with putrescible matter; therefore, the first duty of the sanitarian to a town is to cleanse and purify its sewage, so that it may be turned into a watercourse without dangerously contaminating and discolouring it. Certain standards of purity have been suggested by a Parliamentary Commission to which these towns are required to conform, and the first and primary condition to be exacted from a sewage cleansing scheme or process is that is should purify the water sufficiently to come within the prescribed limits of safety.   The consideration then follows: Is it possible to do this without loss or at a trifling expense, or are there means by which the valuable consituents of sewage can be so completely extracted and utilized as to make them a source of actual profit?

There are three systems by which the solution of this problem has been attempted: irrigation, precipitation, and filtration.   By the first, the manurial ingredients of sewage are passed into the land directly; by the second, they are extracted with the view of applying them subsequently as a dry manure.   Both of them aim at a utilization of the sewage for the purposes of agriculture, and at a return to be derived from the improved condition of the land, or the sale of a chemical manure.

Filtration, which is the third system, on the other hand, merely changes the condition of the sewage, and is purely destined to render it innocuous when discharged into water courses.

Our first patent falls into the category of precipitation processes, and the second is a chemical substitute for filtration.

I would here remark that precipitation and irrigation have been quite unnecessarily placed in hostile juxta-position.   Everybody who candidly considers the question must admit that no precipitation process is able to extract the fixed ammonia from solution, and that irrigation alone can completely utilize this valuable body; on the other hand, there is no doubt that in order to irrigate successfully, the suspended and putrescible matter *ought to be removed by chemical precipitation before the sewage is applied to land.*   Moreover, it would be an immense boon to the irrigationist, were he able in wet weather to dispense with the necessity of over drenching his fields, merely in order to purify his sewage.   This is especially the case in England, where the clouds usually are merciful enough.   When precipitation and irrigation can be combined, they should be so, in order to recover the greatest possible amount of value; but it is evident that in the great majority of cases, where large quantities of sewage have to be dealt with, irrigation is impossible from want of land, while in others the land is not suitable for the purpose.   A precipitation process which throws off a pure effluent and yields a deposit of value, must therefore, in most cases, be a necessity in the utilization of sewage.

In our endeavours to cope with the great difficulty of the age, we have kept two objects constantly in view.   First, to produce an effluent below the standard of the Rivers Pollution Commission; and, secondly, to do so with a fair chance of profit, or at a trifling outlay only. The way to effect this is to consider the varying conditions of sewage, and not to apply the same process everywhere, as a sort of nostrum.

Where sewage is rich in nitrogenous matter, sufficiently rich to yield a fair proportion of ammoniacal substance in the precipitates, we propose to treat it carefully by precipitation, to dry the resultant manure, and to trust to the sale thereof to recoup the cost of the plant and the chemicals, the effluent water being either passed into a water course or profitably turned to irrigation, where that is practicable.

Our process consists in adding dicalcic phosphate dissolved in an aqueous solution of monocalcic phosphate to the sewage as it flows from the sewers, and, when the whole is well mixed, in adding milk of lime in sufficient quantity to precipitate all the phosphates, avoiding an excess of lime.

The reason why we claim a superiority for this method of precipitation over others is simply the following: It not only precipitates the whole of the suspended matters, but it removes the organic nitrogen from solution, and therefore yields a manure really valuable in ammonia, while the phosphate used contains the other base of good manure, namely, phosphoric acid, which is entirely recovered, none of it—practically speaking—passing off with the effluent water.

I am aware that the above is a new chemical fact, but that I cannot help, although, such being the case, it has challenged much criticism. A fact it is, as scores of experiments have proved.

I give you a few very simple figures:

In an experiment on 216,000 gallons of sewage, reported on by Mr. Valentin (Dr. Frankland's colleague), there were in suspension 74·91 lb. of nitrogen, and in solution 50·66 lb. We recovered in the mud 99·77 lb.; that is to say, that 25 lb. of nitrogen were taken out of solution.

In an experiment conducted for the British Association, all the putrescible nitrogen, or protine compounds, were removed from solution.

On the working of our process during a fortnight at Luton, Dr. Corfield reports as follows: "The organic matter in solution is considerably reduced by the process, so as to be decidedly below the standard of purity required by the Rivers Pollution Commissioners."

Dr. Sell (Berlin), after some forty experiments and analyses, reports: " It is a demonstrated fact that dicalcic phosphate has the power of precipitating organic nitrogen."

Dr. Corfield, in a lecture delivered to the Chemical Society last week, drew attention to the above singular features, and remarked that they might be explained by, and explained mutually, some points in physiology hitherto little understood; such as, for instance, the formation of the well-known elastic substance called whalebone, a body made up of the elements of a nitrogenous body albumen, and phosphate of lime, such are likewise the cartilages of young animals. The precipitate which we have obtained has almost invariably contained one per cent. of ammonia to every seven per cent. of tricalcic phosphate, and it must be obvious that a manure which embodies these constituents to a sensible degree, must have a substantial value. We have found that in working with much diluted sewage we could perfectly well pay our way, by selling the manure on the basis of analysis. The precipitate contains no water of combination and is easily dried, thus differing from all precipitates produced by alum in its various forms; when dried it is in itself a desicator and can absorb and deoderize many substances, such as offal, blood, &c., which are now only nuisances, although they contain so many ingredients valuable to the agriculturist.

The effluent water is perfectly innocuous and below the standard of the Rivers Pollution Commissioners. I insist upon this as most important, because so many processes have broken down in this particular, and a notion seems to be springing up that the legal standard is too high. There is no reason whatever why discoloured and unwholesome liquids should be allowed to mix with the sources of water supply.

Dicalcic phosphate can be manufactured in various ways, and there are several English and foreign patents for producing it. Low qualities of phosphates can be used and the necessary compound obtained at a lower price than any other efficacious precipitant. We are aware that a sort of despair exists on the subject of the value of precipitates, but we trust that when the peculiarities and the rationale of the Whitthread process are considered, that the value of a manure containing nearly all the putrescible nitrogen of the sewage treated, and a proportional quantity of phosphoric acid, cannot be doubted, and will secure the attention of sensible men.

Of course, towns where all sorts of chemicals are thrown into the sewers and an immense quantity of suspended matter is carried down in what is scarcely better than dye-water, cannot expect to use the sewers as a public convenience for such purposes without paying for it.   The country and their neighbours will certainly require them to again cleanse the water, and purification in such cases costs money.   Where sewage is comparatively undiluted with anything but water, the quantity of chemicals required is small and the resultant manure as valuable as many guanos.

When sewage is too poor in manurial matters to render it worth treating for the sake of its deposit, we propose to purify it by another very inexpensive process which we have patented, the rationale of which is easily understood.   All know what a powerful disinfectant bleaching powder is.   Bleaching powder owes its power to chlorine; when chlorine is brought into contact with bodies containing hydrogen as one of their elements, such as ammonia, the chlorine seizes hold of the hydrogen to form hydrocloric acid, while the nitrogen is set free.   When, however, the chlorine is brought into contact with oxidizable bodies in the presence of water, no matter whether these bodies are organic or inorganic, they are oxidized.   A fluid like sewage is oxidized by chlorine by a process which is identical with burning all the organic matters present, except the ammonia, which is decomposed, as I have described, while the sulphur compounds which produce the most offensive odours are converted into sulphuric acid.

The compounds we use to effect these changes are some of them little known, but the body which we shall employ most frequently is the tetrachloride of manganese, which evolves in the presence of organic matters a large amount of chlorine in its nascent, and thus its most energetic, condition.   This compound is much cheaper than bleaching powder, much more powerful in its action (an excessively small quantity effecting the desired purpose), while it does not load the water with lime salts as bleaching powder does, and it leaves no objectional by-products in the effluent.

Of course, the little money expended on this process will not yield a return, the precipitate will not be of value, and the effluent useless for irrigation; but if sewage is devoid of valuable putrescible matter, it cannot under any circumstances give a return for treatment.

I say this quite candidly, there is no use in pretending to obtain value in return, when chemical processes analogous to filtration are used.   The object in such cases is to cleanse the sewage at a cheap rate, and when towns determine on this they must look a certain dead loss in the face, and be glad if their primary object is attained.

The object of our first process, then, is to produce a good manure, or the basis of a good manure, by the sparing use of a recognized fertilizing agent, and in doing so to render the sewage harmless by the extraction of the very substances which are of value to the farmer.   The simple object of our second process is rapidly to effect a complete change in the condition of the putrescible bodies, to do the same thing in a few minutes which requires weeks in the ordinary course of nature, and days by filtration through land, with the advantage of doing this in every kind of weather, and at all seasons of the year.

We are aware that the introduction of a new manure may be attended with difficulties, when farmers are told that they must not try it on chemical analysis, but on the faith that there is some unaccountable virtue in it.   If, however, we can offer a manure to the agricultural public at a cheap rate, containing two or three per cent. of nitrogen, and 15 to 20 per cent. of tricalcic phosphate of lime (not of phosphoric acid in an indissoluble shape, calculated as equal to so much phosphate of lime), it will be surprising if such a fertilizer does not find a ready sale.   We can produce this by treating after our method any sewage which at all deserves that name.   This is attested to by the highest authorities of England and the Continent, and we have too much confidence in scientific conclusions very patiently arrived at, to be doubtful of success.

In reply to various questions, Mr. Prange referred the gentlemen present to the figures given in the pamphlet issued last month by Mr. Muspratt, the chairman of the Enfield Chemical Manure and Irrigation Company.   These show that the quantity of chemicals required for the purification of sewage is very small, having sometimes not exceeded one part by weight of the Company's phosphates to 15,000 parts of sewage.   It will be also perceived from the pamphlet that the tanks and mixing apparatus required for the Whitthread processes are similar to those employed in other precipitation processes, but that owing to the rapidity of the precipitation, tank room and cost of plant may be much economized.   Mr. Prange stated that where the Whitthread process did not pay a profit, it would at least recoup the cost of the chemicals used, and pay something towards interest on plant.   He said this from a desire not to overstate his case, which he summarized thus: Where the sewage is moderately rich, employ

Whitthread's process of precipitation; it yields a valuable manure, and the effluent water is purified of all putrescible and suspended matter so as to satisfy the River Conservators, while at the same time it retains the required amount of ammonia so as to be available for irrigation wherever there is land for this purpose.   Where the sewage is weak and comparatively devoid of manurial matter, there employ Whitthread's second process; it is very inexpensive, simply cleansing the sewage so as to render it perfectly harmless and fit for admission into any watercourse.

THE SULPHATE OF ALUMINA PROCESS.

By Dr. ANDERSON.

Dr. ANDERSON read a paper on the "Sulphate of Alumina Process," as carried on at Coventry. As he had not reduced his description to writing he delivered a verbal account of his system. He said : It would take me some time to go through the whole process *seriatim*; and as in connection with the sewage question " seeing is believing," those of you who have any curiosity to witness the process and see the details I shall be glad to see over at Coventry. I will take this opportunity of correcting a few chemical errors, of what is generally received and acknowledged to be the chemistry of sewage. Mr. Angell read just now a statement about the ammonia in solution in sewage. If he would kindly read that passage again I shall make a few remarks upon it. [Mr. Angell read the sentence from his paper, and Dr. Anderson then proceeded:] The Rivers Pollution Commissioners have never given any report on my process, and I am not particularly anxious that they should. Coventry has only been at work lately, and I disbelieve many of the Commissioners' statements *in toto*. Their report as to the average analysis of the sewage of towns is totally erroneous, on practical grounds. Their average is calculated in this way : a definite quantity—the same quantity, say half a pint—of sewage is collected every hour during twenty-four hours. These half pints are mixed together at the end of that time, and a sample of that is taken as the average of the sewage. Now, sewage varies immensely in composition. Oddly enough—reasonably enough, when we come to consider the matter—it is foulest when the flow is greatest. Here are some analyses of Coventry sewage which I took with a good deal of trouble during one day, the 8th April, of this year. I commenced at six o'clock in the morning, and I gauged the flow every three hours, during fifteen hours of the twenty-four. I took a sample of the sewage each time. At six o'clock in the morning the flow of sewage was at the rate of 47,500 gallons per hour. The free ammonia in it (obtained by boiling it) was 1·60 part in 100,000; albuminoid ammonia, 0·80 part in 100,000; chlorine, 4; total residue, 60; of which 32 were organic, and 28 inorganic. At nine o'clock in the morning the rate of flow was 67,500 gallons per hour. The free ammonia obtained by boiling was 3·20 parts per 100,000; albuminoid, 2; chlorine, 6; and total residue, 100; of which 62 were organic, and 38 inorganic. At twelve o'clock the total flow was 80,000 gallons per hour. The ammonia obtained by boiling was 3·35; albuminoid, 3·56; chlorine, 12; and residue, 110; of which 60 were organic, and 50 inorganic. And so on it goes all throughout. I want to draw your attention to this. If we take half-pint samples of each of these analyses and mix them together, it would not give the average of the whole, because at twelve o'clock the flow is at the rate of 80,000 gallons per hour, and the total ammonia 3·35, whereas at six o'clock in the morning the flow is only at the rate of 47 gallons, and does not contain, bulk for bulk, half the organic matter. Any deductions as to average arrived at for calculations made in this way are totally erroneous; they underrate the foulness of sewage very much. The Royal Commissioners also report as to six-sevenths of the manurial constituents of sewage being in solution. That statement I do not acknowledge. I have never been able to discover more than about one-sixth of the actual manurial property of sewage absolutely in solution. If you take raw sewage, filter it, and then apply the Neesler test, you get only the evidence of about one-sixth of the ammonia that actually and truly exists in the sewage. The method in which chemists set to work to determine nitrogen is this: a given quantity of sewage is taken and mixed with distilled water (the purity of which has been previously tested). Then that is distilled. In order to distil it a large amount of heat is applied, and a good deal of the nitrogenous matter by that heat becomes converted into ammonia. But it was not in solution before. The nitrogen which was in suspension is converted by heat into ammonia, and thus the chemists have brought it into solution. It was not in solution before. Then, subsequently, in order to produce a still further decomposition of the nitrogenous material which was not converted by heat, he adds materials rich in oxygen —and of these none is so rich as permanganate of potash—so as to get a highly alkaline material, and highly rich in oxygen. He applies heat again, and produces a further decomposition of the material, and gets off still more ammonia. This he analyzes, still using the same test, and determines the quantity of nitrogen in it.

Six-sevenths of the matter he puts down as matter in solution is not matter in solution, and was never in solution until he made it so.   I do not believe in any bare theoretical facts or highly scientific facts with respect to the sewage question.   You must not look to the aid of the chemists entirely to solve the question; you have to use the evidence of all those interested as ratepayers, and those who represent the ratepayers must consult the evidence of their own senses, and depend less upon chemists and Royal Commissioners than has been the fashion to do up to the present time. Any statements which Mr. Angell has so ably made which militate against the practical results of the defecation process I should ask you to lay on one side until you have an opportunity of judging for yourselves by coming over to Coventry and seeing how it is carried on there.   [Dr. Anderson was about to sit down when he was asked to explain the sulphate of alumina process as carried on at Coventry.   He said:]/The material I make use of is sulphate of alumina.   It is obtained from treating shale with sulphuric acid. The proportions are:

Alumina (that is, the sesquioxide of alumina)	14·
Sulphuric acid	32·70
Residue (insoluble)	43·64
Loss (consisting of moisture and organic matter principally)	9·66

These are parts in a hundred, and that is the matter I make use of. I dissolve that and remove (in round numbers) 50 per cent. of it, which is the residue.   The remainder is in solution, and flows in a state of solution into the sewage as it passes through a part of the works.   It is then stirred up by means of an agitator and passes on into the lime works.   There it receives a small portion of lime. But I should like to impress upon you that lime is not used as a defecator in this process at all.   It is simply used to set free the alumina.   We use it in small quantities, and not in such quantities as to render the sewage alkaline in excess.   I am no friend of lime as a defecator.   When it has received both the alumina and lime it flows into settling tanks.   There it remains.   In its passage from the tanks it settles and deposits a certain amount of mud.   We work each tank for about ten days, when it is swept out into a mud chamber, and the mud is then dried in Milburn's machines, and produces manure, the analysis of which I now submit to you.   I should have stated that before being treated with any of the chemicals, the sewage passes through Latham's extractor, where the manure is extracted containing this composition in its undried state :

Moisture	50·80
Organic matter	44·32
Alkaline and earthy salts (matter insoluble in hydrochloric acid)	2·60
Insoluble matter	2·28

The organic matter contains nitrogen equal to ammonia 3·40. Phosphoric acid exists in very small quantities. Here is an analysis of the Coventry manure:

Moisture	17·40
Organic matter and water of combination	29·90
Alkaline and earthy salts	22·80
Insoluble matter	29·90
	100·00
Containing nitrogen equal to ammonia	2·25
Containing phosphate of lime	3·0

Another analysis of the manure gave:

Moisture	15·40
Organic matter, &c.	31·50
Alkaline and earthy salts	19·10
Insoluble matter	34·00
	100·00
Containing ammonia	1·60
Containing bone phosphate	3·20

The cost of the production of that manure is about 30s. a ton. The effluent is practically clean, and, as conducted at Coventry, the whole process promises to pay expenses and yield a profit. About half the total nitrogen is removed with suspended matter. Before its passage to the river, we propose to run the sewage through a filter-bed, which is not yet completed, but will be in the course of a fortnight.

SEWAGE FARMING.

By Colonel JONES, V.C.

Having been for many years interested in the disposal of town sewage, and having recently published the results of a practical attempt to answer affirmatively the important question, "Will a Sewage Farm pay?" I venture to respond to your invitation to outsiders to join in the discussion at this most important congress.

It would be superfluous to enlarge before such an audience as the present upon the sins of our generation, in respect to the waste of valuable matter, and the pollution of our rivers, because you must all have seen much of the latter in your respective districts, while many of you have had opportunities of studying the chemical analysis of sewage, and observing the marvellous fertility which may be given to the poorest soils by its judicious application in irrigation, and are thus in a position to appreciate the value of the commodity so commonly consigned through our rivers to the ocean.

Nor do I think it necessary to attempt to prove that a sanitary object is gained by well-managed sewage irrigation, for that is, I think, pretty generally admitted; but the question of how far the returns of a sewage farm will recoup the additional labour and expense of cultivation has long appeared to me to be the really important problem.

I shall refer for details to the pamphlet above alluded to, published by Messrs. Longmans, London, and will now, with your kind permission, pass on to a subject, as I think, intimately connected with profitable sewage irrigation, and worth the consideration of all Engineers who may be charged with the drainage of towns.

The small town of Wrexham, with whose sewage I have been lately operating, is sewered in the ordinary manner with street gullies and down-right pipes from the roofs of houses all connected with the sewers, and consequently any fall of rain speedily fills the latter, and comes down to my farm mixed with the sewage. Overflows or connections from the sewer to the brook which flows through the farm, effectually prevent my being overburdened by excess of liquid at such times over and above the capacity of the tanks through which the sewage flows; but the overflow naturally defiles the water of the brook, and carries off a large quantity of sewage matter which would have otherwise come upon my land in due course. It is easy to see, therefore, that an element of uncertainty is thus introduced, which must interfere most materially with all arrangements for applying the sewage to the crops; and that, as the overflow takes place during and after any rainfall, the brook, in a climate like ours, is always liable to excessive pollution.

In the case of towns which are obliged to pump their sewage there seems to be an additional argument for keeping the sewage to itself, and altogether I have come to the conclusion that the separate system of town drainage is much to be desired.

I would ask you, gentlemen, to consider how far in the case of new works you can introduce two pipes into the same excavation, one for sewage proper and the other for rain-water, instead of one intended to perform the double duty; and in the case of towns already sewered to contrive means of diverting a portion of the rain-water, if you cannot abstract the whole of it, from the old sewers.

I am told by Mr. Menzies, the Surveyor of Windsor Forest, that the sewerage of Windsor Castle has been carried out most successfully on the separate system, at a less expense than would have been incurred under the old system, and that some considerable towns are about to adopt it, if they have not already done so. The chairman of the Eton Local Board gave evidence the other day before a Government inquiry, " *that no rain-water reaches the sewers of that town, and that there was no overflow provided.*" I am sometimes told that artificial flushing of the sewers would be required if they were not made liable to natural flushing by rainfall; but is not water a cheap article readily applied in such cases? and is it not better to have the flushing under control, so that there shall be no overflow, rather than in great gushes, bearing the foulest sewage to the river?

Many urge the expense of a double set of drains; but they forget that the pipes for rain-water would run directly to the natural watercourses, and be consequently of short length, while their existence would allow the main sewer to be made much smaller than if its section had to be calculated for the combined duty of conveying sewage and rainfall; and the ordinarily great length of

this main sewer must make every additional inch in its diameter
the cause of great expense.   But when the main sewer is destined
for the combined duty, I believe your experience will confirm the
statement that the pipe provided is *never* equal to that duty in all
weathers, and that overflows are invariably provided for storm-water.

Another argument against the separate system consists in the
alleged unfitness, by reason of impurity, of street-water for direct
admission into a river; and I have had some analyses, by Professor
Way, of the water from some London streets, quoted against me;
but when those analyses are compared with those of the foul
mixture of street-water and sewage entering the river by the overflows, this argument must, I think, fall to the ground.

It is not, I venture to assert, a question of whether the street-
water is as pure as one could wish, but of whether it is not less
impure in its original state, than after admixture with the foulest
sewage.   Moreover, Professor Way's analyses affect the street-water
alone, without dilution by the roof-water which I propose to add to
it, and which must most materially reduce the proportion of impurity in the whole ere the storm-water reaches the river.   When
the streets have been washed by the first downpour, there would,
I think, be but a small proportion of impurity during the rest of
the wet weather, whereas the impurity of the liquid discharged by
overflows must remain more constant during the whole time of
their action.   Professor Voelcker, too, in his evidence at the court
of inquiry above referred to, denies that water passing down the
streets and running from the roofs of houses would contaminate a
river, and when his attention was called to Professor Way's analysis,
he replied, " I have carefully looked into the matter, and I believe
the statement to be grossly exaggerated.   I do not believe that
the conservators of any river would object to it."

It may seem presumptuous to suggest so radical a change of
system to such experienced Engineers as I see around me; but your
free invitation to outsiders to come forward to-day, leads me to
hope that you may not altogether despise the expression of my
experience in dealing with sewage; and I may remind you that the
best instance I know of profitable sewage irrigation, viz. that of
Mr. Blackburn's Camp Farm, at Aldershot, is associated with the
separate system, for I have often heard, from staff officers and
Engineers at the Camp, of the jealousy with which he would re-
monstrate, in case of any accidental admission of rain-water into
the sewers which supply his farm with the genuine article.

In the interest, therefore, of sewage irrigation, I would pray each and all of you who may have new drainage works to carry out, to adopt as far as possible the separate system; and where sewers are already established, as at my own town of Wrexham, I do not see why a great part, if not the whole rainfall, may not be sent direct to the natural watercourses at a very small cost; and I ask, in such cases, what became of your rainfall in bygone years before your sewers were laid down? It must have found its way along street gutters to the river somehow or other; and why cannot you now revert to that old arrangement, keeping your sewers to their proper duty of conveying sewage impure and simple to the land which requires it? Such primitive surface gutters may not answer for large towns in the present day, but in smaller ones would not be objectionable.

I shall now ask you to consider the sewage sludge difficulty, which really gives trouble and dirty work to everyone who has to deal with it; for although it can often be allowed to flow on to the ground along with the liquid when the land is lying fallow, or between growing crops of cabbages and mangolds, it is generally desirable to pass the sewage through some 200 feet length of tank, to allow the heavier suspended matter to subside before the liquid is used in irrigation, and the sludge thus deposited must be taken out of the tank and disposed of somehow or other.

It is well known that this sludge parts with the water it contains very slowly, and I have found it still retaining nearly 70 per cent. of moisture after lying a month or more in a layer 12 or 14 inches thick on the banks of the tank.

I have used a good deal of this sludge on the poorer portions of my farm, and found its effects superior, weight for weight, to farmyard manure; and neighbouring farmers are sufficiently acquainted with its value to be ready to purchase so much as I like to sell at about 3s. per ton, which more than repays the expense of emptying the tank.

Thus, as you will observe, I am not really embarrassed by this sludge difficulty at Wrexham; but I am sufficiently acquainted with the nature of this slimy, offensive looking matter, to appreciate the trouble and nuisance it must create when the sewage of a large town like Birmingham has to be dealt with; and I confess that it appears appalling when all the sewers of such a vast town as this are made to converge to one point, as at Saltney.

I cannot help thinking, however, that we have been mistaken in thus concentrating the sewage of a populous district to form one gigantic nuisance at the focus, instead of dispersing the sewage by pipes radiating to all points of the circumference.

The natural levels of the neighbourhood point to concentration in the direction in which the sewage can be sent by gravitation in the case of small towns; but the expense of pumping a few feet would be nothing to such a town as this, and a few miles of extra pipes should not be considered, if by dividing we can conquer the enemy who appears so strong in his concentrated position at Saltney.

I am afraid that the addition of lime only renders the mass of matter to be dealt with greater than ever; and unless the whole can be profitably converted into cement, one does not see how the mass is to be disposed of.

Within the last month, however, I have become acquainted with a new patent plan for dealing with town refuse, which looks more promising than any other, except the true one of irrigation; and as it is not generally known, although experiments have been carried on for a few months at Salford, I will take the liberty of drawing your attention to this new process, which may, I think, prove valuable to many towns in the cases where irrigation is from local circumstances impracticable.

The United Charcoal and Sewage Co., of Market Street, Manchester, is now bringing out the patent of Messrs. Roby and Chantery, for the carbonization of street sweepings, and with the charcoal thus produced it claims to deodorize fæcal matter and urine collected by the Rochdale pail system from a part of Salford, and thus to form a valuable manure.

— The Company publishes the following analysis of its manure, and is sending out considerable quantities for trial this season:

	In 100 parts.
Moisture	13·880
Organic matter	26·340
Residue insoluble in acids	46·810
Portion soluble in acids	12·970
	100·000

Phosphoric acid	0·6150
Ammonia, by distillation	0·0133
Total nitrogen, by combustion	0·5600

The street sweepings are carbonized by passing through two slowly revolving cylinders, situate one over the other in a horizontal position, over a furnace which raises the temperature of the lower cylinder to about 400° Fahrenheit, and the pair of cylinders are said to be capable of producing about 35 tons of charcoal per week of seven days, at a cost of less than 10s. per ton. But as another set of apparatus could be kept working by the same staff of men, the cost might certainly be very much diminished if the manufacture were carried out on a larger scale than has been as yet attempted.

The analysis given by the Company of the charcoal thus prepared resembles that of animal rather than vegetable charcoal, and is said to be capable of taking up a greater bulk of ammonia than the former, whose porosity is well known to constitute it the most perfect deodorizer we can obtain, and thus I conceive that it will be found superior as a deodorizer to peat or vegetable charcoal, while it can be made at much less cost than the cheapest form of either of these kinds of charcoal.

It is, I believe, the theory of sugar-refiners, that the intimate union of phosphate of lime with about 20 per cent. of carbon in animal charcoal produces the best filter, and the silica and other matter mixed with ordinary street sweepings appear to supply the place of phosphate of lime in the charcoal under consideration.

Being struck with the similarity of the street sweepings used in this process at Manchester with the sludge deposited in my tank, I sent a portion of the latter to Mr. Roby for analysis, and he reports that it (the resulting charcoal) contains carbon in a slightly greater proportion than that made from street sweepings; and therefore I conclude that when the sewage sludge accumulates in embarrassing quantities, a portion of it might be carbonized and mixed with the remainder as an absorbent, to dry and consolidate the rest of the sludge, and form a manure more portable, and therefore more saleable, than the sludge itself.

A DESCRIPTION OF THE PHOSPHATE SEWAGE PROCESS.

By Professor TANNER, F.C.S.

Professor Tanner said: I am under the disadvantage of not having been present until within a few minutes, and, consequently, I trust you will pardon me if I should go over the ground already touched upon. There appear to be three modes of dealing with the sewage of towns, namely, 1st, direct irrigation alone ; 2nd, irrigation aided by a previous partial purification of the sewage ; and, 3rdly, precipitation processes by which the sewage is clarified so as to be discharged into the watercourse without filtration. Now it is clear that where you rely upon irrigation alone—valuable as that system is—you have to contend with the accumulation of solid matter which will deposit in and around the surface vegetation, causing unhealthy growth, and becoming, in some cases, of an offensive character. That difficulty is lessened by extending the ·area which is under action for irrigation purposes, consequently, where the raw sewage is used, a much wider area is necessary than where the sewage has been more or less perfectly cleared from solid matter by some previous treatment. The cases are very exceptional and rare where irrigation, by the use of raw sewage alone, is a profitable speculation. But if you take irrigation as a means of purifying sewage, after a partial purification has taken place, very much less area is required, and the vegetation is of a more healthy character. As a rule, this combined system is attended with greater profit, because less area is required, and the clarified sewage can be used more freely and with less detriment—generally without any detriment—arising to vegetation, or to the atmosphere from accumulations of putrefactive matter. No local board wants to encumber itself needlessly with the trouble and outlay involved in a sewage farm, and, consequently, if the sewage can be purified at a small cost by chemical and mechanical arrangements, it is manifestly a preferable course of procedure. After the fecal and waste matter has been precipitated, or otherwise separated, although the effluent water may be fit to go into any river, yet this mode of dealing with it leaves the question entirely open as to whether it may be desirable at any future time to utilize this water for irrigation purposes. The points which have to be attained in working out any precipitation process are three.   First, the process should in itself be inoffensive; second, the effluent water should be within a moderate conservancy standard ; and third, there should be produced from the sewage a marketable material, which shall go far towards repayment of the costs of working.   In the phosphate sewage process the first stage of operation is to use phosphate of alumina which has been treated with sulphuric acid so as to bring it into an active condition.   This prepared phosphate is added to the sewage after it has been reduced in strength by the addition of water so as to make it intermix readily with the sewage. After four or five minutes, the action of the phosphate of alumina appears to be thoroughly completed by its coagulating the fecal matter in the sewage.   Milk of lime is then added, and this brings down from the clear water, which is intermixed with the coagulated matter, the phosphoric and organic acids which may be present.   After such treatment the sewage is passed into settling tanks, constructed so as to enable the precipitation to be carried forward in the most perfect manner. The extent to which precipitation takes place in any body of liquor is necessarily influenced by the quiet condition of that liquor.   If a strong current be allowed to disturb any portion of the tank, a certain amount of tank space is thereby lost.   By a plan of construction which I recommended to the Phosphate Sewage Company, the working power of their precipitating tanks has been trebled, and this represents a proportionate economy in the original outlay. This arrangement has a further advantage, inasmuch as a constant flow through the tanks can be maintained with very little agitation. The clarified sewage which runs off from these precipitating tanks is thoroughly cleared from all suspended matter ; but where it is required to get the effluent water of a higher purity, it is run through a filter-bed, constructed according to local requirements and conditions.   The deposit which has been precipitated in the tanks is periodically discharged into shallow draining beds, in which it remains until it gets into the condition of clay, when it is moulded into bricks, and dried in the air.   The character of the deposit is one that admits of a ready sale.

THE SEWAGE LIME AND CEMENT PROCESS.

By MAJOR-GENERAL H. Y. D. SCOTT, C.B.

THE action taken by the Association of Municipal Engineers, in making the sewage question the most important feature of their deliberations, augurs well for its speedy solution ; and I have great satisfaction in at once complying with the request of your President, that I would explain to you my plan of dealing with sewage sludge, by the lime and cement process. Your President's exertions merit the warmest support, not only of your own body, but of all who take an interest in sanitary questions.

So far as I have been able to gather from the papers I have heard and from the observations which have fallen from your Members, there is more unanimity of opinion amongst your body on the bearings of the sewage difficulty than is to be found among other eminent authorities on this subject, and I apprehend that the following observations would be generally accepted by your Members as being in the main correct :

1. Whatever system of dealing with excreta be followed, there will be in all large towns a sufficient quantity of fouled water to be got rid of, to entail a sewerage system and an outfall.

2. In the case of sea-coast towns the cheapest and most efficient mode of getting rid of sewage water will generally be to take it well out to sea.

3. For inland towns, although irrigation may sometimes afford the cheapest mode of disposing of sewage, and although in sandy porous soils raw sewage may be at once applied to the land with advantage, yet in the majority of cases where irrigation is resorted to, depositing tanks will sometimes be a necessary, and generally be an advisable, adjunct to a sewerage system.

4. On the other hand, when tanks are regarded as a main element in the purification of sewage water, irrigation or filtration through earth will always be a beneficial adjunct. No known means can purify foul water as well as filtration through earth.

5. Although for small places provided with depositing tanks simple deposition of suspended matters may be a sufficient prepa-

ration for earth filtration, some mode of precipitation must be resorted to in large towns, both for obtaining rapid deposition of suspended matters, and for the avoidance of nuisance. The Select Committee of the House of Commons to inquire into the Birmingham Sewerage Bill, laid it down as an axiom that *no sewage should " be thrown upon land unless previously defecated in tanks,"* and by defecation, in this case, precipitation with chemicals was obviously intended.

6. In the generality of large towns in which precipitation must be resorted to, the sludge will occasion serious difficulties. In some instances it may be possible to bury it, but at a considerable outlay. If the option lie between removing it to a distance in its wet state, or drying it previous to removal, the latter would prove the cheaper way of getting rid of it. Sewage sludge, on the average, consists of one part of solid matter mingled with nine parts of water; and assuming that the expense of the removal of this wet sludge is 2*s*. 6*d*. per ton (which is a moderate estimate), the cost of the removal of its solid matter would be 1*l*. 5*s*. per ton. As the cost of drying and of subsequent removal would not exceed one half this sum, the removal of the deposit in the wet state is not to be thought of unless it can, as at Saltley, be at once run into the soil, without cartage, and be dug in.

7. Of all the modes of precipitating sewage which have yet been proposed, the lime process is the simplest and the cheapest.

The following extracts, though the Report from which they are taken was made fifteen years ago, will be found to afford an excellent *résumé* of the sewage question, and of the arguments in favour of precipitation by lime :

" The use of lime to separate the solid matters of sewage is founded on the following circumstances : Sewage of itself, from the slimy, glutinous character of the matter floating in it, and from the specific weight of that matter being so nearly the same with water, will only separate very imperfectly, and after a length of time, into a clear liquid and a solid deposit. The addition of lime, however, by the chemical changes which it induces, but which we need not here describe, causes a separation of the solid suspended matter in a state of flocculence, in the same way that white of egg clears coffee or isinglass fines beer. The result is that the sewage rapidly changes its character, separating readily into a deposit which falls to the bottom, and a clear liquid.

" We may at once state our belief, that as far .as present know-

ledge goes, this very simple process offers as much prospect of
commercial advantage in respect to the manufacture of a solid
manure from sewage as any patent process that has been proposed.

" But with reference to the prospect of obtaining any very large
profit from the treatment of sewage, we see no reason to dissent
from the view that has been individually held and promulgated by
several of our members, that neither the lime process nor any
other existing method of precipitating sewage is likely to be
commercially advantageous to those who engage in it.   We consider that this is, however, not the light in which the matter should
be viewed.   The great problem is to get rid of sewage, advan-
tageously to agriculture if it may be; if not, at the least expense
to the community at large.

" Throughout the discussions that have hitherto occurred upon
this question, the real issue has been left comparatively in abeyance.
The primary consideration is not whether the sewage can be made
serviceable to agriculture, but whether or not there exists any
method which, consistently with a fair expenditure of money,
falling on those who ought in justice to bear it, will practically
rid us of the nuisance and danger attendant upon town sewage.

" Without going so far as to say that the precipitation by lime
is a perfect success, or that it can in all cases be adopted, we feel
satisfied that it does to a great extent fulfil the purpose for which
it is employed, so far, at least, as the purification of rivers is
concerned.

" By far the largest amount of nuisance and danger arising from
the pollution of rivers by sewage is due to the solid suspended
matters, which give off noxious effluvia throughout the period of
their decomposition.

" This is especially the case in our tidal rivers, where these
deposits form shoals and cover the banks, and at low water offer a
vast surface of offensive matter for the contamination of the air.
The lime process does effectually remove this solid suspended
matter, and in so far accomplishes a great and manifest good.   It
also destroys the immediate influence of the noxious gases of
sewage, and although it may be open to the objection of still
leaving matter capable of further putrefaction in the liquid, we are
of opinion that wherever this liquid is thrown into a body of water
considerably larger than itself, no evil results will be practically
experienced.

" Our conclusion, then, is that the absence of the means for the direct application of sewage to land, the methods of precipitation at command do actually offer remedial measures of a very satisfactory character. It remains to consider whether these remedial measures are within the fair limits to which a town population may be taxed for the suppression of the sewage nuisance.

" We have already stated our belief that, unless some new process of greater efficiency should be discovered, the formation of a solid manure from sewage will not be remunerative; that is to say, that the amount realized by the sale of the manure will fall short of the cost of its production. Neither is this to be considered as a condition dependent on want of appreciation of the manure, which time and better information on the part of the consumer will remove; on the contrary, the tendency has been hitherto to put the price above the value which a sound acquaintance with the nature of manures would attach to it. It is even questionable whether, in some instances, any money at all would be given for this deposit, and in considering the practicability of carrying into effect plans for the precipitation of sewage we must be prepared for this eventually."

The Report is signed—

" Essex.
Henry Ker Seymour.
Robert Rawlinson.
J. Thomas Way.
J. B. Lawes.
T. Southwood Smith.
John Simon.
Henry Austin.

" 12, Great George Street, Westminster,
    26th March, 1858."

Your President, in his report on the West Ham sewage, states his opinion to be decidedly in favour of the use of lime as the precipitant.

8. If the foregoing observations are correct, it must obviously follow that towns cannot look to get rid of their sewage excepting at a considerable cost to the ratepayers.

After the precipitate is dried two plans of disposing of it are available. It may be sold as manure; or, if lime be used as the chief precipitant, it may be burned and be converted into cement or agricultural lime. If agricultural lime is required, no other precipitant than lime is necessary. If cement is aimed at, any deficiency in the silicious constituents, which are an essential element in hydraulic cements, is made up by the addition of clay to the lime precipitant.

In the case of the West Ham deposit, Dr. Voelcker reported to the board of that place that agricultural lime derived from the deposit had a value of 1l. per ton, *in addition to the value of the lime;* and the Engineer, Mr. Lewis Angell, reported that the cement he had prepared, though not equal to Portland, was apparently a good building material. It is true that Dr. Voelcker also reported that the dried sludge was worth 2l. per ton, if the farmers could be induced to buy it; but, unfortunately, herein consists the difficulty: the farmers will not buy it, preferring to purchase guano. In the presence of inventors, who are more sanguine than myself on the subject of feeble manures finding a market, and are pecuniarily interested in their doing so, I should be unwilling to depreciate the agricultural value of sewage precipitates; but to make my own argument clear, I am compelled to call attention to the fact that though farmers still purchase and appreciate manures having a value of 6l. or 7l. per ton, yet the tendency is more and more in the direction of the purchase of high-class manures worth 12l. or 13l. per ton, and upwards. It is not, therefore, surprising that the Leicester deposit should have failed to find a market, nor that Mr. Lewis Angell, remembering the Leicester failure, should doubt whether the dried West Ham sludge would fetch one tenth part of the value which Dr. Voelcker assigned to it. I am not disputing the fact that such deposits have manurial value: I merely assert that if a farmer has a haulage of a few miles to his land, it is cheaper for him to purchase guano, than to cart dried sewage deposit gratis. The cost of cartage and spreading more than eat up the whole value of the latter. I also maintain, that unless a market can be found for the deposit close to the works, a better return will be obtained by burning it, and selling it as an agricultural lime (though the nitrogenous constituents are destroyed in the process), than in selling it as an organic manure. Dr. Voelcker reported to the West Ham Board that agricultural lime prepared from the sewage deposit of that place would have an agricultural value, owing to the phosphoric acid it would contain, of 1l. per ton *over and above the value of the lime.* It is manifest, therefore, that wherever lime is now carried by the farmer, it would pay him better to carry the sewage lime than ordinary lime of less than half the agricultural value of the sewage lime.

In concluding my remarks on this part of the question, I may call attention to the strong testimony which has been given by learned and practical authorities on the value of the cement process. I have only to mention the names of Drs. Frankland, Odling, and Voelcker, amongst chemists, and those of Mr. Thomas Hawksley and Mr. Bramwell amongst Engineers, who were unanimously of opinion that this process was the best which Birmingham could adopt, to convince you that this scheme is not a fanciful theory. It may be difficult without special tank arrangements to produce Portland cement, but cement of fair character can be produced, and has been produced, at Birmingham and elsewhere, without more precautions than would be necessary on any system of dealing with sludge.

The chief difficulty in the process, and this is not peculiar to the cement process, and applies equally to the manufacture of manure, is the drying of the sludge. We have tried drying it on hot iron plates, on porous plates, by Needham and Kite's pressing machines, by centrifugal action, and by the application of heat after draining off as much of the water in open reservoirs as could be removed in this manner. The results of these experiments have left no doubt on my mind, that the last method is by far the cheapest. My belief is, that whereas the cost of drying by pressure is about 1l. per ton of cement made (or 10s. on the dried deposit) by the method indicated, which is now in operation at Saltley, the drying can be effected for one-half of this sum.

With reference to the whole cost of the cement process, I may say that at Birmingham, including drying the sludge by means of presses, grinding the cement under edge runners and sifting it by hand (the whole process being conducted, in fact, on an experimental scale), the cost of production has been 2l. 5s. 6d. per ton of 30 or 31 bushels, and the cement may be assumed to be worth from 1s. to 1s. 3d. per bushel. At the former price sales were made to a contractor at Ealing, of cement made at that place; and he was prepared to purchase at this rate all that could be produced. Up to the present time the whole of the cement produced at Birmingham has been used on the corporation works. With increased appliances, we hope to produce the cement at Saltley at a cost of 1l. 10s. per ton, every expense included, and it is now intended to throw the cement into the market, to test its commercial value more thoroughly.

Before concluding this brief statement of the cement process, I should wish to guard myself from the idea being entertained that I put forward the cement process as the panacea for all the difficulties of the sewage question. This is very far from being my view. I do not even advocate it as a process of cement making simply as such. I merely state that lime is the cheapest precipitant; that if the deposit is to be sold as manure, the use of lime offers the best prospect of a return being made for the cost of the process; that when the deposit cannot be disposed of as a manure, the cheapest plan is to burn it; and that inasmuch as a saleable agricultural lime or a cement results from the burning process, this mode of dealing with the sludge, considered without reference to midden towns, will be the least expensive to large communities.

As to the larger question, of the best process of collecting and removing excreta, considered from the economical (and even, perhaps from the sanitary) point of view, much can be said in favour of more primitive methods than the water-closet system. By your permission, at your next annual meeting, I will explain the mode in which I think the sewage of midden towns should be disposed of.

The PRESIDENT said he was sure the Association felt very much obliged to the gentlemen who had given them so much information as to the various processes which they advocated for dealing with sewage; he thought they were entitled to their best thanks, which he tendered to them on behalf of the Association.

The subject was then thrown open to general discussion.

DISCUSSION.

Mr. MILBURN said they could all hope that the discussions which had taken place from time to time amongst the Members of that Association and other bodies would help them to extricate the vexed question of the utilization of sewage from its present unsatisfactory position. A great difficulty with which they had to deal was sludge, so as to convert it economically into manure. By the process he had to introduce to their notice the difficulty had been in a great measure solved. [Mr. Milburn here described his process, which is by heat.] At Coventry, where the machines had been tried, the cost of producing dry manure from sludge was somewhere about 7s. or 8s. a ton. An average of 3 tons of manure can be produced for farming purposes with a ton of common slack coal. One of the objects of the Town Manure Company was to combine liquids with solids. They wanted the liquid for the large amount of ammonia that was contained in it, and the solids were used as the base. In West Bromwich the system had been successfully tried; and only a week or two ago the company sold all the manure they could make at the high price of 8l. per ton. He believed the Bilston authorities paid the company a certain subsidy, so satisfied were they with the system of the company.

Mr. LEMON (Vice-President) asked what were the financial results of the Whitthread process?

Mr. PRANGE said that where they had been working upon this plan the cost of a ton of manure, including the cost and interest of the plant, and the cost of pumping and chemicals, was about 1l. 12s. Where there was no pumping to do, and where the sewage was not so very filthy as it was where this process was adopted, the financial results would be better. The manure has realized 3l. a ton, a little more or less. He did not at all pretend, unless in exceptional circumstances, that the precipitation process would afford a "mine of wealth" to any town that adopted it, but it would repay the greater proportion of the expenses connected with it.

In reply to questions, Dr. ANDERSON said that the sewage at Nuneaton very nearly paid the working expenses, but there was heavy pumping to be done there. The average value of the manure was about 2l. per ton there. The effluent was very clear, and cattle would drink it in preference to ordinary water, if allowed.

In reply to questions, Professor TANNER said that the selling value of the manure approaches very closely to the cost. The cost of manufacturing is about 4l. per ton; that is, for the dried material. There is no difficulty in meeting a variable flow of sewage. The supply of phosphate is easily kept under control. The phosphate costs about 3l. 5s. per ton. We get about 4l. per ton for the manure.

In reply to questions, Col. JONES said he was led to believe by the advertisement, when he took the farm, that the population of Wrexham was 9000. He had since learned that from three to four thousand is the outside of those who are connected with the sewers, and therefore he did not get the value he might expect from 9000. He paid for the land, which measures eighty-four acres, 350*l.* a year, and the sewage is included. The sewage comes direct on to the farm by gravitation. It is carried over the ground in the simplest fashion, by gutters all round. The subsoil is sand.

In reply to questions, General SCOTT said he believed the cost of grinding at Birmingham was 3*s.* 6*d.* per ton. There were about 36 bushels in a ton, and 2*l.* 5*s.* per ton would be the value of the cement produced. His belief was that with a proper system of drying, they should be able to make the cement for 1*l.* 10*s.* per ton. They could never expect to make a cement from sewage equal to Portland cement. There had been no comparison of cements made except in this way: A series of blocks were made in Birmingham, and they were put into water and kept there about a month. Alderman Avery and others put marks upon the blocks. There was Staffordshire cement; second Portland, *alias* lime cement; Roman cement; in fact, there were five sorts of cement. When the blocks were taken out and examined, the gentlemen agreed in putting "No. 1" upon the sewage cement.

Mr. FOWLER said that sewage contained a large amount of common salt, and it appeared to him that sewage cement would therefore be materially affected by the weather. Would the cement be suitable for plastering rooms?

General SCOTT said he had a room in his house plastered with the cement, and had not found the least dampness arise from it. He was of opinion that the cement would not be affected by the weather. The question is a somewhat novel one. Of course, there may be matters of detail in which improvements might be carried out. The only idea that would occur to him in connection with the matter is, that the question will not apply to this cement alone, but to all cements. In Roman cement there is a certain amount of potash, and there is a tendency in it to deliquesce.

Mr. MONSON expressed himself in favour of applying sewage to the land. It is absurd to say that the sludge which comes from the main thoroughfares in London can be treated as sewage and made into manure. Wherever there is a stream near a town all the surface water should be turned into that stream. Instead of dealing with sewage by means of chemicals, or chemical apparatus, he should pass it through the land. He considered the lime process a mechanical, not a chemical, action.

Mr. GRINDLE could not agree that there is no chemical action in connection with the lime process. In no case had he found any profit derived from sewage by precipitation, and in very few cases from the irrigation process. Chemists are wrong when they say that sewage is a profitable article to deal with; therefore towns must be prepared to pay in order to get rid of what is likely to become a nuisance to them. He firmly believed in the lime process.

The VICE-PRESIDENT (Mr. Lemon) thought it was the fault of gentlemen who wished to save their boards money, that the settlement of the sewage question had been delayed. As a rule, boards were waiting to see how cheap the thing could be done, or to see if they could get some one to do the work for them. He thought the time had arrived when it would be necessary for boards to subsidize companies or do the work themselves. He did not think that sewage could be made to give a profit except under very exceptional circumstances indeed. Birmingham had done more to elucidate this question than any town in England. He had gained much valuable information from a report issued by the Sewage Committee, and he wished to express his thanks to Alderman Avery and the Sewage Committee for the efforts they had made in the elucidation of this difficult problem. The scheme which had been prepared was the best that could have been drawn up for dealing with the question, and he regretted that the Report of the Select Committee had been defeated in the House of Commons. In dealing with the sewage they should try, if possible, to make a small profit, or to get enough to pay expenses, or they must get rid of it as cheaply as possible. He thought the only way in which they could obtain any profit was by applying it to the land. If precipitation by lime were adopted, as at Birmingham, he considered the best way to dispose of the sewage sludge was to dig it in. In towns where there were 10,000 inhabitants a field of five acres would be large enough for the purpose. He disagreed with General Scott as to the wisdom of making cement from sewage. He could not really see how they could expect to make a good cement from sewage deposit or the washings of the streets. He was an advocate for a separate system of drainage for sewage. If the surface drainage could be put into rivers, what on earth was the good of putting it into the sewers, thus increasing the sewage difficulty? The sewage difficulty was enormously increased by the large quantity of sewage water that ran into the sewers.

Mr. C. JONES, Hon. Sec., thought the separate system of dealing with the sewage had no doubt its advantages, but he was not altogether in favour of an absolute separate system. He thought the rain water from the roads might be kept from the sewers; but so far as the water from the roofs of houses is concerned, it would be better to allow it to pass into the sewers. If, however, a system of flushing could be obtained by any other than mechanical means, all the better. Whilst he agreed in the advisability of having a separate system of drainage, he would confine the new system to the water from the roads, and not include the water from the roofs of the houses. In regard to the sewage difficulty, every town must be dealt with upon its own peculiar characteristics. He could not help referring to an original mode which had been suggested for getting rid of the sewage difficulty. It was unique in its character. The *Standard* of that morning contained a letter which stated that in a certain town the sewers are at present running into the Thames. The Conservators served a notice on the authorities to take the sewage out of the Thames, and they, in their turn, served every individual householder with a notice to cut off all sewage connection from the sewer.

Mr. DUNSCOMBE thought many Engineers present believed that the only means of dealing with sewage was by irrigation over a large area, or filtration over a small area. Corporations and local boards must eventually pay a considerable subsidy in any process which they may finally adopt. The cheap precipitation process is a very good and valuable adjunct to either irrigation or intermittent filtration, and the companies recently started are entitled to great praise for their efforts in that direction, more especially as they do not now profess to make a large profit.

Dr. WILSON said it was satisfactory to find that people were beginning to discuss the question in a much more temperate fashion than had been the case hitherto. It appeared to him that the sewage question, like politics, had all along been made too much a party question. Various systems had been advocated, and the usual course adopted by the advocates had been to begin by vilifying every other system. The consequence had been that a great deal of distrust had been created in the public mind in reference to the matter. Many of the processes had been made Stock Exchange speculations, and had not therefore been put before the public so honestly as they might have been. Looking at the question from a purely medical point of view, he believed the water-carriage system was the best system, and he had no hesitation in recommending the adoption of water-closets in all towns where there was a good water supply.

Mr. PRITCHARD (Local Secretary, Warwick) said he had found great advantage result from having a duplicate system of sewers. At Warwick the surface water was partially taken to the river, and the work of dealing with the sewage at the outfall was rendered much easier in consequence. He also spoke in reference to the treatment of sewage on Lord Warwick's farm, and he contended that it was possible to make a profit from the produce of a sewage farm. He also spoke of the Warwick sewage farm; although it did not pay the whole of its expenses, still produce had been sold in Birmingham market from small portions of land, specially prepared, at the rate of 100l. per acre (gross). He also contended that there was not any great difficulty in dealing with the sewage sludge. He advocated precipitation and irrigation, or downward intermittent filtration, combined, as the most effectual method of dealing with the disposal of sewage.

Mr. BUCKHAM (Ipswich) thought that corporations ought to be very careful and consider the matter well before they resolved to enter into irrigation schemes of any kind. He did not believe there is a single irrigation farm that can show a satisfactory balance-sheet. Sewage will do for all kinds of crops if properly applied. He had great faith in the purification of sewage by filtration through land, as practised at Merthyr Tydvil.

The PRESIDENT, in concluding the discussion, said that many important points had been raised, and much valuable information elicited, as to various schemes, and their thanks were due to those gentlemen who had accepted their invitation to the conference, and taken part in the proceedings. In reply to Dr. Anderson, who had disputed the statements of the Royal Commissioners, he could only say, if the Doctor spoke with authority, we should be deeper in the mire than ever; but if we are not to believe Royal Commissioners, how are we to believe Dr. Anderson? Hence the necessity, as he had stated yesterday, of some searching and independent examination on authority. With regard to the various processes which had been discussed, no doubt there were good features in all, and the requirements of different places varied. The chemical processes were very costly, and it yet remained to be seen whether the values could be recovered. He had seen every process in the country, and was satisfied that where absolute purity was required they must go to the land. The lime process had many friends, because it helped us over the stile, and in many instances it was quite as suitable, and very much cheaper, than other chemical processes.

With regard to the separate system of drainage, he had come to the conclusion, having regard to purification, that it is desirable to keep out of the sewers as much water as possible consistently with continuous flow; the very large volume of water coming to the outfall was one of the difficulties of purification.

The general outcome of the discussion was that, under any circumstances, towns must not expect, either by chemical means or by irrigation, to make any profit. It was not the fault of Engineers, nor the fault of the public, that they have been led to expect it: it is the fault, if any, of the Government Reports. We all know what we have read about the "mine of wealth" and the waste of sewage. Having led us into this error, it was the duty of the Government to assist us out of the difficulty.

GAS STREET LIGHTING.

A PAPER was read upon this subject' by Mr. T. A. SKELTON. He referred to the great waste of light which attended the present system of lighting the streets. He pointed out that by the use of "catoptric" reflectors fixed in a lamp, the light radiating upwards would no longer be wasted, neither would it be concentrated below, but it would be thrown forward, and dispersed or concentrated as might be required along the usually dark interval between the lamps. He illustrated his paper by reference to a specimen of a catoptric lamp and diagrams.

The VICE-PRESIDENT said that in High Street, Southampton, sixty or seventy of the catoptric lamps had been erected, and the street was much better lighted than it was formerly. If corporations would reduce the quantity of gas used in the street lamps from 5 feet to 4 feet per hour, and adopt the new lamps, about 20 per cent. of the cost would be saved, and the streets would be better lighted than at present.

VOTES OF THANKS.

AT the conclusion of the business of the meeting, the PRESIDENT said that he desired, in the name of the Association, to express their hearty thanks to the Mayor and Corporation for their kindness in placing the Council Chamber at the disposal of the Association ; also to Alderman Avery (Chairman of the Sewage Committee) for the attention he had shown the Members, and for his invitation to inspect the Birmingham Sewage Works on the next day.

Alderman AVERY, in reply, said he was sure the Corporation felt highly indebted to the Association for their indefatigable labours in the cause of sanitary work.

A cordial vote of thanks was accorded to Mr. Angell (President), for his conduct in the chair.

The PRESIDENT, in reply, thanked the Members for the honour they had done him in re-electing him President, and for the support he had received, not only during the present meeting, but on all occasions. He also congratulated the Members upon the success of the present meeting. It had been said at their last meeting that it would only be a nine days' wonder, and he had replied that he never identified himself with a failure. He had worked throughout with that feeling, and all the Members had worked together with a will, especially the District Secretaries, in promoting the interests of the Association. Having achieved so much success it was impossible to go back. In thanking them on his own behalf, he also thought their thanks were due to Mr. Pritchard, of Warwick, and to Mr. Till, the Borough Engineer of Birmingham, for organizing the local arrangements, which were so satisfactory in every respect.

Mr. PRITCHARD and Mr. TILL having acknowledged the compliment, the proceedings terminated.

ANNUAL MEETING OF THE ASSOCIATION OF MUNICIPAL AND SANITARY ENGINEERS AND SURVEYORS.

MAY, 1874.

THIRD DAY'S PROCEEDINGS.

Visit to the Birmingham Sewage Works.

ON Saturday morning, the 30th May, at the invitation of Alderman Avery, a number of the Members of the Association paid a visit to the Birmingham Sewage Works and farm at Saltley. Many of the Members, including the President, were obliged to leave Birmingham at the close of the Second Day's Proceedings; but in most cases those who were called away had previously inspected the works. The following were the gentlemen who formed the party: Messrs E. PRITCHARD, Warwick (Local Secretary); W. S. TILL, Birmingham; F. ASHMEAD, Bristol; T. W. GRINDLE, Hertford; J. LOBLEY, Hanley; T. W. BAYLIS, Redditch; B. H. VALJE, Stow-on-the-Wold; E. DAVY, Maidenhead; J. CARTWRIGHT, Dukinfield; J. MITCHELL, Hyde; J. ROBINSON, Ashton-under-Lyne; A. COMBER, Kidderminster; J. BANKS, Kendal; G. COLE, Hereford; B. BAKER, Willenhall; J. A. HALL, Toxteth Park, Liverpool; J. MARTIN, Radford, near Notts; E. MONSON, Acton; E. BUCKHAM, Ipswich; E. KENWORTHY, Barnsley; J. W. FEREDAY, Wednesbury; and J. WOOD, Sidmouth.

On their arrival at the Saltley Works they were received by Alderman AVERY and Major-General SCOTT, C.B. Alderman Avery is the Chairman of the Sewage Committee of the Birmingham Town Council, under whose directions the works at Saltley are carried on. Not only did Mr. Avery invite the Association to visit the works, but he also willingly undertook to act as their guide, and to explain the different processes. As the Sewage Committee have made a gigantic, and in several respects a novel effort to deal with the sewage difficulty, an effort which, so far as it has gone, has proved eminently successful, a description of the works will be of interest.

Formerly, the Birmingham sewage was emptied from the sewers into the river Tame, at a point near to the present works, in its impure and normal condition. The Tame is an insignificant stream scarcely worthy of the name of river, and before it reaches Saltley its waters are defiled to a great extent; so much so that it looks little better than an open sewer. In the year 1858, a landed proprietor occupying property on the banks of the Tame below Saltley, obtained a Chancery injunction against the Birmingham Corporation, restraining them after the lapse of a certain period from polluting the stream. Insignificant and dirty though the Tame is, it flows in the only watercourse which the Corporation can obtain to carry off their superfluous water, and the authorities had to turn their minds to the question of clarifying the sewage so as to make it fit to enter the river without creating a nuisance. As the population of Birmingham is 360,000, and the whole of the sewage of the borough, with the exception of a small quantity taken to Smallheath, is conveyed to Saltley, it is hardly possible to over-estimate the magnitude of the work thus left to the care and judgment of the Sewage Committee. If the undertaking was large, the difficulties to be surmounted were greater and more formidable. No scheme for the disposal of sewage that had been adopted elsewhere seemed suitable for a great inland town like Birmingham; and having no satisfactory precedent to follow, and but little extraneous assistance to guide them, the Committee were in great measure thrown upon their own resources; and the result has been the construction of the present works. Before entering into details, the mode of operation may be summed up as follows:—1st. Mixing the sewage with lime to promote precipitation; 2nd. Precipitation in tanks; 3rd. Disposal of the sludge by burying it, or digging it into the land. The great feature of the system is, the " digging-in " process, by which the sludge is completely disposed of and rendered innocuous.

The Saltley Sewage Works and farm are situated at some distance from the outskirts of the town, and about two and a half miles from its centre. The level of the farm being lower than that of the town, the sewage is conveyed to the works by gravitation. In ordinary weather the average quantity of sewage brought down by the two main sewers is about 12,000,000 gallons per day; and in wet weather this amount is considerably increased, the sewers having to convey the surface water from the streets, as well as the offscourings of the kitchen, and the sewage of the water-closet. The first part of the works consists of what may be called the lime mill. It stands at the junction of the main sewers, about a quarter of a mile above the settling tanks. Here between twelve and thirteen tons of lime are daily mixed with the sewage after having been slaked, and diluted with water until it has acquired the consistency of cream. On the ground floor of the mill there are two steam-engines and pumps'; upstairs there are two large circular slaking tubs. The lime is elevated to the tubs by pockets fixed on endless leather bands, and the pumps on the ground floor supplying them with water. Lime and water are constantly dropping in small quantities, and they are mixed together by a stirring apparatus turned round by steam. Near their upper edge the tubs are fitted with taps by which the lime and water run off into long troughs communicating with an opening in the arch of the sewer. Instead of falling into the sewage in one stream, the milky-looking substance is divided into several jets, and is thus spread over the whole surface of the flowing sewage. The end of the trough crosses the sewer at right angles and the jets of milk of lime meet the current. The lime is therefore almost at once diffused amongst the whole body of sewage, and long before the tanks are reached the two are thoroughly intermixed. The reason for having the lime-works at a distance of a quarter of a mile from the tanks is because a canal crosses the sewer at this part, by which the lime is brought in boats. As explained by Alderman Avery to the Members of the Association, the lime is used for the twofold purpose of accelerating precipitation at the tanks, and for deodorizing the deposit. Lime does not prevent, but only arrests putrefaction for a limited period, a period, however, sufficiently long to enable the sludge to be dried and dug in before it can create a nuisance.

There are two tanks, or rather two series of tanks, through which the sewage has to pass before it is fit to flow into the river. In the first, which for the sake of distinction may be called the A tanks, the grosser particles of the sludge are deposited; and in the second, which may be designated the B tanks, the finer matters in suspension are allowed to settle. Taking the two series in their natural order we will begin with a description of the A tanks. These comprise two tanks of exactly similar construction; and they are used alternately every fortnight, the one being cleaned out while the other is filling. The dimensions of each of these tanks are as follows: length, 340 feet; breadth, 90 feet; depth, varies from 4 to 10 feet. The walls of the tanks are constructed of solid brick masonry, and the bottom is paved with bricks. On emerging from the sewer into the A tank, the sewage is seen to be completely intermixed with lime. It does not flow into the tanks in one stream, nor into the bottom of the receptacle; but is made to flow from several orifices on a level with the top of the water when the tank is full, and all of them are in a row at the upper end. At a distance of about 100 feet from the orifices of the sewer a partition runs across the tank dividing it into two portions. This is intended to stop commotion of the sewage and thereby facilitate precipitation. The heavier matters in suspension fall to the bottom of the first division, and the partially-clarified sewage flows over the top of the partition into the second and larger division. Here there is little or no movement in the water, and precipitation proceeds rapidly. Around the inner sides and base of this division there is a low wall about a yard from and parallel with the wall of the tank. This wall serves as a weir, and the water, now considerably improved in its character, flows in a sheet over it into the channel between it and the side of the tank. From this channel the water is led by a conduit to the second or B tanks.

The B series comprises four tanks, each of them being subdivided into four parallel compartments. As yet, only one of these tanks has been completed, but the others are in course of construction. The two A tanks are ample enough for the purpose of precipitating the heavier parts of the sewage; but three B tanks are necessary to give the partly-clarified water sufficient rest to deposit the finer particles. The fourth B tank is requisite, partly for use when the flow of sewage is exceptionally large, and partly because one of the series will, as a rule, be getting cleaned. Only about a third of the sewage at present passes through the one completed B tank, the remainder flowing into the river as it leaves the A tanks. The B tank already completed is divided into four compartments, lying side by side, each of which is practically a separate tank. The compartments are all of the same size, the following being their dimensions: length, 140 feet; breadth, 45 feet; depth, varies from 8 to 10 feet. Along the upper end of the compartments there is a channel into which the sewage flows after leaving the A tanks. This channel is about a yard in width, and is divided from the water in the compartments by iron "shuttles." These shuttles are simply a sort of sluice forming one end of each compartment, and regulating the inflow of the sewage from the cross channel. They can be raised up or down at will by a craning apparatus, so that the quantity of water flowing through the tank is entirely under control. The sewage flows over the top of the shuttles into the compartments; but it is proposed in the remaining three B tanks to make it enter at the bottom of the shuttles, it being believed that the commotion of the water will thus be reduced to a minimum. The present method, however, is practically perfect, there being so little motion in the tanks that four hours are necessary for its passage from one end to the other. The effect of giving the water entire rest by raising the shuttles and preventing inflow for a few hours has been tried, but the result was practically the same as when the sewage slowly passes through the tank. At the opposite end of the compartments the water runs over a weir into a channel leading to the river. The principle upon which precipitation takes place and the construction of the compartments will be best understood by a familiar illustration. Let a common oblong street drinking-trough, having the sides raised an inch or two higher than the ends, represent one of the compartments. If the ends are movable, and can be raised or depressed, the simile is all the nearer to the reality. Both ends should be of the same level. Let the sewage flow over the one end of the trough in a broad continuous sheet, as over a river weir, and as soon as the water rises to the level of the two ends, commotion from the inflow will cease. The sewage will enter over the one end and flow out over the other, calmly and quietly, and the great bulk of water inside the trough will have full opportunity to deposit suspensory matters.

On leaving the B tank the sewage water is clear and innocuous. It enters at A tank filthy, black, and vile; it goes from the conduit beyond B into the river Tame perfectly clarified, but, of course, containing valuable matters in solution which the tanks cannot retain.

The sludge deposited in the tanks is disposed of by digging it into the ground—burying it, in short. When it is remembered that about 350 tons of sludge are brought down the sewer to the tanks daily, and that the same portion of ground will not be used for burying purposes more than once in two years, it will be understood that a large area of land will be needful. The Saltley farm contains 180 acres, all of which is to be utilized for digging-in purposes. The A tanks are cleaned out every fortnight, and the B tanks

alternately in about the same period.   As soon as one of the. A
tanks is full, the sewage is turned into the other.   A few days are
required to drain the water off the sludge and get it dry enough for
removal.   When ready it is lifted out of the tank by a bucket
pump resembling a river dredger, worked by steam.   The dredger
is fixed at one side of the tank and works in a drain cut along the
bottom of the first division, already referred to.   This drain is the
lowest portion of the tank, and the wet sludge flows to it by gravitation aided by the operations of the workmen, who, in long leggings
and armed with drags, push it before them from the second division
towards the dredger.   The buckets of the dredger raise the sludge
to a height of from 20 to 25 feet above the ground, and empty
themselves into a rectangular wooden trough, 2 feet broad and 18
inches deep.   By this trough the sludge is conveyed with ease to
any part of the farm.   Being made in movable lengths, which can
be closely fitted together, the sewage sludge can be carried by them
as in a channel to any distance.   They are supported on wooden
pillars, and as a long trough is seen stretching to a distant part of
the farm, it might be aptly likened to a miniature viaduct.   The
reason of elevating the troughs to a considerable height above the
ground is obvious : gravitation can thereby be brought into action,
and the irregularities of the land, were the trough carried along
the surface, are avoided.   But there is little " flow " in thick sludge,
consequently it is necessary for men to push it along by a wooden
piston, fitting the sides and bottom of the trough.   The digging-in
process is thus conducted : The field or portion of the farm to be
operated upon is stripped of its turf, which, by being built into dykes
a couple of feet high, forms the walls of square reservoirs 18 or 20
feet in length and breadth.   When thus prepared the ground has a
honeycombed aspect, the cells or reservoirs being the receptacles of
the sludge as it issues from the troughs.   As soon as one cell is
filled, the end of the trough is turned on to another.   The sludge
is left in the cells for three or four days to dry by draining and
evaporation.   As the land itself is, or should be, first well drained,
the drying process proceeds rapidly.   The bulk of the sludge quickly
diminishes as the water—which when it comes from the tank is
nine-tenths of the whole bulk—leaves it, and when it has attained
the consistency of paste it is ready for burial.   Along the side of
the cells a trench is dug by manual labour.   Into this a layer of
the sludge is thrown, and the earth on which this layer rested is
dug up to the depth of the former trench and cast upon the top of

K

the sludge. A second layer of sludge is deposited in the bottom of the second trench and covered up in the same manner, and so on until the whole has been dug in. The whole process merely consists in making the sludge and the earth on which it rests, to a depth of a foot or so, change places; but simple as this may seem in theory, much labour is required to carry it into practice. A steam plough was once tried to effect the digging in; it made a splendid trench to commence with, but when its powers to bury the sludge therein were tried, it proved a failure. The sludge, instead of quietly dropping into the bottom of the trench and stopping there until the soil was laid on the top of it, oozed out at the top of the furrow. From that day onwards the plough has been discarded. After the sludge has been decently buried, the lumps of earth on the surface are carefully pulverized, and the ground is planted with rye grass, cabbages, peas, celery, and various other vegetables, all of which grow luxuriantly upon it. Rye grass and cabbages seem to be best fitted for the soil after it has received a dose of sewage. It is intended not to use the same land for digging-in purposes more than once every two years. The Committee, however, have been assured by an eminent chemist that the land may receive a dose with safety every year; but inasmuch as a larger quantity is buried in the land than he suggested, it has been thought advisable to give it a rest for two years. The whole question is as yet problematical, and experience must be the guide of the Committee in testing the matter. In turning the sludge over into the trench a slight odour is emitted, but this is imperceptible at a few yards distance, and as soon as it is covered up with the earth all smell disappears. Wherever the land has received a dose of sludge, and been planted, it looks natural and healthy, and there is every likelihood of its being able to take a dressing once in two years.

Taking the works as a whole, the Sewage Committee have every reason to feel proud of them. Gravel walks are formed around the tanks, and with the addition of shrubbery (as was suggested by a Member of the Association), they would be more like pleasure grounds than sewage refineries. Compared with what it was previously, the sewage farm has been immensely improved by the presence of the tanks and the manure which has been applied to it.

- The party having carefully examined all the works under the guidance of Alderman Avery, was taken in hand by Major-General Scott, who explained the cement process. As his paper is given elsewhere,* it is unnecessary to advert to it further than to say that the sludge from the tanks is dried slightly by evaporation, mixed with lime, and then thoroughly dried by artificial heat in a kiln, and burnt, after which it is ground into cement. It is only being tried on an experimental scale, and therefore it would hardly be fair to speak of the results yet obtained.

At the close of the inspection, Mr. HALL (Toxteth Park) said the Association were greatly indebted to Alderman Avery for the trouble he had taken in showing them over the works, and for the courtesy he had shown the Association during their stay in Birmingham. He thought that Birmingham, by the gigantic experiments it was making with regard to the disposal of sewage, was solving the question to the entire kingdom. It was a shame that the town should be left to struggle single-handed in such a great undertaking, and he thought it would only be right and fair for the Government to step in and bear a portion of the cost, seeing that the question was of national importance. He hoped and believed that General Scott would continue his experiments, and that the result might be very satisfactory.

Mr. PRITCHARD (Warwick) said he would supplement Mr. Hall's remarks by moving a vote of thanks to Alderman Avery and General Scott, for their kindness to the Association. He said it would be very remiss on their part if they did not give these gentlemen a hearty vote of thanks for the manner in which they had explained the different processes to the Association. He expressed the great pleasure and gratification they had experienced in witnessing the admirable results the Sewage Committee had attained, and hoped that the town, though beset on every hand by difficulties of no common nature, would struggle through them and bring the sewage question to a successful issue.

Mr. BUCKHAM (Ipswich) seconded the motion, which was carried unanimously.

Alderman AVERY, in replying, said it was a pleasure to him, as the representative of the Corporation, to meet a body of gentlemen so experienced in engineering matters as the Members of the Association, and to afford them pleasure or instruction through the work that was being carried on there. He had had great pleasure in visiting other towns to make inquiries relative to drainage, and on these occasions he had always found the Members ready to answer his questions and exchange ideas upon this most interesting topic.

* Page 110.

Major-General SCOTT briefly acknowledged the vote of thanks, after which the party returned to Birmingham.

The Members of the Association had intended to pay a visit to the sewage works at Coventry, or to West Bromwich, where Milburn's drying process is carried on, but some time was necessarily spent at Saltley, and several gentlemen having to leave by early trains, neither of the projected visits could be carried out.

Thus terminated the First Annual Meeting of the Association—a meeting which was most successful in all its features.

The Second Annual Meeting of the Association will be held at Manchester, in May, 1875.

DISTRICT MEETINGS

OF THE

ASSOCIATION.

DISTRICT MEETING AT MANCHESTER.

A MEETING of the District Committee for Lancashire and Cheshire was held, by the kind permission of the Mayor, at the Town Hall, Manchester, on Saturday, October 4, 1873. The following Members of the Association were present:

J. G. LYNDE, Manchester; A. W. MORANT, Leeds; A. M. FOWLER, Salford; A. JACOB, Barrow-in-Furness; R. VAWSER, Warrington; JOHN ROBINSON, Ashton-under-Lyne; H. ROYLE, Hulme; J. CARTWRIGHT, Duckinfield; J. PROCTOR, Bolton; R. BRIERLEY, Newton-in-Makerfield; F. SMITH, Blackburn; J. NEWTON, Bowdon; J. WILSON, Bacup; J. STANDING, Allerton and Garston; J. JACKSON, Stockport; J. A. HALL, Toxteth Park; A. G. McBEATH, Sale; HENRY HALL, Waterloo; JAMES HOLLAND, Witton; T. C. THORBURN, Birkenhead; W. B. BRYAN, Burnley; J. WOOD, Manchester; G. WATSON, Crewe.

Letters of regret for non-attendance were received from several Members of the Association.

Mr. Lynde, City Surveyor, Manchester, having been voted to the Chair, the circular convening the Meeting was read, and the minutes of the former meeting were read and confirmed.

It was unanimously resolved:

"1. That the Hon. Sec. convey to the Worshipful the Mayor of Manchester the unanimous thanks of this Meeting for his kindness in permitting the use of a room in the Town Hall.

"2. That the next meeting of this Committee be held in Liverpool, on the first Saturday in January next.

"3. That Messrs. Lynde, Fowler, and Thorburn be a Sub-Committee to confer with and assist the Secretary as to the arrangements and business of this Committee.

"4. That a copy of these proceedings be sent to the Secretary of the Association."

It was determined that the meeting in Liverpool should be chiefly devoted to reading and discussing papers on Engineering and Scientific subjects.

The Members then proceeded to inspect the Salford Intercepting Tunnel Sewer, in course of formation; they likewise visited the Manchester Abattoir and Wholesale Meat Markets, the Sanitary Depôt and Stables, and the New Town Hall and the Fire and Police Stations.

Before separating, the unanimous thanks of the Meeting was voted to Mr. Lynde and Mr. Fowler for their exertions during the day, and for their arrangements for the pleasure and convenience of the Members.

DISTRICT MEETING AT LEAMINGTON.

A MEETING of the Midland District Committee was held at Leamington, on Saturday, October 25, 1873. Leamington was selected " as being the most convenient town for the proposed meeting, in consequence of the intention to hold the annual meeting for 1874 in Birmingham," and also to afford the Members an opportunity of visiting the sewage irrigation works at Leamington and Warwick.

Amongst those present were: Messrs. LEWIS ANGELL, President of the Association; J. LEMON, Vice-President; C. JONES, Ealing, Hon. Secretary; E. J. PURNELL, Coventry; R. DAVIDSON, Leamington; E. PRITCHARD, District Secretary, Warwick; G. HODSON, Loughborough; C. LYNAM, Stoke-upon-Trent; W. BATTEN, Aston; E. CLAVEY, Burton-on-Trent; H. WALKER, Basford, Notts; T. T. ALLEN, Stratford-on-Avon; J. W. FEREDAY, Wednesbury; R. VAWSER, Warrington; J. LOBLEY, Hanley; E. BETTRIDGE, Balsall Heath; G. COLE, Hereford; C. MUMFORD, Wisbeach; B. H. VALLE, Stow-on-the-Wold; J. H. PIDCOCK, Northampton; E. DAVY, Maidenhead; E. MONSON, Acton; B. BAKER, Willenhall; J. HILDRED, Batley; E. L. STEPHENS, Leicester; J. BUTLER, Wolverhampton; Dr. GEORGE WILSON, Medical Officer of Health to the Warwick Union Sanitary Authority; Dr. BALY, Medical Officer of Health to the Leamington Local Board; Mr. C. S. WOODS, Sanitary Inspector of the Warwick Union Sanitary Authority.

Mr. LEWIS ANGELL, President, occupied the chair. He said that the present gathering was an important one, because the Members represented large populations, large industries, and large sanitary requirements, and each one represented a community. Such a meeting as the present, and that which had recently been held in Manchester, were calculated to be of immense advantage, not only to Members themselves, but also to the respective communities with which they were connected. He thought that they might now congratulate themselves on the position their Association had attained, and the interest that was taken in it in different parts of the country, and the public attention it already commanded. That, however, was not a meeting for congratulation, but for work, and he would, therefore, call upon the Secretary to read the programme for the day's proceedings.   He highly eulogized the exertions made by Mr. Pritchard, and the services rendered by him to the Association, and said that, if they had only some half-dozen energetic secretaries like Mr. Pritchard, the Association would soon be a very great and decided success.

STATISTICAL INFORMATION.

The PRESIDENT incidentally expressed an opinion that statistical facts were of more value than theories, and that the Association would be of most service by collecting statistical information on matters of general interest to Surveyors and Engineers, and furnishing it by circulars to the various Members.   He had received a communication from Mr. Wheeler (Boston), suggesting the Association should collect statistics on all matters of interest to Town Surveyors, and have them printed, and furnish copies of the same to all the Members of the Association.   This, he pointed out, would obviate the necessity of sending out circulars to various Engineers whenever information was required, as they would, in the suggested statistics, have it ready to hand.

Mr. PIDCOCK (Northampton) said he was very glad that this subject had been mentioned, because he thought one of the principal objects of the Association should be to circulate useful and valuable statistics amongst the Members.   Town Surveyors were constantly receiving applications for information on some particular subject, and if the Association were to furnish such statistics they would be ready to hand when wanted, and Members would not be troubled with applications and correspondence.

Mr. G. HODSON (Loughborough) said that nearly the whole of the information applied for by Surveyors was for the benefit of the governing body of their respective towns; and he thought, under the circumstances, the Town Council or Local Board, when the information was obtained, should be at the expense of publishing it, and should furnish a copy to each person who had assisted to contribute the desired information.   He had resolved to make it a rule not to furnish information applied for unless a promise was given to supply a copy of the statistics when they had been collected from the various Surveyors to whom application was made.   Mr. Baldwin Latham had recently done so, and Mr. Pritchard furnished the information he obtained with respect to the proposed new waterworks at Warwick.   The information thus given was most valuable,

and was material for reference when required. He thought the
Local Boards of Health should always be at the expense of publishing such returns, and that a copy should be furnished to each of
the persons who had contributed it.

The PRESIDENT remarked that this was a question which would
shortly come under the notice of the Council of the Association,
and he believed it would be proposed that the Association should
collect and publish statistics for the use of the Members.

Mr. HODSON said what he wished to lay stress upon was, that as
the information they were frequently asked to supply was for the
benefit of a Town Council or Local Board, they should publish the
returns, and furnish a copy to each person who had contributed the
information. He had made it a rule not to furnish any returns,
unless a promise was given that a copy of the statistics collected
would be supplied.

A MEMBER: Local Boards and Town Councils will doubtless
show their gratitude by subscribing to the funds of the Association.

The Members then proceeded to the Pumping Station of the
Leamington Sewage Works.

DESCRIPTION OF THE LEAMINGTON SEWAGE PUMPING STATION.

By Mr. ROBERT DAVIDSON, Town Surveyor.

THE sewage of Leamington was formerly treated by the lime process, which did not, however, save the town from an injunction in Chancery for polluting the river Leam. At this time the Earl of Warwick offered to receive the whole of the sewage of the district for a term of thirty years, and to pay a rental of 450*l.* per annum. The Board accepted this offer, and undertook, in consideration of this rental, to erect a pumping station, reservoir, and rising main, and deliver the sewage at certain points on Lord Warwick's estate.

Whilst these negotiations were pending, the Native Guano Company asked for and obtained from the Board a concession of the sewage works, and the whole of the sewage of the town, for the purpose of treating it by the A B C process. This they did for two and a half years, relieving the Local Board of all expense in connection with the works up to the 5th of October, 1871, when the first pumping engine was set to work, and the sewage question as regards Leamington was solved.

The sewage is received into a large reservoir, which, with the old precipitating tanks of the lime process, is capable of containing over a million of gallons; it is then conveyed by a culvert to the wells under the pumping engines. The sewage is not treated in any way, and only passes through an iron screen sufficiently close to prevent anything passing that would damage the pumps. The ordinary dry weather flow of sewage is about 600,000 gallons, in twenty-four hours, but in wet weather it increases to 1,500,000 gallons. The population contributing to this flow is 23,500.

The engines are of the high pressure, condensing, beam type, each of 180 indicated horse-power: there is only one fly-wheel of 35 tons weight with two cranks, so arranged that the connecting rods of either engine may be coupled to the crank shaft as required; the engines may therefore be worked together or independently. The cylinders are steam jacketed, 36 inches diameter, and 8 feet stroke. The beams are 32 feet long between centres, and are each in two flitches. Each engine works a couple of ram pumps, 26 inches in diameter and 5 feet stroke, one on each side of the beam centre. The two pumps of each engine are connected by a delivery pipe, with a capacious air vessel situated below the engine-room floor. There is also a safety valve attached to the delivery pipe, to prevent accidents. There are three Lancashire boilers, 24 feet long by 7 feet diameter, arranged so that the whole or any of them can be used for supplying steam to the engines.

The beam floor is reached by a spiral staircase, which is also connected to the cylinder packing stages. There is a powerful travelling crane capable of lifting the heaviest portions of the machinery. The governor, like the fly-wheel, is mutual, and can be attached to either engine. One engine is capable of doing the whole work, and the other is kept in reserve. Each of the pumps stands in its own well, and the pumps of each engine are calculated to raise 1,500,000 gallons in twelve hours, when the engine is working at the rate of 12½ revolutions per minute. The engine-house is ventilated by an arrangement on the roof, and to prevent the sewage gas rising from the wells to the injury of the workmen, a 12-inch pipe is inserted through the wall of the building under the pump-room floor, and carried underground to the chimney-stack, inside of which it is carried up a sufficient height to catch the upward draught. By this means the engine-house is kept sweet, and the sewage gas destroyed.

The sewage is conveyed to Lord Warwick's sewage farm through a rising main 20 inches in diameter at the pump end, and 18 inches in diameter for the greater part of its length. The main is about two and a quarter miles long, and rises to an altitude of 132 feet above the pumping station. The sewage is delivered by eight hydrants on the main, situated at various points on the farm, from thence it is conveyed in earthenware pipes and open carriers over the land; self-acting air valves are attached to the main at the highest points, and waste pipes and sluices at the lowest points.

Communication is kept up between the pumping station and the sewage farm by means of a telegraph of a very simple and easily understood construction.

The cost of the various works was—

	£	s.	d.
Engines and boilers	5,383	18	3
Buildings, reservoir, and culverts	4,940	4	6
Rising main and laying	5,059	2	4
Telegraph	100	0	0
Incidental expenses	756	7	0
Total	£16,239	12	1

The works were designed and carried out by Mr. R. Davidson, C.E., the Town Surveyor.

The working expenses fluctuate with the price of coal from 900*l.* to 1000*l.* per annum.

THE LEAMINGTON SEWAGE FARM.

From the Pumping Station the Members proceeded to Lord Warwick's sewage farm, about 400 acres in extent, but a thousand acres can easily be brought under the irrigation process, if required.

The land is gravel with mixture of clay, and the sewage is applied at the rate of about 90,000 gallons to an acre at one time. The land receives from three to twenty such dressings in a year, according to crops; and in winter the sewage is applied principally to fallow land.

The Members of the Association appeared greatly pleased with what they saw at the farm, which is under the able management of Mr. Tough. Captain Fosbery, his Lordship's agent, most courteously received the Association. A close inspection was made of the land during the process of irrigation and the crops grown.

The following crops have been successfully and profitably grown, viz., wheat, barley, oats, beans, peas, potatoes, cabbage, mangolds, turnips, parsnips, carrots, onions, strawberries, rhubarb, celery, and kohl rabi; but the principal crop has been Italian rye grass, for which there is a considerable sale in Leamington, and the surplus is used on the farm for rearing cattle. The grass is cut as often as eight or nine times during the season. There has been no statement of accounts published by Lord Warwick, but there is no doubt that the farm has proved a very profitable concern, and there is equally no doubt that the people of Leamington are very well satisfied to get rid of their sewage at the price.

WARWICK SEWAGE FARM.

From Lord Warwick's farm the Association proceeded to the sewage outfall of the Warwick Corporation, and afterwards to the irrigation farm, of which some particulars were furnished by Mr. E. PRITCHARD, the Borough Engineer. The sewage of the borough, with 11,000 population and 2500 houses, was estimated at 528,000 gallons per day, equivalent to 2357 tons in every four hours. There were two engines of 25 horse-power each, and the pump made twenty strokes per minute. The rising main was 16 inches in diameter, and 1400 yards in length. The sewage flows over the farm by gravitation. Originally there were only 102 acres, 0 rood, 17 perches; but an additional 33 acres, 2 roods, 4 perches had been obtained. The land was leased from Lord Dormer, until 1887. The total cost of the works had been 10,084l. 18s. 1d. Some very fine sewage products were also seen growing on this farm. The annual cost of pumping is between 500l. and 600l. The products were greatly admired by the Members, who warmly commended Mr. Pritchard's management of the works and farm.

From this farm the Members returned to the Pump Rooms, at Leamington, which had been placed at the disposal of the Association. The reading of the following papers was then proceeded with.

SANITARY IMPROVEMENTS AT STRATFORD-ON-AVON.

MR. T. T. ALLEN, Borough Surveyor, Stratford-on-Avon, read a paper on sanitary improvements in that town. Premising that the town was well known throughout the civilized world as the birthplace, the home, and the grave of the bard, he remarked that it was a very ancient town, and had been traced to a period of 300 years before the Norman conquest; and it derived its name from being on the great North road from London to Birmingham, which passed straight through a wide part of the river Avon, close to the town. Soon after the passing of the Public Health Act of 1848, it was adopted, mainly through the exertions (in the face of much opposition) of the late Dr. Thomson, a name well known in Leamington, then resident at Stratford-on-Avon. After stating the various improvements which had been effected, he mentioned that Mr. Knott, the District Auditor, at the last audit of the Local Board accounts, said that he did not know any town where so many improvements (considering the size of the town) had been carried out at so moderate an outlay as at Stratford-on-Avon. A very complete system of sewerage and main drainage had been carried out, and the whole of the private property throughout the town connected with the sewers. The outfall sewer at present conveys the sewage into the river Avon, at a considerable distance below the town, and, as the population was small, this did not cause much pollution of the stream. This, however, would not long be continued, as the Local Board were anxious to obtain the best information as to the disposal of the sewage of towns, and the most economical and least offensive method of dealing with the matter, on which there are so many conflicting and opposite opinions at the present time. The attention of the Board had recently been directed to the surface repairs of streets, which he considered might well be classed as sanitary improvements. Within the past five years the Board had newly paved nearly every street in the town, and had

expended about 5500*l.* on the work.   The main streets had the
footpaths laid with York stone, and the others with the best of the
old paving stone and blue bricks.   The result had been that the
appearance of the town had been greatly improved, and from
being one of the untidiest it was now one of the cleanest in the
Kingdom.

THE DISPOSAL OF SEWAGE—A QUESTION FOR LEGISLATION.

Mr. E. Bettridge, Surveyor to the Balsall Heath Local Board, read the following paper:—The disposal of sewage, including in that term, excrements, house slops, and, in industrial districts, chemical refuse from manufactories, is the most important sanitary question of the day. Many large towns, Local Boards of Health, urban and sanitary authorities, are completely at a dead-lock in this matter; and the interest at stake—the well-being of whole communities—is so vast that the subject should, in my opinion, be thoroughly ventilated and dealt with by the Legislature. It is not necessary to go far afield for examples of the difficulty sanitary governing bodies are labouring under. Take the case of Birmingham. It will, probably, be within the knowledge of all that the Corporation of Birmingham is, by an injunction of the Court of Chancery, forbidden to contaminate the river Tame, into which the large system of sewers of the town now debouches; and we also know that, an elaborate and extensive scheme of sewage irrigation having been defeated in Parliament, the system known, I believe, as General Scott's (that of causing the weightier ingredients of the sewage to deposit in tanks by an admixture of lime), is being vigorously and thoroughly tested. Whether this plan will answer is not yet determined; but when we consider that the storm-water from the many miles of Birmingham streets has its only outlet through the same sewers which convey the' usual flow, it will be apparent that no possible system of tanks could catch and retain the insoluble sewage matters which would be hurried into and through them during heavy rainfall. To further illustrate the subject, I will instance Balsall Heath, possessing a Board of Health, to which I am Surveyor. The district adjoins Birmingham, comprises an area of about 450 acres, and contains a population rapidly increasing (having doubled itself during the last ten years), and numbering at the present time about 15,000. The district is divided into two nearly equal parts by the main road from Birmingham to Alcester, called the Moseley Road, which in itself falls

slightly towards Birmingham, and is the back-bone, so to speak—
the watershed falling from it on either side.   Balsall Heath is
bounded on the western side by the river Lea, which flows through
Birmingham and into the Tame; and into the river Lea the drains,
such as they are, run on that side of the Moseley Road.   On the
eastern side the drains run into a feeder of the Warwick Canal, the
Company of which have obtained an injunction from the Court
of Chancery to prevent the pollution of their stream.   The Board
has done a great deal to lessen the evil complained of, by keeping
the clear water, as far as practicable, apart from the sewage, and
by putting down settling-tanks and a filter-bed (the filtering
medium being gravel) through which the sewage water has to pass.
Several years ago the Board consulted Mr. John Lawson, C.E., as
to the drainage of the district, and he gave it as his opinion that
the natural and proper outlet for our sewers was through Birmingham.   On application being made to the Birmingham authorities,
to allow us to connect with their drains, we were referred to landowners on the river Tame, who had then begun to complain of
Birmingham, and they, as a matter of course, emphatically refused
to consent to the proposed addition of our sewage to that already
flowing into the river.   Things went on for a few years, and then
(last year) came the action on the part of the Warwick Canal
Company, which we are endeavouring to meet as best we can.
From the proximity of our district to Birmingham, all the land
within its boundaries and immediately adjacent may be considered
as building land, and far too valuable—even if the land-fall admitted
of it—for any system of irrigation, without pumping to a great
distance, which would be ruinously costly to so small a community.
Enough has, perhaps, been said to show how completely we are at
a standstill.   The feeling of the Board and of the ratepayers is to
carry out an efficient system of drainage; but which are we to
adopt?   We have no outlet.   Our neighbours will not have us at
any price; and we are unable to irrigate.   I believe I am right in
saying that scores of other towns and districts are somewhat
similarly situated.   Surely this is a matter for Government to take
in hand; and my object now is to ask the opinion of this meeting
as to the desirability of memoralizing the Imperial Authority on
the subject, suggesting that commissions be appointed to examine
into such cases as I have described, to advise the local bodies
what course to take, and to authorize their carrying out the
necessary works.   I imagine that any recommendation coming from

this Association of Municipal and Sanitary Engineers and Surveyors, as a body, would have weight with the Government; and I feel sure that we, as Sanitary Engineers, could not bestir ourselves in a more important and beneficial way than by calling the attention of Government to the matter, urging the appointment of commissions to report on the disposal of sewage in various districts; and that Government itself, by dealing authoritatively with the subject, would earn the gratitude of this and all future generations.

THE SEPARATE SYSTEM OF DRAINAGE.

By Mr. E. MONSON, Surveyor to the Acton Local Board.

Mr. Monson gave a description of the works designed and carried out by him at Halstead, in Essex, where the surface water, being kept entirely free from sewage, was discharged into the Mill Head, while the house drainage was conveyed in small drains to a point beyond the town, to be afterwards dealt with. The plan of the works was that of the separate system and back drainage, the sewers being coterminous with the water supply, sluice valves being placed at the ends of the water mains, and the whole of the sewers being flushed by the discharge of water for cleansing the water mains, or from a pond adjacent. The old sewers, after being cleansed, repaired, and reconstructed, where necessary, were used for the most part for surface drainage, which included street drainage in most cases, land drainage, storm-water, and springs. For the sewage, almost entirely new lines of pipe-sewers were laid, which also received the rainfall from houses and yards. The sizes of the sewers were calculated according to the square of their diameters, so that by no possibility could those in the lower part of the town be required to do more than that of which they were fully capable, and the least inclination given to any of them was 1 in 273. Great attention was paid to flushing. The main sewer in Head Street commenced at Paynter's Pond, at the top of the hill, and this pond flushed the greater part of the system. The lower portion could be flushed from the Mill Head if required. In this system the sewage, from its entry into the sewers to its discharge, continued to flow on so that it had no time to decompose and liberate noxious gases, and the formation of sewage gas was prevented to a considerable extent by keeping the sewers free from deposit, by keeping down the temperature of the sewers, by flushing and by ventilation. The branch sewers were flushed by the water mains, which communicated with the sewers in the following manner. Sluice valves were placed at the ends of the mains, and when the sluice valves were raised to cleanse the mains it flushed the sewers. In the neighbourhood of London this water would be discharged upon the surface of the street, washing it away. In other cases it was arranged to flush the sewer from the hydrants with the fire-engine hose, and private drains could also be cleansed by the same means. There were the usual manholes and inspection shafts; and the sewers were ventilated by means of the rain-water pipes, properly jointed, and carried up to the roofs of the houses at places where the gases would not be discharged into the bedrooms. He stated that the compensation paid to owners was only at the rate of 9d. per rod; that there was no objection to back drainage on the part of the owners, because, being less costly, it was to their advantage, and that there were only two or three claims for owners' compensation. The total length of new sewers was 5900 yards, and the cost 1500l. The execution of the works cleansed the Mill Head, situated in the centre of the town, which had previously been a constant nuisance, and restored all streams and watercourses to their original purity. The water which would otherwise have been contaminated with sewage, was preserved fit for domestic or manufacturing purposes, and being conveyed to the Mill Head, was utilized to supply the river and drive the mill. The back drainage was most efficient, a short length of pipe sufficed for a connection, and the drains being kept outside of the houses, there was no necessity for long lengths of drainage pipes under the floors. The sewage was reduced in bulk, and was, therefore, more constant in quantity, more convenient for treatment, and, in its concentrated form, more valuable for irrigation. The advantage of the separate system was that it combined efficiency with economy, and was especially applicable to country towns, although, with suitable modifications, it might have been applied to the Metropolis, which would have materially reduced the first cost for main drainage, and saved a large annual outlay for pumping water that ought to have been conveyed at once to the river without being contaminated with sewage. The system, as modified at Halstead, was to separate the sewage from the rainfall, not the rainfall from the sewage, and the works conveyed the water to the river, and prepared the sewage for the land. Although Halstead was an agricultural district, and there was not a superabundance of manure, there did not appear to be any great wish on the part of the farmers or landowners whose land was near the sewage outfall to employ the

sewage for the purpose of irrigation or improving their land.—
Mr. Monson, in the latter part of his paper, argued that the
method of utilizing sewage by irrigation alone was insufficient,
and that in connection with irrigation there should be works which
should be used when there is a large amount of rainfall and the
land was saturated with water, so that the farmer might not
be compelled to pour the sewage upon his land when it does not
require it. He urged that the sewage should in no case be used
raw; that the insoluble elements should be removed; and that the
sewage should in some cases be chemically prepared before being
applied to certain crops; that the supply to the farmer should be
intermittent; that the rainfall should be, as far as possible, kept
separate from the sewage; that each farm should have its own
manure tank, so that the scientific farmer could add any chemical
to it that the soil or crop might require, and be able to neutralize
or precipitate what he might find to be injurious, or liberate any
element, or restore any property that might have been lost by
chemical combination whilst passing through the sewers.

As so much time had been occupied in inspecting the farms
earlier in the day, there was none left for discussing the papers.

The PRESIDENT made a few general remarks. The disposal of
town sewage was a most pressing and vexed question. There had
been a little too much enthusiasm respecting the subject. The
advocates of the various systems had too often seen no good in any
other principle than that to which they had pledged themselves.
The public had been told that in sewage there was a mine of
wealth, and towns had been led to expect great things and much
profit from the disposal of sewage. That was a mistake, and more
sober views must prevail. The first consideration in connection
with such matters was the getting rid of a nuisance. Cleanliness,
comfort, and health were of much more importance than local
rates, or the question of profit and loss. If they could get anything out of sewage, well and good; but the old proverb was
applicable to sewage, " You cannot expect to make a silk purse out
of a sow's ear." Analysis showed that the outside manurial value
of a ton of liquid sewage was twopence. More could not be got
out unless it was first put into it. If expensive manipulation
and costly chemicals were employed, he did not think there would
be any other result than disappointment and loss. The various

chemical systems before the public had, for the most part, been stock-jobbing concerns, and thus their value had been lost, some of them having been entirely wrecked on the Stock Exchange. Profit and loss was a purely local question, and depended on local circumstances. He was bound to confess, using his knowledge and experience as an Engineer, and his common sense as a citizen, that there was nothing which had hitherto proved so efficient a disinfectant as the earth. If the circumstances were favourable, there was no better way of utilizing sewage than irrigation. Members must guard against being possessed with one idea. Because irrigation was good and proper in one place, it did not follow that it was the only system. Various chemical systems had been propounded: some were in abeyance, and others in incubation. The Association was not pledged to irrigation. It might be, as Mr. Monson had suggested, that a tank or chemical system, combined with irrigation, would be of great service. It was not the right thing in all cases—he hardly thought it was the right thing in any case—to put raw sewage on the land. Such a course had given rise to the observations of Dr. Smee and others, as to the poisoning of crops and land. The separate system must be adopted, if the sewage was to be disposed of by any chemical process. .

The thanks of the meeting were tendered to the local authorities for the use of the Pump Room, and to Mr. Pritchard for his exertions as District Secretary.

The Members then dined together at the Crown Hotel.

DISTRICT MEETING AT LIVERPOOL.

On Saturday, Jan. 3, 1874, a meeting of the District Committee
for Lancashire and Cheshire in connection with the above Associa-
tion was held at the Town Hall, Liverpool.   There were present—
Mr. J. LEMON, Southampton (Vice-President of the Association), in
the chair; Messrs. T. C. THORBURN, Birkenhead; A. M. FOWLER,
Salford; J. G. LYNDE, Manchester; G. F. DEACON, Liverpool;
R. BRIERLEY, Newton-in-Makerfield; J. A. HALL, Toxteth Park,
Liverpool; W. A. RICHARDSON, Tranmere; JAMES STANDING,
Garston; H. ROYLE, Manchester; S. KELSALL, Stretford; J. LOBLEY,
Hanley; H. S. ASPINWALL, Macclesfield; J. JACKSON, Stockport;
J. D. SIMPSON, Buxton; W. CRABTREE, Southport; H. HALL,
Waterloo; A. JACOB, Barrow-in-Furness; EDWARD PRITCHARD,
Warwick; J. PROCTOR, Bolton; A. W. MORANT, Leeds; J. CART-
WRIGHT, Duckinfield; J. WILSON, Bacup; G. WATSON, Crewe;
E. SMITH, Oswestry; J. NEWTON, Manchester; J. ROBINSON, Ash-
ton-under-Lyne; J. HARTLEY, Lancaster; JAS. HOLLAND, Witton;
W. H. CLEMMEY, Bootle; W. B. BRYAN, Burnley; J. G. HOLT,
Manchester; W. KELLY, West Derby; R. VAWSER (District Secre-
tary), Warrington; and Dr. VACHER, Medical Officer of Health,
Birkenhead, as a visitor.

The circular convening the meeting was read, and the minutes
of the previous meeting confirmed.

THE MERSEY TUNNEL.

Mr. SIDES, from the office of Mr. Brunlees (Engineer to the
tunnel in course of construction between Liverpool and Birkenhead), attended with plans and sections, and explained the chief
features in connection with the undertaking.   He said there
would be two distinct tunnels, each tunnel having a diameter of
15 feet, and supported by six courses of brickwork built against
the red sandstone rock.   Between the tunnels there would be a
space of 10 feet of rock, and the up and down lines would merge
into one at the shore ends.   Beneath the tunnels, and about mid-
way between them, there would be a subway of 5 feet diameter,

for the purpose of leading the water to two pumping shafts. The shaft on the Birkenhead side had been driven about 90 feet deep. Very little water was found until a depth of 45 feet was reached, and the quantity now being pumped was 7000 gallons per hour, which was done easily with a Tangye's six-inch pump. The shaft had already reached the level of the tunnel, and there was rock all the way through. The boring would be performed with a diamond drill, the work going on simultaneously at each end. The tunnel would be a little over three quarters of a mile from shore to shore, and the gradient 1 in 37. With regard to ventilation, Mr. Brunlees thought that as the trains would always run in one direction, and would nearly fill the tunnel, they would carry with them a column of air sufficient to secure ample ventilation. If not, it would be easy to fit to the tender a large diaphragm which would drive the column of impure air before it, and drag the column of fresh air after it.

Mr. VAWSER proposed, and Mr. FOWLER seconded, a vote of thanks to Mr. Brunlees and Mr. Sides for the use of the plans and the information furnished to the Members of the Association.

Mr. SIDES, in reply, said it had afforded him much pleasure, and he would be happy to give any further information to any gentleman present who might wish to communicate with him on the subject.

Mr. DEACON (Borough and Water Engineer for Liverpool) said it was desirable, before the Members present proceeded on their tour of inspection, to give them some idea of the use of the water meter, upon which he would read a paper. The object of the meter was to register on a diagram the absolute quantity and rate in gallons, per hour, passing through the meter at any instant, and at all instants of time, for a whole week. In other words, the entire quantity for an entire week would be recorded on one diagram. The essential difference between this meter and others was, that in ordinary meters they had the quantity of water between the two times when observations were taken, whereas in this meter, the exact quantity passing through it at any given moment was recorded. Its usefulness in detecting waste was obvious, because they had the maximum as well as the minimum readings, corresponding to the different times of the day and night. In one district where the meter had been put up, the quantity of water which passed through a four-inch main during the night was 3600 gallons per hour, but it had now been reduced to 700 gallons per hour—a bad condition of things certainly, but remarkably good compared with what it was. Having explained the construction of the meter and its mode of working (which will be found detailed in the paper), Mr. Deacon handed round, for inspection, some diagrams showing the result of a series of observations taken on several successive days.

The Members then proceeded to carry out the programme previously arranged, and which it was intended should include an examination of the Liverpool and Birkenhead tramway systems; the Mersey Tunnel; the method of street formations recently adopted in Liverpool; the new water meter; and visits to the river approaches and the Central Station. The weather was, however, most unpropitious, and had the effect of modifying the arrangements so far as a visit to Birkenhead was concerned. Mr. DEACON accompanied the party to Tithebarn Street, where a water meter was at work attached to one of the mains, and the principle upon which it worked having been explained, the party proceeded to the Hotham Street Corporation Waterworks. Here a water tank had been erected, having a glass gauge and graduated scale showing the exact quantity of water contained in the tank. The water main was above the surface of the ground, so as to facilitate examination. The experiment was conducted by Mr. Deacon first regulating the indicator upon one of the lines of the diagram, and the tap in the main having been turned, and the water kept flowing for three minutes, it was found that it registered at the rate of 2190 gallons per hour, the exact quantity passing through the pipes, as recorded by the gauge, being 2200 gallons. The discrepancy, however, was satisfactorily accounted for by the fact of the indicator not having been set exactly upon the line. Mr. Deacon said not a drop of water could pass through the main (a four-inch one) without being recorded, and the meter would register up to 5000 gallons per hour, the variation between the gauge and diagram being not more than one per cent. A man and a boy could attend to fifty meters in the course of the day. It took about five minutes to take off the diagram, place another upon the cylinder, and adjust the indicator. About half an hour was spent in examining the meter, and the tests were regarded as most satisfactory, the instrument being most sensitive to the slightest alteration in the flow of water.

RANELAGH STREET STATION.

The party next proceeded to the new Central Railway Station, in Ranelagh Street. On the way Mr. DEACON pointed out a length of Val de Travers asphalte footway which had just been completed, and which had every appearance of a good job. The carriage-road at this point was laid with Penmænmawr sets in concrete. Arrived at the Central Station, which is in course of completion, the party were met by the Resident Engineer, Mr. MORTON, who gave some particulars relative to the construction of the station. The roof is 65 feet high and 160 feet span. It covers seven lines of rail, three single platforms and a double one, the length of each being about 700 feet. The ribs are 55 feet apart, with a tie rod beneath each, so arranged as to relieve the roof of undue pressure caused by an accumulation of snow, and allowing for contraction and expansion. The roof is further strengthened by purlins between the ribs, and the appearance of the work is extremely light and elegant. The station will be completed in the course of a month, and is intended to be used for passenger traffic only, the Brunswick Station being kept for goods traffic.

THE NEW RIVER APPROACHES.

The new river approaches on the north side of the Mersey are now in course of construction between the Prince's and George's Docks. Mr. T. C. THORBURN, Town Surveyor, of Birkenhead, in the absence of Mr. Lyster, the Dock Engineer, took the party in charge, and explained the nature of the work which was going forward. The approaches consist of an immense pontoon floating bridge, which will rest on a stone incline at low water, and float at high water. When completed it will greatly facilitate the traffic between Liverpool and Birkenhead, and it is expected that the work will take twelve months to finish.

The party then returned to the Town Hall, when the following papers were read.

WASTE OF WATER AND CONSTANT SERVICE.

By Mr. G. F. DEACON, Borough and Water Engineer,
Liverpool.

In the following paper I propose to state, first, what appear to
me to be the inducements to undertake systematically the prevention of waste; next, my experience as to the working of the
district waste-water meter system; and [I will begin by submitting
to you the three following propositions, which have failed in gaining
universal acceptance, owing principally, as I believe, to the superficial manner in which the subject has been considered :

Proposition 1.—The prevention of waste of water, or, in other words,
the conservation of all water not actually required for domestic or
manufacturing purposes, is or may be accompanied by vast sanitary
benefits, arising from the more efficient action of existing drains, as
well as from the dryness of the subsoil of dwellings.

Proposition 2.—The prevention of waste by the system hereafter
described is practicable, and, apart from all sanitary considerations,
it is by far the most economical mode that can be resorted to for
increasing the available water supply, while it will always diminish
the working expenses in cases of supply by pumping from wells.

Corollary.—Towns and districts at present supplied on the intermittent system, when the total supply is more than sufficient to meet
the necessities of the people, which is the case when more than ten or
fifteen gallons per head per day are taken for domestic purposes, may
obtain constant supply, accompanied by a surplus of water or by a
corresponding reduction in the working expenses of the supply.

With respect to the first proposition, that the prevention of
waste is or may be accompanied by vast sanitary benefits, arising
from the more efficient action of existing drains, as well as from the
dryness of the subsoil of dwellings, I would call attention to the
very prevalent notion that a town cannot have too much water, and
that all the water which can be passed into the mains should, if
possible, be given to it, as it is conducive to cleanliness, and as the
sewers require it. The prevention of waste is assumed to be
equivalent to stinting the supply, when in reality it may have the

contrary effect. Take the common case of a town demanding 25
gallons per head per day for domestic purposes. Now 10 gallons
per head per day is probably the maximum quantity actually used
for such purposes. Of the remaining 15 gallons a large proportion
is lost by defective pipes and fittings and by misuse, and flows down
a few isolated drains to the sewers. But the maximum waste due
to this cause considerably exceeds the average, and it exists where
the pressure on the mains is greatest, viz. in the lower parts of the
town, so that the greater part of such waste water enters the sewers
near their outfalls, where it is useless; while at their upper ends,
where water is most required, the supply to the sewers from this
cause is trifling. Among the sewers of a town many are or ought
to be permanently self-cleansing, and without entering upon the
consideration of the various circumstances which conduce to so
desirable a condition, I may say that all sewers which are not self-
cleansing, with the reasons why they are not self-cleansing, should
be systematically tabulated, and if want of water is the cause—
which is certainly not always, and, I think, not usually so—the
cure is very simple when you have a surplus of water, formerly
wasted, to use for this most beneficial purpose.

Imagine the influence on a single system of sewers, if only a
quarter of a gallon per head per day of the population whose drains
fall into it were used for flushing that system. I will give, as an
example, a single existing case, and in most towns there are many
cases more striking. The sewer system to which I refer carries
away the refuse of 52,000 persons. There are in it about 250
dead ends of branch sewers, of which probably 100 require artificial
flushing to keep them absolutely free from deposit. A quarter of
a gallon per head per day will give 4000 gallons for each of those
sewer ends every month, a quantity which, whether flushing direct
from the mains, or the tank system, which is by far the best, be
adopted, is more than ought ever to be used. It would, in short, fill
a 3 ft. by 1 ft. 10 in. sewer to the crown for 145 feet of its length.

But the private drains also require flushing. It is certain that
the dribble of waste water will never flush them ; the small pipes of
ordinary water-closets kept running all night will never do it ; but
the regulating cistern delivering its two gallons through a 1½-inch
pipe will do it most effectually, and that cistern will help you
greatly in your work. Of course, there are other private drains, but
the dribble of waste water, if it exists, is no advantage to them.

I have spoken of the proportion of the lost, 15 gallons due to

defective fittings and misuse, and I now come to the remainder of
that quantity which leaks from innumerable defects in public and
private service pipes. This water sinks into the subsoil; it renders
healthy soils unhealthy; it makes the houses damp, and certainly
militates against the cleanliness of the lower orders. But its influence for harm does not end here. Part of it reaches the sewers,
and even though it may get into them, it can only do so by
damaging the brickwork and mortar.

The second proposition and its corollary is to the effect that the
prevention of waste by the system hereafter described is practicable,
and that it is, apart from all sanitary considerations, by far the
most economical mode which can be resorted to for increasing the
available water supply, and that it will always diminish the working
expenses in cases of supply by pumping from wells; while towns
and districts at present supplied on the intermittent system, when
the total supply is more than sufficient to meet the necessities of
the people, which is the case when more than 10 to 15 gallons
per head per day are taken for domestic purposes, may obtain constant supply, accompanied by a surplus of water, or by a corresponding reduction in the working expenses of the supply.

I think I may satisfy you as to the truth of this statement by
giving an example of the cost of the work in a district of Liverpool,
where, although the consumption was 20 per cent. below the average
before the prevention of waste under the new system was commenced, the pipes being very old required in a great number of
instances to be entirely renewed. Add to this the fact that the
corporation relaid at their own cost all defective private service
pipes not within the dwellings, and you can understand that I have
good grounds for saying that while the saving was a minimum, the
cost was a maximum.

The district in question contains 31,000 persons; the saving of
water between former constant and present constant supply was
21·38 gallons per head per day, and between former intermittent
and present constant 7·42 gallons per head per day; and the saving
of water between former and present constant service was obtained
at a cost to the corporation of less than a farthing per 1000
gallons. In districts containing a better class of property the
saving is often greater, while the work to be performed in obtaining
that saving is far less. When we consider this in connection with
the actual cost of water when obtained from other sources, we must
admit the last proposition as an established fact.

The inducements to undertake systematically the prevention of waste have been laid before you in what appear to me their most striking aspects. But to those who have taken up the subject in practice many other important features, which I am unable to consider in a short paper, suggest themselves. I will, therefore, at once describe to you the method by which the prevention of waste and restoration of constant service is being rapidly carried on in Liverpool.

I believe a suggestion to place meters upon water mains has been made in former times; but it remained for Mr. J. H. Wilson, the Chairman of the Liverpool Water Committee, to propose the systematic adoption of the plan, and to see it carried out with the most complete success, and with results far surpassing anything that could be anticipated.

The system I now practice and the reasons for it may be better explained if I premise that the piston meters at first used, and which were placed upon the 3- and 4-inch service mains, indicated the necessity for obtaining not merely the total consumption for the 24 hours, but the minimum consumption during the night, and, if possible, the consumption at short intervals during the whole 24 hours. It is evident that such results could only be obtained from the ordinary meters by constantly watching and even counting the strokes. A short experience of the system, notwithstanding its great success, showed the enormous advantages which would accrue from the use of a meter so arranged as to draw a diagram representing graphically the exact quantity of water flowing through any main at every instant during the 24 hours. The great cost and wear and tear of all meters which I have tried was an additional incentive in my endeavours to produce such an instrument.

The best form of the waste-water meter may be described as follows: It consists essentially of a vertical tube lined with brass, and equal in diameter at the upper end—where it is connected with the inlet from the main—to the diameter of that main, but larger at its lower end. In the tube is a horizontal disc of the same diameter as the main, with a vertical spindle on the centre of its upper face, from the end of which the disc is hung by a fine wire passing into the dry chamber above, through a brass gland. This wire is connected above with a counter balance weight, which, when the water is at rest, retains the disc at the top of the tube, which it completely fills.

It is obvious, then, that if water is caused to flow through the instrument, the disc will find somewhere in the tube a position which it will retain until the velocity of the water changes. The lower end of the conical tube being about double the area of the main, no obstruction to the flow can take place, such as must necessarily be the case in all piston meters, while the motion for any given increment of velocity near the top, or place of minimum flow, can be made equal to, or even greater than, that due to an equal increment at the bottom or point of maximum flow, so that its sensitiveness is not diminished at low velocities—a feature which is unattainable in any meters constructed on the turbine or analogous principles.

In order to ensure the absence of any friction sufficiently great to prevent the disc and wire from reaching the exact point at which they would stand if perfectly free during the continuance of each particular velocity, I found it desirable to abandon the use of a stuffing box, properly so called, and to substitute a single brass gland, the hole in which fits the wire accurately, but not tightly. This wire being an alloy of iridium and platinum, maintains its condition for any length of time, and the small quantity of water which oozes past it is allowed to drain away. The almost absolute accuracy and freedom with which the meter acts have been proved by the strictest tests. The vertical motions of the wire are registered by a pencil, connected with it, on a drum revolving once in twenty-four hours, the paper on which can easily be removed at any time, and replaced by a sheet with horizontal lines, each of which corresponds with the height at which the pencil stands when the number of gallons per hour marked upon the line is equal to the quantity passing through the meter. The essential peculiarity then of the waste-water meter is that it registers on paper the exact quantity of water passing at every instant, and the exact time and rate at which that quantity changes. The meter is fixed close to the curb, just beneath the footpath. A single length of the main is removed, and a loop formed to it by two double elbow pipes. Access to the drum and clock is easily obtained, by simply lifting the parapet cover and opening the inner lid.

I will now as shortly as possible describe the process of detecting the various kinds of waste, and the system to be ultimately adopted in order to prevent its recurrence. A· district (of about 2500 persons) supplied by a 3- or 4-inch main having been chosen, a waste-water meter is placed upon that main, and diagrams are

M

taken for a few days before the condition of supply is disturbed. If stopcocks outside all premises do not exist, they are at once fixed under the footway on every service pipe; and, at the same time, a day inspector calls at each tenement and fills up a suitable form. Besides giving much information with respect to the fittings, the forms afford, in connection with the diagrams already taken, the means of tabulating the normal condition of the supply, as in the first three lines of the following form.

Example of form used to record information contained on waste-water meter diagram.

———— Street, District No. —

Population—Day occupants 263
Day and night occupants 1,110

Total 1,373

Date.				Total Consumption for 24 hours in gallons.	Rate of Consumption in gallons per head per day	
					Average for the 24 hours.	Average from 1 to 5 A.M.
Oct. 4, 5,* 1873	..	..	..	80,183·2	58·4	50·4
„ 5, 6,† „	..	..	..	81,693·5	59·5	52·44
„ 7, 8,† „	..	..	..	81,418·9	59·7	50·0
„ 10, 11,‡ „	..	..	..	69,479·3	54·1	49·0
„ 29, 30,§ „	..	..	..	35,698·0	26·0	21·0
Dec. 10, 11,‖ „	..	..	..	28,252·0	20·5	15·0

* Saturday afternoon and Sunday morning.   † Normal condition of district.
‡ Taking census, inspecting and making sundry small repairs.
§ Fixing stopcocks.   ‖ Stopcocks fixed.
NOTE.—The figures are those of an office district in Liverpool in connection with which the operations for the prevention of waste are incomplete, the next step being to serve general notices and proceed with the detail examination.

In this form column 4, headed "Average from 1 to 5 A.M.," contains information peculiar to the waste-water meter of the greatest value. The result of deducting any one of the figures in it from the corresponding one in column 3, headed "Average for the 24 hours," is generally found to be about equal to the actual quantity of water used. Thus, from the 4th to the 5th October, 8 gallons per head per day was about the actual quantity used, while 50 gallons per head per day was about the waste from all sources. The line on the diagram due to water running continuously to waste is distinguished by its steadiness from the line due to water being used, and therefore fluctuating in amount from minute to minute. The use of column 4 in the detection of waste is further shown by the following table, the figures in which are those which actually occurred in the district:

Night Readings of Meters between 1 and 4 A.M., at various dates, in No. 1 District.

January 22, 1873, 30·0 gallons per head per day.
April   19, „   9·4   „   „
June   27, „   ·74   „   „

After stopcocks have been fixed, it is desirable to issue official notices to all tenants and owners of property in the district under test, embodying the full powers of the corporation or company with respect to fittings, and explaining the steps which will be taken upon the discovery of the waste of water within any premises.

At this stage the work of discovery is commenced in earnest. At twelve, on the first fine night, a waste-water inspector sounds each stopcock, partly closing it, if necessary, in order to contract the passage and increase the noise. In this test the inspector uses his turning key after the manner of a stethoscope. If the inmates have retired, and a flow of water is heard, the stopcock is closed, its number and time being accurately noted. At the same instant, the meter registers the reduction in the flow of water, and the time at which it takes place. In some cases the house is visited by the inspector early on the following morning, and if while he is within another inspector outside turns on the stopcock, there is generally no difficulty in detecting the source of waste at once. If, however, the waste is not superficial, sounding with the teeth at the taps and other fittings will generally discover a leak in the buried pipes. Each source of internal waste having been discovered by these means, the greatest care must be exercised by the inspectors to ensure its remedy in the best possible manner.*

In most districts the whole of the stopcocks may be sounded by one inspector in a single night; but several such night inspections, followed by day inspections and repairs, are always necessary before the waste is prevented.

A test for the condition of pipes is conducted as follows, and generally with most valuable results. Any convenient section, say one-fourth of the district, is isolated from the remainder by a valve,

* *March,* 1875. Since the date of this paper the practice has been somewhat modified. At present the night inspectors open all the stopcocks they have closed before leaving the district. They thus leave on the meter diagram indelible evidence of the time of commencing and completing their work. On reaching the office they write in copying ink a complete report as to the stopcocks passing water, and before nine o'clock a copy of this is ready for the day inspector.

and commanded by the meter. In this sub-district all the fittings are closed and tied with a string, a number of men being employed for the purpose, and each having several houses to watch. The stopcocks are then closed one by one, and, the time being noted, waste in the pipes of any premises is thus discovered and measured.

The following statement shows the various classes of defects in fourteen waste-water districts in Liverpool, containing an aggregate of 30,000 persons :

	Notices Issued for Defects.					Simple Repairs by Inspectors.					Total noticed and re-paired.
	Cocks.	Ball Cocks.	Water Closets.	Pipes.	Total.	Cocks.	Ball Cocks.	Water Closets.	Pipes.	Total.	
Total for 14 Districts	713	5	555	1,232	2,665	253	58	55	28	394	3,076

Tests for leaks in public pipes are conducted as follows. The condition of the main and branches to the stopcocks may be ascertained by closing those stopcocks entirely when any flow must be due to leakage. By sounding closed stopcocks, and all other exposed metal work connected with the pipes, the leakage may often be localized. An internal examination of the neighbouring sewer on a dry night may lead to many important discoveries, especially if large isolated leakages exist.

It only remains for me to point out the means by which I propose to maintain the condition of comparative freedom from waste in those districts in which a fair normal consumption has been attained. Taking, for example, a town of the size of the borough of Liverpool, containing 500,000 persons, there will be about 300 waste-water districts, and 300 waste-water meters. Unless the consumption of a district has suddenly become abnormal, it is not objectionable to leave each diagram on for a week, and to allow the seven diagrams to be superimposed upon each other. Each day fifty diagrams will be removed and replaced by blank sheets, and brought to the office.

The work can easily be performed by two meter inspectors and two boys, with the reserve of one inspector and one boy, who, in addition, will wind up the clocks, and do any other necessary work in connection with the meters.

Any district, the consumption in which the diagrams brought in, show to have increased unduly, will be excluded from the general inspection, and omitted by the ordinary meter inspector. Two or three special inspectors will at once be sent into it, and there is no doubt that a few days' work, or even less, will generally bring it back to its normal condition.

The advantage of such a system is manifest. Without it, waste-water inspectors discover only superficial defects, and spend their time equally on good and bad ground; but the best evidence of its value is the unprecedented success which is attending its adoption in Liverpool.*

⎯I do not now propose to speak of what I really think we shall be able to do here, but the result up to the present time is, that out of a population within the borough of about 500,000 persons, with eight to ten hours' supply, and without the borough of about 125,000 persons with constant supply, taking in each case about 24 gallons a head (excluding only water used for trade purposes), we commenced work in a district within the borough of 31,000 persons, who were taking only 19½ gallons a head in the eight or ten hours, and 33½ gallons per head per day when on constant service, and that we have given and continued the constant service, and reduced the consumption to 12·17 gallons per head per day, which is maintained without the slightest difficulty.

* At the present time, March, 1875, the district waste-water meter system has been carried out in the greater part of the borough of Liverpool, and no fewer than 358,000 persons are receiving constant service, while, notwithstanding a great increase of private consumers, and of manufacturing supplies, the consumption of water has greatly decreased. The system is now being extended to the whole town.

The following table is taken from the fortnightly report of the Water Committee, made March 19th, 1875:

DISTRIBUTION OF WATER FOR FORTNIGHT ENDING THE 16TH INSTANT, AND FOR THE CORRESPONDING FORTNIGHTS OF FIVE PRECEDING YEARS.

Year.	Mean total weekly delivery. Gallons.	Rate per head per day. Total Domestic.†		Total Population supplied.	No. receiving constant supply.	Average intermittent supply.
		Gallons.	Gallons.			
1870	111,778,285	27·47	24·79	581,340	93,367	11¼
1871	122,309,685	29·55	26·50	599,224	98,076	10⅞
1872	117,636,576	27·94	24·57	601,398	103,023	10¼
1873	117,402,726	27·41	23·88	611,848	114,744	10¼
1874	123,310,780	28·29	24·29	622,627	165,259	10¼
1875	116,829,203	26·33	22·14	633,725	358,052	10½

† The term domestic supply includes all water used for sanitary and other purposes, excepting only the supplies by meter for trade purposes.

THE FORMATION OF STREETS AND HIGHWAYS.

Mr. Hall (Toxteth Park), in introducing his paper, referred to the importance of the question of road making from a social, sanitary, or commercial point of view, and after referring to the rapid changes rendered necessary by the vast increase of traffic, and the absolute necessity for closer intercourse between towns and communities, he spoke of the early steps taken by the Legislature to make highways and to keep them from becoming impassable. In the middle of the last century there were 7000 miles of public highways in this kingdom, but their condition was disgraceful, even the best of them being incomparably worse than an average county road of the present day. · But great as was the progress that had been made, it was insignificant compared with the necessities of our own time, and the tramway and the steam engine would soon supersede all other means of locomotion. Mr. Hall's paper did not extend to practical details.

Mr. Thorburn said Mr. Hall had omitted to make mention in his paper of Macadam, who, with the exception, probably, of Telford, did more to improve the roads of this country than any other man. There was also another man who deserved to be mentioned—a countryman of Mr. Hall. Whilst travelling in the neighbourhood of the lakes of Killarney, he (Mr. Thorburn) came across some remarkable roads, with tunnels half a mile long, and these had been made by a blind man. He was in hopes that the paper would have taken a wider scope, and pointed out some of the difficulties, more especially in regard to the making of streets by property owners, which they had to meet in the course of their experience. Probably on a future occasion Mr. Hall would extend his paper.

Mr. Fowler said he would have preferred, instead of Mr. Hall dealing so largely with the historical part of his subject, if he had said something with reference to the relative merits of macadam sets, asphalte, and the Patent Wood Company's pavement.

Mr. Deacon said it had never been settled among Engineers, and he should like to hear the opinion of those present, as to the harm done by putting sand or binding upon macadam. He knew it was difficult to do without it, but if they could use a roller sufficiently heavy to lay the macadam in its clean condition, so that the stones would lock into each other, the road would be much stronger than if any material was put between the stones.

Mr. FOWLER said he found great difficulty in making good roads with a steam roller and stones broken by Blake's machine. They were not sufficiently cubical, although they did very well for the bottom. By using the revolving screen the small pieces were separated, and were used for the binding, and answered very well. Broken granite, trap rock, limestone chippings, and gravel, were equally serviceable; but it was a bad plan to throw upon a newly-macadamized road scrapings which had all the nature taken out of it, and which wound round the wheels of vehicles passing over it, like so much tape.

Mr. VAWSER said his opinion was that they could not, within a reasonable time, get a good macadam road without using some kind of binding. No roller would so thoroughly consolidate a road as to prevent horses' feet pulling it to pieces again, and he fancied the macadam in the streets of Liverpool would be found as loose and rough at the end of twenty-four hours as when just put on. It was a mistake to lay macadam on too thick. He always put it on in layers not exceeding three inches in thickness, having first opened the road with a pick, and afterwards put some macadam scrapings on the surface, which caused the macadam to set fully a fortnight quicker than it otherwise would have done.

Mr. LOBLEY thought it possible that in the course of a few years a stone-breaking machine would be invented which would cut cubes, say two inches square on the top, and as deep as they liked. Another machine could lay them close together very rapidly, and without sand or any other dressing, a roller could then be passed over them, and a good solid road made.

Mr. NEWTON said his experience convinced him that it was better not to put anything on the road rather than use sand and scrapings, especially limestone.

Mr. THORBURN said the great thing to remember was to get the stones as nearly cubical as possible. In putting down new macadam, if the angles got rubbed off by the wheels of passing vehicles, they would never interlock, and would be always on the roll. Sand was a very good thing to bind with, but dry road scrapings were better. He had seen a steam roller, 20 tons weight, used for

road making, and it made an admirable surface.   There was no
country in the world that excelled France in road making.   Even
in the Pyrenees there were capital roads, 8000 feet above the level
of the sea.

The CHAIRMAN said he had lately made some experiments in
road making, and had found granite siftings admirably suitable as
a binding material.   He obtained it from Guernsey, where the
best roads in England were to be seen.   The granite siftings were
rather expensive, and although vessels came from there to Southampton very readily, they cost 6s. 6d. per ton as against 2s. 6d.
per ton for sand.

Mr. HALL said his paper was more an introduction to the subject
of road making and the formation of streets than an exhaustive
treatise.   He was glad that his paper had elicited such an interesting and useful discussion, and would probably return to his subject
at a future meeting.

SEWER VENTILATION.

By Mr. T. C. THORBURN, Town Surveyor, Birkenhead.

It must be patent to all, that the matter conveyed in the sewage conduits or channels, being mainly composed of animal and vegetable matter, is in a state of more or less decomposition, and must be highly charged with gases, that when given off are likely to prove prejudicial to the health of those whose duties require them to enter the sewers, as also to that of the public, should the escape take place in the thoroughfares or into the houses.

Some idea of the deadly nature of the gases, whose complete removal is now very generally admitted to be necessary, may be gathered when we remember the fatal accidents that so frequently occur to those employed in the sewers, as well as to recent events which have drawn general attention to the influence which this gas has on the production of typhoid or enteric fever; and these accidents and dangers to health are sure to recur unless efficient means are taken to remove the gases as they are created.

Very great stress has been laid by some upon the value of a copious supply of water as a means of neutralizing the odours given off by the sewage channels, and there is no doubt that water is one of the best deodorizers at our command.

Nearly the whole of the present water consumption finds its way into the sewers, but it has not proved itself sufficient to destroy their offensive exhalations, and in the face of this fact it would be inconsistent to suppose that we might rely upon such an additional water supply that further action in the ventilation of sewers would be unnecessary.

In the elementary maxims for town drainage issued by the General Board of Health, in the year 1852, it is recommended "to make proper provision for the ventilation of all sewers and drains in such manner that there may be a free current of air through them in the direction of the sewage flow." This result cannot be attained in the manner suggested; the air and water in a sewer being controlled by laws involving an opposite issue to each; the one seeking by its rarefaction the highest possible point of discharge, the other by its gravity the lowest outlet.

This recommendation has been supplemented by " suggestions as to the preparation of plans as to main sewerage and drainage, and as to water supply," issued by the Local Government Act Office in 1866.

In these suggestions the Local Government Board advise that—

" House drains should not pass direct from sewers to the inside of houses, but all drains should end at an outside wall.   House drains, sink pipes, and soil pipes, should have ample means for external ventilation.

" Sewers having steep gradients should have full means for ventilation at the highest point.

" Tall chimneys may be used with advantage for sewers and drains ventilation, if owners will allow a connection to be made.

" Manholes should have movable covers at the surface of the ground.   There should be a side chamber for ventilation, which may have a charcoal screen or filter."

These suggestions of the Government officers are good so far as they go, and have, I believe, in many towns and districts been carried out with comparative success.

The experience, however, gained through the great attention that has of late been paid to sanitary science, also the close connection that has been proved to exist between the disregard of healthful condition of building, and disease, and the interest that has been awakened in the public mind by the extensive operations undertaken by the authorities for the main drainage of towns, have prominently brought to the front the best means to be adopted to regulate the disposal of the sewage of towns, and the forms, sizes, and best means of constructing the sewers and drains designed to effect that purpose.

The normal condition of the generality of houses has had an important bearing on the necessity for the ventilation of sewers and drains.   The superior temperature of the air of houses and the draught caused by chimneys have the effect of causing the various traps that are used to seal the inlets to the drains, to be relieved from pressure ; consequently as there is less atmospheric pressure upon traps within houses than upon external traps, and moreover, as many of the traps used within a house have far less seal than those usually employed out of doors, when no ventilation is provided, gases are sure to escape into a house at the least point of resistance.

Mr. Deacon, the Borough Engineer of Liverpool, says, in a recent report on the ventilation of sewers, that, "It is no exaggeration to say that there is great popular ignorance on sanitary matters, as the utter indifference with which persons build houses to live in, and the open direct communication between them and the air of the nearest sewer, clearly show.

"For, if even water-traps of the best construction be fixed in connection with water-closets, baths, wash-basins, and sinks; sewer air is allowed to pass, by absorption and emission, which as a matter of fact it does frequently by imperfections of workmanship in the longitudinal joint, or holes in the lead soil pipe, which is a frequent occurrence where the lime of the plaster comes in contact with the lead. These pipes are frequently fixed entirely within the house; the connection of the soil pipe with the drain, or other drain connection within the house, is sufficient in most cases to account for the offensive smells, which it is frequently difficult to trace to their source."

In the basement of many houses there are drains, the traps at the inlets of which are seldom supplied with water, thereby allowing the sewer air to rise throughout the house.

Mr. Baldwin Latham, C.E., says, in his recent excellent work on sanitary engineering, that, "The evil effects of the want of ventilation were conclusively shown in the early sewerage works of Croydon, in which place no sooner were the works of drainage drawing towards completion, than the town was visited by an epidemic of typhoid fever, which was traced entirely to the absence of ventilation in the system of sewers.

"It may be said as Croydon was sewered on the small-pipe system, the result of non-ventilation was attended with more marked results than is the case in towns where sewers of larger size are in vogue, as the fluctuation in the rate of flow, and the effect of sudden changes of temperature, which have an extraordinary influence on the air of sewers, in this case exercised a more marked effect in increasing the pressure of the imprisoned sewer air."

Since the introduction of systematic ventilation, there have been no periodical outbreaks of fever; and the general rate of mortality has so declined, that, in a district having a population of nearly

60,000 persons, the rate of mortality rarely exceeds 18 in the thousand, which is a standard of health unparalleled in the history of sanitary science for a district having so large a population.*

The case of London affords another striking example as to the influence of sewer ventilation. Here the sewers are ventilated, though no general plan is adopted for dealing with the noxious effluvium escaping from the ventilators, and yet London stands at the head of all large towns by reason of its small death-rate, which has been ascribed by more than one eminent authority to the somewhat rude ventilation provided for the sewers.

Medical men say that it is true that in a very dilute form some of the gases are innoxious, but it is not so much the presence of gases of known composition that is so injurious, as the organic vapours and germs of disease which are carried in the air of sewers, and which are ever active to feed or spread disease until effectually destroyed. Sewer gas escaping into the streets, and combining with large quantities of atmospheric air, is less injurious than when allowed to escape into the more limited atmosphere of our houses.

Chemists say that pure atmospheric air has the power of oxidizing or destroying organic compounds; but when sewer air enters the generality of houses, especially at night, when the house is closed, and the whole atmosphere has been robbed of its vital properties, the gas carrying the elements of decomposition or the germs of disease becomes a deadly poison.

Experiments made by Dr. Letheby on the generation of sewer gas from sewage, show that a gallon of sewage, containing 128·8 grains of organic matter, when excluded from the air, gave in nine weeks 1·2 cubic inch of gas per hour, consisting of 73·833 of marsh gas, 15·899 carbonic acid, 10·187 of nitrogen, and 0·081 sulphuretted hydrogen.

It should be noted that this is the result of a laboratory experiment, and after decomposition has purposely been allowed to take place.

" When atmospheric air is present in sewers, the gases found are carbonic acid and nitrogen with but mere traces of sulphuretted hydrogen." The air in a sewer of the city of London, ventilated and fitted with charcoal for deodorizing the escaping gases, was found by Dr. Letheby to contain 79·96 per cent. of nitrogen,

* The borough of Portsmouth, containing a population exceeding 113,000, which was drained upon a system designed by the Editor, almost invariably shows the *lowest* death-rate in the Returns of the Registrar-General.—ED.

19·51 per cent. of oxygen, and ·53 per cent. of carbonic acid, with mere traces of ammonia, marsh gas, and sulphuretted hydrogen.

Dr. W. I. Russell, in September, 1870, collected the air from the Ranelagh sewer, at Paddington, which was ventilated by open shafts of the ordinary London type, and he found that it contained 0·40 per cent. of carbonic acid, 20·79 per cent. of oxygen, and 78·81 per cent. of nitrogen; and when tested for sulphuretted hydrogen, by allowing the air to pass over acetate of lead paper, after five minutes' contact, no discolourization took place.

An examination of the forces at work within a sewer will show how necessary it is that ventilation should be provided; and from a study of the forces at work, the Engineer will be led to form correct opinions as to what measures should be taken for the purpose of securing perfect ventilation.

The difference of temperature between the external atmosphere and the internal air of a sewer is one of the forces at work by which the ventilation of sewers is effected.

The following table, compiled by Mr. William Haywood, in 1858, shows the difference of temperature between the internal air of the City sewers and the external atmosphere.

SUMMARY OF OBSERVATIONS AS TO THE TEMPERATURE OF THE CITY OF LONDON SEWERS.

Time of Year.	Temperature in External Atmosphere in Shade.			Temperature in Sewers.			Mean Temperature of Sewers.	
	Highest.	Lowest.	Mean.	Highest.	Lowest.	Mean.	Above External Atmosphere.	Below External Atmosphere.
	°	°	°	°	°	°	°	°
Summer ..	72	55	65·04	68	56	61·92		3·12
Winter ..	34	30	32·37	52	40	43·98	11·61	..
Spring ..	61	46	52·46	59	48	52·52	0·06	..
Autumn	68	48	59·90	70	53	62·97	3·07	..
Average of whole year	..	..	50·24	..	..	55·35	5·11	..

By reference to this table it will be seen that on the average of the year the internal temperature of the sewers was 55·35°, and the external atmosphere in shade 50·24°, so that on an average of the whole year the sewer possessed a temperature of 5·11° only above that of the atmosphere.

In the summer months the average temperature of the sewer was below that of the atmosphere.

In the spring the temperature of both sewer and air is equal, while in the autumn and winter the average temperature of the sewer was in excess of that of the atmosphere.

During the year 1870, Mr. Latham, from experiments made at Croydon, found that on 220 days the external air rose to a higher temperature than the highest temperature of the sewage, and on 145 days the highest temperature of the air was lower than the temperature of the sewage. There were 313 days when the external air fell to a lower temperature than the lowest of the sewage; and 52 days when the lowest temperature of the sewage was less than the lowest temperature of the external air. It may be here noted that the temperature of the Croydon sewers is pretty nearly uniform during the whole year; this is due to the water supply of the district being taken from an artesian well.

The varying ebb and flow of the sewage, leaving the sides of the sewer alternately wet and dry, naturally leads to much vapour, or sewer gas; it has also the mechanical effect of compressing or . diluting the air present in the sewers. According to the law of the diffusion of gases, the pressure is inversely as the space occupied, it is therefore pretty clear that unless openings are made as outlets and inlets, the natural consequence of the rise and fall of the sewage in the sewer must be to draw in and expel foul air at points out of control.

In consequence of this rate of fluctuation, it appears to be clear that all those propositions which have been made for the purpose of the ventilation of sewers will prove comparatively abortive, as the sewers have within them a force which at one period naturally expels air. It is clear that all shafts, whether upcast or downcast, will at that period become upcast shafts; and when the air is drawn into the sewer, they will naturally become downcast shafts. If sufficient openings are formed in the sewers or drains, air will naturally be drawn in at these openings at one period of the day.

This fluctuation in the flow of sewage which takes place in every sewer or house drain, may be augmented so as to lead to an artificial filling and discharging of the air of certain sections of a system of sewers. Self-acting flushing valves may be used, as has been recommended by the Government Engineer, so arranged that certain sections of the sewer would be filled with pent-up sewage at certain periods of the day, and then be rapidly discharged, so that the double purpose of flushing and ventilating the sewers would be secured.

Barometric changes, it is said, affect the amount of sewer gas present in sewers. The diminution in barometric pressure leads to the escape of gases which are stored in the interstices of the sewage, and favours decomposition. An increase of barometric pressure enables sewer air to carry a larger amount of the vapour of water.

The vapour of water may be considered a force within a sewer affecting ventilation, as it gives lightness to the air. At 32° the vapour is about one three-hundredth part ($\frac{1}{300}$) the density of air; and at 212° it is nearly half as dense as air, so that at all ordinary temperatures the vapour of water will materially affect the density of the air of sewers.

Wind blowing over the surface of ventilators in a street has a material effect in changing the currents of air within the sewer. The position of the outfall of a system of sewers in reference to the prevailing winds of a district has also a material effect upon their ventilation. If an outfall sewer is open to the prevailing wind, rapid currents of air are certain to be produced in the sewers, and will escape so quickly at the ventilating shaft as not to be under control. To prevent this, every outfall so situate should be protected by tidal flaps or gates to control strong currents from entering the sewer in gusts.

Friction and leakage within a sewer materially affect the general question of ventilation.

When sewers have great falls, they may act like an ordinary chimney shaft, so that when there is a comparative uniform rate of flow through the sewers, there is an invariable tendency for air to enter the openings or shafts at the lower levels and escape at the top or higher points of the system.

In Paris and Antwerp, shafts have been tried for the purpose of ventilating the sewers, but the results were not sufficiently satisfactory to admit of their use as a general system for promoting ventilation.

Numerous experiments have also been made with shafts and furnaces as a mode of sewer ventilation. In the report of Sir J. W. Bazalgette, C.B., on the ventilation of sewers, addressed to the Metropolitan Board of Works, in January, 1866, some results as to the efficiency of this mode of ventilation are given.

Quoting from evidence given by himself and Mr. Haywood, before a Parliamentary Committee, in 1858, Mr. (now Sir J. W.) Bazalgette said, " A down draught so complete as to be superior to the diffusive power of the gases, you cannot start with less than

two miles an hour; and suppose the whole district has been so
arranged as to have a sufficient exhaustive power, the mere opening
of a water-closet, or the enlarging or putting in of a new drain
into a sewer, or the making a hole a foot square, or a servant
taking up a bell-trap in a sink, or a sewer-man lifting a side entrance
covering, would very much destroy the power of the furnace; and
unless you had a gigantic power sufficient to guard against all
these casualties, the system could only be a failure."

Mr. Haywood, in his evidence before the same committee, says,
" A furnace ventilating any large district would require to produce
a very large volume of air, and to keep up a velocity sufficient to
ventilate all the branch sewers, and the drag would consequently
be so great through the main that it would force open any house-
drain traps or water traps we could form before it would influence
the remote branches; but putting these difficulties out of the question,
which appeared to us insuperable, we found that the consumption
of coal to extract the required quantity of air, supposing that the
sewers could be laid like the channels of mines, would be something
enormous."

Speaking of the ventilation experiments with the Clock Tower of
the Houses of Parliament, he says: " I found that the furnace of
the Clock Tower of the Houses of Parliament was supposed to have
been connected with the adjoining district to the extent of about a
quarter of a square mile, and, with about six and a half miles of
sewers in length when added together, but that the ventilation had
in reality been intercepted by a flap, so that the benefit supposed
to be derived therefrom was purely imaginary.

" Having come to that conclusion, the next thing I directed my
attention to was, supposing the whole of the air extracted from
that furnace was produced from the sewers, and supposing that all
the intermediate channels could be stopped, and that it could be
directed from the most remote end of each of the sewers, and distributed over those sewers with the most perfect theoretical accuracy,
so as to have a uniform current passing through each of the sewers
towards that chimney, still the effect upon those sewers would be
nothing; and the way in which I prove my statements is this: The
total area of the six and a half miles of sewer now connected with
the furnace is 713 feet, the total area of the channel through which
the air has to be brought from them is 8 feet—that is about the
90th part of 713—the air was passing at the rate of 542 feet
per minute through the 8-feet area. Therefore, if I could divide

that over the whole district, the velocity in all those sewers would be 6 feet per minute, or $\frac{1}{13}$th of a mile per hour.

" But we have shown already that there exist in sewers, from other causes, velocities amounting to 100 feet per minute and upwards, and 6 feet per minute is, practically speaking, stagnation, and not ventilation."

He further stated, " that supposing you could obtain theoretic perfection, and all the air produced by this furnace was spread through this district, you could only get up a velocity of $\frac{1}{13}$th of a mile per hour, which is no ventilation whatever.

" The areas of the branch sewers discharging into any one main sewer are probably much more than a hundred times its capacity; therefore, even if it were possible that they could be all hermetically sealed at all points excepting the extreme ends, a velocity of current equal to 100 miles an hour (which is next to impossible) would have to be obtained in order to secure a current of one mile per hour in each of the branch sewers.

" But it is not possible to obtain such a condition of things; and this difficulty lies at the root of all proposed modes of ventilation for extracting the foul gases by furnaces, fans, or such other appliances."

A glance at a few of the propositions which have been made at different times for the purpose of preventing the formation of sewer gas, or for the purpose of ventilating sewers, will not be without interest.

Natural ventilation embraces all those methods which cause the air to move by reason of difference in temperature or weight of the respective columns of air.

This method of ventilating sewers has been extensively adopted in London and a few other large towns. Ventilated openings or shafts have been formed from the sewers to the surface of the streets, which have had the effect of removing the point of escape of the sewer air farther from the pedestrian traffic and from the houses, and of aiding the dilution of the escaping gases.

In the Metropolis these ventilating openings have frequently been the subject of complaint, and in Southampton gratings in the road gave off such offensive effluvia that the inhabitants of the neighbouring houses stopped them up with pieces of wood.

The rain-water pipes or conductors from the roofs of houses have been connected with the sewers without trapping in many towns, with a view of their assisting in the ventilation of the sewers;

N

and a great number of the Engineers and Surveyors in charge of town
sewers have endeavoured to carry the proposition into practical
effect; but although it is undoubted that the emanations from the
street gratings have been lessened in consequence of the extra
height of the rain-water pipes directing the current of sewer air
towards them, and the condition of the sewers thereby improved,
this result has been attended by a nuisance of so serious a character
that it is questionable whether it may be regarded in the light of
an improvement.

The evil most complained of, in the employment of the rain-
water pipes as a means of sewer ventilation, is that the vapour
carried off by them is emitted at such a level that it becomes a
nuisance to the occupiers of rooms in the upper stories of our
dwellings. It has been suggested that this nuisance might be got
rid of and the ventilation of sewers still further improved by
carrying the pipes to the tops of the chimney-stacks, but on trial
it has been found that in certain conditions of the atmosphere the
vapour has descended, and has been conveyed by the flues to the
room below. Great difficulty, moreover, would be experienced in
getting the owners of property to consent to these pipes being
affixed to their premises, and a very heavy expense would be
entailed upon the authorities, first in erecting, and, secondly, in
maintaining them in repair.

There are, however, further serious objections to this method of
ventilating sewers besides those above named, viz. that the pipes
are not generally so well jointed as to prevent an escape of sewer
gas, and that whenever there is a considerable rainfall, the escape
of gas by these pipes is prevented by the presence of the water
coming down them, and that the sewer air on these occasions is
frequently driven into the houses.

Mr. B. Latham says, that "at Croydon it was found that the
more rigorously the system of ventilation by rain-water pipes was
pursued, the more unhealthy the district became, and it was not
until special means were used, at his recommendation, for the ventilation of house drains, and the establishment of an efficient system
of ventilation for the public sewers, that the death-rate of that
town was at all reduced."

Special pipes, usually made of metal, have in many districts been
used for the ventilation of sewers and drains. They are usually
connected with the crown of the sewer and carried under the
roadway and up the external walls of the adjoining houses. One

objection to the use of these ventilating pipes is, that in cold weather, when the sewers have such a temperature as to produce a natural tendency to discharge their gaseous contents into the air, the vapours ascending by these long metallic tubes become so chilled as to condense the aqueous portion, and check the natural tendency to ventilation.

Such pipes may be used in many places with advantage, and especially in connection with the ventilation of house drains, or soil pipes, as they will act efficiently for the purpose of allowing air to escape when it becomes compressed; as, for example, when any water is passed into a sewer or drain it causes a displacement of an equal amount of the sewer air; thus in a system of sewerage and drainage, the same volume of water may be made to displace several times its volume of sewer air.

Suggestions have been made from time to time in reference to the use of the large lamp columns in our streets, roads, and open places, as ventilators for the sewers; and it has been suggested that the ventilation tube should be aided by the combustion of gas, or that the lamp columns should be simply used as ducts for conveying away the gas. This system has been adopted in a few cases in London.

It has been proposed to supplement the ventilation of sewers by special pipes with mechanical agency. In Liverpool, 1064 ventilating pipes have been fixed to buildings, and fitted up with cowl-heads and Archimedian screws, for the purpose of exhausting the air from the sewers. When the wind blows it causes the cowl-head to revolve, which gives motion to the screw, and the action is to more or less withdraw the sewer air.

Mr. Deacon says, in his recent able report on the ventilation of the Liverpool sewers, in reference to the Archimedian-screw ventilators: " After a careful test of the efficiency of these ventilators, in Hornby Street "—the experiments were conducted continuously for several days and nights, during which time the ventilators of the court in question, as well as those in the adjoining courts, were in good working order—" it was found that there are currents in the sewers of far greater potency than any which the ventilators produce, and that, on the whole, it could not be ascertained that the ventilators produced an effect which, considered in relation to the work they were called upon to perform, could be said to approach to successful ventilation.

" The reason why ventilating shafts such as those on which the

Archimedian screw is fixed are insufficient even in cases where the sewers contain no air-currents of greater strength than might be fairly assumed by calculation to be produced by the ventilators is not entirely so because they do not extract large volumes of air, but because the air extracted is not replaced by the really offensive sewer air requiring removal, but by small quantities only of that air highly diluted with pure air drawn into the drains close to the ventilators."

It is reported that the use of the steam jet was proposed by Sir G. Gurney in combination with properly-constructed shafts for the ventilation of sewers. The action of the steam jet is due in a measure to the rarefaction of the air, the partial vacuum created, and to the velocity of the escaping vapour which drags along with it the sewer air. The efficiency of the steam jet for the purpose of promoting ventilation was fully tested some years ago by Mr. Nicholas Wood, and he stated, in a paper read by him, when president of the North of England Institute of Mining Engineers, that the practical result of all these experiments is, that within the limits or range of furnace ventilation the steam jet acting as substitute is attended with an increase in the expenditure of fuel of nearly 3 to 1, without any corresponding advantage either in the steadiness, security, or efficiency of ventilation. On the contrary, from its simplicity of construction, the steadiness of its action, its less liability to derangement, its economy and its efficiency in cases of emergency, the furnace is more secure, more safe, and a more eligible mode of ventilation than the steam jet.

Chemists say that "all porous substances have more or less the power of condensing gases in their pores."

Wood charcoal, as an absorber of sewer gas, is decidedly generally acknowledged to be the most efficient and the cheapest agent that has hitherto been used for the purpose of absorbing or destroying the noxious properties of sewer gas.

Professor Muspratt says that "the absorbing powers of charcoal are so great that some have doubted whether it is really a disinfectant. This opinion has probably arisen from imperfect views of its *modus operandi*, since it not only imbibes and destroys all offensive emanations and oxidizes many of the products of decomposition; but there is scarcely a reasonable ground of doubt remaining that it does really possess the property of a true disinfectant, acting by destroying those lethal compounds upon which infection depends.

A piece of charcoal placed in a volume of sewer gas will absorb that gas effectually.

"It is not necessary for the gas to be brought mechanically into contact with the material, but just as the loadstone attracts iron, so charcoal is sure to attract the noxious ingredients of sewer air."

Dr. Voelcker says of charcoal, "it possesses the power not only of absorbing certain smelling gases, sulphuretted hydrogen, and ammonia, but also of destroying the gases thus absorbed, for otherwise its purifying action would soon be greatly impaired.

"It is very porous, and its pores are filled with condensed oxygen to the extent of eight times its bulk. We have therefore in charcoal oxygen gas (which supports combustion or lights fires) in a condensed and more active condition than in the common air we breathe.

"Hence it is that organic matter in contact with charcoal is so rapidly destroyed.

"The beauty of charcoal is, that the destruction takes place imperceptibly, and that its power of burning organic matter is continually renewed by the surrounding atmosphere, so that it is a constant carrier of atmospheric oxygen, that acts on organic matter and burns it up, is speedily replaced, and the process goes on continually.

"Hence it is that a comparatively small quantity of wood or peat charcoal is capable of destroying a very large quantity of organic matter."

TABLE, COMPILED BY DR. STENHOUSE, SHOWING THE QUANTITY OF GAS, IN CENTIMETRES, ABSORBED BY HALF A GRAMME OF CHARCOAL.

Kind of Charcoal.	Ammonia.	Hydrochloric Acid.	Sulphuretted Hydrogen.	Carbonic Acid.	Oxygen.	Sulphurous Acid.
ood	98·5	45·0	30·0	14·0	0·8	32·5
Peat ..	96·0	60·0	28·5	10·0	0·6	27·5
Animal ..	43·5	..	9·0	5·0	0·5	17·5

Professor Liebig says, in his 'Letters on Chemistry,' that one cubic inch of beechwood charcoal contains pores equal in area to 100 superficial feet.

As to the efficiency of charcoal for ventilation, Dr. Stenhouse says, "the efficiency of the charcoal appears never to diminish if it is kept dry, and its pores are not choked up by dust.

" The only precautions to be observed are, that while the filters shall be sheltered from rain and moisture, free access shall be given to the air."

He also says, with regard to the construction of filters, " I should prefer using two or more thin filters placed at short distances, say two inches from each other. These thin filters disinfect the air quite as efficiently as a single thick one."

Dr. Letheby recommends charcoal as being the cheapest and best, as well as the most effective, plan for dealing with noxious exhalations from sewers.

He says that charcoal has the power of absorbing and oxidizing the miasma of organic decomposition, when, with atmospheric air, they are passed over it. The charcoal used in the ventilators of the City sewers has been examined, and in the joint report of Mr. Haywood and Dr. Letheby on the use of the charcoal ventilators, it is stated, " Charcoal from the ventilators has been submitted to chemical examination, after having been in action for nine to twenty months, and when treated with water it yields abundance of alkaline nitrate, showing that some of the organic miasma has undergone complete oxidation. But besides these compounds, others are present, namely, peculiar alkaline salts, which indicate the fixation not only of ammonia, but also of other volatile nitrogen bodies, which are peculiar to organic decomposition.

" The nature of these compounds has yet to be determined upon, for all that can be said of them is that they have a remarkably bad odour, compounded of urine, sewage, bad meat, ammonia, and stale tobacco. Attempts have been made to isolate them, without success.

" This, however, is not surprising when we consider that chemists have hitherto failed to separate and identify the miasmata of organic corruption."

In the same report it is further stated, as to the power of charcoal, that, " let them, however, be what they may, either physically suspended organic molecules, or complex volatile alkalies, and be the morbific agent either the one or the other, there is in charcoal a perfect means of arresting and oxidizing all the noxious compounds contained in these gases.

" This is demonstrated not merely by their absence in the sewer air which has passed over charcoal, but also by the presence of the alkalies, and the changed molecules in the charcoal itself."

From what has been stated by chemists and others, it is clear that charcoal kept dry is, practically, a most efficient material for purifying sewer air, as it is not only a disinfectant, but it destroys or burns up the noxious gases. Some doubts may arise as to its use in connection with sewer ventilators, on account of the escaping vapours being highly charged with moisture; therefore, on this point, it is well that we should be assured that the moisture taken up from the sewer air rather improves than impairs the efficiency of the charcoal.

In a paper on " The Absorbtion of Mixed Vapours by Charcoal," read before the Chemical Society, on the 20th January, 1870, J. Hunter, Esq., M.A., gives the results of experiments with charcoal and moisture.

" These experiments show that if charcoal is introduced into a mixed vapour, the vapour which is nearest to its point of condensation is first absorbed, and this in its condensed state in the pores of the charcoal aids the absorbtion of the other vapour." According to this view a succession of condensation is going on.

" The theory is strikingly illustrated in experiments with a mixture of water vapour and ammonia gas (obtained by heating an aqueous solution of ammonia, of specific gravity $0·88$), when the mixture is much more largely absorbed than either the gas or vapour separately.

" The mean of a set of experiments made at $100°$, and a mean pressure $706·2$ mm., was $316·6$ volumes of the mixtures absorbed by one volume of charcoal."

Mr. B. Latham, in speaking of charcoal, says, " these experiments confirm our faith in charcoal as an absorbant of sewer gas, for they prove that the vapour of water when near the point of condensation, as is the case with sewer air, instead of being prejudicial, greatly assists the absorbing power of charcoal."

Other materials have been proposed to be used in connection with the abstractions and destruction of sewer gas; such, for example, as carbide of iron, lime, chlorine gas, sulphurous acid gas, and chloride of calcium in a powdered form, to disinfect the sewage.

Various methods of fitting up the charcoal-filter in the sewer manhole ventilators have from time to time been adopted, all more or less so arranged as to partially obstruct the natural ventilation.

Experience in the use of charcoal for sewer ventilation shows that it is better to place the charcoal in thin layers close together than in a mass, completely filling the aperture provided for ventilation.

In the construction of charcoal sewer ventilators, provision should be made for surface water and the water produced from the condensation of moist vapour. So long as charcoal is brought in contact with the moist air of sewers it will retain its efficiency ; should it, however, become saturated with water, the condensed oxygen within its pores is driven out, and it ceases to absorb or destroy the noxious gases.

Mr. Haywood and Dr. Letheby stated, in their report to the City authorities, that " if the ventilators could be so arranged as to keep the charcoal dry, we are of opinion that it would not require renewal more frequently than once a year; but under existing circumstances, many of them require to be changed not less than once a month."

The introduction of vertical trays of charcoal into manholes, as recommended by the Local Government Board, and extensively used by many Engineers in sewage works, is to some extent objectionable, as the charcoal materially interferes with the natural ventilation. They also do not fit tightly round the sides of the manhole, and thereby allow a certain quantity of sewer gas to pass without being deodorized.

The plan adopted by the Metropolitan Board of Works for experimental purposes consists of a single tray containing charcoal placed over the top of a vertical pipe leading directly from the crown of the sewer. The objection to this plan is, that the charcoal is placed in a mass, and little or no provision is made for getting rid of the surface water.

The experimental system adopted in the City of London sewers in fixing the charcoal trays, is to leave a space each side of the aperture between the trays and the side of the special shaft. Six trays containing charcoal are fixed in each shaft in a zigzag manner, the surface water being allowed to drain down between the trays and the sides of the shaft. . This arrangement exposes the charcoal in thin layers to the sewer gas, and is decidedly superior to placing the charcoal in a mass. An opening is left communicating with the atmosphere on one side, and with the sewer on the other. The objections to this system are stated to be that the ventilating trays cannot be made to fit tightly at the sides, and thereby allows a small part of the sewer gas to escape without oxidation, and that the dirt-box is too small and inadequate, in cases of heavy rain-fall.

In reference to the experiment with charcoal for ventilation in the City of London sewers, Dr. Letheby, the Medical Officer of Health, says, in his recent presidental address on the use of disinfectants, read at the opening meeting of the present session of the Society of Medical Officers of Health of the Metropolis, in respect of charcoal as a disinfectant, that " sewer gases are easily disinfected by vegetable charcoal in the manner already explained, the charcoal being placed upon trays in boxes which are situated in the course of the ventilating shafts from the sewers or drains.

" The air-filters consists of an iron box, 18 inches deep and 14 inches square, containing a movable frame of six trays or sieves, upon each of which there is a layer of wood charcoal in pieces as large as filberts, about 2 inches deep.

" Our experiments were commenced in 1860, and they have been maintained with perfect success until the present time, for they are still in action.

" I have repeatedly submitted the charcoal from the ventilators to chemical examination, and have always found that it contains abundance of nitrate, together with a peculiar alkaline salt of a nitrogenous nature with associated hydrocarbon.

" These ventilators are best fixed where they are protected from actual wet, as against the sides of houses, or in the course of a shaft or pipe, carried up from the soil pipe of the closet.

" In such situations their action is continuous for many years, and they should always be thus used where foul gases escape from the soil-pipe, the drain, or the closet of a house."

Mr. B. Latham says: " After having used this description of ventilation extensively, I found that charcoal got speedily destroyed through becoming saturated with surface water, and introduced an improved method of spiral arrangement of charcoal trays, so that the surface water, after filling the dirt-box, could pass away to the sewers in such a manner as not to destroy the charcoal, and at the same time provide for the escape of the surface water, without the sewer gas being brought into contact with the charcoal."

In Brooks's patent ventilator the charcoal is placed in mass in a single tray placed upon the top of the ventilating shaft in a manner somewhat similar to that adopted for experimental purposes by the Metropolitan Board of Works. No provision is made for getting rid of the surface water, which is allowed to soak away or overflow and destroy the charcoal.

Messrs. Brooks have also another form of ventilator used in connection with street gullies. The charcoal in this case is fixed in a tray placed in the cesspit, above the mouth of the outlet drains, between the dip plate and the side of the pit.

Mr. A. Jacob's patent charcoal sewer ventilator is very compact, and is intended to be used in combination with the manhole. The charcoal is placed in a perforated cylinder in mass, fixed at the top of the manhole immediately under the cover, with a small receptacle on each side for dust, dirt, and surface water; the means of disposing of the latter being somewhat defective, and the apertures provided for the ventilation being liable to be choked with dust or mud. The surface water is intended to be got rid of by small syphon pipes dipping into the dirt-box, which are liable to be choked up with mud, or occasionally frozen up in winter.

In Harrison's patent, the arrangements for fixing the charcoal trays are somewhat similar to one of the methods suggested in the Local Government Board recommendations; the improvement consisting of a movable dirt-box, fixed at the top of the manhole immediately under the street grating, with an overflow pipe extending down the manhole, so as to dip into a pool of sewage, obtained by sinking part of the invert of the sewer. The charcoal tray is fixed vertically on one side of the manhole, near the top, with a special shaft for the escape of the sewer gas.

In Hildred's patent ventilator, the charcoal is placed in a mass near the top of the manhole in a tray provided with a syphon trap, to get rid of surface water, which, like the other syphons previously referred to, is liable to get blocked up with mud, and occasionally frozen in winter. In summer, unless regularly supplied with water, the evaporation would unseal the trap.

The experience of Mr. B. Latham goes to show that the sum total of the area of the ventilating gratings should equal the discharging capacity of the sewers. The discharge from the ventilators should be computed as taking place under a pressure not exceeding $\frac{1}{10}$th of an inch head of water.

The ventilators should be placed closer together in the lower parts of a district, and the space between them may be somewhat increased in the upper part of the district. In no case should the distance between the ventilators be more than 200 yards.

In the district under the control of the Birkenhead Commissioners there is a length of about 60 miles of roads and streets laid out or constructed; and the length of main or common sewers laid down or constructed under roads and streets is about 43 miles.

The drainage area of the town and part of the out-townships is divided into three districts, each of which has a separate tidal gate locked, or flood-flapped outlet into the river.

In Birkenhead, inclusive of the surrounding townships of Tranmere and Oxton, there are, according to the official returns in 1869, 14,156 houses, with 7279 water-closets, and 7745 privies and middens; the cost of cleansing the latter being returned at 2336*l.* annually; to an estimated population, in 1869, of 77,570, spread over an urban and suburban area of 7385 acres.

The length of streets laid out and sewered in Birkenhead proper (which includes the townships of Birkenhead and Claughton-cum-Grange) is at present out of proportion to the number of buildings (of which 7750 are inhabited houses, with 4600 water-closets, besides privies and middens), and a population of over 50,000, giving a density, including the area occupied by the Dock Estate, of 30 per acre, and exclusive of the same about 41 per acre, or something like one third the density of the population of Liverpool.

The dual use, therefore, for which the sewers are ultimately intended to answer, if they are continued to be used as at present, viz. for the carrying off by suspension in water of the sewage matters discharged from the dwellings of the inhabitants, as well as the surface drainage, is therefore limited, and out of proportion to their capacity or to the purposes that they will ultimately be used for, when the town becomes more closely and fully built upon. Hence we have not in Birkenhead the same amount of deleterious gases to contend with in the sewers as is to be found in the sewers of Liverpool, where the population is so much greater per acre, and the sewage largely diluted or mixed with the refuse from chemical or other similar works, and steam and hot water from manufactories.

The principle of the ventilating shafts erected in Birkenhead by me, of recent years, will be understood from the drawings submitted.

These ventilators are for the most part constructed adjoining the vertical manhole entrances to the sewers from streets and roads.

Each shaft is provided with a galvanized iron wire basket of $\frac{1}{4}$-inch mesh, 10 inches square, filled with small pieces of wood charcoal for a width of 6 inches, and fixed in a short horizontal gallery between the opening through the crown of the sewer and the upcast shaft, terminating at the surface of the street in a position so as to protect the charcoal from being saturated with rain water falling through the surface cast-iron grating, fixed on the top of the shaft level with the street. Each ventilating shaft is provided with a cesspit as a receptacle for surface water and road drift falling through the street grating, having a bottom formed of porous stone, which permits the surface water to permeate and drop into the sewer.

The manhole entrances are found in most cases to act as downcast shafts, thereby facilitating the draught of gas through the charcoal-filter fixed in the ventilating or upcast shafts, very much on the principle of syphon ventilation.

These ventilators are found to answer their purpose effectually, and very little if any trace of deleterious gas or unpleasant smell is perceptible at the grating in the street, it being estimated that about 90 per cent. of the sulphuretted hydrogen or other gaseous emanations from the sewers is intercepted in passing through the charcoal filter.

The number of these sewer ventilators constructed in connection with new works are 6 double, 36 single; and the number in connection with old sewers, 198.

In the latter case the charcoal basket is fixed in a horizontal gallery constructed near the top of the manhole entrance, with an outlet to the street similar to the others, the total number of ventilators constructed up to the present time being 240.

The principle upon which they are arranged is on the main line of sewers at every junction, and at the termination of the collateral sewers in the side streets and courts.

It is intended to extend the system to the drains in courts and back passages, where they will be constructed at the termination of each line of drain.

Many of these ventilators have been in use for upwards of eight years; and while we have had complaints of unpleasant smells emanating from untrapped gullies, we have never had any complaints during that period of any disagreeable emanations from the grids over the ventilating shafts.

Vertical shafts provided with baskets filled with charcoal, which answer all the purposes of a deodorizer, are, in my opinion, better adapted for rendering innocuous the aqueous gases emanating from the sewers than either chimney shafts or Archimedian-screw ventilators, as they allow of a natural diffusion of the deleterous gases by their own specific gravity, and pass them into the air of our streets comparatively harmless.

The extra cost of *constructing the ventilators*, according to the various arrangements, varies from 31s. 6d. on court ventilators, to 3l. 2s. 6d. for a double ventilator at summit levels.

Various propositions have been made for the ventilation of house drains, viz. by pipes, shafts, and other means; all such systems more or less fail to properly ventilate sewers. When applied to house drains, the failure is more marked and decisive, as the forces at work within a house drain are the same which have already been pointed out as at work within a sewer, but they are much more violent and irregular in their action.

Experience shows that the safest way to ventilate house drains is by carrying up ventilating pipes at the heads of the drain and its branches. The point of exit should neither be near a window nor the top of a chimney, as there are at certain periods currents of air at these points into the house, so that if the point of discharge is permitted to terminate near these openings, sewer gas may be drawn into our habitations.

On the whole, then, the evidence would seem to show that the best plan to ventilate house drains and water-closet soil pipes is to have special pipes raised high above the roofs of the houses, provided with Archimedian screws at the top, and a charcoal-filter immediately underneath.

The system adopted for trapping and ventilating sewers, drains, and soil pipes in Birkenhead, is set forth in a circular, from which it will be observed, that "The Health Committee feel it their duty to point out and call the attention of the public to the general absence of the necessary safeguards for the prevention of the escape of sewer gas into their dwellings through drains and water-closets, in order that owners or occupiers may take the necessary precautions to secure protection from the evil effects of sewer gas on themselves and their families, and require that the following general principles should be observed in constructing private drains, soil pipes, and water-closets.

"1st. Where water-closets are placed within a dwelling, the communication of the soil pipe with the drain should have double traps, immediately outside the external wall of the building, with an intermediate ventilator between the traps, and the soil pipe carried up through the roof, at a point removed from the chimneys, windows, or sky-lights; the connecting pipe between the water-closets, baths, and sinks being securely trapped.

"2nd. All pipes conveying waste water from the interior of a dwelling into the drains should have their continuity broken, where practicable, and terminate over a trapped gully placed in the ground, in the open air.   Care should also be taken that such pipes are syphoned so as to prevent an inward draught of air.

" 3rd. Syphon, or 'hopper closets,' should invariably be used in preference to 'pan closets.'   Where pan closets are now fixed, the apparatus should be provided with efficient ventilation by means of an air pipe extending from the top flange, at the bottom of the basin, through the external wall.

"4th. The water supply to all closets should be through a proper, *separate and distinct* service box, which is recommended to be provided with double valves; and in no case should such service box be connected with or fixed to the cistern supplying the house with water.   The water used for drinking and culinary purposes should be drawn from the service in direct communication with the water main.

" 5th. No water-closet to be perfectly safe should be constructed inside a house without an intermediate vestibule with a cross current of air, so as to cut off the air in the house from that in the closet.

" These observations point out the more general defects of the present arrangements of private drains, soil pipes, and water-closets. Cases may occur requiring special precautions to be taken.   The Health Committee and their officers will at all times be ready to afford every assistance, by way of advice or explanation, to meet such cases."

The CHAIRMAN having invited discussion,

Mr. DEACON thought too much stress had been laid in the paper upon sewer gas.   His own impression was that in well-constructed sewers gases capable of doing harm ought not to exist.   Where mephitic air existed the germs of disease were carried with it and propagated, but the real secret seemed to him to keep the mephitic air in the sewers, or oxidize it before it found its way into the external air.   The system of open ventilation was gaining ground, and he believed would be the only one adopted, when once the sewers were in good condition.   A constant flow of pure air into the sewers would oxidize and so dilute the mephitic air that it would rise through the open ventilating grids, and be so attenuated as to be innocuous.   He was informed that in the Jews' quarter, in London, it was impossible to have open grids, owing to the habits of the people and the peculiar character of the exudæ, and charcoal baskets were substituted.

Mr. LOBLEY said he was glad to find the system of ventilating sewers by means of open grids was becoming so general. During the last four or five months he had put down 150 manhole covers in Hanley, and had not heard a single complaint.

Mr. FOWLER agreed with what Mr. Deacon said, and thought, as much attention ought to be given to get air to circulate freely in the sewers as there was to allow the gases to escape.

Mr. PRITCHARD was strongly in favour of the system of open ventilation of sewers.

Mr. HALL said that, instead of putting ventilators in the centre of the street, he utilized the side grids by making an opening in the dipstone, about nine inches from the top. Tests had shown that a strong current of air passed through it, and no complaint had been made of any nuisance arising.

Mr. MORANT said that, in Leeds, the whole of the street gullies, 11,300 in number, had been made into ventilators, and not a single complaint had been made.

The CHAIRMAN endorsed what Mr. Deacon said, that there would be little need of ventilation if sewers were properly constructed. His experience in connection with the Metropolitan Board of Works, and also at Southampton, led him to think there was an unnecessary outcry made about sewer gases. He had known men, upwards of sixty years of age, who had been engaged in cleaning out sewers ever since they were twenty years old, and they were as healthy as any class of men in London. There was a good deal of prejudice in regard to this particular question, and he did not agree with much that had been said. With regard to flushing the sewers with water, they all knew that in times of epidemic there was a large and unnecessary consumption of water. He remembered that during an outbreak of cholera, the medical men recommended the people to turn on their taps, and the consequence was, the consumption went up to 40 gallons per head per day ; but a bucket of water thrown down a closet would do more good than if the tap was left running ten hours.

Mr. THORBURN, in replying, said although Mr. Deacon and others had argued that there ought to be no gases of a deadly nature in well-constructed sewers, he was afraid they would always have an existence, and therefore provision should be made to get rid of them. Where open ventilation had been adopted, as in the case of the Metropolis, ·it led to constant complaint. With reference to the plan of making ventilators of the side gullies, they would be simply going back to the time when they were untrapped, and when there were constant complaints made about them. As to the employment of charcoal baskets, no doubt if they were placed in a ventilator they prevented the flow of the gas in proportion to the space taken up with the charcoal, but the remedy for that was by increasing the number. Possibly they would not be found to answer where a large quantity of hot water and steam went into the sewers, and they required constant attention and renewal where employed; but in regard to removing and remedying certain nuisances of which the public complained, he thought they would be found well worth the money expended on them.

THE UTILIZATION OF SEWAGE WATER AND WATER OF POLLUTED STREAMS.

By Mr. A. M. FOWLER, Borough Engineer and Surveyor, Salford.

In introducing this subject, I feel sure it will occur to you all that there has been a great deal written and said on the question, but very little done to show municipal bodies the best course to adopt for dealing with sewage, and I therefore feel it a somewhat delicate matter to bring the subject before you; but I am prompted to do so, knowing that you are better able to judge from your knowledge of the configuration of the counties you represent, and the nature of the trade and manufacture carried on in each town, than those not particularly acquainted with the difficulties to be overcome. There have certainly been very able men called upon to give evidence, but the questions introduced to them have generally been leading *up to* and *upon* irrigation, and their scientific knowledge has been sought as to the best means of distribution. Elaborate displays of figures have been given as to the cost of constructing and maintaining, and of the estimated results.

Royal Commissions have been instituted and the country has been scoured to obtain information; Blue Book after Blue Book has been published, but to what purpose? Why, to submit a standard of purity to the country that cannot possibly be realized.

This island is now becoming so thickly populated, that unless the iron arm is stretched forth with a determination, something very serious will be the result ere long. We *have had, and are still having*, repeated warnings from rich and poor in the large number of lives that are daily sacrificed, through the want of reform to aid the practical Engineer in maturing his schemes so as to grapple with the crying evils of the present day. Would it not have been far better to consult those who know the difficulties to be met with in large towns, than to frame a Bill which sets the country in alarm, rouses the public to such an extent that deputation after deputation has urged upon the Home Secretary so to frame his Bill that the interests of manufactures should not be jeopardized? It was stated

o

(in fact, I have heard it frequently) that should such a measure as that first proposed become law the trade would be driven out of the country.   The Bill therefore, as enacted, is of little or no use.

The first Royal Commissioners were blamed for not recommending some plan of fixing a standard of purity by which the refuse should be dealt with.   The second Commissioners were blamed for recommending irrigation, and fixing a standard of purity.   Practically, neither could be carried out.   This has been proved to be the case when the question was fought out in the House on considering the private Bills deposited by Birmingham, Rochdale, and West Ham.

So far as I am able to judge, irrigation, for universal adaptation, is out of the question for the towns I have principally been engaged in, viz. Rochdade, Leeds, and Salford.

It is labour in vain to attempt to do anything satisfactory with respect to our polluted rivers, unless a more united action is taken, and a proper understanding come to between the authorities of large towns and the owners of manufactories carried on along their banks.

This can only be done by careful legislation on the part of the Government, and the united action of Borough Engineers and Surveyors, and Officers of Health, to obtain something within the bounds of practice.   As science progresses let the standard of purity be a more stringent one.

One would be led to think, seeing the great sacrifice of life and property daily going on in the present fever of politics, that domestic reform is neglected.

Never was there such a state of things for the Engineer to contend with ; he has not only to fight for the land and way-leave for his works, but he has also to combat with the evidence brought against him as to the *principle* to be adopted, although the Government has virtually told him what is best to be done.

It would appear that the valuable evidence and Reports of the Royal Commissioners are shelved, or at least come to a dead stand, for want of some practical way by which to deal with the refuse poured into each particular stream ; and it is to you, gentlemen, that I particularly address myself, knowing that you are more cognizant of the facts bearing upon this subject than any body of gentlemen in the country—knowing the difficulties to be overcome where water is impounded by weirs for the supply of mills for motive power and for navigation, and knowing the serious loss which would ensue in the event of the supply of water obtained from streams being cut off from the manufacturer along the course of our large rivers and streams in the counties we represent.

The manufacturer cannot always turn the refuse from his works into the sewers; as in the case of Leeds, nearly the whole of the refuse from works is turned back again into the river and streams, the undertakers of the Aire and Calder navigation there having the whole of the water rights *in* and *above* the town under their control.

At Leeds, in 1866, I ascertained that there were no less than 217 manufacturers, employing 35,142 hands, discharging refuse (from the trades there carried on) into the river and streams within the borough.

The river Aire at Leeds, the Irwell at Salford and Manchester, are very little better *above* the town than below it.

The Legislature, about forty years ago, evidently did not contemplate the necessity of guarding against and making provision for the existing state of things, for it does not appear that agitation on the subject of public health was commenced until moved by Dr. Southwood Smith, in 1832.

The Acts of Parliament which were obtained years ago for the construction of canals (say, since the Duke of Bridgewater's time, 1759), and for the purpose of making navigable many of our large rivers, of which we have, including canals, about 2500 miles, are now a stumbling-block in the progress of sanitary reform. These and other grand engineering works have to a great extent, no doubt, been the making of this country. Look at the towns in Lancashire and Yorkshire: would they have been the centres of wealth and industry if it had not been in a great measure for canals? Those works gave our large cities and towns a start, and they have never looked back since, and are now clothed in princely wealth; master and workman were never better paid for their services than at the present day, therefore we should all try to help in obtaining the object before us, although it may be to some a sacrifice of money. To see our sturdy fellows at work a stranger would think the country was rich in health as well as coin; but if this were said it would be far from the truth. We see the poor children in the gutters, and wonder how it is many of them look so well and hearty; but it is easily accounted for when we look at the very high death-rate amongst children—none but the strong are left, the delicate children are like plants blighted in the bud.

I may here remind you that the death-rate within the Borough of Salford, comprising the townships of Salford, Pendleton, and Broughton, between 1861 and 1868, averaged respectively 30·81, 22·59, and 16 per thousand. Salford ranged from 41·47 to 62·8, and was on the average for seven years *nearly* 50 *per thousand*, or 5 per cent. Of children under five years one dies out of every 64 of the inhabitants in Salford, one in 94 in Pendleton, and one in 231 in Broughton, or nearly one-fourth of the number in the Salford township. The old portion of the town of Salford is surrounded by a loop of the river, the houses are thickly packed, and in some parts there are as many as 144·3 persons per acre. The land in this particular part of the town is very low, two railways are built over it at a very high level, and many manufactories are in its midst, ventilation is thereby much impeded. These drawbacks may, to some extent, account for the high death-rate as compared with the more elevated and less built on localities.

Fresh sewage is *said* not to be dangerous, but I contend that the polluted state of the air and rivers in many of our large towns must have a very deleterious effect upon the health of the inhabitants. Can municipal authorities avoid this? I say no! It is out of their power to *entirely* do so. Most municipal authorities are at work in earnest in carrying out sanitary measures, in constructing main drainage works, and putting in force the Acts of Parliament to be applied within the boundary of their jurisdiction.

I feel sure the results sought to be obtained will not be acquired unless some central authority is formed, with power to act with promptitude, to compel the various local boards, millowners, and others to be prohibited from fouling the river above the town where sanitary regulations are carried out.

We all know that water once polluted cannot be appropriated for drinking, washing, or domestic use, although after treatment by chemicals, filtration, or irrigation, it is made bright and clear.

Officers of Health have been appointed to assist in remedying the evils; but I am sorry to say that Government has not in like manner taken the opinion nor thought fit to strengthen the hands of the Engineer and Surveyor who has really to point out the best means of remedying the defects complained of, because he has to show the necessity for the expenditure of money, and it is when you touch a man's pocket that he generally finds an excuse to grumble.

I feel convinced that justice has not been done to the Borough Engineer or Surveyor with whom offending parties are daily brought in contact, knowing as I do, from many years' experience in sanitary matters, that reform cannot be obtained if the advice of the Engineer is not secured.

We know quite well that the requirements for making a town healthy are difficult and most expensive to acquire, principally owing to the want of a cheap and an abundant supply of water.

Water carriage is the cheapest and most effective, and where the water-closet system is adopted the death-rate is low, saying nothing of the comfort and economy thereby secured. I may say that in Leeds the estimated cost of emptying middens and taking away refuse was, for the year ending June, 1871, 4800l. Since the tub system has been in operation the cost of removal, disinfectants, &c. (for the system brings its expenses), is estimated to be for the year ending June, 1874, 20,509l.

Fresh air and a fresh and abundant supply of water are the two first essentials to be secured for the preservation of health, and it is with this end in view that I propose to show a means by which our bright spring waters can more permanently be secured for the legitimate use of drinking, cooking, and washing, instead of such waters as at present (in many towns) being appropriated for, say, fellmongers and for various sorts of manufacture, when water of an inferior quality would do quite as well, and in some cases (especially for the boilers in generating steam) much better than bright spring water. Many manufacturers in Leeds prefer the polluted waters of the becks to the town's water, inasmuch as the boilers are less affected thereby.

The supply of water in most of our large towns has, during the past ten years, trebled in quantity, and the population has during the past twenty years (in some towns) doubled. This increased water supply beyond the proportion of increased population is principally owing to the great demand for water for manufacturing purposes.

It is fearful to look forward to the quantity of water likely to be required in the next generation, or say in thirty years' time; we have only to look back during this period of time to form an opinion. As the population increases and mechanical science progresses, in the same rate so will coal and water be consumed, and our rivers will become more and more polluted.

Twenty gallons per head may be said to be the water supply to large towns, and about one half of this quantity is generally sold to manufacturers, at about 6*d.* per thousand gallons. But this demand by manufacturers is rapidly increasing according to the prosperity of the country, and we must not forget that where the commodities for manufacture exist, as in the coal-fields of Lancashire, the population has, during the past fifty years, been twice doubled, and is rapidly on the increase at more than this rate.

The following table, from information I have recently obtained, will give some idea of the amount of water consumed by manufacturers in addition to the quantity used for water-closets:

Name.	Supply per day of 24 hours.	Supply per day to Manufacturers.	No. of Closets.	Population of District Supplied.
	gallons.	gallons.		
Morley	90,000	45,000	15	10,000
Oldham	2,000,000	1,000,000	800	120,000
Huddersfield	500,000	20,000	1,100	45,000
Halifax	2,000,000	1,250,000	2,200	70,000
Manchester	10,700,000	5,300,000	..	700,000
Bury	800,000	200,000	220	70,000

From the evidence of thirty manufacturing firms, it appears that to them *alone* the restoration of the river to its original degree of purity would be worth more than 10,000*l.* per year.

Compensating reservoirs would be very useful, and in some cases the cost would not be excessive, considering the benefits to be derived from a constant supply of water during working hours.

Dr. Henry Letheby tells us that " the ordinary sewage of a town may be so defecated, by easily-managed chemical processes, that when it is mixed with not less than twenty times its value of good water in a river, and has a run of eight or ten miles, it is not merely harmless but is actually discharged, and the water is fit for domestic use."

I have heard it said that the rinsing of a teapot, or a lump of sugar put into a gallon of water, would not admit of such water being turned into a running stream, according to the standard of purity fixed by the last Royal Commissioners, of which Dr. Frankland was a member.

Dr. Henry William Fuller states the effect of running water

in oxidizing or otherwise destroying organic matter is very remarkable.

It is clear that Parliament will not grant schemes on a large scale for irrigation.

From my observation of almost all the large irrigation works in this country, and from the opinions given by scientific men from time to time, the land irrigated is not free from noisome effluvium, the area required is very great—from twenty-five to fifty persons per acre—the crops of grass are so very coarse that there is a difficulty in disposing of them, and the farms are not profitable.

One has only to walk along the roads adjoining the irrigated fields at Harrogate and Rugby to realize the offensive smell at certain times.

Leeds would require, at 25 persons per acre, 160,000 con-⎫
   tributing sewage .. ..⎬ = 6,400 acres.
Bradford (Yorkshire) about .. ..   6,400 ,,
Salford .. ..   5,200 ,,
Manchester, population 300,000 .. .. 10,400 ,,

Therefore these towns would require a small county each for the disposal of their sewage by irrigation.

At Leeds it would require at least a conduit twenty miles in length, costing 10,500l. per mile, before the fields could be reached, saying nothing of the cost of way-leave, purchasing, and laying out the land.

It is proved by the gauging of the flow of sewage from a number of towns that the discharge is about 2½ times more than the water supply, owing to the influx of subsoil and spring water intercepted by the sewers; it is therefore easy to imagine the quantity of water to be dealt with.

The flow of sewage at Leeds in a dry time is about 11,000,000 gallons per day from 160,000 inhabitants.

The flow of sewage in Salford will be about 9,000,000 gallons per day.

From experience in carrying on the precipitation process for dealing with sewage at Leeds, I am satisfied that sewage can be so treated by the process known as precipitation that an effluent water can be produced so as not to be a nuisance.

The sewage at Leeds was discharged into a tank 183 feet long, 28 feet wide, and 11 feet deep, and after being treated with crude alum, clay, and animal charcoal, was allowed to flow constantly through the tank at the rate of 1½ to 2½ million gallons per day with the following results, without being filtered :

ANALYSIS.

EXPRESSED IN PARTS PER 100,000.	Grains in an Imperial Gallon.
Free ammonia	0·64
Albumen or ammonia	0·17
Chlorine	9·83
Fixed salts in solution	60·90
Dissolved organic and volatile matter	11·90
Total solid matter in solution ..	72·80
Suspended mineral matter	0·48
Ditto organic matter	0·70
	1·18

A sixpence could be clearly seen at the bottom of the running stream nine inches deep. I have had fish living in the water so produced for upwards of five months.

I obtained in February, 1872, four fishes, all about the same size (four inches long), and placed three in the town water, and one in the effluent sewage water taken from the overflow from the tank ; they were kept in my office in globes, the water being changed twice or three times a week. One of the fish died in the town water on the 28th February, 1872, three days previous to the one fish in the sewage water.

In the first Report of the Rivers Pollution Commission, 1868, in reporting on "polluted liquids from calico print, dye, and bleach works," it is stated that every form of pollution arising from the operations carried on in these works can be satisfactorily remedied by subsidence or filtration. We have seen these operations performed with perfect success upon water of the foulest description ; indeed, water so polluted, and even with the further addition of sewage, is constantly so purified in most calico print works which have not the good fortune to be situated near the source of a stream. The process is everywhere in operation, and in this way the water of a river is often purified, over and over again, in its passage down to the sea. Unfortunately, however, the riparian owners other than manufacturers, and the public generally, derive no advantage from these purifying processes, the clarified water existing only within the premises of the manufacturer. We collected several samples of water before and after these processes of purification, and the results of the analyses of these samples given in the following table show how well the purification was effected :

" Waste Water.—Effects of Filtration and Subsidence . Results of Analysis expressed in Parts per 100,000.

Description.	Total solid matter in solution.	Organic Carbon.	Organic Nitrogen.	Ammonia.	Nitrogen as Nitrates and Nitrites.	Total combined Nitrogen.	Hardness.			Suspended Matter.		
							Temporary.	Permanent.	Total.	Mineral.	Organic.	Total.
The Roach at Messrs. Wrigley's Paper Mills	43·30	4·518	·288	·512	·230	·940	8·83	7·57	16·40	2·82	3·18	6·00
Ditto, after treatment with lime, subsidence, and filtration	30·10	·368	·010	·020	1·710	1·736	1·72	9·25	10·97	0	0	0

" In the purification of the water of the Roach for Messrs. Wrigley and Son's paper manufactory, the water is first mixed with slaked lime, in the proportion of from five to seven grains of lime per gallon; it is then admitted into capacious subsidence tanks, the largest having an area of one acre; thence it passes on to the sand filters, of which there are nine, each forty yards by nine yards. These filters deliver 600 gallons per minute of splendidly bright water. The deposition tanks are cleaned out twice a year; a process which occupies only four hours: the sludge is thrown into the river. The filters require cleansing once a fortnight, two men half a day suffice for each filter. . . . .

" The effluent water is considerably superior to the water of the Thames as delivered to consumers in London—a result which could hardly have been anticipated, considering the very foul condition of the Roach at this part of its course."

In the Report of the Commissioners on the " Mersey and Ribble Basins," p. 65, the experiments on the filtration of sewage through the Beddington soil show how satisfactorily the sewage is purified at the rate of 7·6 gallons per cubic yard of soil per diem.

Therefore, if filter-beds were resorted to, after precipitation, for the further purification of ordinary sewage, I am satisfied that such water would be exceedingly valuable and perfectly satisfactory for the objects I have in view. Having these facts before me, and dismissing from my mind all the views of enthusiastic advocates of various schemes, I feel convinced that water can be produced from sewage by precipitation and filtration for a second source of water supply to towns.

I therefore propose to pass the effluent water through filter-beds, allowing about 118 gallons per cubic yard of filtering medium.*

The tanks for precipitating the sewage to be similar to those I have designed for Leeds, and now in course of construction, which are so arranged that any one tank can be shut off at pleasure, or the sewage be allowed to rest or flow in a continuous stream through a series of reservoirs.

The cost of obtaining a water supply to large towns is, say, from $2\frac{1}{2}d.$ to $3d.$ per 1000 gallons, but with the present high rate of wages and price of materials it will be impossible to obtain water at such a price in future when the filtering is taken into account.

The greater the demand for water the greater the necessity for filtering, unless the Lake Districts are resorted to, because we must not forget that wherever the tributaries of large rivers are intercepted it is only the picked waters that are selected.

Seeing the difficulties to be overcome in the event of compelling all persons to discharge the refuse of works into the sewers instead of discharging the same into the river from whence the supply is generally obtained, it is necessary to compensate in some way or other the parties affected by any enactments which may be considered arbitrary.

For the reasons before given it is out of the question for manufacturers or authorities in the populous cities and large towns to think of irrigation.

From experiments on works I have been engaged on, some time before the high price of coals began, 1000 gallons were raised 240 feet high for $1d.$, including all wear and tear, interest on capital, &c., and I estimate that this quantity can now be raised for $1\frac{1}{4}d.$, or say $6d.$ per million gallons 1 foot high.

The following is an estimate for filtering and raising, say, $4\frac{1}{2}$ million gallons per day, or half the estimated quantity of effluent water for disposal at Salford :

	£	s.	d.
Cost of filter-beds, four acres, 24,000*l.*; interest at 5 per cent. on capital	1,200	0	0
Cost of land, five acres, at 200*l.* per acre, 1,000*l.*; interest at 5 per cent. on capital	50	0	0
Working expenses of filter-beds and repairs	250	0	0
Cost of iron mains, 2 feet diameter, 1·125 miles, at 4,000*l.* per mile, 4,500*l.*; interest at 5 per cent. on capital ..	225	0	0
Cost of raising $4\frac{1}{2}$ million gallons 220 feet, at $6d.$ per million gallons, 1 foot high, including coals, wages, and interest upon buildings and machinery	9,033	15	0
Total cost per year.. .. .. ..£	10,758	15	0

Or 1·58*d.* for raising 1000 gallons per day 220 feet high.

* Being more than allowed at the works of Messrs. Wrigley, before referred to.

The estimate for raising 5½ million gallons per day in like manner for Leeds would be as follows:

	£	s.	d.
Cost of filter-beds, five acres, 30,000*l.*; interest at 5 per cent. on capital	1,500	0	0
Cost of land, six acres, at 200*l.* per acre, 1,200*l.*; interest at 5 per cent. on capital	60	0	0
Working expense of filter-beds and repairs, say	300	0	0
Cost of iron mains, 2 feet diameter, 1·61 miles, at 4,000*l.* per mile, 6,400*l.*; interest at 5 per cent on capital ..	320	0	0
Cost of raising 5¼ million gallons per day 195 feet high, at 6*d.* per million gallons, 1 foot high, including coals, wages, and interest upon cost of buildings and machinery	9,786	14	3
Total cost per year.. .. .. ..£11,966	14	3

Or 1·43*d.* for raising 1000 gallons per day 195 feet high.

The cost of distribution would be about ¼*d.* in each case per 1000 gallons per day.

In Leeds the effluent water can be raised 195 feet to a point near York Road, with a length of conduit of 1·61 mile. This would give an elevation above the centre of the town of 105 feet, and of 125 feet above the streams where the mills are principally situated.

For the town of Salford the water can be raised 220 feet to Barr Hill, with a length of conduit 1·125 mile. This would command an elevation above the town of from 115 to 150 feet.

This does not take into account the cost of providing tanks and machinery for the purification of the sewage, except filter-beds, as some plan in all towns must be adopted before such water is allowed to pass off into any stream.

Works for a precipitation process will cost from 7*s.* 6*d.* to 10*s.* per head of the population, in addition to the above estimate.

It was decided to postpone the discussion of Mr. Fowler's paper to the next meeting.

Vote of Thanks to the Mayor.

The CHAIRMAN proposed, and Mr. LYNDE seconded, that a vote of thanks be given to the Mayor of Liverpool and the Finance Committee, for having placed the Council Chamber at the disposal of the Committee.

The resolution was unanimously passed.

Thanks to Mr. Deacon and Mr. Thorburn.

Mr. VAWSER said that at their previous meeting at Manchester the Members paid a well-deserved compliment to the gentlemen resident in the town, by formally recording their thanks for the efforts that had been made to ensure a successful meeting, and he thought they should now pay a similar compliment to Mr. Deacon and Mr. Thorburn, by thanking them for all the trouble they had taken in connection with that meeting, and which had been so highly successful.

Mr. LYNDE seconded the proposition, and it was unanimously carried.

Mr. DEACON and Mr. THORBURN severally expressed their acknow-ledgments, and the proceedings were brought to a close.

The Members then adjourned to the Royal Alexandra Hotel to dine.

DISTRICT MEETING AT LEICESTER.

On Saturday, March 14, 1874, a well-attended meeting of the Members of the Association was held in the Mayor's Parlour of the Town Hall, Leicester, under the Presidency of Mr. LEWIS ANGELL, the President of the Association, when there were also present Messrs. J. LEMON, Southampton, Vice-president of the Association· C. JONES, Ealing, Honorary Secretary; E. PRITCHARD, Warwick, District Secretary for the Midland Counties; R. VAWSER, Warrington, District Secretary for Lancashire and Cheshire; E. L. STEPHENS, Borough Engineer, Leicester; J. PROCTOR, Bolton; E. J. PURNELL, Coventry; R. DAVIDSON, Leamington; E. R. L. ESCOTT, Halifax; J. H. HALL, Canterbury; H. WALKER, Basford; J. LOBLEY, Hanley; A. COMBER, Kidderminster; R. HODGE, Plymouth; E. BETTRIDGE, Balsall Heath, Birmingham; E. CLAVEY, Burton-on-Trent; G. HODSON, Loughborough; W. BATTON, Aston Manor, Birmingham; E. MONSON, Acton; E. SHARMAN, Wellingborough; T. T. ALLEN, Stratford-on-Avon; E. DAVEY, Maidenhead; J. DEVIS, Oldbury. The visitors included Messrs. T. STOPHER, Architect and Surveyor, Winchester; W. HUMBER, Assoc. Inst. C.E., London; W. BOON, Coventry; T. COLTMAN, Borough Accountant, Leicester; and J. BAKER, Assistant Surveyor, Warwick.

Mr. E. PRITCHARD, Hon. Sec. of the Midland District of the Association, read the minutes of the meeting held at Leamington, which were confirmed. Mr. Pritchard also read a number of apologies from several gentlemen who were unable to be present. Among the letters received was the following from Mr. R. Rawlinson, C.B., C.E. :

ʼ "LANCASTER LODGE, BOLTONS, WEST BROMPTON, S.W.
March 3, 1874.

"DEAR SIR,—I am much obliged by the invitation from the Municipal Engineers to meet at Leicester on the 14th inst., but my health will not permit me to accept it. Please to make my respects to the assembled Members, and say that I wish the Society success.
" Yours truly,
" R. RAWLINSON."

Mr. PRITCHARD added that he had had a personal interview with Mr. Rawlinson, and that gentleman had expressed his strong desire that the Association might be a great success, and promised to assist in the formation of a library in connection therewith. Mr. W. S. Till, Borough Surveyor of Birmingham, had become a Member of the Association.

A Sub-Committee to assist the Honorary Secretary for the Midland District was then appointed, consisting of Mr. W. S. Till, Birmingham; E. L. Stephens, Leicester; E. J. Purnell, Coventry; and R. Davidson, Leamington.

THE WATER-WORKS.

The Members then proceeded to the Bradgate Water-works. By the kind permission of the Earl of Stamford and Warrington, they were allowed to drive through Bradgate Park, thus giving a full opportunity of seeing the reservoirs and catchment area. The reservoir, which is a very large one, contains about 500,000,000 gallons. It is constructed by an embankment thrown across the valley. At the foot of the ravine are placed engine-house, four filter-beds, pure-water tank, by-wash, engine-house, and buildings. The engine-house contains two splendid steam engines of the Woolf description. The works generally are most elaborate, and have been most successfully carried out by T. Hawksley, Esq., C.E., at a cost of somewhere about 40,000l. By the kind permission of E. S. Ellis, Esq., the Chairman of the Leicester Water-works Company, the Members were allowed to visit the works, and the manager, Mr. Tebbett, very courteously explained each object of interest. In the Board Room a splendid *déjeuner à la fourchette* was provided by Mr. Ellis for the party, and Mr. Pritchard, as Hon. Sec. for the District, was requested to convey the thanks of the Association to that gentleman for his kindness. The Association also expressed their indebtedness to Mr. Tebbett. Not only were the water-works open to inspection, but copies of the plans were placed for inspection by Mr. T. Hawksley. The general opinion, as expressed by the Members, was that the works were a masterpiece. Mr. Hawksley had wished that the Association had deferred visiting Bradgate till the summer time, when they would have seen not only the works, but the grounds, which are tastefully laid out, to great advantage.

The party then proceeded to the Leicester Sewage Works.

The Sewage Works.

Mr. Stephens, the Borough Surveyor of Leicester, took great pains to carefully explain all matters connected with the works, which were about the first of the kind constructed. They are by Mr. Wicksteed, and have been frequently pointed to as being one of the best illustrations of purification of sewage by lime.

Upon the return of the Members to the Town Hall, the President said he had prepared a paper having especial reference to the legislative aspect of the sewage question, and the failure of chemical systems, but he preferred deferring the reading of his paper till the annual meeting at Birmingham, in May, in order that the meeting might hear the paper to be read by Mr. Stephens, explaining more fully the interesting works they had just left.

A CONCISE DESCRIPTION OF THE SEWERAGE AND SEWAGE WORKS OF THE BOROUGH OF LEICESTER.

By Mr. E. L. STEPHENS, Borough Engineer.

THE town of Leicester extends over an area of nearly 1000 acres, containing a population of about 105,000. There are 450 streets in the town, the total length of which is about '45 miles. The greater number of the streets have a double system of sewers, the original sewers having been constructed to deliver into the river at various points on its course through the town. In 1851 an Act was obtained for the construction of a second or deep system of sewers, which has been carried out in all the streets, and, being chiefly for basement and closet drainage, are made at a minimum depth of 10 feet, varying in size from 12 to 36 inches in diameter.. These sewers are all connected with main sewers passing along the lower portion of the town, varying in depth from 10 feet to 30 feet, and in diameter from 30 to 60 inches; by these sewers the whole of the sewage is conveyed to an artificial outfall, formed by the engine well at the sewage works. The old sewers are left intact throughout the town, receiving, as previously to the construction of the new sewers, all the surface water from the streets, thus preventing the heavy *débris* from them finding its way into the deep sewers. At the various points where the new sewers pass under the old sewers, which are in each case within a short distance of the old outfalls, connections are made between the old and new sewers to prevent the sewage entering the river; but when the junctions are gorged by storm-waters the bulk passes on to the river as of old, the sewage at that time being so diluted as to be innoxious. The sewers are ventilated by various methods, the most efficient of which are numerous connections with boiler chimneys, which, from their great height and high temperature, form very powerful exhausts. The other modes are by pipes carried up the sides of public buildings, the rain spouts from high buildings, open ventilators in the centre of streets, and

by ventilators furnished with charcoal trays at the summits of
sewers, which trays, being easily removable, serve the purpose also
of flushing places.   The flushing of the sewers is effected by means
of a portable waggon constructed of boiler· plate, and capable of
holding 1000 gallons.   This waggon is furnished with a disc valve
in the bottom of 12 inches diameter, below which is fixed a strong
leather hose of the same diameter.   The waggon is drawn over the
flush, the grating and tray removed, the leather hose inserted into
the mouth of the flush pipe, the waggon filled from a hydrant fixed
near, the disc valve is raised by a lever attached thereto, and the
whole 1000 gallons thrown down the sewer in about two and
a half minutes.   The Sewage Works are situate in the Abbey
Meadow, about half a mile from the town, and were designed and
constructed by the late T. Wicksteed, Esq., C.E., of London.   The
site contains an area of about four acres of land, on which are
erected engine and boiler houses, large covered settling tanks, lime-
house, coal-house, and various other sheds, and four cottages for
foreman and staff.   At these works the whole of the sewage,
together with a large quantity of subsoil water, amounting together
to an average quantity of five millions of gallons per diem, is
raised by steam power 20 feet, into reservoirs placed at an elevation sufficient to allow the purified water to flow off into the river.
The steam power consists of two single-acting Cornish pumping
engines, each of 20 horse-power, and one rotary engine of 10 horse-
power to drive the machinery.   The Cornish engines are so con-
· structed that at each stroke pumps are worked which mix with the
sewage water a certain portion of the cream of lime, the effect of
which is a rapid and perfect precipitation of all the matters held
in suspension.   The lime is slaked in pits constructed for the
purpose, furnished with sluices, and when the lime is thoroughly
slaked it passes into circular tanks, in which agitators constantly rotate to prevent a deposit.   It then passes to the suction
pipes of the lime pumps, which are attached to the beams of the
pumping engines, and is, as before stated, raised and mixed with
the sewage in its course from the sewage pumps to the settling
tanks.   The sewage thus mixed with the lime passes through
settling pits, each 20 feet long, 8 feet wide, and 10 feet deep, in
which the heavy *débris* is precipitated.   It thence passes through
covered troughs to pits beyond, in which other agitators are kept
in constant motion by the machinery engine for the purpose of
more intimately mixing the lime with the sewage, from thence it

P

passes through chequered walls into the settling tanks. These tanks are divided into four compartments, the first two, which receive the mixed sewage on passing through the chequered walls, are each 60 feet long by 45 feet wide, and are formed with sloping sides to prevent, as far as possible, the deposit settling on them. At the bottom of these slopes, at 12 feet below the water line, inverts are formed of 3 feet diameter, in which Archimedean screws are fixed, which are driven by the machine engine: the action of which is to draw back the solid matter as it is precipitated into wells, from whence it is lifted by sets of buckets attached to endless chains to troughs on the upper portion of the buildings, whence it is delivered by gravitation into large open tanks, where it lies until the supernatant water is drained off by open shafts into the engine well; by this means, and by evaporation in the atmosphere, the matter, amounting to about 4000 tons per annum, becomes solidified and is disposed of as manure. The farther compartments of the settling tanks are in three divisions, each 140 feet long by 45 feet wide, the central portions being level and the sides made sloping towards the centre to facilitate the removal of the deposit. These compartments are arched over, the upper surface forming a drying floor of 140 feet by 90 feet. The outlet for the effluent water at the north end of the settling tanks is by weirs extending the whole width, over which it falls on to a screen of pebbles and gravel resting on gratings, and thence over a series of weirs, by which means the water is further purified and aerated previous to passing into the river. When the pumping engines are overpowered by storm-waters, at which times the sewage is highly diluted, the storm-water sewer constructed for that purpose is brought into action, and the storm-waters are carried another quarter of a mile into the tail water of the Belgrave Mill below the town, which is 7 feet below the level of the town pond, into which the greater number of the old sewers have their outfall. I have made various alterations on these works for their improvement during the seventeen years they have been under my charge. In the first place, the boilers were fixed at so low a level that even in flood time it was imperatively necessary to continue pumping to prevent their being flooded. To prevent this calamity, I had the boilers raised 6 feet to lift them above flood level. I also altered their position, and placed them so that their steam chest was brought in close proximity with the cylinders, thus effecting a great saving in steam. In the next place, I found both engines pumping into one delivery pipe. This was very costly, as it necessitated double supervision of the engine-drivers to keep the engines in a regular rotation of stroke to prevent the two volumes of water jostling in the one pipe. This I remedied by giving to each engine a separate delivery pipe, and by constructing large catch-pits beyond, not only to relieve their delivery, but to detain the heavy *débris* brought down with the sewage. The effluent end of the settling tanks was originally furnished with a set of twenty-four sluices, all of which had to be opened and closed to meet the varied stream of sewage. Those I removed, and constructed the effluent weirs as they now exist. I have also added the gratings and gravel screen, and constructed the catch-pits and weirs beyond, the beneficial effects of which must be patent to all. I have now in contemplation, what I feel certain will be a still further improvement in the effluent water, viz. a filtering tank of about an acre, in which I shall lay bare the water-bearing gravel, and pass the clarified effluent water into it by the pressure of some ten feet of head.

In reply to questions, Mr. STEPHENS said that it took nearly two years to dry a tank of manure, and that in connection with the Leicester Sewage Works, they had about two acres of tanks. The working expenses were about 1800*l.* or 2000*l.* per annum, and there was a dead loss in connection with the works of between 1400*l.* and 1500*l.* annually.

The Members afterwards dined at the "Bell," where they were joined by the Mayor and other Members of the Corporation.

DISTRICT MEETING AT CHESTER.

A MEETING of the Lancashire and Cheshire District Committee of the Association was held, April 10, 1874, in the Committee-room of the Town Hall, Chester, kindly placed at the disposal of the Society by his Worship the Mayor. The object of the Committee's visit to Chester was to inspect the Main Sewerage Works, now in course of construction, under the direction of Mr. G. A. BELL, and afterwards to resume the discussion on the papers read at the Liverpool meeting by Mr. G. F. DEACON, Liverpool, on "Waste of Water," and Mr. A. M. FOWLER, Salford, on "The Utilization of Sewage and the Water of Polluted Streams." The following Members were present: Mr. R. VAWSER, the Secretary, Warrington; Messrs. MATTHEW JONES, Chester; J. PROCTOR, Bolton; P. SMITH, Blackburn; S. KELSALL, Stretford; G. DICKINSON, Westleigh and Bedford; J. WILSON, Bacup; A. JACOB, Barrow-in-Furness; W. A. RICHARDSON, Tranmere; G. WATSON, Crewe; JOHN D. SIMPSON, Buxton; JAMES HOLLAND, Witton-cum-Twambrooke; JOHN JACKSON, Stockport; JOSEPH LOBLEY, Hanley; J. G. LYNDE, Manchester; A. M. FOWLER, Salford; and R. HUGHES, Rhyl.

Mr. THORBURN was called to the chair, and the minutes of the previous meeting were read and confirmed.

Mr. VAWSER then read letters of regret from several gentlemen unable to be present, and stated that Mr. Bell, the Engineer, would presently escort them over the Main Sewerage Works of the city, and explain to them everything connected therewith. Members would also have the privilege of inspecting the Chester Waterworks.

The CHAIRMAN had much pleasure in proposing a vote of thanks to the Mayor and Corporation for granting them the privilege of meeting in their noble Town Hall. Those present who had not been over it, would find that it contained many matters of interest. The Hall was indeed well worthy of the people of Chester. And the least thing they could now do would be to give the Mayor and Corporation a hearty vote of thanks for their kindness.

The motion was seconded and carried unanimously.

The CHAIRMAN announced that there would be an important meeting in London, on the 24th of this month, interesting to Members, and it was proposed that they should on that occasion examine the sewerage works of the Metropolis. He was sure they would find such a visit very interesting. It would be only by this means that they would be able to fully realize the magnitude of works of this kind. These works he believed were successful; but he thought they were still capable of further development, and there were plenty of other things that would interest them there. The annual meeting at Birmingham next month would extend over two days, and the Chairman expressed a hope that Members would be able to attend it, when they would have an opportunity of seeing the large works now about to be commenced in that town.

DESCRIPTION OF THE CHESTER SEWERAGE WORKS.

By Mr. G. A. BELL, City Engineer.

THE following description of the main outfall sewers now in course of construction in Chester was then read by Mr. BELL, the City Engineer, in charge of the works:

I beg to submit for your information a brief statement of the purposes and character of the sewerage and outfall works which are now in course of construction in this city, and which it is the intention of your Association to examine.

Like the existing practice in many other towns, the sewage of Chester is discharged into the river at many independent outlets; and the internal sewerage is so arranged that the greater part of this sewage enters the upper length of the river above the weir or mill-dam which is adjacent to the old Dee Bridge. The bottom of this part of the river is not under the influence of scour from tidal action, and consequently a considerable deposit of solid matter has taken place in the river in front of each outfall; and this is an evil which would naturally continue to increase. In addition to this there has also been a constant fouling of the river from the liquid parts of the sewage.

This was a condition of things which the Corporation determined to remedy, and the manifest course to be taken was to construct an intercepting sewer along the right bank of the river, and thereby convey the sewage to some point on Sealand, where it could either be utilized by irrigation or conveyed directly into the tidal part of the river after undergoing that degree of clarification which would render its discharge unobjectionable.

The committee of the Corporation charged with this work gave long and anxious consideration to that part of the question which regarded the point of outfall. After the suggestion of many different sites at a greater or lesser distance from the city, the present ground was selected and adopted as the one combining great advantages either for ready and rapid discharge into the river after clarification or (by an addition of a stand pipe and main of iron pipe) from which to convey the sewage on such part of Sealand as might be adopted for irrigation.

Another purpose to be attained was the internal drainage of the north-west part of the borough, which is a rapidly increasing district, and which in consequence of there being no proper outfall, no lines of sewer had been laid. The provision of sewerage for this district became a growing and a very pressing demand upon the Corporation, and the first step towards this end would necessarily be the laying of an intercepting sewer somewhere near the north and west boundary of the borough.

This was accordingly determined upon—the sewers in course of construction consisting of one for the southern and principal part of the city, and the other for the north-west district—as they are shown upon the plan and section.

The southern sewer will be two and a half miles in length. It will be circular in form, and vary in size from a diameter of 4 feet to a diameter of 1 foot 6 inches. The 4 feet and 3 feet 6 inches diameters will be brickwork, in two 4½-inch rings set in hydraulic lime mortar. The 2 feet and 1 foot 6 inches diameter will be stoneware pipes. The line will be carried by inverted syphons under a brook and under the canal basin. Each syphon will consist of two lines of cast-iron pipes of 2 feet in diameter. The pipes have been cast with the joints patented by Mr. William Williams, of Liverpool, which allows of the required curvature being readily obtained, and affords great facility of laying.

In use and action each of these lines of pipes will be in work together or singly according to the amount of the flow of sewage. Their combined or single action will be regulated by means of gates within the manholes which join the brick sewers to the syphons.

On certain parts of the line, as shown on the section, heading is necessary, and at these points, while retaining the same width of the sewer, the internal height will be increased to 4 feet 6 inches.

The line is also to be carried through Chester Castle, the boundary walls of which are of great thickness; and beyond this point and the Bridge Gate a heading is required through and under a projecting angle of a very old portion of the city walls.

On the north-west line of sewer, which is one mile in length, the only part of any importance or difficulty is the passage under the Dee and Mersey Canal. The intended direction of the line has here been changed, so as to carry the heading through more solid ground, and clear of the Canal embankment.

The southern sewer will drain an area of 502 acres, and the north-west sewer an area of 232 acres, being a total of 734 acres.

The minimum flow of sewage will be 1¼ million gallons in twelve hours, and I calculate the maximum flow at about 8 million gallons. We provide storm-water overflows along the lines of sewer to meet the emergency of very heavy rainfall.

At the outfall works one set of tanks will receive the sewage and discharge by gravitation so long as the level of the tidal water in the river will permit.

Another set of tanks built above the level of the ground will receive the sewage by pumping; the lift being 12 feet, and the pumping machinery to be provided being two 10 horse-power horizontal engines, and four of Gwynne's centrifugal pumps.

It is intended to work these tanks by continuous flow, and to precipitate and deal with the mud according to the system of General Scott, by which I anticipate that the whole operation will proceed without causing any public offence or annoyance, and the river will be kept entirely clear of the passage into it of any of the solid constituents of the sewage.

The Members then inspected the works in company with Mr. Bell, who explained the various details.

On returning to the Town Hall, Mr. BELL volunteered to give any further information the Members might require, and stated that the sewage in the tanks would have a steady and continuous flow, and that it was expected the solid matter would precipitate at about one inch per minute, and the effluent water flow off perfectly clear. The working expenses are estimated at 600l. per annum.

After some further conversation,

Mr. LYNDE proposed a vote of thanks to Mr. Bell for his paper, and for conducting them over the works, and answering the questions which had been put to him.

Mr. BELL, in acknowledging the vote of thanks, said how much honoured he felt by their coming to see the works, and how glad he was to see them.

In the absence of Mr. Deacon, it was determined not to discuss his paper on " Waste of Water," read at Liverpool Jan. 3, 1874.*

* Page 157.

Mr. FOWLER then read the greater part of the paper prepared for the Liverpool meeting,* and a general discussion followed.

The CHAIRMAN said the idea was a novel one, and there might be cases where such a process might become a source for supplying water for a specific purpose. They knew that the population of this country was growing at a rapid rate, and it would soon become a serious question where water was to come from to supply the towns. He thought the day might arrive when such a process might provide the additional supply necessary in large manufacturing towns for trade and sanitary purposes. Until that day arrived they could hardly expect that the experiment would be tried.

A vote of thanks to the Chairman terminated the proceedings.

* Page 193.

DISTRICT MEETING AT WEST HAM.

• A MEETING of the Members of the, Home Counties District was held at West Ham, on Friday, April 24, 1874, for the purpose of inspecting the Abbey Mills Metropolitan Pumping Station, the West Ham Sewage Works, and the phosphate process and irrigation farm at Barking. The meeting was attended by Mr. LEWIS ANGELL, C.E., President; Mr. LEMON, Borough Engineer, Southampton, Vice-President; Mr. C. JONES, Ealing, General Hon. Sec.; Mr. ELLICE CLARK, Hon. Sec., Home Counties; Mr. PRITCHARD, Borough Engineer, Warwick, Hon. Sec. for Midland Counties; and the representatives of about forty towns, including Bilston, Birkenhead, Croydon, Canterbury, Cambridge, Stoke-on-Trent, Folkestone, Lowestoft, Richmond, Hereford, Maidenhead, Reading, Boston, Hanley, Watford, High Wycombe, Epsom, Maidstone, Acton, Eaton, &c. Letters were received from Liverpool, Manchester, Salford, Leeds, Norwich, Birmingham, Portsmouth, and other towns, regretting non-attendance through business arrangements. Sir JOSEPH BAZALGETTE, C.B., Engineer to the Metropolitan Board, and Mr. HAYWOOD, C.E., Engineer to the City of London, were elected Honorary Members of the Association.

A visit was paid to the Metropolitan Pumping Station at Abbey Mills. The Members inspected the large iron cages for straining the coarser matter out of the sewage in the sewage wells, which averages two or three tons per day, and is taken away by a contractor, who applies it as manure. It consists of garbage, dead animals, rags, and miscellaneous articles, which, if allowed to pass into the pumps, might do some mischief. The contractor takes all these away, as well as the ashes from the boiler furnaces, under a contract which for the present year is 28*l.* Apart from the aforesaid cages the freedom of the Pumping Station from all disagreeable odour was remarkable. The paint and the gilding on the engines and framework were bright and fresh, although six years old. The boilers are heated with the best anthracite coal, of which 1000 tons per annum are consumed. Only the low-level sewage has to be pumped, the remainder flowing by gravitation.

From Abbey Mills the entire volume travels off through three large culverts in an embankment a distance of four miles down to the Thames, near Barking Creek, where it is stored in a reservoir during the flow of the tide and discharged at the ebb. One of the curiosities of the main-drainage system consists in the much larger proportion of sewage, considering the population, discharged into the river on the southern side, at Crossness, compared with the northern. Hence the southern sewage at the outfall is comparatively deficient in ammonia, being evidently very much diluted.

From Abbey Mills the Association proceeded to a pumping station of less magnificence and cost on the banks of the river Lea, in Canning Town.

On arriving at the West Ham Pumping Station, the President, Mr. LEWIS ANGELL, who is the Engineer to the West Ham Local Board, explained that the whole sewage of the district, containing a population of 80,000, flowed into the river Lea. The conservators of the Lea and the Thames had each given notice to the Local Board calling upon them to clarify and disinfect the sewage of the district by the best known practicable means before discharging it into the stream. The Board were simply anxious to know what process to adopt. Originally, and, as they thought, in accordance with the views of the Government, they had secured 750 acres of land, situate between the Lodge Farm, Barking, and the Thames, far away from human habitation. Here they proposed to utilize the sewage by irrigation, and they so contrived the financial point of the scheme as to reduce the local burdens of the ratepayers, instead of increasing them, and that without any reference to profit from the use of the sewage. But to their great surprise, after preparing their plans, they were told by the Local Government Board, then newly appointed, with Mr. Stansfeld at its head, that they need not go to so much trouble, and they were advised to adopt the tank system, purifying the sewage as far as they were able. The Government sanction to the irrigation scheme was positively refused, and the Local Board were left in the difficulty of not knowing what to do. The Metropolitan Board would not take them. Mr. Angell stated that they had tried several plans, including General Scott's lime process, producing Portland cement, on which method they had expended 1400l. The drying of the sewage sludge connected with General Scott's process was going forward at the time of the visit, by Needham and Kite's patent presses. A new process for purifying sewage was also in view,

being the invention of Mr. Goodall (Leeds). But the operator
had only been a week on the ground, and had not been able to get
his system into full working order. The materials employed con-
sisted of gas-lime, animal charcoal, and certain salts of iron—a
mixture which, in the first instance, seemed to make the sewage
rather worse than it was before.

The next visit was to the Lodge Farm, near Barking. Here
Mr. HENRY J. MORGAN explained the operations of the Metropolitan Sewage Company. A portion of the sewage of London is
conveyed from the contiguous line of the great outfall sewer and
distributed over the farm by means of open carriers. The area of
the farm is 212 acres, and a portion of the sewage is previously
treated by the Phosphate Sewage Company. The sewage so treated
is speedily rendered clear and inodorous, and at the same time
enriched, by the presence of phosphate. The deposit is dried by
exposure to the air, and is said to give off no smell during that
process. When dried, it is ground and sold as a portable manure,
stated to be valuable, having a large portion of phosphate for its
base. The original precipitating mixture consists of a phosphate of
alumina, ground to powder and treated with sulphuric acid. The
effluent water was extremely clear, and without perceptible smell,
and some of the deposit, only very partially dried, gave no offensive
odour, even when stirred with a stick. The farm itself was in
excellent order, and no smell of sewage was apparent anywhere.
The Italian rye-grass, some of which was being cut for the second
time this season, was exceedingly clean, and all the live stock
appeared in very good condition.

The Members afterwards dined in the Town Hall, Stratford; the
Chairman, Medical Officer, and several Members of the West Ham
Local Board being present.

APPENDIX.

ADMINISTRATION OF THE SANITARY LAWS.*

By LEWIS ANGELL, President of the Association of Municipal and Sanitary Engineers and Surveyors.

"Great is the *vis inertiæ* to be overcome, the repugnance to self-taxation, the practical distrust of science, and the numbers of persons interested in offending against sanitary laws, even amongst those who must constitute chiefly the local authorities to enforce them." Such was the language of the Royal Sanitary Commission in 1871, and such, during twenty years' official experience, have I found to be the fact.

Notwithstanding the great advance recently made in sanitary knowledge, the real work is yet to be done; as yet we have only attacked the outposts, for, to quote the words of Dr. Guy, Professor of Hygiene, in King's College, London: "Most of our towns, and all our villages, are still untouched by the hand of the Sanitary Engineer; a great work of cleansing has yet to be done in all our rivers and streams; there are swamps and marshes still undrained. When," continues Dr. Guy, "I bear all this in mind, I cannot condemn as extravagant the estimate of those who think that a fourth part of our actual mortality may be ultimately averted."

Perhaps the greatest difficulty we have to encounter is the want of appreciation of sanitary principles by the population at large— that "practical distrust of science" referred to by the Royal Commissioners. Nor do we encounter this difficulty among the illiterate or the poor alone; we know from practical experience how constant must be the effort to maintain domestic sanitary arrangements, and how frequently such efforts are regarded as "fussy." We have, of late, heard much about sanitary science, but what we hear comes from the active and the thoughtful few; the mass of the people are utterly indifferent; indeed, not a few, who claim to be in-

* A paper read at the Social Science Congress, Norwich, October, 1873.

fluenced by common sense as well as religious feeling, still attribute ancient plagues and modern epidemics either to Providence or occult causes beyond the influence of hygienic or engineering efforts. Those who ignore the work of Howard and Jenner in the past, as well as modern experience and undoubted statistics, will at least admit that pollution of the air, impurity of water, adulteration of food, and overcrowding of dwellings, are productive of disease, and are preventible. Before we charge Providence with the results of pollution, we should at least enforce the maxim that " cleanliness is next to godliness."

The " repugnance to self-taxation " is another great difficulty the sanitarian has to encounter. To the mere " ratepayer " sanitary science means officials, public works, and taxation; an investment which gives no dividend, matters which may be postponed. The value of health, comfort, and prosperity, or the loss of labour and waste of capital consequent upon disease and pauperism, are matters of social economy of which the average ratepayer takes no account: he will endure poor-rates, and tax himself for luxuries, but he will not willingly submit to taxation for preventive sanitary measures.

The independence of the British character, the freedom of our institutions, and the theory that " an Englishman's house is his castle," do not conduce to that efficiency which involves sanitary house-to-house inspection, interference with domestic habits, and compulsory obligations.

Another obstacle to sanitary efficiency is the excessive cumbersomeness of sanitary legislation, which was recently pronounced by one of our judges to be the greatest muddle with which the Courts have to deal. For several sessions past all attempts at sanitary legislation have proved abortive. Social questions give place to political and party considerations. There is necessity for " home rule " in England, as well as for Imperial legislation.

Many radical reforms will occur to those experienced in sanitary administration, especially with regard to boundaries, governing bodies, and officials; but there is an instinctive feeling in Englishmen to maintain and utilize old institutions, and to effect reforms by engrafting improvements. I shall not therefore venture to advance any new theories in local government, but suggest improvements in existing arrangements.

Notwithstanding the difficulties and defects attending legislation, our existing opportunities for promoting sanitary work are very

considerable, if we only choose to avail ourselves of them.   Our
municipal corporations and local boards already possess great
powers, and if such bodies were constituted of proper persons, and
their powers judiciously exercised, a great improvement might be
speedily effected in the sanitary condition of the country; but unfortunately we too frequently find that the energy of such bodies
is expended in finding out " how not to do it."

The great principle of local government is based upon the
theory that representative men of intelligence, business ability, and
disinterested motives shall constitute the governing body; but in
practice local affairs are too frequently avoided by those who are
most fitted to take part therein.   Local power and patronage are
objects of ambition to persons of mediocre ability, and the position
is frequently sought from personal and interested motives; thus
local government may degenerate into littleness and obstructiveness
in the hands of uninformed, prejudiced, or interested persons, to
the exclusion of intelligence, sound judgment, and progress, a fact
recognized by the Royal Sanitary Commissioners, who say " that
no code of laws, however complete in theory, upon a matter of
such importance and complexity as the health of the community,
can be expected to attain its object, unless men of superior education and intelligence throughout the country feel it their duty to
come forward and take part in its working.   The system of self-
government, of which the English nation is so justly proud, can
hardly be applied with success to any subject, unless the governing
bodies comprise a fair proportion of enlightened and well-informed
minds.   It seems, therefore, peculiarly incumbent on those who
have leisure to take their share in administering these laws."
There are many who, while considering it *infra dig.* to associate
themselves with local matters, write to the leading journals to
denounce local authorities and public officials; but such persons
would do far better service to the great principle of local government, by taking their proper part therein.

Too much of our sanitary legislation is permissive instead of
obligatory; " shall " might be substituted for " may," in many
instances, with advantage.   The duties of local authorities should
be more precise and obligatory, and there should be more ready
means of compelling negligent or evasive authorities to the per-
formance of their duties.   There should be general building
regulations, applicable to the whole of the country.   It should be
absolutely obligatory· upon all river-polluting, air-poisoning, or

smoke-producing manufacturers to purify their refuse and consume their smoke. Local officers should be in a better position as to qualification, remuneration, and protection; their office should be more ministerial; that is to say, in matters of detail and within well-defined limits, it should be the duty of the local officer to put the law in force directly, as is done, for example, by the metropolitan building surveyors, without the delay, intervention, and sometimes favouritism of the local board. If we infringe an excise law, give incorrect measure, or omit to register a dog, we are subject to summary proceedings upon the action of an official upon whom we cannot possibly retaliate; but if we infringe some wholesome regulation as to building or drainage, or poison our neighbour, there is delay; the offence must be reported to and discussed by the local authorities, among whom the offender may find a friend and the means of retaliating upon a "meddlesome official." A dependent officer is tempted to become a time-server and respecter of persons, and thus discharge his functions from considerations of policy rather than of duty.

There is great room for improvement in this respect. Local officers are frequently badly paid, injudiciously selected, and in all cases too dependent on local influences to be thoroughly efficient. Their duties bring them into antagonism to the pecuniary interests of large sections of the ratepayers, and sometimes even to their immediate masters; upon this point I could produce an amount of recent evidence from local officers, detailing acts of retaliation and evasion of the law under local government, such as would hardly be credited. Local officers ought not to be placed in any such position, and I will venture to assert, that had such officers from the first been judiciously selected, adequately remunerated, and duly protected, their influence upon sanitary progress would have been much more conspicuous. Speaking generally, neither the position nor the pay of local sanitary officers is such as to attract or retain efficient service. Every Poor Law official under the Local Government Board is protected, but sanitary officers under the same department, viz. the Medical Officer of Health, the Surveyor, and the Inspector of Nuisances, are not so protected, but generally subject to the will or caprice of local feeling; this, I assert, from long experience, is one of the greatest defects in local sanitary administration, and yet one which may be easily remedied.

In claiming protection for local officers I do not advocate centralization; I would maintain the great principle of local government as a bulwark of social and political freedom; but local government is under constitutional control, and I claim that the protection which is enjoyed by other classes of officials should be extended to the important functions of the local sanitary officer. I would insist that all officers of a local authority should be properly qualified, adequately remunerated, and that in the honest discharge of their duties they should be protected from the effects of ignorance and interested clamour; in short, that they should be able to discharge their duties efficiently and impartially, without fear of consequences.

Insufficiency of staff in large towns is a general defect in sanitary administration. The constructive details of house drainage require active supervision. Scavengering arrangements are generally imperfect. "Scavengering," said Mr. Rawlinson, in a recent letter to the *Times*, "is a matter of police." We have already in the country an organization which might be made extensively useful in the detection and abatement of nuisances, as well as of crime: every corner of the land is supposed to be daily patrolled by a police-constable. A recent return shows that there is an average of one police-constable to each 770 of borough populations; these men are local officers, maintained at a great cost, and have comparatively little to occupy their time and thoughts; they might render considerable assistance in preserving physical as well as moral order. In many towns constables are told off to discharge the duties of nuisance inspectors. The subdivision of a sanitary district into smaller areas, making each constable an inspector on his beat, would secure much more efficient sanitary supervision. The most elementary instruction from a medical officer would convert an army of idle men into a health-preserving as well as a peace-preserving force.

We are justly jealous of any system of espionage; but within proper limits inspection is necessary, and there can be no greater objection to a local constable promptly reporting to his superior officer an offensive dustbin, foul drain, a stagnant ditch, than to the intermittent visits of the special constable, designated a sanitary inspector.

In conclusion, I would urge that the object of future legislation should be to promote greater simplicity, completeness, and certainty in the operation of sanitary laws, and especially to secure greater efficiency in their administration, by affording protection to local officers.

Concurrently with the above we require the moral influence of a higher tone of intelligence in the constitution of local authorities, and a better appreciation of sanitary principles by the public, without which, as the Royal Commissioners say, no legislation of this class can " be applied with success."

There are indications that the elements of natural science will, before long, form part of the curriculum of school education; and especially should sanitary science be taught, from the lowest grade board school to the college, because it affects alike the welfare of the prince and the peasant.

It is not to local authorities nor to Government influence that we most look for reform—reforms seldom arise from within; it is by the power of public opinion, guided by such influences as the Social Science Association, that we hope for sanitary progress. The efforts of boards of health, medical officers, and Sanitary Engineers, however well directed, will fall short of their mark, unless there be also an intelligent appreciation of sanitary principles by the population at large.

COPY OF CORRESPONDENCE BETWEEN MR. ANGELL, AND THE ROYAL SANITARY COMMISSION, THE HOME SECRETARY, AND THE LOCAL GOVERNMENT BOARD, 1870-71.

(No. 1.)

ENGINEER AND SURVEYOR'S DEPARTMENT,
TOWN HALL, STRATFORD, LONDON, E.
February 18, 1870.

SIR,

I wish to bring under the notice of the " Royal Sanitary Commission " a *very great defect* in the administration of the Public Health and Local Government Acts.

Without question the most important office, practically, in connection with these matters is that of the " Town Surveyor," but, as a rule, neither the pay nor the social consideration for the office is such as either to attract or retain the services of qualified Surveyors or Engineers—those who hold the office are subject to the dictation of Boards and the public, who resent any approach to independence of action or the administration of office upon *principle*.

Boards are not guided by precedent. The same Board at different meetings, will decide similar questions in different ways, according to its humour or the interest brought to bear. Their officers, being unprotected, must do their bidding and discharge their duties according to *policy* and not *principle*. Speculating builders, small property holders, and other interested persons, averse to the cost of sanitary works, too frequently form the majority of a Local Board; against such influences the Surveyor is powerless.

The Surveyor of a Local Board ought to be protected in a similar manner to the Poor Law officers, and there should always be an appeal to some power above, say the Local Government Act Office.

The Surveyor's office should also be to a certain extent ministerial and independent of his Board, as in the case of the District Surveyors of the Metropolis under the Building Act, that is to say, *it should be the duty* of the Surveyor to put the law in force in the matter of building and sanitary works as is done by the District Surveyors of London. An officer charged with such duties as a Town Surveyor must necessarily find himself in frequent antagonism with the builders and small property holders; it is a common thing, within my own experience, for persons to get elected on the Board to defeat and, if possible, remove the Surveyor.

The duties never will be properly carried out until the officers are (1) fairly paid and (2) duly protected.   There is no reason why such appointments should not have social consideration and be sought by qualified men, like the office of town clerk or medical officer . of health.   An experience of seventeen years has shown me this great defect in Local Board appointments.

I have not myself any personal grievance.   I have at present a good Board and am fairly paid ; but a change of Board, public agitation, &c., might reverse circumstances ; therefore on principle, and on behalf of less fortunate officers, I submit this statement, quite unofficially, with the hope that it may receive the consideration of the Royal Sanitary Commission.

I am, Sir,

Your obedient servant,

LEWIS ANGELL, M. Inst. C.E.,

Engineer to the West Ham Local Board.

To the Right Hon. Sir C. B. ADDERLEY, M.P.,
Chairman of the Royal Sanitary Commission.

Note.—The receipt of this letter was acknowledged, but no further correspondence took place thereon.

(No. 2.)

ENGINEER AND SURVEYOR'S DEPARTMENT,

TOWN HALL, STRATFORD, E.

SIR,   *February* 22, 1871.

On February 18, 1870, I wrote to Sir C. B. Adderley, Chairman of the Sanitary Commission, submitting certain views with reference to the position of Engineers and Surveyors employed under Local Boards.

On the 13th of the present month it was stated in Parliament by the Home Secretary that the Government had the Report of the Sanitary Commission *under consideration,* and that in three weeks from that date the result would be announced.

On inquiring at the Local Government Act Office I cannot ascertain either the recommendations of the Commission or the proposals of the Government.

It is the desire of officers holding appointments under the Local Government Act, that they should have at least the same protection in the discharge of their duties as is extended to officers employed under the Poor Laws.   The individual constitution of Local Boards renders it, in most cases, impossible for officers properly to carry out the duties imposed by Act of Parliament without such protection, consequently the Surveyors holding such appointments throughout the country contemplate united action by deputation, memorial, or otherwise, in order to secure if 'possible the advantages I have indicated in any legislation which may take place in connection with sanitary matters.

If the Government, in drawing the Bill, will accede to our views much trouble and expense to us will be saved, and I would also submit that such a clause would be much more likely to pass if introduced into the original Bill than if proposed in the House as an amendment, thereby challenging the opposition of interested parties out of doors.

I shall be glad if you will be good enough to forward this representation to the proper quarter. I am also prepared to attend any appointment in explanation of the views of Local Board Surveyors, of whom there are some hundreds in the kingdom, and without whose intelligent aid no real progress can be made in sanitary work.

I am, Sir,

Your obedient servant,

LEWIS ANGELL.

To W. H. BIRLEY, Esq.,
Secretary to the Royal Sanitary Commission.

(No. 3.)

ROYAL SANITARY COMMISSION,

ROOM E, HOUSE OF LORDS, WESTMINSTER.

SIR, *February* 23, 1871.

I am directed by the secretary to acknowledge the receipt of your letter of the 22nd instant, and in reply to inform you that the Report of the Commission was presented to Parliament on Tuesday last; but the copies are not quite ready for circulation yet.

Herewith I send you a copy of the recommendation of the Commission as bearing upon the point named in your letter. ,

I remain, Sir,

Yours obediently,

L. ANGELL, Esq., F. QUAIN.
&c., &c.

(ENCLOSURE.)

" 21. That the officers of every Local Health Authority should be appointed and removed by such authority; but medical officers of health should be appointed subject to the veto, and should not be removed without the sanction of the Central Authority; and inspectors of nuisances should be removable either by the Central or Local Authority."

CIRCULAR LETTER TO THE TOWN SURVEYORS OF ENGLAND AND
WALES.

WEST HAM LOCAL BOARD OF HEALTH,
ENGINEER AND SURVEYOR'S DEPARTMENT,
TOWN HALL, STRATFORD, LONDON, E.

DEAR SIR,   *February* 27, 1871.

The Royal Sanitary Commission have presented their Report
to the Government, and it was officially stated in the House of Commons, February 13, by Mr. Bruce, the Home Secretary, that the
Government had the recommendations of the Commission under
consideration, and that in about three weeks from that time the result
would be announced.

The Chairman of the Sanitary Commission, Sir C. B. Adderley,
has stated publicly that the object of the proposed legislation is to
consolidate the "confused and multifarious sanitary laws" in one
comprehensive Act, so as to "render uniform, general, and *active*, the
powers of Local Government in every place, under the inspiration and
stimulus of a central authority."

There cannot be any doubt as to the necessity for such legislation,
and it is highly desirable that Engineers and Surveyors employed
under the Public Health and Local Government Acts should embrace
this opportunity of improving their position in connection with the
independent discharge of their duties.

It must be within the experience of every such officer that it is
almost impossible to discharge, faithfully and impartially, his numerous
duties without giving-offence to interested parties, and becoming
subject to some degree of unpopularity. The duties which a Local
Board Surveyor has to perform and enforce are frequently such as
are opposed to the prejudices or to the pecuniary interests of large
sections of ratepayers or owners of property, who may have influence
in the Local Board. The prominence of the Surveyor's public position and the general nature of his duties render him especially
liable to attack, while the constantly changing constitution of the
Board leaves him without friends.

The Public Health Act of 1848 contained a clause which prevented
the removal of the Surveyor without the sanction of the General
Board of Health. Since the General Board was suppressed no such
protection has existed, and there does not appear to be any intention
of introducing such a clause in the proposed new Act, although it *is*
proposed that the medical officer of health shall have the protection
of the central authority.

From a Surveyor's point of view it is difficult to understand why
such a distinction is to be made. I have therefore taken the initia-
tive in endeavouring to induce Engineers and Surveyors throughout

the country, holding such appointments, to unite for obtaining, if possible, the same protection as is to be extended to the medical officer—which is at present possessed by officers acting under the Poor Laws —and which *was* included in the original Public Health Act of 1848.

I have already been in correspondence with the Sanitary Commission and the Local Government Act Office, and believe that with a little energy on our part our object will be attained.

My suggestion is to act by conference, petition, and deputation; and as I represent a large and important district immediately adjoining the metropolitan boundary, and am in frequent communication with the Local Government Act Office, I am favourably situated for assisting my brother officers in any combined action. I shall therefore be glad to receive immediate communications and suggestions, and to associate myself with other Surveyors in the conduct of this movement.

May I append your name, stating position and titles, to a petition for promoting the above object ?

I shall be glad to meet any gentleman who may happen to be in London to discuss this matter.

The subject of an "Association of Local Board Surveyors" is worthy of consideration.*

I am, dear Sir,

Yours faithfully,

LEWIS ANGELL, M. Inst. C.E.,

Engineer and Surveyor for the District of West Ham, London.

(No. 4.)

Engineer and Surveyor's Department,
Town Hall, Stratford, E.
March 9, 1871.

Sir,

Engineers and Surveyors holding Local Board appointments are disappointed that *their* evidence has not been taken with reference to the *working* of their department. The efficacy of sanitary legislation will always depend very much upon the professional skill and intelligent aid rendered by the Surveyor.

I for one should have been glad to have tendered important evidence (*vide* my letter, February 18, 1870). We are, as a body, most anxious to aid sanitary efforts, but we cannot be really useful unless we have protection such as you propose to give to medical officers (Clause 21,

---

* An immense number of letters of approval were received from Local Surveyors in reply.

page 126, 2nd Report), which even workhouse masters and relieving officers at present have under the Poor Law Board.

The Local Board Surveyors have agreed upon united action in this matter, and hope to have the sympathy and assistance of the Sanitary Commission.

I am, Sir,

Your obedient servant,

LEWIS ANGELL.

To the Right Hon. Sir C. B. ADDERLEY, M.P.

(No. 5.)

ROYAL SANITARY COMMISSION,
ROOM E, HOUSE OF LORDS, WESTMINSTER.

DEAR SIR,   *March* 12, 1871.

I am directed by the Chairman to acknowledge the receipt of your letter of the 10th instant, and in reply to inform you that it is now too late for the Commission to take any further evidence.

I am, however, to add that the Chairman will attend to the point named in your letter when legislation on the subject of the report comes on.

I am,

Yours truly,

LEWIS ANGELL, Esq.,   W. H. BIRLEY,
        Stratford, E.   *Secretary.*

(No. 6.)'

ENGINEER AND SURVEYOR'S DEPARTMENT,
TOWN HALL, STRATFORD, E.

SIR,   *March* 13, 1871.

At a meeting of Civil Engineers and Surveyors holding appointments under the Public Health and Local Government Acts, held March 11, 1871, it was resolved :

"That Mr. Lewis Angell, C.E., be requested to communicate with the Home Secretary, to request the favour of the reception of a Deputation of 'Local Surveyors' upon the subject of the proposed New Sanitary Act, and that Mr. Angell take such action for the purpose as he may deem advisable."

In accordance with the above resolution I beg most respectfully, on behalf of more than 500 Engineers and Surveyors holding such appointments in England and Wales, to request, before the proposed Bill is introduced into the House of Commons, that a deputation be received at the Home Office for the purpose of submitting to your consideration certain important matters connected with the Surveyor's department under a Board of Health, upon which the efficiency of sanitary efforts and results so much depends.

I have the honour to be,

Your most obedient servant,

LEWIS ANGELL.

To the Right Hon. HENRY AUSTIN BRUCE, M.P.,
Secretary of State for the Home Department.

(NO. 7.)

LOCAL GOVERNMENT ACT OFFICE,
8, RICHMOND TERRACE, WHITEHALL, S.W.
March 28, 1871.

SIR,

I am directed by Mr. Secretary Bruce to acknowledge the receipt of your communication of the 13th instant, requesting the Secretary of State to grant an interview to a deputation to submit certain matters connected with the Surveyor's department of a Local Board for his consideration.

I have to ask the deputation to submit their views and suggestions in writing first, in order that they may be considered before the new Act is framed. This step may more usefully be taken before than after any visit of a deputation to the Home Office.

I am, Sir,

Your obedient servant,

To LEWIS ANGELL, Esq.,
Stratford, E.

J. MONTAGUE,
Chief Clerk.

(No. 8.)

ENGINEER AND SURVEYOR'S DEPARTMENT,
TOWN HALL, STRATFORD, E.
March 29, 1871.

SIR,

In reply to your letter of the 28th instant, requesting that the views of the proposed deputation of Surveyors upon the subject of sanitary legislation be submitted in writing, I have now the honour, on behalf and with the authority of Engineers and Surveyors holding Public Health and Local Board appointments in the chief districts in England and Wales, most respectively to submit :

That the general nature of the duties of a local Surveyor, especially in connection with sanitary work, are such as, if actively and impartially performed, bring his office into antagonism with popular prejudices as well as to the pecuniary interests of ratepayers and property owners, and not unfrequently to the personal interests of members of the Local Board, his employers. The Sanitary Commission recognizes this fact when referring to "The number of persons interested in offending against sanitary laws, even amongst those who must constitute chiefly the local authorities" (page 31, Second Report). The Report also refers to "exemptions which, although mischievous, are not unpopular." Hence the local Surveyor becomes the object of personal attack, and is forced by circumstances to elect between policy and duty in the exercise of his functions.

That the experience of local Surveyors ·has taught them that sanitary work cannot be made, to use the words of the Commissioner's Report, "active and effective" so long as they continue to be "too dependent on their immediate employers to be thoroughly efficient."

That officers employed under the Poor Law Board, to which department the Sanitary Commission desire to assimilate the Health Board, are thoroughly protected in the exercise of their duties.

That during the existence of the General Board of Health local Surveyors had such protection. (Sec. 37, Public Health Act.)

That Surveyors at present holding office under the Towns Improvement Clauses Act have such protection.

That the Sanitary Commission advise the re-enactment of the sections as to the *protection* and correction of officers (page 85, Sec. 7, Second Report).

That the Commission recommend, "In order that *medical officers* of health may be able to discharge their duties *without fear of personal loss*, they should not be removed from office by any local authority except with the sanction of the Central Authority" (pages 35 and 176, Second Report).

That the Sanitary Commission, while thus recognizing the importance of protecting officers, have omitted in terms to recommend the extension of protection to the Surveyor, although in our experience the reasons apply with greater force.

That the *results* of the medical officers' recommendations depend to a very great extent upon the zeal and efficiency of the Surveyor's department; it is also through this department that the medical officer derives much of his information.

That in many cases the unprotected Surveyor may be required to report, to a protected medical officer, the negligence of his own employers, who will have it in their power to reward his sanitary zeal by dismissal.

That no local Surveyor or Engineer can be expected to give cordial and active assistance in compulsory sanitary work while he is conscious that his action would be opposed to the views or the interests of his employers, the public, upon whom he is dependent.

That the very existence of such a distinction between the medical officer and the Surveyor under the same Local Board is calculated to produce a want of harmony in interest, and will probably lead to a divergence of action in the two departments.

We beg therefore most respectfully to submit that in the proposed legislation the Surveyor should have the same protection as the medical officer, and that the protection should extend also to the *salary*, experience having shown that when Local Boards cannot resort to direct dismissal they accomplish their object by the reduction of salary.

We beg further most respectfully to suggest that as the Sanitary Commission recommend the union of the poor laws and sanitary laws under one administration, the various officers of the proposed Health Boards should also possess the same advantages as to position, salary, and superannuation as are extended to officers employed under the Poor Law Board.

There are other matters connected with the pay and qualification of a local Surveyor, and the efficiency of his department, which would be introduced in a conference with a deputation, but are not included in the present communication.

I am, Sir,

Your obedient servant,

To J. MONTAGUE, Esq.,   LEWIS ANGELL.
Chief Clerk Local Government Act Office.

(No. 9.)

' LOCAL GOVERNMENT ACT OFFICE,
8, RICHMOND TERRACE, WHITEHALL, S.W.

SIR,   *April* 19, 1871.

I am directed by Mr. Secretary Bruce to acknowledge the receipt of your letter of the 29th ult. As to the views of the proposed deputation of Surveyors on the subject of sanitary legislation, I have to inform you, that the suggestions contained in your communication have been considered, and are such as may very properly be submitted by the Secretary of State, on behalf of the Surveyors employed by Local Boards, to the minister or department charged with the preparation of any Bill for carrying out the recommendation of the Sanitary Commissioners.

By far the best mode of bringing forward these suggestions, and any others which the Surveyors may wish to add to them, is by written communication like that of March 29th;—and I have to suggest, that if the additional suggestions to which you refer at the conclusion of that communication be drawn up in writing with the same fulness of statement and distinct enumeration of reasons to be found in the communication of March the 29th, they will be more effectually brought to the notice of that branch of the Government to which the framing of the new Sanitary Bill is entrusted than by a conversation between a secretary, or under-secretary, and a deputation.

I have therefore to request that you will submit, in this way, the additional suggestions of the local Surveyors.

I am, Sir,

Your obedient servant,

LEWIS ANGELL, Esq., C.E.,   T. TAYLOR.
   Town Hall, Stratford.

(No. 10.)

RATING AND LOCAL GOVERNMENT BILL.

ENGINEER AND SURVEYOR'S DEPARTMENT,
TOWN HALL, STRATFORD, E.

SIR,   *May* 6, 1871.

In reply to your letter of the 19th ult., requesting me to submit for the consideration of the Secretary of State the additional suggestions referred to in my letter of March 29, I beg to state that a conference of Engineers and Surveyors affected by the proposed Bill has been held at the Institution of Civil Engineers; and taking into consideration the postponement of the consideration of the various Sanitary Acts, &c., we are of opinion that it would be premature to enter at present more fully into matters of detail.

There is, however, one feature in the proposed Bill to which I am desired to draw the attention of the Secretary of State as seriously affecting our interests.

The effect of the proposed Act will be to abolish many important " *established* " paid offices.

Immediately following the schedule, in Clause 18, it is provided that where a parish is co-extensive in area with a Local Government District 'some other authority, viz. Improvement Commissioners, Council or Parochial Board, " *and not a Local Board*, shall be the sanitary authority." In many important districts, West Ham and Tottenham, near London, for example, the local government district *is* co-extensive in area with the parish, consequently, if our reading be correct, the new " *Parochial Board*," and *not* the old established Local Board, " shall be the sanitary authority; " and by Clause 80, Sec. 3, it is provided respecting " All officers whose duties are trans-ferred to the Parochial Board "—" that their offices shall be vacated and cease to exist ; " but under Section 5 of the same clause the new authority " may " grant compensation.

Many Engineers and Surveyors therefore who fill important positions, and have worked hard for many years, will be deprived of office and subjected to the chance of re-election and alteration in salary by a new authority, or left with such uncertain compensation as " may " be granted, while in less important districts, under the schedule, Clause 18, the Local Board and their officers will be continued in authority.

I beg therefore most respectfully to submit, that the provisions of Clause 84, introduced for the protection of those officers who are at present employed at the Central Office, should be extended to any "established paid office " under the existing District Boards, and that Surveyors at present holding office shall, under the new " Sanitary Authority " in the words of Clause 84, " hold their offices by the same tenure, and upon the same terms and conditions, and receive the same salaries as if this Act had not been passed."   And in the event of the abolition of an " established paid office " it would be but a simple act of justice, in accordance with established practice, recognized by the 84th clause of the Bill, that adequate compensation *shall* be made for the loss of office consequent upon the passing of the proposed Act.

The conference were also of opinion that there should be established some recognized standard of remuneration and qualification in the case of all new appointments to the office of Surveyor under the re-constituted sanitary authorities.

In conclusion, I beg to request that my letter of March 29 and the present communication may be read together, and to express the hope that the propositions which we most respectfully submit may receive the favourable consideration of the Secretary of State.

I am, Sir,

Your obedient servant,

LEWIS ANGELL,
Chairman of the Conference of " Local

To TOM TAYLOR, Esq.,   *Surveyors" (April 29, 1871).*
  Local Government Act Office.

(No. 11.)

LOCAL GOVERNMENT ACT OFFICE,
8, RICHMOND TERRACE, WHITEHALL, S.W.
May 9, 1871.

SIR,
        I am directed by the Secretary of State for the Home Department to acknowledge the receipt of your letter of the 6th instant with reference to the " Rating and Local Bill," &c., &c.

I have to state in reply that you will have observed from the reports of the proceedings in Parliament last evening that the "Rating and Local Government Bills" are withdrawn.

I am, Sir,

Your obedient servant,

T. TAYLOR.

To LEWIS ANGELL, Esq.,
  Town Hall, Stratford, E.

*

(No. 12.)

SANITARY LEGISLATION.

ENGINEER AND SURVEYOR'S DEPARTMENT,
TOWN HALL, STRATFORD, LONDON, E.
July 20, 1871.

SIR,
 I am informed that you have charge of a Bill upon the above subject. I was in former correspondence with the Royal Sanitary Commission with regard to the position of local Engineers and Surveyors. I was also in correspondence with the Secretary of State upon Mr. Goschen's Bill.

The Surveyors of the country have (in conference in London) appointed a committee, which I represent, for watching their interests. I trust therefore that the points already submitted to the Secretary of State will have consideration in the proposed measure under your charge.*

I am, Sir,

Your obedient servant,

LEWIS ANGELL.

To the Right Hon. C. B. ADDERLEY, M.P.

(No. 13.)

LOCAL GOVERNMENT BOARD.

INSTITUTION OF CIVIL ENGINEERS,
25, GREAT GEORGE STREET, WESTMINSTER.
July 24, 1871.

SIR,
 As Chairman of a conference of Engineers and Surveyors holding permanent appointments under the Public Health and Local Government Acts, recently held at the Institution of Civil Engineers upon the occasion of the introduction of Mr. Goschen's Bill, I wish to bring under your notice a resolution of the conference that it was the

---

* Sir Charles Adderley introduced into his Bill, 1871, a clause, 57, for the protection of Local Surveyors.

desire of such officers to be brought under similar protection as to their duties and salaries as is at present enjoyed by officers under the Poor Law Board districts. I have only just discovered that the Bill is fixed for committee this evening, but I shall be glad to enter into further explanations.

I am, Sir,

Your obedient servant,

LEWIS ANGELL.

To the Right Hon. J. STANSFELD, M.P.

(No. 14.)

POOR LAW BOARD, WHITEHALL.
July 25, 1871.

SIR,

I am desired by the President of the Poor Law Board to acknowledge the receipt of your letter, dated yesterday.

In reply I am to state that it appears you have not read the Bill introduced by Mr. Stansfeld.

That Bill does not propose to alter the law regarding officers of Local Boards, who are not at all in the same position towards the Home Office as Poor Law officers are towards the Poor Law Board.

Perhaps you will explain more precisely what the officers holding permanent appointments under the Public Health and Local Government Act are desirous of obtaining.

I am, Sir,

Your obedient servant,

L. ANGELL, Esq. C. F. D'ANGERS ORRED.

(No. 15.)

LOCAL GOVERNMENT BOARD.

ENGINEER AND SURVEYOR'S DEPARTMENT,
TOWN HALL, STRATFORD, E.
July 27, 1871.

SIR,

I beg to acknowledge the receipt of your letter of the 25th inst., in reply to my letter of the 24th inst. upon the above subject.

You say that the Bill "does not propose to alter the laws regarding the officers of Local Boards, who are not at all in the same position towards the Home Office as Poor Law officers are towards the Poor Law Board." We entirely agree with the above proposition, and desire that in the proposed legislation we, the officers of Local Boards, may have corresponding advantages, as to protection, as are enjoyed by medical and other officers under the Poor Law. At present we are at the mercy of our Boards in the discharge of important sanitary duties and the enforcement of works which are distasteful to ratepayers, and not unfrequently to interested members of Local Boards, upon whom we depend.

A considerable correspondence has already taken place with the Home Office with reference to Mr. Goschen's late Bill; and Mr. Tom Taylor, in a letter dated April 19, 1871, in reply to my letter (copy enclosed) of March 29, states:

"*I have to inform you that the suggestions contained in your communication have been considered, and are such as may very properly be submitted to the Secretary of State on behalf of the Surveyors employed by Local Boards to the minister or department charged with the preparation of any Bill for carrying out the recommendation of the Sanitary Commissioners.*"

Subsequently, however, I received a communication from the Home Office, May 9, stating that the Bill was withdrawn.

The reasons we have already advanced, the force of which was acknowledged by the Local Government Act Office in the above communication, have, we respectfully submit, equal weight in any new proposal relating to the same subject. We submit that the sanitary laws can never be effectually administered until the sanitary officers are free from undue local influence and intimidation.

I am, Sir,

Your obedient servant,

LEWIS ANGELL,

Chairman of Executive Council, appointed at a Conference of Surveyors (April 29, 1871).

To the President of the Poor Law Board.

——— ———

(No. 16.)

POOR LAW BOARD, WHITEHALL, S.W.
August 11, 1871.

SIR,

I am directed by the Poor Law Board to acknowledge the receipt of your letter of the 27th inst., and to state that the subject to which it relates shall receive due consideration whenever a general measure is prepared in connection with the Report of the Royal Sanitary Commission.

At the same time the Board think it right to state that the Commissioners recommend that the officers of the local authorities should be exclusively appointed and removed by those authorities, with the exceptions that the medical officers should be appointed subject to the veto of the central authority, and should not be removed without the sanction of that authority; and that inspectors of nuisances should be removable either by the central or local authority.

I am, Sir,

Your obedient servant,

H. HENRY,

To Lewis Angell, Esq., M. Inst. C.E.,   *Secretary.*
Town Hall, Stratford, E.

Proposed Sanitary Legislation.

Universities Club, Jermyn Street.
November 29, 1871.

Sir,

Understanding that it is the intention of Her Majesty's Government to re-introduce, during the next session of Parliament, a Bill for amending and consolidating Sanitary Legislation, I beg permission—as Chairman of a Conference of Civil Engineers and Surveyors holding appointments under Local Boards, held at the Institution of Civil Engineers in April last, and as Chairman of the Executive Committee appointed at that Conference—to bring under the consideration of the Local Government Board the following facts:

That in April, 1869, a Royal Commission was issued "to inquire into and report on the operation of the sanitary laws of England and Wales."

That among the various official and representative persons who were invited to give their evidence and opinions before the Commission, as to the practical working of the existing Acts, there was not one Civil Engineer or Surveyor holding office under a Local Board, although there are several hundreds of such officers actively employed throughout the country who have great experience in the details, and are too conscious of the defects of the present arrangements.

That the general experience of such officers is that the duties which they are called upon to perform and enforce are frequently such as are opposed to the prejudices and pecuniary interests of large sections of the ratepayers and of property owners who have influence with or in the Local Board. This fact is recognized by the Sanitary Commission (page 31, Second Report), when referring to "the number of persons interested in offending against sanitary laws, *even amongst those who must constitute chiefly the local authorities.*"

That it is almost impossible for the Surveyor to discharge his duties faithfully and impartially, without giving offence to interested parties; while the prominence of his public position, and the general

R

nature of his duties, especially in connection with a large expenditure upon works from which there is no return, excepting in health and comfort, render him liable to harassing attacks from which he has no protection under existing Acts, and the constantly changing constitution of a Local Board leaves him also without friends.

That in the more important and populous districts the local Surveyor is generally prohibited from the private practice of his profession; hence he may find himself in middle age, driven from office without a practice to fall back upon; and in consequence of the limit of age which Local Boards now impose upon candidates, he will also, notwithstanding his experience, be ineligible for another similar office, and this after the best years of his life have been devoted to the public service in a branch which is under the direction of a great Government Department. At the present time Local Boards have not the power, like other corporate bodies, of granting pensions to their officers. The result is that these appointments are not calculated to either attract or retain the services of qualified Surveyors of character and experience.

That it is due to such officers, so long as their duties are efficiently discharged, that they be protected in their position and emoluments from the consequences of personal malice, local prejudices, and party strife, as is the case in the Department of the Poor Laws under the Local Government Board.

That the recommendation of the Royal Sanitary Commission—" In order that medical officers of health may be able to discharge their duties *without fear of personal loss* they should not be removed from office by any local authority except with the sanction of the central authority "—applies, in our experience, with equal and even greater force to the office of Surveyor. It is through the Surveyor's department that the medical officer must derive much of his information; it is by the Surveyor's department that his recommendations must be carried out. Such an invidious distinction between the two departments must inevitably lead to want of harmony and a divergence of interest and action; the unprotected Surveyor cannot render cordial assistance to the protected medical officer; the obvious *policy* of the Surveyor will be to side with his Board in all points of difference with the medical officer.

The Surveyors are fully conscious of the difficulty as well as the inexpediency of introducing any approach to centralization in connection with local appointments, nor do they desire it. Local Boards will continue to make their own arrangements and select their own officers, subject only that an appointment shall not be rescinded, *nor the salary reduced*, without a good and sufficient reason being submitted to and approved by the Local Government Board.

I beg to enclose a Correspondence which has already taken place with other Departments with reference to the Royal Sanitary Commission and the Bills proposed last session. Your attention is particularly directed to Letter No. 9, wherein the Local Government Act Office recognizes the views advanced on behalf of the local Surveyors. Another recognition was contained in Clause 57 of Sir Charles Adderley's Bill of July last, wherein it was provided that the surveyors should not be removed without the sanction of the central authority.

A small deputation of Surveyors will be glad to have a conference with the Local Government Board to explain more fully the matters herein referred to. I have, therefore, on their behalf, to request that the favour of such an interview be accorded.

In conclusion, I may be permitted to quote the words of the Royal Commission, with which we most fully concur, viz. that sanitary work will not be "active and effective" so long as local officers continue to be "too dependent upon their immediate employers to be thoroughly efficient."

I am, Right Honourable Sir,

Your most obedient servant,

LEWIS ANGELL.

To the Right Hon. J. STANSFELD, M.P.,
  President of the Local Government Board.

EVIDENCE.

EVIDENCE OF SURVEYORS HOLDING OFFICE UNDER LOCAL SANITARY AUTHORITIES.

THE following extracts are taken from a great number of letters received from Surveyors employed under local sanitary authorities, representing districts in all parts of the country, from the largest to the smallest. They all ask for *protection*. The statements were made spontaneously, and many of the letters detail facts of gross personal injustice and public wrong-doing, to the great detriment of sanitary progress. Names, places, and special facts are, for obvious reasons, omitted :

" With twenty years' experience in various parts of the country as a Sanitary Surveyor, I could relate very many instances of injustice, jobbery, favouritism, and evasion of the law. Clever indeed must be the officer who could, through so long a period, escape the consequences of factious clamour, party strife, and personal enmity. The effect of leaving local Surveyors entirely dependent upon local feeling, without power of appeal, is to paralyze their energies, and convert them into mere time-servers ; we cannot afford to quarrel with our bread and butter for the sake of consistency and the public good. A permanent qualified officer has knowledge of the law, of his own duties, and of the special requirements of his district ; his instincts and experience would lead him to act, if protected, with a purpose and with consistency, but a Local Board is ever changing in personality, in views, and in tactics. Our best policy, therefore, is inaction, for no officer can be expected to render active and cordial assistance in carrying out compulsory sanitary legislation so long as he is conscious that his action is opposed to local feeling and the safety of his own position."

" I am perfectly convinced that until Government secures us against local tyranny and oppression, we shall never be in a position to carry out the sanitary measures which may or have become law. No matter what you may think necessary to be done for the sanitary improvement of a place, my experience proves that there is such local influence brought to bear upon you, that in nine cases out of ten the law is null and void, because, however necessary it may be, you dare not carry out its provisions under penalty of dismissal."

" That it is impossible for a Surveyor to carry out faithfully and impartially his numerous duties without giving offence to interested parties is an undoubted fact. We are appointed to carry out most important duties, involving a practical and professional knowledge of all branches of the profession ; and instead of being placed in a position to carry them out without fear or favour, we are subject to the will and caprice of those to whom we may have rendered ourselves obnoxious by the faithful discharge of our duties, and then dismissed at a short notice, without opportunity of appeal, to make room for a more subservient officer, or for another victim to ' local influence.' "

" The duties required to be performed by the Surveyor in almost every instance affect the pecuniary interests of the ratepayers or owners of property, and the effect is that a conscientious and impartial Surveyor is nearly always unpopular. My experience has long shown me that while our local authorities are constituted for the most part of owners and agents of property, there will be comparatively little advance in sanitary improvements, and but a small share of honest dealing and fair play to the local officers engaged in carrying out and enforcing such improvements."

" My experience during twenty years has been that it is absolutely necessary to make the Surveyor independent of the Board in carrying out his duties. No Surveyor, under the present law, will dare to serve a notice on the chairman or other members of the Board unless he is prepared to undergo the most petty annoyances and exactions, until he is *wearied into resigning, as I have done."*

" Ever since I have held office I have felt how insecure my seat has been, and that I am at the mercy of a few capricious people, who, for no fault or error of mine, may at any moment discharge me. It is simply an impossibility for a Surveyor to carry out his multifarious duties impartially without giving offence to some of the ratepayers or members of the Local Board ; *and if you give such offence you are entirely at their mercy."*

" I suppose no official is more subject to unpopularity, or so liable to petty tyranny, as the Surveyor to a Local Board. I have known factious oppositions raised against Surveyors, which have terminated in their removal; and I am of opinion that as much benefit would accrue to the public as to the Surveyors, were they to have the protection of the central authority."

" I consider it an essential measure in the development of sanitary reform that Surveyors employed under the Public Health Acts should be protected in the faithful discharge of their several duties."

" Protection would not only be a personal advantage, but it would also effect a public good by enabling us more faithfully to carry out the objects for which we hold our appointments."

"I am fully convinced that if such protection is given, a much better class of officers would be obtained, and the public become very great gainers. I wonder the Government cannot see that the law would be more fully carried out by giving us such protection."

"The peculiar duties of a Surveyor to a Local Board, if they be honestly discharged, imperatively demand for him protection against the caprices of those possessing fancied grievances, and in whose power he may be placed by the changing character of the body who have control of his position."

" From my own experience I feel the necessity of such a protection, as it frequently happens that a Surveyor in the exercise of his duties not only comes into collision with ratepayers and owners, but with *members* of a Local Board; and it is impossible for him to carry out such duties faithfully and impartially."

" We are at present entirely at the mercy of a clique, by which our tenure of office is rendered most insecure."

" Many a man who wishes to perform his duties honestly and honourably is driven to lend himself to jobbery, through fear of offending an influential member of his Board, and thereby running the risk of dismissal."

"I conceive it is next to impossible that the Surveyor should discharge his duties in a fearless and impartial manner, unless he be a man of iron will and nerve, and of means independent of the salary received from his Board."

" I have held the position of Surveyor to the ——— Local Board for seven years, and am at this time the *most unpopular man in its service.* It is to me a source of constant regret that I have been able to do so little for the sanitary improvement of the district."

" In consequence of the extraordinary treatment I have received from the Local Board at ——— I have *resigned my appointment.*"

"I have long felt the need of some protection, so that we are not subject to the whims and caprices of a certain class of men who generally constitute Local Boards. I have had a great deal to put up with lately." (*Since resigned.*)

" I am ruled by a Board of the strangest and most unreasonable body of men in existence : they tell me I must either submit or go about my business. I have been badgered and bullied by them beyond description."

. " Members of a Board of Health will drive away any Surveyor who does his duty fearlessly, but not satisfactorily to some one or two members who can often lead a whole Board. I *was* Surveyor to the ——— Local Board, therefore I can speak from my own experience."

" During my two years' employment here as the first Surveyor appointed since the adoption of the Local Government Acts, my experience has been that the opposition and animosity I have endured from some quarters have varied in the exact ratio of my activity in carrying out certain provisions of the Acts."

" It is almost an impossibility for a Surveyor to perform his duties impartially. I have been in public offices for fifteen years, and *have always been hampered* in my desire to carry out sanitary improvement, from the want of a shield from private clamour."

" Town Surveyors should not be subject to the vagaries of Local Boards, which, I am sorry to say, are becoming very common, should an officer carry out his duties strictly and impartially."

" The Surveyor renders himself very unpopular if he evinces any energy in carrying out the sanitary requirements in his district."

" My experience is that the most scrupulous and conscientious Surveyor may have the most numerous opponents."

" In Wales especially your action will not be appreciated, for of all parts I have been located in, nowhere is protection more needed."

" In carrying out my duties (Wales) I am frequently attacked, not only by ratepayers, but by members of the Local Board."

" Owners of small properties and tenements not unfrequently take an active part in politics and local affairs, and are sometimes members of corporations and Local Boards."

" Some of the members of the Local Board here are owners of house property in the town in the worst possible sanitary condition, and are, consequently, always opposed to the enforcement of sanitary matters. *These men have much power on the Board* and in the town, and the Surveyor cannot possibly act freely in the present state of things."

" I can say from experience that it is requisite that something should be done for the protection of Surveyors to Local Boards from the undue influence of ratepayers."

" I have been Surveyor to a large borough several years.   I found the town in a most deplorable condition; the corporation, being in a difficulty, treated me very well.   I designed and carried out their drainage works, and the death-rate was reduced to less than 20 in the 1000. *Great changes have since taken place;* inferior men have made their way into the Council; the result is a complete system of annoyance to the officers who desire to carry out the Sanitary Acts. Do-nothing members of my Board obstruct me all they can in my duty. I am convinced there is only one way of improving the health of towns, viz. *by protecting the executive officers.* Government inspection now and then will not do it."

" I hope you will be able to do something to protect us against the caprices of interested and meddling local grumblers, who have nothing better to do than annoy public officers in the discharge of their important duties.   We should be placed in the same position as Poor Law officers, who cannot be dismissed without the approval of the Poor Law Board."

ON THE COMPARATIVE MOR-

By Dr. B.

TABLE OF MORTALITY PER 1000 INHABITANTS FROM ALL CAUSES AND
DURING THE TWENTY YEARS,

REGISTRATION DISTRICT.	Decades. 1851 to 1860. 1861 to 1870.	Death-rate from all Causes.	Fever (Typhus of Registrar-General).	Diarrhœa and Cholera.	Diph-theria.
Twelve Healthy Rural Districts	51 to 60 61 to 70	17·1 17·4	·6 ·59	·4 ·38	·18 ·22
England and Wales ..	51 to 60 61 to 70	22· 22·4	·91 ·88	1·08 1·08	·1 ·18
London	51 to 60 61 to 70	23·7 24·3	·85 ·89	1·5 1·29	·08 ·18
Bristol (Parish) ..	51 to 60 61 to 70	26·9 26·9	·95 ·93	1·3 1·2	·07 ·18
Liverpool	51 to 60 61 to 70	33·3 38·6	1·35 3·1	2·9 2·9	·05 :17
Manchester	51 to 60 61 to 70	31·5 32·8	1·25 1·7	2·4 2·6	·04 ·16
Leeds	51 to 60 61 to 70	27·7 29·8	1·1 1·4	2·25 2·37	·05 ·13
Sheffield	51 to 60 61 to 70	28·4 29·	1·3 1·4	2·2 2·1	·2 ·19
Birmingham (Parish)	51 to 60 61 to 70	26·5 26·6	1· ·79	2·2 2·	·07 ·34

TALITY OF LARGE TOWNS.

FOSTER.

CERTAIN SPECIAL CAUSES IN BIRMINGHAM, AND EIGHT OTHER DISTRICTS, 1851 TO 1860, AND 1861 TO 1870.

Scarla-tina.	Total Zymotic death-rate.	Proportion of deaths from each cause to deaths from all causes.		Under 5 Years.			15 to 55 Years.	
		Zymotic per cent.	Diarrhœa per cent.	All Causes.	Diarrhœa &c.	Lung Disease, excluding Phthisis.	Phthisis.	Other Lung Disease.
·53	2·9	17·	2·3	38·8	1·4	6·6	3·2	·7
·45	..	..	2·2	38·7	1·6	5·8	3·	·8
·87	4·95	22·5	4·9	67·6	5·2	9·1	3·8	1·
·97	..	..	4·8	68·3	5·9	11·	3·7	1·1
·93	6·1	25·7	6·3	78·	7·1	14·7	3·9	1·3
1·14	..	..	5·3	81·6	7·5	15·	4·	1·4
·98	5·75	21·4	4·8	88·1	7·7	17·1	4·5	1·4
1·27	..	..	4·4	90·2	7·2	15·5	4·1	1·6
1·5	9·4	28·2	8·7	132·	16·2	24·8	5·3	2·6
1·47	..	..	7·5	139·5	17·	24·2	5·7	3·5
1·5	8·	25·5	7·6	117·2	15·8	17·6	5·1	2·4
1·56	..	..	7·9	111·8	17·1	17·9	5·	2·7
·97	6·8	24·5	8·1	102·7	13·	17·3	3·9	2·
1·26	..	..	7·9	104·6	15·2	18·9	4·	2·3
1·24	7·9	27·8	7·7	100·2	11·5	15·9	4·3	1·6
1·42	..	..	7·2	99·	12·4	18·5	4·	1·8
1·06	7·15	27·	8·3	94·4	12·9	17·	3·9	1·5
1·32	6·98	26·3	7·5	94·	12·8	16·5	4·	1·5

SEWER VENTILATION.

By E. B. Ellice-Clark.

REPLIES FROM TOWNS.

TOWN.	What system is your town drained under—small pipe, or otherwise?	What is the nature of the outfall?	Are your sewers ventilated? and if so, what description of ventilation, and distance apart?
ASHTON - UNDER - LYNE.	Most generally brick sewers, but house drains all socket pipe; brick sewers from 2 to 5 feet diameter.	The river Tame, which is about 290 ft. at its highest point, and 250 ft. above mean-water level.	Ventilated by drop spouts only, which all communicate with the sewer.
ACTON	Otherwise.	An open sewer in the Metropolitan district.	Yes; Brooks's.
BACUP	Our main sewers are of various sizes, viz. 3 ft. by 2 ft., 30 in. by 20 in., and 24 in. barrel sewer, all in brickwork. The branch sewers are formed of pipes, varying in size, from 9 in. up to 21 in. in diameter.	At our outfall, we have constructed subsidence tanks, provided with filters or strainers charged with coke and charcoal, through which the sewage passes, and the effluent water is discharged into the river Irwell at a point about a quarter of a mile below the tanks. We are never troubled with back water, however high the river rises.	I have ventilated all our sewers. I have used various kinds of ventilators for experiment, viz. Clark's of Carlisle, Brooks's of Huddersfield, Haworth's Archimedean-screw ventilator, and Baldwin Latham's spiral ventilator. All the above, except the "screw," are charcoal ventilators. Clark's ventilators consist of a perforated cast-iron basket filled with charcoal, and placed in the manholes so that the gases in passing through the perforations are brought in contact with the charcoal; after which they pass into the open air. Brooks's ventilators are similar to Clark's in principle, the charcoal being placed on a wire tray, through which the gases pass, and they are mostly used at the top end of pipe sewers, or in lamp-holes. I have discontinued the use of these two ventilators some time since, as I consider them useless as ventilators. I have used Latham's spiral ventilators, and I consider them the best charcoal ventilators at present before the public. At the top end of all my pipe sewers, I put in an Archimedean - screw ventilator, and I may state that I find them to answer very well. I place my ventilators 60 yards apart.
BURY	The main sewers are made of bricks; the minor sewers are tile sewers, varying in size from 21 in. to 12 in. diameter.	We have two outfalls: one into the river Roch, and the other into the river Irwell.	Only by the gully girds in the street. I use very few traps.

SEWER VENTILATION.

By E. B. Ellice-Clark.

REPLIES FROM TOWNS.

Have you used charcoal ventilation in any form? if so, with what result?	Give me the size, gradient, and length of a sewer ventilated, and the results?	Have any experiments been made by you to obtain the velocity of air in sewers, or the compound gases? if so, will you state them?	If your outfall is a tidal one, is it tide-locked at high water?
No.	See 3. Our minimum fall is 1 in 90, and about 1¼ mile long, 4 ft. by 4 ft. 6 in. drain. Our minimum fall will be 1 in 144, and often 1 in 36.	No.	Not tidal, being 250 ft. above the tidal-wave.
Yes. No good.		No.	No.
Yes; in the form described in No. 3. The result of my experience I sum up as follows: Charcoal ventilators to be of any use must be completely protected from the weather, and the basket containing the charcoal must be constructed so as to prevent the charcoal becoming consolidated by the tremulous motion caused by the heavy traffic passing over the streets. Latham's ventilators comply with these conditions better than any I have seen, and they have given me great satisfaction.	Six months ago I completed a brick sewer, 1000 yards in length, 480 yards 3 ft. by 2 ft., and 520 yards 30 in. by 20 in.; gradient 1 in 81·75. The air is kept continually in motion by the ventilators, and the sewer is comparatively quite pure or free from bad gases. The ventilators are Latham's.	No; I have not.	Our outfall is not a tidal one.
Never used them.		No.	No.

TOWN.	What system is your town drained under—small pipe, or otherwise?	What is the nature of the outfall?	Are your sewers ventilated? and if so, what description of ventilation, and distance apart?
BRADFORD	Large brick main sewers, smaller brick street sewers, and earthenware pipe drains for houses. Sizes of main sewers vary from 8 ft. 6 in. diameter to 2 ft. 6 in. by 1 ft. 6 in.; street sewers, from 2 ft. 6 in. by 1 ft. 6 in. to 2 ft. by 1 ft. 3 in.; house drains, 9 in. diameter to 4 in. diameter.	A stream in the valley below the town, called the Bradford Beck, a tributary of the river Aire.	The sewers are ventilated by means of vertical pipe shafts and open grates at the street surface, by means of the rain spouts of buildings, by untrapped gully grates in the streets, and in one case by a shaft 50 feet high at the upper extremity of a long line of main, forming a complete opening from the end of the sewer, and conveying any vapours to a height above the surrounding houses.
BIRKENHEAD.. ..	Brick and pipe sewers.	Tidal.	Yes; by vertical shafts, as per accompanying plans; about 60 to 120 yards apart.
BLACKBURN	Brick main sewers, 6 ft. by 4 ft. to 2 ft. diameter; pipe tributary mains from 21 in. to 9 in. diameter. Provision made in several places in the town for the discharge of sewer water direct into the river. In the house drainage not a single house is connected direct with the sewer.	A small river.	Yes. The fall of the sewers being very great, the velocity of the sewage carries all with it. I do not see any necessity for artificial ventilation. The end of each tributary main is connected with the street by an open grate; all other mains have also an open connection at each manhole, by which we have obtained a constant current of air through them.
BARNSLEY	All drains under and inclusive of 15 in. diameter are pipe; all above this size and up to 7 ft. diameter are in brick with glazed inverts, varied of course in thickness.	By open channel into the river Drarue for about half a mile in length; but a Bill is now pending in Chancery calling upon us to adopt some means of purification previous to entering same.	Most of our sewers are ventilated with Brooks's patent charcoal ventilators, and in one or two cases by a method of my own. Brooks's patent acts extremely well, and the gases remaining in the sewers (if any at all) are very slight. Placed about every 100 yards in highest levels.
BOLTON	The sewers of Bolton are constructed to receive both storm-water and sewage; storm overflows being provided at all available points.	The sewage is intercepted from the river in its course through the town, and discharged into it above flood level at the extremity of the borough.	The sewers are not efficiently ventilated, but we are now engaged upon that work. The ventilators are perforated oviform grates, and are placed about 100 yards apart.

Have you used charcoal ventilation in any form? if so, with what result?	Give me the size, gradient, and length of a sewer ventilated, and the results?	Have any experiments been made by you to obtain the velocity of air in sewers, or the compound gases? if so, will you state them?	If your outfall is a tidal one, is it tide-locked at high water?
No.	All the sewers are ventilated. The vertical shafts and grates are about 100 yards apart. The results are much more sentimental than real. The question is one about which an alarming quantity of twaddle has been written and talked.	No.	
Yes; satisfactory.	A main brick sewer, from 4 ft. by 2 ft. 8 in. to 3 ft. 9 in. by 2 ft. 6 in., with gradients of 1 in 300 and 1 in 68; about 690 yards of each size in length, with satisfactory results. *Vide* Dr. Corfield's 'Digestry Facts relating to the Treatment and Utilization of Sewage.'	Yes. *Vide* accompanying paper.	Yes.
All are provided with arrangements for fixing charcoal ventilators, if found requisite.	See above.	No.	No.
See above.	2 ft. 6 in. diameter in the centre of the town; 1 in 60. The neighbourhood in which this sewer is situate is densely populated, and all sinks trapped, and the inhabitants are tolerably healthy from the fact of the ventilator having acted satisfactorily and efficiently.	No.	See No. 2. The river Drarue is not a tidal river.
No; as we do not appear to require them.	The sewers of Bolton have an average gradient of 1 in 150, and are self-cleansing. The result of the ventilation, so far as we have gone, appears to be quite satisfactory.	Have not made any such experiments.	Outfall is not a tidal one.

TOWN.	What system is your town drained under—small pipe, or otherwise?	What is the nature of the outfall?	Are your sewers ventilated? and if so, what description of ventilation, and distance apart?
BARROW - IN - FUR-NESS.	Main sewers of brickwork; tributaries, pipes from 18 in. downwards.	Outfall tidal locked for about three hours out of twelve.	I am remodelling the sewer-age system, which was ventilated by a few street gratings only. I use my own patent in all new works that I construct, placing the ventilators at distances varying from 100 to 150 yards, according to circumstances.
BIRMINGHAM .	Combined system of brick and pipe; sizes vary from 5 ft. 9 in. by 3 ft. 6 in. to 9 in. pipes.	There are two outfalls, 5 ft. 9 in. by 3 ft. 6 in. each, and one 3 ft. 6 in. by 2 ft. 6 in., which discharge into the rivers Rea and Cole, both small streams and tributaries of the river Tame.	Yes; by means of shafts carried from crowns of sewers to surfaces of roads generally speaking; in some instances down spouts are used. Distances vary very much.
COLCHESTER	Part small pipe, and part brick sewer.	Tidal river.	No.
CHICHESTER	No system of drainage.		
COVENTRY	Brick sewers principally, but about four or five miles of pipe sewers have been laid by land societies.	The outfall is at present through rough filtering tanks into a small river, called the Shabourne, but very complete filtration and deposition works are being erected.	The sewers are ventilated by being connected with engine stacks, of which we have about seventeen in the city; also by down spouts from houses, No. 1230.
CHATHAM, EXTRA..	Surface water drainage only. We have two sewers—the high level, egg-shape, 3 ft. 9 in. by 2 ft. 6 in.; and the low level, 3 ft. by 2 ft. 3 in.	Both sewers empty themselves into a chamber on the quay, and from these it is conveyed to low-water mark by iron pipe 15 in. diameter. The low-level sewer has a pen-stock, which shuts down to keep the tide from flowing up; and when the tide has receded, it is opened. One man is paid extra to attend to it night or day, according to the tides. The high level is above high-water mark, and empties itself at all times.	They were ventilated by small pipes brought up to the centre of the roads, and covered by an iron grating, which was very objectionable, and I have done away with them in most cases.
CHELMSFORD	Small glazed stoneware pipe drains.	A sewage well, from whence the sewage is raised and pumped on to land.	Not systematically ventilated; only at places by means of rain-water pipes.
EALING	Both pipe and brick. Pipes from 12 in. to 18 in.; brick, from 2 ft. circle to 3 ft. 6 in. by 2 ft. 3 in., egg-shape: in all, about 13 miles.	Effluent water from works passes into small stream, thence into Thames.	Charcoal baskets in man-holes, about ten to the mile; also rain - water pipes, where they can be obtained, above roof of house.
EASTBOURNE.. ..	Brick sewers, 5 ft. 6 in. by 3 ft. 6 in.; and subsidiary drains, 12 in. glazed pipes.	The sewage is carried three miles from the town, and discharged by a 3-foot iron pipe into the sea.	The sewers are ventilated by cast-iron open ventilators immediately over the sewers, 100 yards apart. The ventilators are made to contain charcoal, but none is at present used.

Have you used charcoal ventilation in any form? if so, with what result?	Give me the size, gradient, and length of a sewer ventilated, and the results?	Have any experiments been made by you to obtain the velocity of air in sewers, or the compound gases? if so, will you state them?	If your outfall is a tidal one, is it tide-locked at high water?
See enclosed description.	My main outfall is 3 ft. 4 in. by 2 ft. 6 in.; slope from 1 in 700 to 1 in 1000. At present there is a considerable draught through this sewer, but no sewage has yet been admitted.	I have not yet made any experiments, but propose doing so.	See answer to No. 2.
Not on any scale worth speaking of.	Our sewers vary in gradients from 1 in 12 to 1 in 980. The men find no difficulty in working in same.	No.	It is not tidal, but the whole sewage is discharged by gravitation into the streams named.
No.	.. ..	No	No.
No.	.. ..	No.	No.
No.	3 ft. 9 in. by 2 ft. 6 in.; gradient, 1 in 660. ¼ of a mile we get deposits of heavy sand and flint at the connections from the different hills, which we are obliged to remove twice a year.	None.	See above.
Only by way of experiment. Not satisfactory, to my mind. Emits much smell at times.			
Yes. Very fair results when kept dry.	.. ..	No.	No.
We have used charcoal, but find, after it has been placed in the boxes a few hours, it becomes useless.	Our sewers have many different gradients, and I have made no particular experiments in any particular part.	No.	Yes,

S

TOWN.	What system is your town drained under—small pipe, or otherwise?	What is the nature of the outfall?	Are your sewers ventilated? and if so, what description of ventilation, and distance apart?
FOLKESTONE	Glazed pipes are used for all drains up to and including 24 in. in diameter. The large main sewers are constructed with bricks; they are egg-shaped, 4 ft. 6 in. by 3 ft.	The outfall is to the eastward of the town, and is carried out to low-water mark, ordinary tides, by iron pipes. The set of the tide at this point is always eastward; therefore the sewage is carried away to sea without in any way becoming a nuisance to the town.	Yes. The whole of the sewers are ventilated, either by charcoal ventilators or stack pipes. Two of the main sewers are open at the upper ends, which terminate clear of houses, and through which a good and constant stream of water is always flowing. The ventilators used for the centre of the roads are somewhat similar to the Hastings ones, which I understand Ramsgate has adopted. I also construct my gullies in manner suitable to be used for the purposes of ventilation with charcoal. I have over 100 of them in operation: they answer the purpose well. I have not adopted any definite distance apart, but place them according to circumstances, not exceeding 100 yards.
GRAVESEND	No system of drainage.		
HUDDERSFIELD ..	We have many descriptions of sewers, varying from 3 ft. diameter downwards. We have earthenware tubes 3 ft. diameter, but I do not like them. For large sewers, bricks are much better.	We have several outlets into the river Holme, and have not as yet laid down one general intercepting sewer and outfall.	Our sewers are (in all new works) ventilated with Brooks's, patent charcoal ventilators, and they answer very well.
HARTLEPOOL.. ..	Small-pipe system.	Sea-shore, subject to rise and fall of tide.	Ventilated by rain-water pipes.
IPSWICH	Our drainage cannot be designated as a system at all; the town is, practically speaking, not drained at all. We have in out-streets old sewers, some of which are pipes and others bricks, which carry off about one third of the sewage of the town, and empty it into the river Orwell. We have now under our consideration a complete plan for perfecting the sewerage of the whole borough, and disposing of it by irrigation, or what is better known as intermittent filtration, which is a modification of wide irrigation.	The outfall of our present sewers is direct into the river Orwell, at the docks.	Our sewers are not ventilated by any properly designed means.

Have you used charcoal ventilation in any form? if so, with what result?'	Give me the size, gradient, and length of a sewer ventilated, and the results?	Have any experiments been made by you to obtain the velocity of air in sewers, or the compound gases? if so, will you state them?	If your outfall is a tidal one, is it tide-locked at high water?
Yes; as above described.	A 2-ft. glazed pipe, with a gradient of 1 in 75, and 1000 yards in length. Ventilated as above with fourteen ventilators. Very satisfactory.	No experiments have been made.	It is a tidal one, but not tide-locked at high water. The tide is allowed to flow up the sewer, an air-shaft being erected for the purpose of relieving the same from any extra pressure, besides the two open ends, as mentioned above.
We have, and with beneficial results; but my notion is that any method of ventilation which requires looking after is bad, and that the best means is by tall pipes or chimney-stacks, wherever practicable.	I have a sewer lately put down of 2 ft. circular earthenware tubes in four gradients, 1 in 60, 1 in 42, 1 in 179, and 1 in 38, with one ventilator at the end; and in changing the charcoal once in six weeks or two months, we have found no perceptible effluvia, though the sewer is 2330 feet in length; but this is ventilated as often as practicable with up full pipes.	No.	Our river is not a tidal one.
No.	.. ..	No.	Yes.
I have used charcoal ventilators, but not with the sewers of this town; and my opinion is, to make them effective, they must be at very frequent intervals, and arranged in the shafts so that the charcoal cannot be affected by the rain water. The result of charcoal ventilators, so far as my experience goes, is that they must be fixed throughout in every line of sewer in a system of drainage at not less than 300 feet apart. I like to ventilate into chimney-shafts, where it can be done.	I cannot do so, as there is no sewer here which would give the results and information you want.	I have made no experiments of this kind.	It is a tidal one, and is locked by the tide during two thirds of the rise and fall of the tide.

TOWN.	What system is your town drained under—small pipe, or otherwise?	What is the nature of the outfall?	Are your sewers ventilated? and if so, what description of ventilation, and distance apart?
KINGSTON	Sewers of average capacity.	The Thames, above Teddington Lock.	Partially.
LOWESTOFT	There are four main sewers discharging into as many outfalls. The first is of earthenware pipes, 2 ft. internal diameter, terminating with iron pipes of the same diameter, which convey the sewage into the sea at the Ness Point. The second is 3 ft. 4½ in. by 2 ft. 3 in., egg-shaped: this discharges into tidal water. ~~The other two are~~ 18 in. brick-barrel drains: these also discharge into tidal water. The lateral and subordinate drains vary from 2 ft. 3 in. by 1 ft. 6 in. egg-shaped, to 18 in. brick-barrel, and from 18 in. to 12 in. glazed pipe drains.		No. The subject was under consideration at the time of H.R.H. the Prince of Wales's illness, but since then nothing has been done. I am, however, going to introduce the question, feeling sure that it is one of paramount importance.
LEEDS..	Sewers of all sizes, from 8 ft. diameter to 9 in.	Into a river.	Yes. There are about 500 ventilating shafts, but every gully is also made a ventilator by cutting an aperture in the dip-stone at the top; so that, although the silt is excluded, the gas escapes. There are not any complaints, and no nuisance is experienced, on account, probably, of the very large number, viz. about 10,000.
LEICESTER	Brick sewers, from 5 ft. diameter to 18 in. and 12 in. pipes; side drains from private property, 12 in., 9 in., and 6 in. pipes.	Into an engine well, from which all the sewage is raised 20 feet by pumping-engines into tanks, where the solid matter is precipitated by admixture of lime, and the *effluent water* turned into the river.	Many of our sewers are ventilated by connections to engine-boiler shafts. We have also many open ventilating gratings in the middle of roads, not at any regular distances.
LEAMINGTON.. ..	Main sewers, brick culverts, the largest 4 ft. by 2 ft. 8 in.; side sewers, earthenware pipes, 15 in. down to 9 in. diameter.	A large reservoir, a pumping station, and a sewage farm.	Yes. Ventilating manhole covers at irregular distances.
NOTTINGHAM ..	We have various sizes of sewers, from 9 in. pipe to 7 ft. 6 in. by 5 ft., and 9 ft. by 7 ft. 3 in.	The outfalls deliver into the river Trent below the town, at mean summer level of water. One outfall is 7 ft. 6 in. by 5 ft., the other 9 ft. by 7 ft. 3 in.	Yes. A small shaft is constructed at side of ordinary manhole shafts. In the side of the latter is an opening 1 ft. 6 in. by 1 ft. 6 in., through which the sewer gases escape and go up the side shaft. They are ordinarily about 80 yards apart.

Have you used charcoal ventilation in any form? if so, with what result?	Give me the size, gradient, and length of a sewer ventilated, and the results?	Have any experiments been made by you to obtain the velocity of air in sewers, or the compound gases? if so, will you state them?	If your outfall is a tidal one, is it tide-locked at high water?
Latham's, and Burton, Sons, and Walter's charcoal ventilators.			
No; only a few.	.. ..	.. ..	The sewer is only full at the outfall during floods. Very shortly all the sewage will be pumped into tanks, to be treated by the A B C process works, nearly completed.
The summit ends of sewers generally are furnished with charcoal tray ventilators, which are removed when the sewers are flushed, the ventilating pipe being used as a flush pipe.	The sizes of sewers vary as above described; the gradients vary from 1 in 800 to 1 in 100. The effect of the ventilation is to reduce the pressure of sewer gases in house drains.	No experiments have been made.	Our outfall described above.
Yes. In the manhole covers, where there is heavy traffic the charcoal gets clogged; where the traffic is light, it remains good for about six months. The sewers are sufficiently ventilated to be entered at any time without danger.	Brick culvert, egg-shaped, 3 ft. 9 in. by 2 ft. 6 in.; gradient 1 in 1000.; length 3420 ft. Eight manholes with ventilating covers. Result: can be entered at any time without danger. The manholes have dip holes for catching grit and other heavy matter, and these are emptied every three months.	No.	See No. 2. The outlet is never closed.
We originally used charcoal in the openings at side of manhole shafts, but as they impede the ventilation, we have abandoned them.	The sizes and gradients vary. Have never had any serious complaints as to any nuisance caused by the ventilators.	No.	Our outfalls are not tidal, but the river is subject to very heavy floods.

TOWN.	What system is your town drained under—small pipe, or otherwise?	What is the nature of the outfall?	Are your sewers ventilated? and if so, what description of ventilation, and distance apart?
NORTHAMPTON ..	By brick; 3 ft. oval brick culverts, cement lined.	Into sewage tanks; thence by culvert, four miles, to irrigation farm, with a gradient of 1 ft. in a mile (by gravitation).	By open gratings in centre of roadway, about 60 yards apart; but many of the old sewers have not yet been ventilated completely.
OXFORD	About two thirds of the town is drained into the rivers and streams, the remainder into cesspools. Such sewers as exist are principally of brick, and for the most part very inefficient, on account of defective construction, insufficient fall, and the entire absence of any means of flushing.	The outfalls are into the streams, as above.	There is no ventilation whatever.
PORTSMOUTH.. ..	Brick and pipe. No sewer less than 12 in. pipes; no pipe sewer more than 15 in. diameter.	Into the sea.	By charcoal baskets inserted in the side of manholes, about 100 to 150 yards apart, but dependent on circumstances.
PLYMOUTH	The main sewers and all street drains in Plymouth are built with circular tile bottom; sewers nearly egg-shaped. House drains are all earthenware pipes, not less than 8 in. in bore. Closets to each house supplied with water. No privies are allowed, or any refuse allowed to be collected on the premises longer than two days.	The whole of the sewage is discharged into the sea under water, consequently it is deodorized by salt water, and no nuisance by smell. Formerly, the sewage was discharged on the beach, and very offensive.	The sewers are ventilated by chimneys or shafts into or adjoining house chimneys, where an opportunity occurs. No regular distance has been considered, and very few persons know where they exist, so as to prevent prejudice or imagination from being injurious to the residental property.

REMARKS.— I find the ventilating shafts of the sewers of Plymouth, near the outfall, carry off the foul gases, but the others in the streets take pure air into the sewers. The cold air above rushes after the warmer air below, and mixes with the gases in the sewers.

I have never measured the velocity of air or sewage in any of the sewers, but I find the air in the sewers at the highest point is free from any obnoxious smell; and when I construct any more new ventilating shafts, they shall be made wide at the top, to admit as much pure air as possible, and small at the bottom, so as to increase the velocity of air, as well as the velocity of the sewage.

I may remark that all house drains should have a syphon between the house and the main sewer, so as to prevent the gases in the cold sewer rushing through the pipe-drain into the heated chambers within the inhabited premises.

| RUGBY .. .. .. | Pipes, from 9 in. to 24 in. | Screening tanks, for the purpose of intercepting the solid matter before the sewage flows into the land for irrigation. | Yes. Latham's patent. Distance from 100 to 200 yards. |

Have you used charcoal ventilation in any form? if so, with what result?	Give me the size, gradient, and length of a sewer ventilated, and the results?	Have any experiments been made by you to obtain the velocity of air in sewers, or the compound gases? if so, will you state them?	If your outfall is a tidal one, is it tide-locked at high water?
The ventilators are provided with cages for charcoal to be used in cases of emergency, but for ordinary use, as the charcoal impedes free vent, we do not use it.	Our town rises abruptly from the river, so that the gradients are rapid, generally, with some exceptions, in which the streets contour the hill side. Our worst is for a mile, 1 in 700, running parallel with the river at the foot of the hill. This is an insufficient affair, and will be some day reconstructed.	I have instituted no experiments on this subject.	No. Our outfall vents free into the tanks, but in time of storm, owing to the very rapid fall of all the culverts, and its general level below the river, the bottom or intercepting sewer becomes filled, and overflows by means of a storm outfall into the river.
I have now commenced an entirely new system of sewage for the whole of the district, with manholes, ventilators, flushing-shafts, &c. On an average, there will be an opening at the surface, in the centre of the roads, at about every 100 yards. I do not propose using charcoal or other disinfectant. In one or two cases, where the heads of sewers will be in confined places, I may probably carry pipes to the tops of houses.	.. ..	.. ..	No.
Quite satisfactory, if removed when requisite.	Out of 60 miles of sewers, our gradients vary from 6 in. in a mile to 1 in 150 all.	No.	Yes.
Never used charcoal; but my opinion is, that charcoal will only absorb to a certain extent, and the cleaning or renewing charcoal traps would be very obnoxious, and the cure more injurious than the disease.	Our main sewer is about 2 miles in length; at the outfall, 6 ft. by 3 ft. 6 in.; at the summit, 2 ft. 6 in. by 2 feet. The gradients for 1 mile, 1 in 100; for ¼ mile, 1 in 300; and near the outfall, 1 in 500 for ¼ mile. Another main sewer, about 1 mile in length, the greatest portion through the streets, about the level of the sea, and where the sea flowed 100 years ago; this portion is 6 ft. by 3 ft. 6 in., so that a man can walk through it and prevent any accumulation which may be caused by heavy rains and the washing of macadamized roads. These sewers discharge into covered catch-pits or reservoirs, which are discharged with the tide by self-acting valves.	.. ..	The outfalls are tide-locked only when very high tides, or during a storm; but we have reservoirs at two main outlets, with self-acting valves, and penstock at the very bottom, which is opened two hours after the tide begins to ebb.
Yes, and with good results, provided the charcoal is carefully placed in the basket; if not, the gases are obstructed.	Size, 15 in. and 18 in.; gradient, 1 in 200; length of sewer, about 200 yards.		

TOWN.	What system is your town drained under—small pipe, or otherwise?	What is the nature of the outfall?	Are your sewers ventilated? and if so, what description of ventilation, and distance apart?
SOUTHPORT	We have 24 miles of main sewers; one mile of which is 3 ft. diameter of 9 in. brickwork, the remainder are pipes from 12 in. to 24 in. diameter.	We have three outfalls: one of the older portion into the sea; two flow into a brook, that formed our boundary in land, emptying into the sea, four miles from our boundary,	We have four ventilators to steam-engine chimneys, and the gas chimney, each 6 in. diameter, from our main sewers. Not at any regular distance. 25 in. by 4 in. pipes to high gables, and all the houses built since 1871 have a 2-in. pipe to the highest part of the roof.
SHEFFIELD	Some of the larger drains are circular, but the great majority are egg-shape.	Into the river Don, at several points.	No, except through the manholes and street grates.
STOCKTON-ON-TEES	From large egg-shaped brick sewers down to 9-in. diameter pipes.	Tidal river.	Not uniformly so; chiefly by the down pipes.
	REMARKS.—The corporation are waiting for legislation on town sewage, before they spend reconstruction, that means of ventilation should receive as careful consideration as the plicated. Plain shafts under a regular system would be ample.		
SALFORD	Previous to my appointment here, small - pipe drains. I use from 6 in. to 30 in. by 27 in.* pipes. The main sewer, which I commenced about nine months ago, is equal to a circle 8 ft. 6 in. diameter.	.. ..	My report for ventilating sewers is before our council. At present, I am ventilating by direct openings, similar to London.
ST. HELENS	Having no main arterial sewer in this town (St. Helens), the drains, or sewers, are in one or two cases, are ventilated by means of the tall chimneys of the larger works; sites are ventilated simply by means of open grids at the junctions of streets, or open now, I believe, being adopted by Liverpool and Manchester. We never believe in		
STOCKPORT	Brick and pipe sewers, varying from 4 ft. by 2 ft. 8 in.; 2 feet circular in brick, and from 2 ft. to 4 in. in pipes; socket jointed and circular.	Several outfalls into the river Mersey. The new system all arranged to come to one outlet, and either to filtrate or irrigate: not yet decided.	All new sewers, both by special ventilators, and all down pipes for rain water, connected direct to the sewers. No given distance apart. I have recently had eight Archimedian ventilators fixed at side of buildings, in 6-in. iron socket pipes, and they answer very well.
WARWICK	Small pipe sewers.	Deposits in tank, from whence it is pumped out on irrigation farm.	No, excepting outfall.

Have you used charcoal ventilation in any form? if so, with what result?	Give me the size, gradient, and length of a sewer ventilated, and the results?	Have any experiments been made by you to obtain the velocity of air in sewers, or the compound gases? if so, will you state them?	If your outfall is a tidal one, is it tide-locked at high water?
No.	As they are at irregular distances, I cannot give the information. What I name above are a success.	No.	The outlet to the Irish Sea is tide-locked at high water; the other two outlets are not. There are tidal sluices at the outlet of the brook.
No.	None.	No, I should think it much depends on direction of air currents and size and gradient of sewer.	No.
No.	None.	No.	There are two outfalls: one is at high water; the other is tide-locked a short time.

anything on ventilation. My own opinion is, that in all new systems of sewerage and laying out of the sewerage. I have no faith in charcoal and such like: it is ever com-

I used these, when in Leeds, for some years; also as above described.	* This would take more time than I have at my disposal for collating the information you require.	I have found sewer gas to leave at the rate of about 500 feet per minute.	The outfalls are some fifty into the river Irwell. I am now carrying out works to intercept the whole into our main arterial sewer, to discharge the refuse about 1¼ mile below the town.

discharged direct into the Sankey, which flows through the town. Our main sewers, and in situations where there are no such chimneys, the systems of sewers in elevated places, sufficiently distant from windows and doors of dwelling-houses. This system is charcoal ventilation, and consequently never used same in any form.

Used in a few manholes, but do not think much of them. The surface gratings easily choke upon macadamized roads, and I find they require a deal of attention, and some cease to act.	24-in. and 21-in. pipes; 1900 yards long; gradients various, from 1 in 50 to 1 in 184, with eight ventilators, mentioned in No. 3.	No.	No.
Yes; but I consider the charcoal soon loses its qualities.	.. ..	No.	Not a tidal outfall, but in consequence of the reservoir bottom being on the same level as the sewer, it has every night about 9 feet head upon it.

T

TOWN.	What system is your town drained under—small pipe, or otherwise?	What is the nature of the outfall?	Are your sewers ventilated? and if so, what description of ventilation, and distance apart?
SUNDERLAND ..	Brick mains, and pipe branches.	The sea and river.	The ventilation of 169 acres of sewerage area is nearly completed, by manholes, street grates, lamp-holes, and special ventilators on the surface, being about 100 yards apart.
WARRINGTON ..	The main sewers are brick; the branch sewers are drain pipes.	The sewers discharge into the river Mersey.	Our sewers are ventilated with open grids into the streets, at distances from 80 to 500 yards apart, as they appear to be required.

REMARKS.—I believe careful experiments have been made by the Borough Engineer of

Milton Keynes UK
Ingram Content Group UK Ltd.
UKHW012249290324
440241UK00004B/231

9 783385 383890